GOLD IN THE
SHADOW

*The blood of Isis, the spells of Isis, the magical powers of Isis
shall make this shining one strong, and shall be an amulet of protection
against he that would do to him the things which he abominateth…*

GOLD IN THE SHADOW

Michael Marcotte

Writers Club Press
San Jose · New York · Lincoln · Shanghai

GOLD IN THE SHADOW

Published by Writers Club Press
an imprint of iUniverse.com, Inc.

For information address:
iUniverse.com, Inc.
620 North 48th Street
Suite 201
Lincoln, NE 68504-3467
www.iuniverse.com

ISBN: 0-595-09414-7

Printed in the United States of America

For Robin, Kit and Marissa

Acknowledgements

Although this novel is entirely a work of fiction, I have drawn upon the actual research and expert knowledge of many friends and colleagues. I would like to express my deep appreciation to Merline Lovelace, Carol Burr, Dwight Normile, Dr. J. Madison Davis, Joan Cuccio and Dr. Janis Sacco for the valuable professional advice that they provided.

Special thanks to Serafin Coronel-Molina for the Quechua translations. I take full credit for any language errors that remain.

Thanks also to Dr. Wiley Harwell, Margaret French, David Shauberger and Dr. Don Wyckoff for their suggestions and assistance.

Virtually all of the Egyptian hieroglyphics were derived from various works by the late Sir E. A. Wallis Budge, Keeper of the Egyptian and Assyrian Antiquities at the British Museum. While the translations to English were taken from the Papyrus of Ani and other versions of the Book of the Dead, the contextual interpretations were often irreverently and unabashedly manipulated by myself for the purpose of the story.

Additional thanks to the many other friends and family members who read the early versions of this novel and whose observations improved the final work.

Finally, special thanks and much love to my wife, Robin, for her encouragement, multiple proof-readings and patience.

Introduction

The Amazon Basin. Dark and foreboding to some, to the more intrepid it excites and beckons with mystery and adventure. It is the primeval forest of legend and imagination. Fed by the world's largest river and spreading across portions of Brazil, Ecuador, Bolivia and Peru, the Amazon's vast interior contains the largest continuous expanse of forest in the world.

Encompassing some of the most remote and rugged portions of South America, it is nearly equal in size to the entire continental United States. Much of this immense two-and-one-half-million-square-mile jungle is so impenetrable that it has never been explored. Scientists estimate that hundreds of animal types and thousands of un-catalogued species of plants, birds, fish and insect life exist in these rainforests. That is in addition to the thousands of known species.

In the Amazon River itself, or in its hundreds of tributaries, live several types of South American crocodile, flesh-eating piranha, and monstrously large anacondas. In the rainforest dwell the jaguar, rare black panther, puma, and ocelot. Through the branches and on the ground below slither the bushmaster, the world's largest poisonous viper, as well as the fer-de-lance, coral snake and several of the world's other deadliest snakes. The abdomens of some spiders here grow to the size of tomatoes. Some of these venomous creatures spin webs thirty to forty feet across. One in particular, the Goliath bird-eating spider, reaches nearly a foot in length. Malaria-carrying mosquitoes, leeches and vampire bats are also among the more unnerving denizens of this primordial wilderness. Giant anteaters, tapirs, sloths, giant Harpy eagles, condors, manatees and a variety of monkeys add a softer variety to the more sinister images, but do not serve to make it any less alien.

Some of the fiercest Indians that ever lived, including the Achuara and Auca headhunters, cannibals and poison dart tribes such as the Hivitos, Chuncas and Yagua, called the Amazon their home. Numerous tribes that still practice such customs, have yet to encounter modern man, or who remain hostile, are still known to exist deep within these jungles.

To be fair, the Amazon is clearly not the Valley of Death. Many dangers exist in the jungles, but mankind has co-existed with these for thousands of years. There are many more places for animals to hide in a rainforest, and as wild creatures are generally very reclusive, they most often retreat or remain secluded when humans are present.

Amid this environment, from the fifteenth to the sixteenth centuries, arose one of the greatest empires ever known, and the largest of any native civilization of the Americas, the realm of the Inca. By the time of the Spanish conquest, it is estimated that this empire controlled around twelve million people in what is now Peru, Ecuador, Bolivia, Chile, and northwest Argentina. The Spaniards even reported seeing Inca sea vessels as far north as Panama. Hundreds of stone metropolises, that in their prime must have rivaled our modern cities in size and beauty, still exist in the forests and highlands of South America. Archaeologists have now partially excavated a few dozen of these cities, such as Machu Picchu, Kuelap, and Vilcabamba. Others, reclaimed by the jungle, remain lost, known only from historical accounts or legend.

The Inca called their empire "Tawantinsuyu," meaning "the four parts." The term Inca has come through common usage to mean all the Quechua-speaking tribes who were subjugated by this empire. The Inca, however, was actually a royal title given to the rulers of a minor Andean tribe that gained prominence after conquering its neighbors. Among these were the Chachapoyas, who are believed to have built the incredible pre-Columbian stone highways that criss-cross Peru. These and many other subjugated *tribes were required to pay tribute to the Inca rulers, in gold, silver, and precious gems.*

Known to have accumulated a wealth beyond imagination, the Inca somehow managed to hide this immense treasure. Only a fraction was ever captured by the conquistadors.

When Francisco Pizarro made the Inca ruler Atahualpa his captive, the Inca sought to obtain his release by offering to turn over a great ransom. Only a small portion, although estimated at fifteen million dollars, had reached Pizarro at Cajamarca, in 1533, before the Spaniard foolishly had Atahualpa assassinated! In the chaos that followed, approximately forty thousand Inca Indians fled. Before the Spaniards' very eyes, these refugees took with them huge amounts of treasure. The Indians that remained told the Spanish monks that the treasures the conquistadors already had collected were only "a drop in the bucket," compared to the wealth that the fleeing Indians had taken and hidden.

Not surprisingly, the conquistadors gave pursuit. Ambushed by the hostile Chuncho Indians and their poison darts and arrows, and thwarted by the dense jungle, the Spaniards were delayed. Ultimately they were forced to abandon the pursuit. The fleeing Indians vanished into the jungles east of Cuzco, Peru. Some experts believe that these Indians used a vast network of secret tunnels, the likes of which have actually been discovered in modern times beneath Lima, Cuzco and elsewhere in Peru, to escape the pursuing conquistadors.

Airplanes, satellite images, and other modern technologies have created renewed interest in the search for the lost city and the treasure. Several expeditions over the past five centuries embarked upon the search for El Dorado/Paititi inside Peru, Brazil, Ecuador and Bolivia. Some of the expeditions, such as that of the famed British army surveyor, Colonel Percy Harrison Fawcett, in 1925, and more recently, the ill-fated Franco-American team lead by Bob Nichols, in 1972, vanished inside the immense Amazon jungle without ever having been heard from again. Others returned, but empty-handed. The descendants of the Inca, the

Quechua Indian people of Peru and Bolivia, still speak of great stone cities deep in the forest that contain incredible wealth. The inhabitants of these hidden cities are said to still dress in brightly colored feathers, carry bronze-tipped spears, and live in the ancient ways.

Gran Paititi, the greatest of the Inca outposts, along with the fabulous Inca treasure, remains undiscovered to the present day.

The numerous mythologies of the different cultures of our world often hold as many similarities as differences. It is not at all uncommon, for example, to find extremely similar creation stories between African and Amerindian tribes. Some of these similarities can be explained by the concept that Joseph Campbell called "basic truths."

In other words, some ideas are simply so much a part of our own humanity that they simply find a way to emerge, no matter when or where on our planet the culture happened to arise. Other similarities or identical ideas, legends, language and iconography are less easily explained. Some may be pure coincidence. Sometimes, however, the sheer number of coincidences are so amazing as to make one wonder if they might be something else.

In the second half of this century, there has been an increasing amount of speculation by scholars that ancient times saw far more contact between distant cultures and continents that has been hitherto accepted as factual, and subsequently recorded as history. Expeditions by explorers like Percy Fawcett, Thor Heyerdahl, and Gene Savoy often have had this theme as part of their motivation. Artifacts have been found during several legitimate archaeological digs all around the world, including the Americas, that are unexplainably out of place. The discovery of America, more and more, would appear to have been only the latest of several discoveries throughout earlier history of the two continents.

The premise of this novel is entirely a work of fiction, drawn from such speculation. With the exception of historical figures and documented explorers referenced in this novel, all characters and events are fictional, and are not intended to represent any actual persons or events. You have, *however, heard the expression "Fact is sometimes stranger than fiction." If you want a really mind-boggling experience, check out the actual facts of history, archaeology and linguistics behind this tale of adventure.*

To use a well-known cliché, "It could happen."

Sometimes history, be it truth, perspective or pure fiction, is all in the translation.

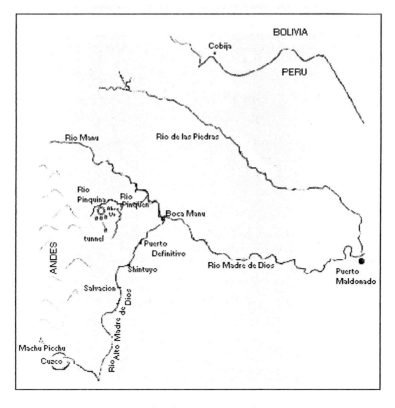

Madre de Dios area of Peru

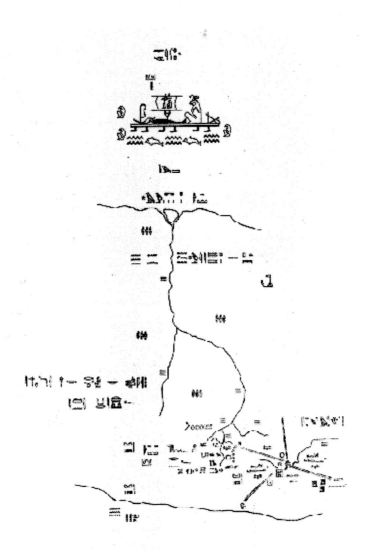

Map of the Tuat/Corner of the Dead

Chapter One

My mother bore me,
And my father begot me,
in the middle of a storm
So I would wander like a cloud

—Ayacucho folk song

✶✶✶✶

Norman, Oklahoma, Wednesday, February 11

Feet apart, fists on her hips and wearing little more than a rumpled, oversized T-shirt, Rachel Carson Aguila looked to her friends Dee and Trish more like a pint-sized Peter Pan than a studious anthropologist. The determined posture would have been more effective had it not been for the obvious worry in her eyes and the infuriating tears that she kept blinking back.

"No," she insisted, with a vehement shake of the head that tumbled a lock of raven-colored hair across one eye. "He's alive, but he'll need help. My brother doesn't know the first thing about jungles."

"I thought you told me the Amazon was one of the most exotic and beautiful places on earth," Dee objected.

"If there is a more remote, uncharted and inhospitable patch of jungle left anywhere else in the world, I can't imagine where it might be," Rachel answered. "That's what makes a jungle exotic. The Madre de

Dios *is* beautiful, but it's a lethal sort of beauty. That's why it's so important that I get there as soon as possible."

As evidenced by the puzzled expressions on their faces, neither of the other two young women had the slightest idea how their friend had strayed to that bizarre conclusion.

"I don't know of a way to put this gently," Trish ventured, "but if Kenny's plane did crash…and in the middle of a jungle…"

"With all those nasty piranha," Dee's eyes widened in alarm. "…and didn't you tell me they still had cannibals down there? Ouch!" She winced and rubbed at the ankle that Trish had just kicked.

Rachel shook her head in vigorous denial. "He's alive. I would know. We're twins."

Dee's son Tyler was the only one in the apartment unaffected by the crisis. The toddler wobbled down the hall from Rachel's bedroom, dumped a shoe in his mother's lap, then wandered off again, unnoticed.

Dee and Trish had instantly known the phone call from Peru was bad news. That much had been evident from the devastation and panic that had flashed across their friend's face.

The caller had identified himself as Kenny's current Peruvian employer. The man had deeply regretted having to confirm that Kenny had failed to report, after a long distance flight over the jungles east of Cuzco. Some hope remained, however, since no crash wreckage had yet been found.

"There's been some sort of mix-up, that's all," Rachel affirmed, nervously combing her fingers through her short dark hair. "I'm sure he survived and just hasn't been able to contact anyone, yet. The radio must have been damaged."

The more she talked, the more her face regained its color. Her conviction grew with each word and, before long, Dee and Trish were adding their own words of encouragement. The almost psychic bond that frequently exists between twins was legendary. If Rachel was so certain that Kenny was still alive, neither friend thought it helpful to contradict her.

"He'll probably need medical attention. There may not even be anyone looking for him, yet. I need to get down there, fast. Kenny could fly a hang glider through a hurricane. If there's anyone who could crash land an aircraft inside a jungle like that and walk away from it, it's him."

"You're right," Trish soothed. "There's probably no reason to overact. So, wouldn't it be best to wait a couple of days? If Kenny's okay—and I'm sure he is—you'll be the first person he'll contact. Maybe the best thing you could do would just be to stay close to your phone."

"She's right," Dee reassured. "You should give it a little time. What about your studies and your job?" In addition to her graduate classes, Rachel worked as a research assistant at the University of Oklahoma's Museum of Natural History. "Spring break will be here in a couple of weeks. Couldn't you wait 'til then?"

Dee's advice went unnoticed, as did the return of Tyler. The toddler now added a sock to the shoe in his mother's lap.

"I'll just have to catch up. Or if not, I'll take the classes over again. The Museum will understand. This is my brother, my *twin*. In two weeks, a person could die, stranded in an environment like that. I'm leaving on the first flight I can get. Where did I put the phonebook?"

Trish tried again, sympathetic, but practical. "What could you do down there that you can't do as well from here?"

"I don't know," Rachel sighed. "I won't know until I'm there."

"Isn't Cuzco the same city where you did your research?" Trish asked.

Rachel shook her head. "I was at Cocha Cashu, in the rain forest. It's just a research station. Cuzco was the closest big city. Kenny called a couple of days ago from there to brag about where he was." She suddenly realized something else. "Dee, I'm sorry…this means I have to cancel the eclipse trip to the Galapagos."

"Let's just say you're putting us on hold. Who knows? You may hear from Kenny at any moment, or he may turn up safe and sound once you get there. Why not keep your options open."

"This isn't the time," Trish admonished.

Dee rarely paid attention to the latter's advice. To her, Trish's sexual preferences were conclusive proof of a truly skewed sense of judgment. She was just about to pursue her argument, but was interrupted.

"No," Rachel explained. "I'll need to leave today or tomorrow, and the money will have to come from what I was setting aside for the Galapagos."

Dee avoided eye contact. Like Trish, she had learned not to look for too long a time into those mismatched irises; they knew it made their friend uncomfortable. Contrary to Rachel's perception, most people found the blue eye/brown eye combination quite fetching. Some, like Trish, thought it irresistibly endearing, in the same sort of way as a snaggle-toothed puppy.

Rachel's insecurity about her minor anomaly had persisted long after the inevitable taunts of childhood had faded. It was one of the physical traits that she did not share with Kenny, and in their youth she had held that against him. If her twin was going to be so much like her, he should have had to share "the mutation" too.

Tyler reappeared from the back of the apartment, clutching another article of clothing in a pudgy fist. He thrust it toward his mother. "Weh!" he announced triumphantly.

"Red," Dee corrected. She took the item from Tyler and examined it. It was a pair of panties. A lacy red thong.

"Oops," said Dee, with an apologetic grimace.

Rachel was far too preoccupied to be embarrassed. She found the phonebook on top of the refrigerator, where she usually kept it, and started leafing through the pages for the airline listings.

Dee looked at Trish and shrugged. Both of them knew that once their friend had thought through the options and made her choice, there would be nothing anyone could do to keep her from following through. In the past five years, Rachel had already lost her father and her childhood sweet-heart—one to cancer, the other to a traffic accident. How much more bad luck could a person stand? Certainly not the loss of her twin.

Outside, large raindrops began to pelt the windowpanes, creating a monotonous background rhythm. Tyler was now cruising the room's bookcases, making Trish nervous. Dee often let her son get too far out of hand before stepping in.

Trish's nervousness was caused by the contents of the bookcases. Besides Rachel's many dictionaries and books on anthropology, the shelves held several irreplaceable possessions. At the moment, a few of these personal treasures rested dangerously near the child's fingers. Strewn across the top of the bookcase was a small collection of fragile Indian necklaces from the Amazon, made from porcupine quills, colored parrot down and sloth toenails.

Many items scattered around the apartment were as much symbols of Rachel's personal journey as they were souvenirs of the places she had traveled. She revealed her thirst for adventure and the unorthodox through the reverent dispersal of such objects around the apartment. There were no archaeological or ancient artifacts. These treasures were rare solely in the sense that a person could only obtain them by remote travel, personal hardship and some danger. The resulting collection and fastidious cleanliness of the apartment caused Rachel's small circle of friends to jokingly refer to her place as "the Museum."

"Look," Trish said. "If you're really determined to go off to South America, maybe I should come with you…"

Trish and Dee had originally invaded the apartment, that afternoon, to exploit their friend's expertise as the trio completed the Galapagos travel plans. Rachel was often in such demand by her friends and acquaintances. Like her famous mountain man ancestor, Kit Carson, Rachel was an intrepid adventurer who found few locations too remote or inhospitable to keep her away. She also spoke over a half dozen languages, another reason her two friends had wanted her to join them.

"Trish, that's sweet of you, but I'll be fine. I spent almost a year in Peru by myself. There's really not that much you could do. I speak the language; you don't. Don't worry about me. Really. When I find Kenny,

I'll just hang around Cuzco for a few days. I'll watch the eclipse from there with Kenny, instead." She put as much confidence into the statement as she could muster.

"Dee, are you going to do something about Tyler?" Trish prompted, nodding toward the child. The toddler was on tiptoe, now banging wildly with a plastic dinosaur, nervously close to a fragile Amahuaca Indian gourd-rattle.

"Oh, my mom lives in Oklahoma City. She's already said she'd be happy to keep him. It's only nine days." Dee belatedly took the hint. "Tyler! No, no. You leave that alone."

A flash of lightning flickered across the room, followed by a loud clap of thunder, which made each of the women jump slightly.

Also startled by the thunder, the youngster dropped his toy tyrannosaurus and began crawling back toward his mother. He started to whimper halfway across the room.

"Tyler, are you already hungry again?" Dee quizzed. "He's hungry all the time. I think he's going through a growth spurt or something. He tries to eat *everything*. Yesterday, I caught him out in the yard about to put a little piece of dried doggy doo in his mouth!"

Trish wrinkled her nose. "Thanks so much for sharing that with us."

While an astonished Trish tried to comprehend how insensitive her friend could sometimes be, Dee continued to spout on and on about how great the Galapagos trip would be. Meanwhile, the toddler's fussing became more insistent. Rachel nervously toyed with a small silver eagle that hung from a delicate chain around her neck.

"If you really think he's hungry, maybe you should put him out in the yard for a while. After he eats, he'll probably go right to sleep."

"Huh? Oh! I get it…" Dee made a face, then laughed. "Don't listen to the wicked lady, Tyler," she cooed.

With her thirtieth birthday only matter of months away, Rachel was beginning to feel the proverbial pressure on her biological clock. Lately, she had found herself wondering whether the sacrifices she had made to pursue her career were excessive. Where had all the time gone? Most days, she leaned more toward forgoing the "Mommy" experience. Her own mother had done little to make the role seem appealing. *But then, her housewife Mother had done little with her life, period. Except to leave Dad, even after he was dying of cancer.*

In the end, Trish and Dee wished Rachel luck, and offered any help that they could provide. All she had to do was call. Trish volunteered to stay at the apartment, in case a message came through from Kenny or another source. Rachel accepted the offer. She hugged her friends and shooed them out, so she could start telephoning airlines and packing what she would need for the journey to Peru.

Despite the brave face she had put on for her friends, Rachel was understandably shaken. Even though she truly did believe her brother was still alive, she knew Kenny had never spent time in a jungle like the Madre de Dios. He was probably injured, and all kinds of danger existed in the Madre de Dios. Kenny would be totally unaware and unprepared. She hoped he had the good sense to stay at the wreckage. He would be far safer and easier for a rescue team to find, than if he tried to walk out of the jungle on his own.

She debated whether she should telephone her mother. Communication was still awkward. When she and Kenny were infants, twins not being the easiest to raise, their parents had split the work by singling out which twin was whose responsibility. Rachel had become the infant assigned to her father, while their mother had mostly cared for Kenny. Each twin's personality and temperament had, to some extent, been affected by those traits in the respective parent. As a result, Rachel did not identify well with her mother. She had later felt abandoned after their parents had separated, and this resentment had grown since her father's death. Age had also led her mother to devote much of their infrequent phone conversations to idle rambling and irrelevant tangents. The more contact she had with her mother, the more depressing Rachel's perception of their relationship became. A more than passing resemblance to her mother only made matters worse. She suffered from the classic fear that she was increasingly *becoming* her mother. She much preferred to retain a mental image of when her father was still alive, and to all appearances, they were all one happy family. Each new phone conversation chipped away at that image.

She decided to wait until she had more definite news, and scribbled a note for Trish with the hotel's telephone number in Peru.

Rachel walked to the desk where stacks of research papers, maps and books formed a daunting pyramid of work from which she had been interrupted. There was no helping that. Kenny was in trouble.

She had been surprised when her brother had telephoned from Cuzco. He had said he was working for a large Peruvian construction company.

"Where the hell is Shintuyo, anyway?" he had wanted to know. Because of on-going border disputes with Ecuador and Bolivia, commercial maps of Peru were notoriously incomplete. This was irksome for a bush pilot like Kenny. He needed to know where the very sparsely scattered airstrips were located in the region. In an area as densely forested as the Madre de Dios, maintained airstrips were the only place to land any aircraft other than a seaplane, in which case there are a multitude of suitable rivers and tributaries.

"Can't you remember where you put anything?" she remembered joking. The exchange no longer seemed a laughing matter.

Tacked to the wall above the desk was a heavily annotated map of the northern half of South America. A provocative eleven-by-fourteen-inch, framed photograph of Trish in a revealing leotard and erotic ballet pose hung beside the map. Originally a publicity photo for a University of Oklahoma ballet production, hand-written words in black magic marker now scrawled across the image: "To dearest Rachel, all my love—Trish." The photo startled some of Rachel's acquaintances, which she, in turn, found wickedly amusing. Trish and Dee were the closest things to "best friends" that she had been able to make since moving from California. The two very opposite friends found common ground mostly via Rachel. Rachel, in turn, increasingly wondered which of the two she might be becoming more like, and whether she should worry about it, in either case.

Tacked next to Trish's photo were several postcards from Kenny and a couple of old snapshots of the twins. She unpinned one of these and held it cupped in her hands—a terrible dread again wrapping icy fingers around her heart.

On the edge of the desk a clock radio was playing Melissa Etheridge's *Nowhere to Go*, while outside the rain continued to beat a sympathetic accompaniment against the apartment's windowpanes.

Rachel returned to making her travel preparations and murmured a silent prayer for the umpteenth time in the past hour. *Don't abandon me, Kenny. Not you, too.*

Chapter Two

****

Cuzco, Peru, Friday, February 13

Rachel arrived in Cuzco. Because of the short notice, she had been unable to find a timely flight through Houston with connections onward to Lima and then Cuzco. That meant she had to travel a different route by way of Miami to La Paz, and spend an extra night there. During the layover she had contacted Trish, but had learned that there was still no news from Kenny.

She took a taxi from the airport directly to the Hotel El Libertador. The Libertador was an old colonial mansion, which had been transformed into one of Cuzco's more expensive lodgings. The hotel boasted perhaps a bit fewer amenities than others, but it was quiet, elegant and Rachel liked its charm. An interior courtyard provided an antiquish warmth that Rachel found somehow comforting amid the backdrop of the unsettling crisis she had traveled to confront.

Rachel let the desk clerk know that she might need to extend the reservation for several more nights than previously arranged. Because the hotel was not heavily booked at this time of year, the clerk believed this would present no problem.

Rachel's first order of business was to again telephone home. In the space of a moment, her sprits plummeted from hopeful to despondent.

"Still no news," Trish told her. "Anything there?"

"Nothing yet. I didn't want to go to the police, until I'd heard from you."

"Sorry. You'll check in every day or two?"

"Yeah," she mumbled. As she hung up, she slumped onto the edge of the bed. Although exhausted from the trip, Rachel knew she would be unable to sleep until she checked with the local authorities for news about her brother. She groaned and pushed herself back onto her feet. After a quick shower and change of clothes, she was soon on her way to the tourists' police office next to the Plaza de Armas, just a few blocks away.

The police were sympathetic and seemed genuinely concerned, but no one had heard about the plane crash. The officer-in-charge offered to help arrange transport and guides, but this, he apologized, would take a couple of days. However, if Rachel had a few minutes, he would be happy to telephone to the headquarters of the Guardia Civil y Policia. Perhaps someone had reported the crash at one of their field offices or checkpoints.

After what seemed like an eternity of irrelevant phone conversation, the officer told her that the police officials of the Guardia Civil near Shintuyo had received an inquiry from the construction company for whom Kenny was working. The investigation was still tied up in official channels. The officer warned that it would be very difficult to reach the wreckage, once it was sighted. He understood that the flight plan her brother had filed crossed a large area of jungle that even the Guardia did not patrol, because of the sometimes hostile Indians and dense forest conditions. Perhaps the best thing, he suggested, would be to wait in Cuzco until an aerial search of the region was completed. Meanwhile, it would be necessary for the Señorita to register a missing person's report. Without the report, the police would be unable to enlist the help of the Servicio Aereo Fotografico Nacional or other official channels.

By the time Rachel finished the required paperwork and left the police station, she had developed a splitting headache.

She hailed a taxi at the Plaza de Armas for the short trip back to the hotel. At the front desk, she again stopped to check for messages. The desk clerk shook his head sympathetically and turned his attention back to a tall sandy-haired stranger that had been inquiring about interpreters.

"What about Amahuaca?" asked the stranger.

The desk clerk shook his head no. "I don't think so, Señor. You could try the University of Cuzco. Do you need directions?"

The stranger shook his head.

"If you want a local guide, you'll need one who speaks Quechua," offered Rachel. "None of the Indians near here speak Amahuaca."

"I don't need them for near here."

The man's tone was just a little curt, and Rachel was already a bit edgy due to her headache.

"That should work out well. The Amahuaca don't need you near them, either."

The stranger blinked once, but otherwise allowed no change of expression. His gaze insolently traveled the length of Rachel's slight form, before he turned his back to resume his conversation with the desk clerk.

At the edge of the lobby, she glanced back across her shoulder in confused irritation. *That was really my fault,* she admitted. *Oh, well.* She had far more important worries.

She retired to her room, resigned to tackle the crisis again in the morning when she was more recuperated from the effects of the long airline flights and Cuzco's high altitude. She shrugged her way out of her clothes and crawled into bed. Seconds after her head touched the pillow, she was asleep.

Chapter Three

hieroglyphic determinative for a foreign country, distant land

****

Cuzco, Peru, Saturday, February 14

Max Arnold shivered inside the "Bar-Marques" adjacent to the hotel courtyard, sipping a brandy. His gaze meandered through the window across the Libertador's carved boulder foundations. He knew that like many such walls in Cuzco, these stones had been placed there by the Incas, a half millennium earlier. A treasure hunter by profession, Max had educated himself in both the country's legends and its history. Visible just beyond the walls and rooftops, the brownish slopes of the Andes Mountains ascended into the dreary cloud cover obscuring the ancient peaks.

He had arrived in Cuzco late the previous afternoon, accompanied by his partner and jungle guide, Tristan Sloan and an Egyptologist, Dr. Harold Gallagher. Although a stranger to South America, jungles and the local languages, Gallagher's skills were expected to be useful, if not essential. Max was paying Gallagher a large bonus to placate him for the absence from his wife and children.

All things have their price, he smirked.

Max didn't much care for Peru, and subsequently was spending most of his time in the hotel bar. Tristan, on the other hand, was never more at home than in cities like this. Since his arrival, he had spent most of his time recruiting guides, translators and porters. Before leaving Los Angeles, Max had arranged for Dr. Jorgé Ramón from the University of Trujillo's Archaeological Museum to join them in Cuzco. Max and Tristan both recognized the wisdom of including such a representative. Many doors that would have otherwise remained closed to the group would open graciously to the Peruvian. The two professors had already established a rapport with one another. To Max's pleasant surprise, the late inclusion of Gallagher had provided exactly the air of respectability needed to persuade Dr. Ramón to accompany the expedition. Max knew that there was a perpetual distaste, if not outright enmity, by archaeologists and anthropologists toward professional adventurers. The first group views the second as little more than unethical looters and grave robbers. Local archaeologists had for many years leveled formal accusations against the most renown of such adventurers. Even Hiram Bingham, discoverer of the lost city of Machu Picchu, was accused of spiriting artifacts out of Peru.

Despite this stigma, Dr. Ramón had found Max's story plausible, and was eager to compare everything he knew on the subject of Peruvian petroglyphs with Gallagher knowledge of Old Kingdom hieroglyphics. The Egyptologist was enthusiastically soaking it up. The local petroglyphs bore only small or coincidental similarities to the sacred writings of the Egyptians, but nonetheless kept the two academics in animated discussions.

Max's gaze momentarily shifted to the Egyptologist, and his face became a marble effigy of contempt. Every time he laid eyes on Gallagher, Max inadvertently recalled the farmer with horned-rim glasses and pitchfork in the painting *American Gothic*. Had they been schoolboys, Max knew he would have been compelled to beat Gallagher to a pulp. Now, however, forcing such men to bend their principles provided Max with the same sense of fulfillment.

Max had already asked Ramón about rumored ancient tunnels near the city. The Peruvian professor had enjoyed telling an apparently famous story about a local peasant who had entered a maze of such tunnels. The man had supposedly re-emerged through the floor of a local church, days later, clutching a bar of gold in each hand, but out of his mind from having been lost in the tunnels for days. The peasant had later died without recovering his sanity. In the aftermath of the disappearance of other local citizens and finally two tourists who were looking for the rumored treasure, the government dynamited the entrance. Many archaeologists had subsequently appealed for permission to reopen the tunnel, but the Peruvian government remained steadfast in its rejection of all such requests.

While enlisting members for the expedition, Max had suggested that Tristan also try to ascertain the church where the storied peasant had emerged. Typically, as when dealing with such local myths, he received a different assurance from each person he asked that it was this church or that one. With a little perseverance, Tristan finally discovered that the church of Santa Domingo—ironically, the one across the street from the Libertador—was the one in question. That made sense. After all, it rested upon the ruins of Coricancha, the Inca's Temple of the Sun. The local caretakers understandably would not allow the treasure hunter more than the same casual look around that was given to tourists. Max and Tristan had agreed that it was improbable that the tunnels would have remained passable all the way to the site they believed to be Gran Paititi. They decided it would attract too much attention and would be a waste of time looking further for such an entrance in Cuzco. For now, they were determined to get as close to the estimated coordinates, as possible. Hopefully, they would be able to do this without running into hostile Indians. Max was anxious to get under way. These damn anthropologists were beginning to get on his nerves. Tristan, however, was insistent that they not go into Yaminhua territory without an interpreter. That problem was the one Tristan was now off trying to resolve. If he failed in that mission, the expedition would be confined to probing the edges of the jungle, checking out caves and tunnels known to local farmers and friendly Indians.

As he listened to Gallagher and Ramón chatting, a few tables away, Max's plans suddenly underwent an unexpected revision.

Dr. Gallagher was verbally fawning over some photographs that Dr. Ramón had produced of petroglyphs from a nearby site called Pusharo. When the Egyptologist abruptly paused mid-sentence, Max twisted in his chair to see what had caused the interruption. Dr. Gallagher was staring at a young woman who was passing through the glassed-in corridor next to the Bar-Marques and interior courtyard. Max was surprised that Dr. Gallagher was taking interest in a woman other than his wife.

Rising from the table, Gallagher proclaimed, "I know that person!" and strode out of the bar in pursuit.

Max watched as the professor caught up with and greeted the surprised young woman and then engaged her in conversation. After the two had talked for several minutes, the young lady went on her way and Dr. Gallagher returned to the bar.

"An old flame?" Max asked. "A clandestine Valentine's Day meeting?"

"No, nothing like that. A former student. Actually, not really one of *my* students. I was just one of the professors who served on her master's thesis committee at U.C.L.A. Quite the linguist, as I recall. She even had a paper published by the Summer Institute of Linguistics. It made quite a hit…dealt with the languages of some of the more isolated and hostile Indian tribes of the jungles here in Peru."

"How fascinating," Max commented, using a sufficiently syrupy tone to disclose that he thought it anything but that.

"I wouldn't be so disdainful, if I were you," Dr. Gallagher countered. "She lived with a couple of those tribes near the same area that your intrepid Mr. Sloan is so reluctant to cross. She spent almost a full year out there in the rain forest. She couldn't have been over about 24 or 25 years old. That was four or five years ago, if I remember correctly."

The professor now had Max's full attention.

"What tribes might those have been?" Max asked cautiously. Dr. Gallagher had left Max's Los Angeles office before Tristan had mentioned specific Indian tribes, but even Dr. Gallagher knew from later conversations, that finding a way past hostile tribes was of great concern to the expedition leaders.

"I'm sure I don't remember the right pronunciations," Dr. Gallagher explained. "Just something like Macarinas and Yabbaduas."

"Machiguengas?" prompted Dr. Ramón. "That's one of the indigenous tribes near here. Dangerous a few years ago, but fairly accustomed to the outside world, now."

"That might have been one of them."

Max was disappointed. Machiguengas weren't one of the tribes that concerned Tristan. "What about the other tribe…Yabbadua?"

"I don't know of a tribe by that name," Dr. Ramón smiled. "There are Yagua, Huarayos…"

"Yaminhua?" Max suggested.

"Ah, yes," said a surprised Dr. Ramón, "Very good, Mr. Arnold. The Yaminhua. Still a very volatile and dangerous tribe. Not many left. Perhaps less than a thousand. You say your young friend contacted them? Learned their language? Impressive. I dare say, I don't believe I've heard of more than one or two outsiders who ever learned to speak Yaminhua. Even among the local Indian guides."

Yaminhua, Max thought. *Well, well.*

"Poor thing," Dr. Gallagher sighed. "She's here looking for her twin brother. His small aircraft was reported missing three days ago. She's trying to get the national aerial surveillance service to look for his plane."

"What's this young lady's name, if I might ask?" Max queried.

"Rachel," Dr. Gallagher answered, puzzled by Max's interest. "Rachel Aguila."

Ramón and Gallagher resumed their discussion of the ancient art of rock writing, and Max shook his head in mild disgust. As he digested the facts revolving around Rachel Aguila, a plan began to formulate in the back of Max's mind.

****

While Tristan continued preparations for the incursion into the jungle, Max spent much of the day on the telephone. At first, his directions were initiated through his secretary in Los Angeles, but by mid afternoon Max had taken over much of the phone contact in person. It did not surprise Max how fast he was able to collect the information he needed. The cash he was willing to spend guaranteed almost anyone's cooperation. By the end of the day, a private investigator had collected and forwarded to Max, by way of the hotel's fax machine, a substantial amount of background information on Rachel Aguila. The investigator had also identified Kenny Aguila's Peruvian employer.

As Dr. Gallagher had claimed, Rachel apparently possessed a basic proficiency in the Yaminhua dialect. The young woman was said to be an adept linguist, and had been able to pick up much of the language in the time she had spent in Peru. Max learned that Rachel had spent a year in the restricted area of Manu National Park in the Madre de Dios Forest. Before that, Rachel had spent earlier stints of six months in the Caixuana Reserve on the Brazilian Amazon, and four months in the nearby rugged Xingu River basin. Besides Yaminhua, the young woman was conversant in French, German, Portuguese, Italian, and Spanish, as well as the Peruvian Indian dialects of Quechua, Amahuaca and Machiguenga. Max began mentally thinking of her as the "idiot-savant."

Max also verified by way of the investigator's information that Rachel's brother was a freelance pilot who frequently flew cargo planes, seaplanes, and other aircraft on short-term contracts all over the world. Max would not have found it surprising if he had employed the brother at some time in the past on a prior expedition.

Kenny Aguila had arrived two weeks ago and had flown a dozen loads of supplies from La Paz to Cuzco for a Peruvian construction company. He had been reported missing three days ago, on the eleventh of February. Rachel's formal request for the Servicio Aereo Fotografico Nacional to do an aerial search of the suspected crash area was still hopelessly embroiled in bureaucratic red tape.

Max continued to refine his scheme. Under the circumstances a monetary offer would probably insult the young woman. He would have to make use of Rachel Aguila's own priorities.

Chapter Four

chm: "the unknown"

****

Cuzco, Peru, Sunday, February 15

"Señorita Aguila," the desk clerk called. "There is a message for you."

Rachel had just started toward her room. She nearly sprinted across the lobby to the reception desk. *Word from Kenny!*

"It's from your American friend, Señor Gallagher."

Rachel found it difficult to keep the disappointment from her face as she accepted the folded note. The clerk smiled apologetically.

Today had been another impossible mess at the police station. The local officials were extremely courteous and understanding, but still were unable to make anything happen. She had wasted another entire morning filling out more forms, talking to new policemen and waiting for hours for word of their progress. The last thing she felt like at the moment was catching up on old times with Dr. Gallagher.

"Dear Rachel," she read. "I have had to leave Cuzco sooner than expected. The expedition is moving today to a base at Shintuyo, from where we will embark into the rain forest on Tuesday morning. I have learned some news from the organizer of our expedition, Mr. Max Arnold, which may bring you some relief. A just-completed aerial survey of the region into which we are headed has produced a sighting of the wreckage of a downed plane! The description matches that of the aircraft your brother was flying. There is apparently good reason to believe that your brother may have survived the crash, as the pilot of our survey plane indicated the wreck was mostly intact and had not burned. Upon learning of this news, Mr. Arnold has instructed me to offer you any help that we might be able to give in enabling you to reach the crash site. There is an airstrip at Shintuyo and the hotel clerk has been given instructions, in case you decide to pursue this offer. If you prefer to wait for more official assistance from the local police, I will, of course, understand."

The note was signed by Harold J. Gallagher, Ph.D.

Even had it been an easier day, the contents of the letter would still have sent Rachel into a whirlwind of emotions. Until now, there had been no irrefutable confirmation that Kenny's plane had crashed. The news of the sighting was a crushing blow. Yet, all signs were on the positive side that the crash had been survivable. Rachel's first impulse was to race immediately back to the police station with the letter. The longer she thought about it, the less attractive this idea became. First, Dr. Gallagher had failed to provide information about the location of the crash site. To get that information, she would have to speak with Max Arnold, who had already relocated to Shintuyo. Second, she had absorbed just about all the bureaucratic entanglement that she could stand. Dr. Gallagher's offer was appealing. The expedition was already en route toward the proximity of the crash. All she had to do was catch up. Besides, she wasn't sure if she could just idly sit by in Cuzco. The waiting was already driving her crazy. She needed to be *out there*—

doing something herself. Rachel made up her mind. The expedition was her best hope of finding Kenny.

Rachel asked the hotel clerk about the instructions Dr. Gallagher had left. She wasn't too surprised to find out that there was no way of communicating by phone. When she had been in Peru before, many places she had visited had been without telephones. Shintuyo was just a mission station then, not even a village. Kenny had teased her about the changes when, during their last conversation, she had lamented the intrusion of his construction company employer into the relatively untouched part of the rain forest.

"At this rate they'll deforest and depopulate the entire Amazon Basin within the next century," Rachel had preached to her twin. "If trees could scream, I wonder if everyone would still be cutting them down so fast?"

"They might…if the trees were screaming all the time, for no good reason."

Rachel had scolded Kenny for his cavalier attitude, but gone on to caution him about the dangers of such an area.

Apparently, the area hadn't changed that much, after all. Access to Shintuyo from Cuzco was still not all that convenient, and the mission station still was without a telephone.

Dr. Gallagher's instructions were not much help. No pilots were available to fly Rachel to Shintuyo by tomorrow evening. The clerk advised Rachel that to make the connection with the expedition, she would have to use ground transportation. This, as Rachel feared, was one of the local truck routes. The clerk had already checked, and told Rachel that the next truck would be departing for Shintuyo from the Avenida Pachacutec at eight o'clock the following morning. There was no advance purchase; seats were "first-come, first-served."

Rachel realized that she had not come prepared for a trek into the jungle. The expedition would provide food, water and shelter, but she could hardly expect them to have suitable clothing on hand for her. At a minimum, she'd need different pants and a pair of knee-high rubber boots. These Rachel figured she should be able to get from an expedition outfitters' shop recommended by the hotel clerk. She would also need to find a local pharmacy and get some Lariam. Optimally, she should have started taking the malaria prevention drug three days before she had left Oklahoma, but there had been no time to get a prescription. She doubted that local pharmacists would require one. In a pinch she could always chew quinine bark. She grimaced at that thought and, checking the time, saw that she might barely be able to get both places before the shops closed.

****

The mission station at Shintuyo might not have a telephone, but in such an age of technological wizardry, that was hardly a barrier for someone with Max's resources. He finished one conversation on his portable Iridium phone, and initiated another. The whole reason for moving the expedition to the river encampment, on such short notice, was to force Rachel away from real reports of her twin's whereabouts that might direct her elsewhere or keep her in Cuzco. Max had purposely not left instructions on how he might be reached via his Iridium phone. He did not want to answer questions from the young woman until it was too late for her to turn back. Dr. Gallagher had written the letter to Rachel exactly as Max had dictated it. Max suspected the professor knew the story about the sighting of the plane wreckage was bogus. Even so, Gallagher had remained silent. If anything had a price, it was ethics, Max snidely surmised.

Although Max had contemplated waiting for Rachel in Cuzco, he had felt safer luring her on to Shintuyo. The faster he could get her away from contact with other sources of information and assistance, the more she would be dependent on him to help find her brother.

As it turned out, Max was now gratified by this decision. If his sources were correct, Kenny Aguila had suddenly turned up. Alive. An

American pilot shuttling cargo from La Paz to Cuzco had been forced on account of mechanical failures to land at a tiny airstrip near Cobija, Bolivia. Cobija was just on the other side of the border from Peru. The airstrip was primitive enough that its only means of communications was through an archaic wireless radio setup. The grounded pilot was trying to have a replacement instrument for his plane flown to the same airstrip near Cobija, but was having trouble getting a complete message relayed back to La Paz.

Through a tangled web of former contacts that Max had made in Bolivia and public officials whose cooperation he had been able to hire, Max was almost certain the American was Kenny Aguila. Max was waiting, at this moment, for the completion of a link that permitted him to converse by way of the Iridium phone, across a Bolivian military communications channel, to the radio operator in Cobija. Finally, a Spanish-speaking voice at the other end of the connection confirmed that Max was indeed speaking to the correct person. Max made certain that the Bolivian had been told of an arranged cash payment to an account in the Bolivian's name. Max gave a few short and simple instructions in Spanish and then asked for confirmation that the man understood and was willing to do as he was asked.

****

In Cobija, the Bolivian told Max that indeed he understood, and would follow the instructions. The Bolivian hung up the phone and turned to the short wave unit. Shrugging, he switched off the power. Opening a panel, he reached inside the unit and removed a transistor, which he dropped in his pocket. He then switched the power back on. The unit automatically executed a self-test sequence, and detecting the missing part, displayed an error code on the diagnostic panel. The Bolivian stood and went outside. Next to a small makeshift hanger, the gringo pilot was leaning against the small Cherokee Piper aircraft.

The American noticed the Bolivian standing outside the communications shack and waved.

"*Buenos tardes, Miguel!*"

"*Holá, Señor Ken!*" Miguel called, waving back to the American. "*Mas problemas.* The radio…he no working no more."

****

Prior to their departure from Los Angeles, Tristan Sloan had obtained several LANDSAT photos of the relevant part of the Madre de Dios jungle. To his disappointment, the results were inconclusive. Three or four different areas showed what looked like partial clearings in the forest, but nothing else of interest. A couple of the photos that were infrared color-indexed showed what possibly could have been stone pyramids or tower structures like those expected to be found in Paititi. Because of the immense distance from which the photos were taken, the structures could just as well turn out to be natural outcroppings of rock. A preliminary fly-over by a hired pilot revealed nothing discernible under the forest's triple canopy. Gallagher had volunteered that even the Pyramid of Mekaurae, also known as Mycerinus, on the Giza plateau, rose only about one hundred fifty feet. The smallest of the three pyramids at Giza, Mekaurae was still monumental in comparison with earlier discovered Inca structures. The third level of the canopy in the destination area of the Madre de Dios reached as high as two hundred fifty feet. This presented the possibility that such ruins might not be visible from an aerial view.

Max and Tristan sat together on the banks of the Alto Madre de Dios, at their encampment a quarter mile from the mission station. They were planning the best approach into the forest, and Tristan was still perplexed by the proximity of their destination to the Yaminhua territory.

"That won't be quite as big a concern," Max said. "…if our interpreter shows up in the next twenty-four hours. I think she'll accept."

Thus far, Max had been fairly close-mouthed about the interpreter. For his part, Tristan had switched his attention to other details and had not had much opportunity to query Max on the subject. This was the first time he had heard anything about the interpreter being female.

"The hell you say!" Tristan exploded. "She? *She's* going to accept? This is the last place in the world to be taking a woman. Are you out of your mind?"

"Relax. She's been here before. According to Gallagher, she lived with these Indians for over a year. Works for a museum now, like Ramón."

"Lived with the Yaminhua? I don't believe that for a second. You don't mean to tell me that this is someone that prima donna Gallagher found for you? He doesn't know one Indian tribe from another."

"He recognized her in front of the Libertador," Max said. "It's karma. Destiny. She may be the *only* Yaminhua-speaking white person in the world. Do you get the picture? We needed one, and she just happened to walk by, in the right place at the right time. Don't look a gift horse in the mouth."

"She was at the hotel? Then, why the mad rush to move everyone out here? What kind of cockamamie story was that about the interpreter only being available if we got here by the weekend?"

Max was starting to get irritated with Tristan. "Look. You didn't find anyone that could do the job; isn't that right? I did. Everything was to our advantage to move out at once. This Rachel, the interpreter, has some other interests down here. She's an anthropologist, working on a doctorate or something back in Texas, Oklahoma or one of those other cowboy states. It turns out she has a brother who's missing out there in the jungle. I simply hinted that we were headed in the direction of the crash."

"Are we?" Tristan asked.

"Everyone believes he crashed in the Madre de Dios. That's east of Cuzco. That's the general direction we're headed, isn't it?"

"When you say everyone *believes* he crashed…I hear you saying between the lines that *you* don't believe so. What are you up to, Max? Is this some sort of shady trick you're trying to pull on this girl?"

"Watch it, Tristan. I *own* this operation. I have the damn map memorized. I can go with you or without you." Max paused and softened his tone before continuing. What he had just said wasn't necessarily true. He still needed Tristan.

"Pal, we go back quite a few years. We've been through a lot together. If this young woman wants any part of this, she'll come on her own accord. If we do find Paititi, this kid will have it made. She can write all about it. It'll make her famous. There's no sense in ending our friendship over something as inconsequential as this." He slapped Tristan affectionately on the back. "C'mon Tris'. We're in the nineties. Women these days look out for themselves. They *resent* gentlemen."

For a few tense moments, Tristan considered telling Max to go to hell. As he began to calculate the costs of paying the men they had assembled, reason overcame his anger. Max had always been more bark than bite, and his thick pocket book tended to offset numerous faults.

"I'm going to straighten this all out with her, if she does show up," Tristan insisted.

"If you do…" Max scowled, dropping the good ol' buddy routine, "…make sure you pick up your things on your way out of camp. We need her help. I don't want her thinking that she's been tricked into being here. Think it over, Tristan. We're not breaking any laws. We're not kidnapping her. I didn't even lie to her." *More or less*, he added silently. "She's free to make up her own mind."

As Tristan glowered, Max offered a compromise.

"If it will make you fill any better, I'll see whether I can get a message through to my secretary. I'll instruct her to spare no expense to locate this young woman's brother, and to return him to Cuzco. Deal?"

"I still don't like anything about it."

"She's our only choice. Take her, or leave her."

"You'll do what you said? Make a sincere attempt to locate her brother?"

"You have my word on it."

"We'll see how she does, as far as Boca Manu," Tristan said. With little lessening of his misgivings, he turned his back on Max and strode back toward the camp.

As soon as Tristan was out of sight, Max returned to his own tent and retrieved the iridium phone. When the connection went through to his secretary in Los Angeles, Max told the secretary that she was to do whatever she could to relay a simple message to a certain Miguel Cordova, at a remote airstrip in Cobija, Bolivia. This task could be complicated, because the airstrip was temporarily without a radio or other means of communications. The message would have to be delivered by a local courier.

"The message is to be worded as follows," Max instructed. "An extra bonus will be paid, if the corpse of the missing American pilot is returned to Cuzco. Use those exact words."

Max had no quarrel with Kenny Aguila, but the fewer people who knew about Paititi, the better. Now, or later.

After all, smirked Max, *I gave my word.*

Gloating over his cleverness, Max whistled cheerfully as he turned to more important matters.

Chapter Five

⌐⌐◯◯⼂

pert: "coming forth"

****

Cuzco, Monday, February 16

Not wanting to miss the truck to Shintuyo, Rachel arrived at the Avenida Pachacutec a half-hour early. Sometimes in Peru, she knew from experience, eight o'clock just as easily might mean seven thirty, eight thirty, or even nine o'clock. Rachel had become almost accustomed to this flexible sense of punctuality and accepted it as a cultural difference. She found it annoying at the moment, but mostly because she no longer had time to waste.

Upon arrival at the departure point, Rachel learned that the scheduled truck had developed mechanical problems. The next truck would not leave until Thursday.

Rachel was despondent until she learned from two other stranded passengers, Australian tourists, that there was a costlier but quicker way of getting to Shintuyo. As it turned out, air-conditioned tourist buses or vans left Cuzco regularly for Salvación, another town not too far from Shintuyo. The cost of the tourist buses was much more—about forty dollars American, maybe more if there wasn't a regular departure. The Australians weren't sure if they wanted to splurge forty dollars each. They were thinking of just hanging around Cuzco until the next truck, on Thursday.

Rachel talked the young couple into showing her the way to the tour bus office. Again, her options were few. The bus company had a handful of other passengers who also wanted to depart today, but too few to make the trip cost-effective. After convincing the Australians to sign up by paying ten dollars apiece toward their tickets, Rachel still had to guarantee the departure by paying the remaining one hundred twenty dollars the company wanted to make up its usual fee.

Once under way, the drive was a little bumpy and at times nerve-racking. The Volvo all-terrain bus wound around the narrow roads leading from Cuzco through a couple of high mountain passes. Rachel knew that the Machu Picchu ruins were not far away, although the route would not pass them. She could, nevertheless, easily imagine the ancient Inca city, perched upon its scenic terraced peak, surreal and serene against a backdrop of clouds and lush high altitude forests. Rachel leaned back in her seat and relaxed, insofar as her state of mind would permit, for the first time in days. The twelve thousand-foot descent from the breathtaking eastern slopes of the Andes was scheduled to take six hours, terminating at the town of Salvación, on the Alto Madre de Dios River. From there, the only means of onward transport would be by river.

Rachel felt guilty, because, in a way, she was excited at being back in Peru. She barely noticed much of the spectacular scenery they passed, as her thoughts drifted back and forth between her brother and the year that she had spent in the rain forest. The irony of the good fortune that had befallen her by way of the tourist bus also bothered Rachel. Although extremely opportune to her present mission, the bus was an ominous sign of human encroachment and exploitation. Once again, she was reminded that only four years ago this had been virgin rain forest. Then, Rachel had come to the Madre de Dios precisely because of its extreme isolation from modern man, and the lack of civilization's taint. The station had been inside a restricted area that permitted only twenty or so serious researchers each year. Even in the unrestricted areas of the national reserve, only a couple of hundred people passed through each year.

Some company was now apparently importing planeloads of cargo to build more lodges for eco-tourism, or worse, a lumber mill. Ultimately, the result would be the same. One of the planet's few remaining unspoiled tropical rain forests would be flooded with unwelcome vehicles, structures and trespassers. Rachel had even felt guilty about her research stay. She remembered how, during the last two months at the Cocha Cashu Biological Station, she had been unable to shake the feeling that, just by studying the Indians, she was meddling and thereby changing their behavior.

"*What next?*" she wondered.

Gazing out the window of the bus as it wound its way onward, Rachel felt almost like she were dreaming as cloud-veiled and forested mountain tops, plummeting cliffs, deeply etched river valleys and white water rapids zoomed past. Her spirits, already low, sank deeper. She began to wonder what craziness was leading her across the Andes and down into the jungle on a hastily planned search-and-rescue effort. What if it turned out that Kenny had to be air-evacuated back to the States? Would she have been better off waiting for more details, like her friends Dee and Trish had urged?

What made her think she had any likelihood of being able to rescue Kenny, anyway? As long as she could remember, Rachel had been trying to look out for him, even if he had been perfectly capable of doing so for himself. She recalled a time when they were kids...*First grade? No, it must have been second.* A pair of bullies had ganged up against Kenny on the way home from school. Rachel had charged the two other boys, flailing away at their heads with her Scotch plaid-colored lunch pail, and shouting, "Run Kenny! Run!" Even second-graders recognized a maniac when they saw one. Rachel's wild charge had driven the bullies off. *This isn't second grade and this isn't Kansas, Dorothy*, Rachel scolded herself.

Raindrops from a somber gray sky began to speckle the windowpane, and soon Rachel was lulled to sleep by the patter of the rain on the roof of the bus.

When the bus finally arrived at Salvación, Rachel was startled to find that she had slept for the last three hours of the journey. She recognized that the drastic change in altitude over the Andes and the marathon jet voyage had tapped her energies. She admitted that it was probably a good thing to have gotten what sleep she could on the bus.

As her first order of business, Rachel asked about transport onward to Shintuyo. Here, she got her first lucky break in days. As luck would have it, someone pointed out a member of Max Arnold's expedition. This man had relatives in Salvación, and was to join the rest of the group later.

Within an hour of her arrival in Salvación, Rachel was in a motorized canoe being transported downriver to Shintuyo.

When they reached the expedition's campsite, Rachel ascended the riverbank and located Dr. Gallagher, who was engaged in conversation with two other men. One of these interrupted Gallagher to shout instructions to one of several Peruvians milling about the camp. Rachel assumed this was Max Arnold, the organizer of the expedition. The third man was tall and rugged-looking with tousled, sandy-colored hair.

Rachel stopped in midstep.

Oh, no. The guy from the Libertador.

The stranger watched Rachel without expression as she resumed her approach.

Max Arnold was a bear of man who resembled what Rachel thought a drill instructor must look like. Rachel figured that Arnold and the other man were probably both in their early forties. All three of the men wore lightweight tropical khaki clothing. Max smiled broadly upon seeing Rachel and strode forward to greet her.

"Miss Aguila, I presume?" Max's voice was deep and resonant. He sounded like a man used to being listened to. He met Rachel's eyes and blinked once, but if the mismatched color of her irises surprised him, he didn't show it by his facial reaction. "I'm Max Arnold. Nice to meet you! Unfortunate circumstances, of course." A concerned look replaced the smile as a more suitable accompaniment to his words. "I see from your bags that you must have decided to accept my offer. Excellent! We're off, first light, tomorrow morning."

"I'll be ready," Rachel replied, forcing a smile. "I want to tell you how much I appreciate your help, Mr. Arnold. There's no telling how long I might have been caught up in Cuzco, otherwise. But tell me, have you been able to find out anything else about the crash?"

The older man shrugged off the thanks with a sympathetic gesture. "Please call me Max. Mr. Arnold makes me feel ancient. In answer to your question, all that I was able to do so far, was to have a second plane fly a few more passes over the wreckage. There's good news and bad news." Max paused for dramatic effect, before he continued the lie. "The bad news is that we still haven't seen any trace of your brother. The good news is that we're not entirely sure now that the wreckage is the plane that he was flying. Our pilot couldn't safely get low enough to make sure, because of the variable heights of the trees in the area. There appears to be some discrepancies between the description the pilot and spotter gave us and the Cherokee Piper that your brother was flying."

"But, if it's not Kenny, why wouldn't someone have heard from him?" Rachel demanded, taken aback by this new information.

"Well, of course, that's the reason everyone thought something had happened to him," Max nodded. "I mean, he wouldn't have just gone off on a wild weekend or anything, would he?" Max again paused and glanced at Rachel, as if for verification.

"Never. Not Kenny," Rachel answered.

"No, I guess not. There's not much around here of that sort, anyway," Max continued. "Anyway, that's why we're still going in—to visit the crash site in person."

Max suddenly realized that he had not yet introduced the third man, and turned, gesturing toward his partner.

"I'm sorry, Miss Aguila; where are my manners? This gentleman is Tristan Sloan, my associate and one of the best jungle guides in the world. You already know Dr. Gallagher, of course."

Rachel smiled as best she could manage, and nodded first at the professor, then at Tristan.

"We've met," said Tristan.

"Um…yes. I suppose I should apologize about that. I was having a really bad day."

She waited to see if Tristan offered a handshake. He did not, but nor did most men. Nonetheless, Rachel had the subtle impression that he was not that happy about her presence. More than just their bad start, back in Cuzco. Something about the eyes and the set of his mouth warned her that the man probably considered her extra baggage.

Tristan gazed for a prolonged moment directly into Rachel's eyes—a deep, penetrating look. Rachel prepared for the usual tired comment, but then realized it wouldn't be forthcoming, after all. He continued to assess her like he might a stray dog—as if deciding whether to shoo her away or just ignore her presence.

Don't tell me he's still nursing a grudge over her retort, back in Cuzco, she thought. Perhaps he was angry that she was causing the expedition to veer off course. She realized that Max had given no indication of the expedition's mission, nor had she yet asked. She had been so preoccupied with the logistics of getting here and with worrying about Kenny that she hadn't even been curious.

"I certainly appreciate you deterring from your route to look for Kenny," she said. "If you don't mind my asking, where was your group originally headed?"

"Now that," the broad smile reappearing across Max's tanned face, "…is something that I look forward to telling you all about…but later tonight. I'll fill you in, over supper. Right now, let's get you settled. We went ahead and put up an extra tent, just on the chance that you might be joining us."

"Chico!" Max bellowed. The shout was directed at one of the Peruvians crossing the campsite. "Have one of the men take Miss Aguila's bag to her tent, and you show her where it's set up."

The man named Chico trotted over.

"*Sí, Señor!*"

Chico gestured at one of the other men, and gave him some directions in Spanish. He then turned to Rachel and pointed at the tents. "Please follow me, Señorita."

In all, Rachel counted nine tents: three large ones and six two-person, all season mountaineering tents. Besides the three that Rachel had already met, about six more men were occupied in various tasks around the camp or were resting in the shade chewing coca leaves. A few others sat near the riverbank. Rachel didn't see any other women, but this didn't surprise her. It just confirmed that the expedition wasn't an ecological adventure trip. Otherwise, as many as half of the expedition might just as well be female.

"This one is yours," said Chico, stopping next to one of the smaller tents. The other man carrying Rachel's duffel bag strode up behind them. Rachel gestured that he could place it inside the tent.

"Make yourself at home, Rachel!" Max called. "Supper will be ready in about twenty minutes."

Rachel waved back in acknowledgment. There wasn't much that she could do in the tent to make herself at home. The tent was only about three feet high and meant solely for sleeping.

She decided to walk down by the river. As she approached, three men sitting there stood to greet her, she saw that one of these was again Dr. Gallagher.

"Hello again," Rachel greeted. "It's turning out to be quite a help, the coincidence of running into you here in Peru. Thanks for getting me an invitation to accompany your expedition."

"Not mine. Max Arnold's. But you're welcome, I suppose. Although, there are few true coincidences, I'm afraid." He was certain that Rachel was unaware of even half the truth.

"This is Dr. Jorgé Ramón," Dr. Gallagher introduced. "Dr. Ramón is a distinguished colleague from the University of Trujillo. I was just telling Dr. Ramón about your scholarly interests and research here in Peru."

"A pleasure to meet you, Señorita Rachel," Dr. Ramón said, greeting her with the traditional *abrazo*, or embrace and kissing of both cheeks, as was the custom in his country.

"Intelligent and such a beautiful young woman, as well," he flattered. "Of course, any help that I can offer you…anything that can help in your studies…please do not hesitate to ask, Señorita."

"That's very kind of you."

"I am very sorry to hear about your brother," Ramón continued. "Let us hope that it is only a problem of not being able to communicate his whereabouts. You realize that here, away from the larger cities, there is often no telephone. It is possible that at this very moment your brother is on his way back to Cuzco."

"I'm praying that something like that is exactly what has happened," Rachel said.

"Permit me to also introduce our associate, Señor Amasu," Dr. Gallagher interrupted. "Señor Amasu is a native Quechua inhabitant of these parts, who will also be a part of the expedition. We've already had some fascinating discussions of local legends."

"*Napaykullayki*," Rachel greeted.

The Indian named Amasu raised his eyebrows a bit. This was the only sign of surprise that a foreign woman had greeted him in his native tongue. The Indian was the oldest of the men she had met so far in the camp. She estimated that he was probably well into his sixties.

"*Napaykullayki*," Amasu replied. "¿Runasimita rimankichu?"

"Yes," Rachel answered, smiling. "I speak Quechua…just a little."

Amasu nodded.

"Good for you." He fell silent again, and seemed to lose interest in Rachel. Rachel wasn't particularly surprised at this reaction. Most of the Quechua-speaking Indians she had met during her previous experiences in Peru were quiet, solitary figures. The caste system of Peru kept these Indians at the peripheries of their society. As if stoically biding time, these modern descendants of the Incas continued to patiently live in the obscurity of prejudice and cultural segregation. It surprised Rachel to find the old Indian in the company of the Peruvian professor. She wondered that the two men would have anything in common.

"Is your father perhaps Hispanic, Señorita Rachel?" Dr. Ramón asked. "I only ask because Aguila is a Spanish name. If you will forgive me for saying so, it is also unusual to find an American who speaks Quechua."

"My great grandfather was Peruvian. I understand that there was even a distant kinship with the conquistador Hernando De Soto and some of his descendants who remained in Cuzco. And yes, you're right about the name. Aguila is Spanish for eagle."

"That's correct," Ramón nodded.

"As for the Quechua," Rachel said, "I picked up a little during the year I spent here. I'm more than a little rusty, you see."

"Yours sounded fine to me," Dr. Ramón said. "I, too, speak the Quechua language. As a matter of a fact, that is one of the reasons I was asked to join the expedition. Amasu speaks such good English, however, that I'm afraid I've not been able to earn my way. I hope you are not also going to put me out of a job, Señorita Rachel," he said, chuckling.

"Oh, no worry on that account," Rachel replied quickly. "I'll be headed back to Cuzco as soon as we find my brother—or find out that the wreckage out there is not his plane."

"He's your twin, I understand?"

"That's right. Maybe that's why I know he has to be okay. Twins are supposed to have this greater than normal connectedness."

The Indian Amasu made an odd clicking sound with his tongue.

"*Apocatequil y Piquerao*," he murmured. Having made the strange pronouncement, he nodded at the group and wandered away.

"Strange old bird, isn't he?" Dr. Gallagher asked. "What was that he said?"

"Just some superstitious nonsense, really. Apocatequil and Piquerao were mythological figures in Peruvian Indian legends," Dr. Ramón explained. "They were the twins Thunder and Lightning. I think he took it that Señorita Rachel being a twin was an ill omen. Many of the older Quechua Indians still believe such foolishness."

The sky was starting to darken, and the mosquitoes were out. Back at the campsite, one of the men was calling to the group at the river that supper was ready. Rachel walked back with the two professors, chatting a bit along the way with Dr. Gallagher about what each other had been up to since Rachel had left Los Angeles. When they reached the tents, Rachel excused herself to go put on some insect repellent and a long sleeve shirt.

A makeshift toilet, consisting of a hole in the ground, powdered lye, a camp shovel and a sheet wrapped around three trees as a privacy screen, was within sight a distance from the tents. Rachel took a flashlight and made a quick visit before joining the others at the campfire. She kept a wary eye out for scorpions and snakes until she was back near the campfire. As much as she advocated preservation of the jungle, it was not because of all the creepy-crawlers that abounded therein.

Dinner consisted of chicken or some sort of chicken-like fowl, lentils, yucca, papaya and other fruit. Over dinner, Max engaged Rachel in conversation. She learned that almost all the porters were Cuzqueños—natives of Cuzco. She wondered a bit about that. Most Peruvians who preferred living in the larger Peruvian cities didn't like spending that much time in the *alta selvas, montañas* or the jungles. She wondered that they hadn't tried to recruit *paisanos* from the river dwellings closer to their destination.

"Dr. Gallagher mentioned that you liked to travel," Max said. "How many countries did he say you had you visited? Thirty?"

Rachel was surprised that Gallagher even knew something like that. Oddly, Dr. Gallagher also looked a bit surprised by Max's remark.

"Uh…yes, that's…about right. One for each of my twenty-nine years of age. That's just coincidence, you understand? Not a goal. Although, I thought if I stayed home this year, I might beat the rap of my thirtieth birthday. I guess I've messed that up. I'd never been to Bolivia before, but I came through La Paz on my way here. You think I'll have to count that?"

"It's not to late to turn back," noted Tristan. "Then you wouldn't have to." *There. At least he had tried. If the damn fool girl was determined to plunge into the jungle, it wasn't really his job to stop her, was it?*

"I understand you spent quite a bit of time near here," Max resumed, scowling at Tristan.

Rachel nodded, her mouth too full of food to explain further.

"Excellent," Dr. Ramón joked. "You will be able to tell us where to find all the best restaurants."

Rachel grinned. The Peruvian obviously knew better than that. During her previous stay, Rachel had spent three to four months at a stretch without being anywhere near a restaurant. When she had finally been able to get to the closest town, the only restaurants were scarcely more than plywood shacks with one or two menu items.

"When you were here," Max asked, "…did you happen to learn any local folklore about the Inca and the lost cities?"

Rachel swallowed part of the food, trying and almost succeeding at not speaking while her mouth was full.

"I'm an anthropologist, remember?" Having said this, she glanced apologetically at the two professors. "Well, almost. At any rate, my dissertation revolves around the native people of Peru."

"Of course. You're familiar, then, with the legend of Gran Paititi?"

Rachel nearly choked on the food she had just swallowed. "You're kidding! Don't tell me this expedition is to look for Paititi?" She hesitated. She was not in a position to be rude with her benefactors. "No offense meant," she added, "…but no one is sure that it was even a real city."

Even if it was, Rachel reflected silently, there was as much evidence to place it in Guyana, Ecuador, Columbia, Brazil, Bolivia, or even Argentina as here in Peru. As she well knew, at least a dozen different theories existed about the "golden city." Many accounts suggested that El Gran Paititi was a person versus a place.

"You know," Rachel said, "Many Paititi authorities believe that the Indians made up the treasure stories to lead the conquistadors off on a wild goose chase, away from their cities."

"There are many Spanish eyewitnesses' journals dating from the sixteenth century that indicate that those sources just might very well be mistaken," Max protested. His overall expression remained affable, but there was a distinct hardening of his eyes.

"What else would the Indians have told them?" Rachel replied. "They hardly could have told the conquistadors, 'Yep, we swallowed all the gold and rubies. So did our daughters, who coincidentally are all virgins.'"

"I'm afraid the Señorita is mostly correct," Dr. Ramón chuckled. "What few truths are *known* are accounts of Lake Guatavita, near the Cundamarca Plateau in Columbia."

At least one of them hasn't lost his marbles, Rachel thought.

Dr. Ramón continued with an explanation. "The chief of the village by this lake exercised a traditional ceremony wherein he covered his entire naked body with gold dust at the dawn of a prescribed day. He rowed out to the center, then threw some jewels and gold into the lake before jumping in. This was all part of legend and ritual to honor a long dead Indian princess who drowned in the lake centuries earlier. Ah, I see you are already familiar with this story…yes?"

Max and Tristan both nodded.

"Probably fifty or sixty different expeditions were launched just in the hundred years after the Spanish landed looking for Paititi," Rachel explained. "Every time the Spaniards thought they were getting close, the local Indians would say something like, 'Oh no, Mr. Conquistador…there's not so much gold in our poor little territory. You obviously mean the city of The Golden One, which just happens to be our neighboring enemy's city. They are just rolling in the stuff.' I think the Indians must have had quite a bit of fun with the story."

Max had waited patiently, hearing out Rachel's bemused interpretation of the Paititi myth.

"Although I've made a very good living at recovering lost treasures, your opinion is much the same as mine was—until a few days ago," he replied calmly. "That's why neither Tristan nor myself have ever gone looking for El Dorado, even though it's reputedly the richest treasure ever lost. That, however, was before Tristan stumbled across a *very* old map that made us think differently."

Rachel glanced around at the men circling the fire. She didn't know how gullible Max Arnold or the man Sloan was, but surely the two university professors should know better.

"Dr. Gallagher, Dr. Ramón…you surely recognize that these men are what the local authorities call *huaqueros*. This is going to sound bad…but bluntly speaking, their purpose is to *plunder* whatever historical artifacts they might find. I am really a bit surprised that either of you is knowingly a participant in such an undertaking, and such a fanciful one, at that."

"You don't understand," Dr. Gallagher protested. "This isn't a treasure hunt for me. This goes far beyond that. Dr. Ramón and I are here with the very noblest of intentions, I assure you. There's a lot you still don't know about this expedition."

Rachel was unconvinced. "You have some special reason to believe that the map Max mentioned is authentic?"

"I'm reasonably comfortable with the notion that it is at least three thousand years old," Dr. Gallagher answered.

"Even papyrus doesn't last *that* long!"

"It's stone," Max answered.

"That doesn't make a difference. Hasn't Dr. Ramón told you that the Inca empire only truly emerged at the beginning of the fifteenth century? The very earliest evidence of their presence is around 1250 AD. Your map would be almost two thousand years older than the Incas and their oldest cities. If it *is* that old, your stone drawing would have to be a map of somewhere other than the Inca empire. Besides, they didn't even use written communication. Their pictographs and rock carvings wouldn't do more than represent a person or a scene of some sort."

"I am sure, Señorita Rachel," Dr. Ramón explained, "…that you are aware of the proposal that the Chavin culture arose from some tribe that originally dwelt in the deepest reaches of the rain forest east of the Andes. We know that the Chavin people lived here as early as nine hundred, BC. The pyramids at Tucumé, Peru, existed by the eleventh century. Certainly, if we have only discovered such evidence in the past few decades, it is within the realm of possibility that the Chavin or some other earlier native culture long before the Incas may have created a civilization and such a city as Paititi within the jungle. Surely, as a fellow anthropologist and one familiar with Peru, you do not subscribe to the belief that only ignorant savages could have lived in such a resource-laden, fertile Eden. This was, you'll recall, at the very same period as the Egyptians, Greeks and cultures of the Far East were building civilizations that we are hard-pressed to equal, even today."

For a moment, after listening to Dr. Ramón, Rachel felt a little bit like an undergrad. The Peruvian professor was unquestionably much more experienced than she. To some extent, however, even Dr. Ramón's explanation was heavier on theory than researched evidence. Rachel thought that the Peruvian professor's nationalistic pride and bias for the theory was also heavily influencing his opinion. As was frequently her habit after having expressed a conflicting opinion, Rachel felt embarrassed for having spoken out. She switched to a more deferential approach.

"Dr. Gallagher, do *you* believe this is a map of an ancient lost city in the Amazon jungle?"

"I'm afraid I don't know the least bit about lost cities in the jungle. As you'll recall, my specialty is Egyptology. I do, however, believe in the authenticity of the map. I've given my utmost scrutiny to its most minute details. It would have to be an incredibly expert forgery. The circumstances and location of its discovery also point toward authenticity."

"Wait, don't tell me. You dug it up in the secret tunnels beneath Cuzco?" Rachel said, in jest.

"No," Max said. "You're just going to love this part. The map is written in Egyptian symbols. Tristan unearthed it in Morocco almost three months ago, hence Dr. Gallagher's involvement. And along with Gran Paititi, it *shows* the tunnels under Cuzco."

Max's smile was broader than ever.

Chapter Six

Egyptian hieroglyph for water

****

Alto Madre de Dios River, Peru, Tuesday, February 17

The month of February is part of the wet season in the montañas and forests east of the Andes. Rachel knew that the Peruvians used the terms "wet" and "dry seasons" comparatively. A rain forest isn't so-named just for the hell of it. An early morning downpour even now pelted the two motor launches, as they made their way northeasterly along the Alto Madre de Dios River from Shintuyo.

The two boats had arrived at dawn. Tristan Sloan, who had said hardly a handful of words the entire previous evening, was transformed as he supervised the transfer of equipment, supplies and team members to the two boats. He took charge with quiet assurance. Shouting instructions here, pointing and waving directions there, he somehow got the entire campsite taken down, packed and stowed on board in under half an hour.

Rachel learned that the expedition included fourteen people, not counting her or the two men who crewed each of the boats. Chico and most of the Peruvians had loaded onto one boat. The two professors, along with Tristan, Max, Amasu, Rachel and a Cuzqueño giant named Raóul boarded the other. The men serving as porters had divided the supplies and equipment evenly between the two boats.

The motor launches were typical of the river craft that Rachel had seen throughout her earlier stay in Peru. Each was about thirty feet long, with most of the deck covered and enclosed. Neither vessel bore much paint above the water line. The hand-painted name, *Asunción*, proclaimed itself from the bow of the boat. The second vessel was christened *Salvación*, like the nearby river town.

Rachel poured a second cup of coffee and wrapped her fingers around the cup, appreciative of the warmth. The morning air was still a bit cool, and the movement over the water caused a brisk breeze to flow through the open-sided boat. As she counted the few blessings of her present situation, she gratefully numbered among them an absence of seasickness. She sniffed the aroma of the coffee as it mingled with the damp smell of the hovering jungle and, for the moment, contentedly watched the other members of the expedition while she deliberately postponed waking up all the way. The men had mostly paired off and begun to converse quietly with one another as the expedition motored down the river.

Trying not to be too obvious, her attention often focused on Tristan. She liked something about the way his blue eyes darted about, curious and absorbing everything, but rarely lighting for more than a second on one person or object. It was almost childlike. *A chink in his armor?* she wondered.

As she took stock of her location and company, Rachel again found herself questioning the judgment that had led her to her present circumstances. *Here I am*, she thought,...*in a floating shack drifting down a river into a primitive jungle. I'm surrounded by a group of loony-toon*

*treasure seekers, headed to check out a crash site that's increasingly starting to
sound like it probably isn't even Kenny's plane!*

What the hell am I doing? she wondered. She engaged in serious
consideration of turning back at the first opportunity.

The expedition packs and supplies had been stacked in the center of
each of the two boats and, as one of the men rose and made his way
toward Rachel, the boat leaned heavily to one side. The culprit turned
out to be Max, who on reaching Rachel, sat down and unfolded a map.

"Here's where we're headed. The site of the wreckage," he indicated,
stabbing a finger at an area circled in red on the map. "And here's where
we are now, on the Río Alto Madre de Dios. We stay on the river until it
intersects at the Manu River late this afternoon. We'll camp there for the
evening, and try to find a couple of Indian guides for the next part of
the journey."

Rachel nodded. "Machiguenga?"

"Preferably," Tristan answered. He had come up silently from behind,
without having caused as noticeable disturbance as Max, and Rachel
had not realized his presence until he spoke.

"If not, then possibly Amahuaca," Tristan added, as Rachel blushed at
the reminder. "I understand that you speak both languages?"

"Yes, a little. How is it that everyone seems to know so much about
me?" It was beginning to make her a bit paranoid.

"I believe Dr. Gallagher may have mentioned it. Something about a
paper you wrote in college."

"Excellent. Maybe that'll even come in handy," Max said. "At any rate,
tomorrow, the easy part of the journey ends. We'll have to go on by foot
from Puerto Definitivo. We'll mostly be dependent upon the Indian
guides to steer us clear of hostile natives."

"And then how long to reach the crash site?"

Tristan remained silent, but Max immediately filled in.

"That depends on how dense the jungle is. We'll have to cut a trail as
we go. I'm guessing it could take two days."

Two days! That would make it over a week since Kenny had disappeared. How long could he survive without adequate medical attention? She wished there was a way to contact the hotel in Cuzco, to see if there had been further news.

For the most part, the river voyage was smooth going. Occasionally, the boats would pass through some very mild rapids, but there was plenty of clearance between the rocks, and the boat captains knew their jobs well.

After the first hour beyond Shintuyo, there was almost no other traffic on the river. Only a couple of times did they see other human beings. Once they met a lone "*piroque*," a notoriously unstable canoe, made from a hollowed-out tree trunk. The Indian paddling it was transporting a large bundle of palms and other plants. Everything the Indians needed they found in the jungle. Rachel wistfully longed for the simplicity of the native's lifestyle, even though she knew it was his alone.

Why is that? she asked herself. *Why can't that be mine? Because everyone expects more? The problem is,* she reflected sadly, *there's never enough. Enough of anything…time, energy, cooperation.*

She could never trade places. The Indians and she lived in radically different realities.

A bit later, they passed a couple of riverside shacks built upon stilts on a steep embankment. Through the open doors and windows of the ramshackle structures, naked children peered out inquisitively at the passing boats, and an older youth hauled up an empty wire-mesh fish trap. *Even the ones with simpler worlds are screwed,* she thought.

Apart from the scarcity of human presence, there was a variety, if not abundance, of life along the riverbanks. Rachel spotted a few pairs of macaws, toucans, and other bird life, and marveled at their glorious colors. Once, as their boat approached a bend in the river, a dozen brown capuchin monkeys filled the air with alarmed shrieks and chatter. Leaping from the overhanging branches to treetops farther back from the river, the monkeys noisily retreated from the intruding motor launches. Rachel's smile at their chaotic flurry turned into a frown as she conceded that she was part of that intrusion.

On another occasion, Rachel saw movement in the water near the shore and asked one of the crew if it had been a caiman. The crew member thought a fish biting at an insect was more likely. During the day the caimans were most likely several hundred meters up inside the smaller streams that fed into the river at regular intervals. The engine noise frightened away most wildlife long before the boats reached them.

Gradually, Rachel grew bored of watching the passing shoreline. After a hour or two, even a passing jungle is just a bunch of trees. She began to engage various members of the expedition in conversation. After visiting briefly with Max, Dr. Gallagher and then Dr. Ramón, Rachel was about to work up sufficient nerve to chat with the enigmatic Tristan Sloan. As she rose to shift places in the boat, she nearly knocked heads with someone coming from the opposite direction.

"Oh! Excuse me, Amasu…*Napaykullayki,*"

"*Napaykullayki, Doña Rachel,*" the old man answered, taking a seat.

"Not Doña…just Señorita, I'm afraid. I have no claims to nobility or station."

"You are of the Aguila family? The Aguila of Cuzco are of the *ayllu* of Quilaco."

"I'm afraid you must be mistaken. My father's surname is Aguila, that's true, but he was born in the United States, as was his father. My great grandparents are the ones who came from Cuzco. They were related to the De Sotos of Cuzco, a *mestizo* family. Not Spanish nobility, but descendants of the conquistador Hernando de Soto." One of two famous ancestors, Rachel thought. Both of whom, she was embarrassed to admit, had been instrumental in opening virgin territories to colonial expansion. The other—Kit Carson, through his vast explorations and later scouting for the American military—had done much to open the American West. Well, all families have their skeletons in the closet, she reflected. She wished she could be more like Kenny, who never found the family ancestry bothersome. Genealogy was all ancient history to Kenny—"dead and buried," as he would say.

"*Arí*…yes, yes." Amasu was undeterred. "…De Sotos, but by the line of the daughter of Doña Leonor Cori Cuillor."

Rachel shook her head, still confused.

"Cori Cuillor, the Golden Star. The wife of Quilaco, of the *ayllu* of Atahualpa."

"Really? I'm afraid that's a new one on me. I have never heard anything like that from my father or grandfather. You're saying that you believe I am somehow related to the Inca Atahualpa?"

"Not directly. But to Quilaco, yes. He was one of Atahualpa's captains and a relative."

Rachel smiled slightly. "All right, I guess I'll have to take your word for that." She decided that Amasu must have her family mixed up with some other one. Her ancestors had left Peru in the early 1900's to find greater opportunity for those with mixed racial ancestry. They had wound up in California. Nonetheless, perhaps once she found Kenny, it might be interesting to see what history she could dig up on the Aguila line. From what she knew of Atahualpa, she would just as soon Amasu's lead be mistaken. Spanish monks had chronicled the inhuman atrocities that the famous Inca and his half-brother Huascar had inflicted upon one another's families. Rachel had long ago reached the conclusion that the Inca empire had come to a timely end during the Spanish conquest.

Rachel noticed that the old man was staring at her eyes and didn't stop this when Rachel made eye contact. For some reason, this irritated Rachel slightly. He probably thought she had the "evil eye."

"Is there a problem?" she asked tersely.

"Your eyes speak of an imbalance."

"And your mouth speaks of a lack of diplomacy," she shot back.

Amasu seemed taken aback. "*Manan*…inside." Rachel understood from his gestures that he meant her heart or soul.

"Eyes are only the windows…This is an English saying, yes? I see in your eyes a *lost* look. This says to me, 'Here is a soul, searching for balance.' I meant to speak no offense."

"I'm sorry. I didn't mean to snap back at you. I've had a rough couple of days. At any rate, it's not something inside that's lost. It's my twin brother."

"Perhaps. It is possible, however, that you look for the wrong thing in the right place."

"I don't think I understand. I'm just looking for my brother. There was a sighting of a plane's wreckage in the jungle. The crash site is near this expedition's planned route; just a couple of days from here."

Amasu shook his head. "Your brother does not need you. If you go into the jungle, it is better for you that you look for the right thing. There are many dangers there."

"Did Max put you up to this? Are you trying to tell me I should be looking for the treasure?"

"*¡Waw!*" Amasu shook his head in disgust. "Not the treasure."

"What then? My brother's the only reason I'm even here."

"*Ignotium per ignotius,*" Amasu, replied like that answered everything. "Look for the gold, but not the ancient ones' gold. Look for the gold in the shadow."

Rachel stared at the old Indian for a few moments in confusion. What in the world was he talking about? And Latin? A Latin-quoting Quechua Indian! He must be certifiably off his rocker! She mumbled an excuse about needing to speak with Max and started toward the back of the boat where Max had rejoined Tristan. *Ignotium per ignotius,* Rachel thought. *The interpretation of the unknown, by way of the even more unknown. Where in the world had the old man picked up that?*

By nine o'clock a.m., the temperature had already climbed to eighty degrees. The humidity made it feel warmer. Because of many large logs, the boat had been forced to reduce speed, lessening the earlier breeze that had kept things comfortable. By noon, it was sweltering, and

Rachel began looking for clouds, hoping that the rain would return to cool things down.

Finally after lunch, Tristan suggested to Max that they stop for a brief swim.

Max was suffering at least as much as anyone else, and after a few moments' consideration, agreed on a short rest stop. The two boats pulled up at a small cove where the current would present less danger. In minutes, Max, Tristan and Gallagher had stripped off their shoes, socks and shirts and were in the water, along with most of the men from Cuzco.

"The water's great," Max called. "Come on in."

The water really did look appealing, and Rachel was not yet accustomed to the tropical heat and humidity. Still, she wasn't sure how safe the river might be.

"Are you sure there are no caiman around here?"

"Not during the daytime. They're strictly nocturnal. Go for it!" Max urged.

"What about piranha? We used to catch piranha all the time in the *igarapes* around the Manu Biosphere."

"I assure you, Señorita, no piranha in this river," the foreman Chico answered. "The Alto Madre de Dios is too fresh and fast flowing. The piranha like the back streams."

Rachel figured if there had been piranha, the men would be scream-ing and flailing about by then, so she stripped down to her tank top and pants and jumped in. The water was surprisingly cool and refreshing. Dr. Ramón, however, leaned over the side of the boat and called to Rachel.

"I think it is not so good, Señorita, for you to go in the river."

"No?"

He shook his head, displaying a genuine look of anxiety.

Rachel decided a quick dip was enough, anyway. Why push her luck, if Dr. Ramón didn't think it was safe? She climbed back on board, allowing Dr. Ramón to give her a hand getting back up over the side. She used the dry outer shirt she had left on board to dry her face and hair.

"Chico said there were no piranha or caiman," she said, wondering at Dr. Ramón's concern.

"No caiman, perhaps, but other things. It is not so safe, Señorita Rachel. They're are probably four or five different species of piranha. Here, they won't bother you unless you were bleeding profusely, but there are still some nasty parasites and other dangers."

"Okay," she replied, shrugging.

By that time, the others were starting to pull themselves back on board, as well. Max had Chico tell the stragglers to load up, and soon they were again on their way.

It didn't take long for their clothes to dry. Soon, almost everyone was beginning to sweat again.

About forty minutes later, one of the crew whistled loudly and pointed to the river, between the boat and the shore. Two, then three humps appeared like a miniature Loch Ness monster. A few minutes later the humps reappeared behind the first boat.

"What was it?" Rachel asked.

"I'm not a hundred percent sure, but an anaconda, I think." Tristan answered. "Huge one, if so."

Dr. Ramón caught Rachel's eye and nodded. Her eyes round as half-dollars, Rachel glanced at Chico.

"I thought you said it was safe!"

Chico grinned weakly. "No caiman," he said.

Rachel thought she saw the ghost of a smile on Tristan Sloan's face.

"No caiman," she muttered.

****

Cobija, Bolivia, Tuesday, February 17

If it hadn't been for the *chapo*, there's no telling how long he would have been stranded.

In the few days following his emergency landing at Cobija, Kenny had been able to establish an easy-going rapport with the Bolivian, Miguel. This afternoon, Miguel had even brought Kenny home with him. "Home" for Miguel, was a ramshackle lean-to on the banks of a nearby tributary. Miguel shared the structure with his wife and three children, who were now working or playing outside. After an ample lunch of many items Kenny was at a loss to identify, Miguel had produced a large pot of the local beverage called "*chapo*." Fermented mashed bananas was not Kenny's favorite drink. For that reason, he sipped his portions much slower than did his host. After a couple of hours and most of the brew, Miguel was feeling no pain. Almost every sentence either of the two men uttered struck the Bolivian as hilarious. Kenny still did not feel even a slight buzz.

Things could be worse, he figured. Surely, the replacement compass and other parts were on their way. The plane's radio was another instrument that had been incapacitated. Kenny wondered if there had *ever* been anyone assigned to the aircraft's maintenance, and what else might be on the verge of failing. After Miguel's radio failed, there had been no way to verify when to expect delivery. Until a courier landed at Cobija, Kenny figured he had no choice and therefore might as well enjoy Miguel's company and hospitality. His thoughts turned to his twin. Rachel would probably be getting anxious about not hearing from him, by now. He almost never went this long without contacting her. He worried a lot about his sister. In her struggle to avoid becoming like their mother, his twin failed to see that she was doing everything possible to recreate herself as their father. He wished he could help, but realized Rachel's was a singular journey that not even a twin could share.

"Unless those instruments arrive soon, you may have to adopt me," he joked to Miguel.

Miguel guffawed and slapped his knee. Having forgotten he was holding his mug of chapo in the same hand, Miguel giggled uncontrollably as the liquid inundated his trousers. Kenny shook his head at how easily it was to amuse a person who alcohol has rendered feeble-minded.

"*Mañana, amigo,*" the Bolivian said, after he regained his composure. "Tomorrow, I make radio La Paz. I tell somebody they come *pronto.*"

"No kiddin'? How are you going to radio La Paz? I thought the radio was still broken. Did you find a way to fix it?"

Miguel winked at Kenny and put down his drink. He staggered to a wooden box that served as a dresser, and dug something out of the pocket of a wrinkled pair of pants. When he brought it over to Kenny, the American recognized a transistor of some sort.

"You have a spare part for the radio?" Kenny asked. "What? You just now remembered that?"

Miguel guffawed again. "The gringo…he say I should make the radio no work. He no say how long."

All of a sudden, Kenny grew deadly serious. "What gringo? Are you saying you intentionally disabled the radio?"

Miguel pawed for the nearly empty pot of chapo, found it, and sloshed more of the liquid into Kenny's cup.

"*No problema, amigo. Mañana.*"

Kenny calmed himself for a few seconds, then renewed the question. "Miguel. Tell me about the gringo. What's his name?"

Miguel shrugged, then giggled again. "*El gringo con muy dinero.* He no say hees name. He just say call my brother in La Paz…to know what he says about dee money ees true. I call my brother…he say Sí, the bank receive muy dinero por Miguel. The gringo say thees money ees all mine if radio no work for a few day."

Miguel waved off the rest of Kenny's questions as unimportant. The Bolivian suddenly grew very tired and stretched out on the ground. Despite Kenny's efforts to pry more information from his host, Miguel was soon snoring loudly.

What was going on, wondered Kenny. Who would bribe an airstrip attendant in an obscure border town to disable communications? Did it have anything to do with him, or was he just an innocent bystander? Did someone want him stranded on purpose? Environmentalists, looking to sabotage the construction company's efforts?

Kenny wasn't sure what course of action he should follow. It would be dangerously unsafe to fly the plane to Cuzco or La Paz without the replacement parts. The only place between Cobija and Cuzco with an airstrip was Shintuyo. That was also too far. Puerto Maldonado was a little less than half the distance, but out of the way. Yet, there were more open spaces where he could land if necessary. The most sensible thing would be to wait.

In the state Miguel was in, he'd probably sleep straight through to morning. Once sober, would the Bolivian be contrite and helpful, or sullen and tightlipped?

Kenny extracted the transistor from Miguel's hand. He hadn't the slightest idea where inside the radio it might belong. He gave his situation closer consideration. How far would someone go to keep him stranded here? Life was cheap in the third world, and he already seen that something underhanded was afoot. If he stayed, was he in serious danger? Miguel didn't seem the cutthroat type, but the Bolivian had, after all, taken money to shut down the airstrip's communications system. Who else knew of Kenny's whereabouts? Rachel knew he was near Cuzco, but she was a continent away. People disappeared all the time in South America. Kenny's world and the jungle where he found himself stranded suddenly seemed more sinister and dangerous. He evaluated his present physical status. Thanks to Miguel, he had spilled more of the chapo than he had consumed. Unless the concoction packed a delayed whammy, he'd be able to fly just fine. The plane was still the big question mark. Would it perform well enough to reach Puerto Maldonado? He looked at the unconscious Miguel and figured he still had a few hours to decide.

Chapter Seven

"Narti-ankh-em-senf"
first of the nine snakes infesting the way between this
world and the next, according to the Papyrus of Iuaa.

****

Puerto Maldonado, Peru, February 18

Kenny landed in Puerto Maldonado only moments before the sunrise.
Both his nerves and the plane had remained more or less intact.

A symbiotic relationship? he wondered.

Luck and an uncanny sense of direction had favored him, and Kenny
had found the small city without serious course deviation.

It took a while to persuade anyone, but finally one of the airport
officials allowed him access to a telephone. That was only after the
American had shown that he had plenty of cash. Many locals hoarded

dollars as the only safe method of beating the country's rampant inflation. A glimpse of the greenbacks Kenny flashed probably worked as well as any verbal plea he had made.

He first placed a call to his construction company employer in Cuzco. He was surprised to discover that everyone had given him up for dead, and worse, that Rachel had already been notified as next-of-kin. The company had already hired a new pilot, so Kenny was also out of a job.

He immediately placed a new call to Rachel's apartment in Norman.

When Trish answered the phone, Kenny was startled. One of his ongoing jokes was to tease his sister about her ballerina friend. Was Trish having the last laugh?

"Uh, hello…" he said. "This is Kenny. Is Rachel there?"

He jerked the handset away from his ear, in reaction to the shriek that came in response. He alternately listened then asked questions, as Trish filled him in on what had happened. Yes, he was fine. No, he hadn't crashed. Who had said so? When had Rachel left? Had Trish heard from Rachel or have a newer number for her in Peru? No, he hadn't already contacted the hotel. He wrote down the number. Was Trish sharing an apartment with Rachel, now? Oh, well, that was very considerate. He'd better go.

As Kenny initiated a third call, the airport official was loudly repenting that he had allowed Kenny use of the phone. When the Hotel Libertador answered, Kenny learned that Rachel had already left. There was, however, a message for Mr. Aguila from his sister. The message briefly explained that Rachel had learned of the plane crash, had come to Cuzco, and was now en route to the crash site with Max Arnold's expedition team. If he received this message, Kenny was supposed to contact the expedition, through the mission station at Shintuyo.

The hotel desk clerk was very helpful in helping to fill in missing pieces of the puzzle. Kenny found out that Rachel had met an American professor that she had known in California. He also learned what little the clerk knew about Max Arnold and the treasure expedition. No one had told the clerk that the group was looking for lost treasure, such men and their expeditions had been departing from Cuzco since the days of the conquistadors. This was nothing new. The most valuable piece of information that the clerk provided was the news that one of the expedition members, Tristan Sloan, had asked for the hotel's help in locating an interpreters for the Amahuaca and Yaminhua Indian languages. The clerk had been the one who delivered the faxes to Max from the private investigator, and he also shared that knowledge with Kenny.

Oh, what a tangled web… Kenny thought, as his concern for Rachel's well being doubled.

After the call to the Hotel Libertador, Kenny tried to fit the pieces of information together. Why would Max have pretended to have sighted Kenny's plane wreckage?

With the airport official wagging a finger at him, Kenny made one last call, this one again to the construction company. When he found out that Max Arnold had indeed been in contact with them and had been asking questions about him, his route and other matters that were none of Max's business, Kenny knew he had his answer.

"The son of a bitch!" he exclaimed. Max was almost certainly the one who had bribed Miguel. Max wanted him out of the way, to trick Rachel into a supposed emergency rescue. All this just to enlist her services as an interpreter? The lunatic had even fabricated a story about finding her brother's plane in the jungle!

Kenny knew the expedition's general direction because of the mention of the Yaminhua Indians. From Rachel's previous trip, he knew that was somewhere along the Río Pinquina, northeast of Boca Manu. One thing was for sure. He now had to find Rachel and remove her from whatever scheme Max Arnold had planned. If the treasure hunter was so devoid of ethics to have made up the crash story, Rachel might be in extreme danger.

Kenny's first problem was transport. The Cherokee Piper wasn't safe enough in its present condition to go anywhere else. Even if it could be repaired in time, the Piper was the wrong plane for scouring the jungle. He needed one with seaplane floats. The only landing places he could rely on were the rivers. The only promising place to arrange such an aircraft would be the capital.

Kenny found another pilot who was leaving Puerto Maldonado and who was willing to make room. Not long afterwards, they were aloft, headed west, toward the Andes and beyond, to Lima.

****

Boca Manu, Wednesday, February 18

The convenience of Boca Manu, at the juncture of the Manu and Madre de Dios Rivers, had made it a logical base camp location for many expeditions into the surrounding reserves. Max's plan was to spend the night in Boca, then backtrack the next morning by truck a short twenty-five kilometers to Puerto Definitivo. A new road paralleled the river to the spot that Max and Tristan had chosen for the expedition's entrance into the jungle.

Rachel was curious why Max hadn't flown the expedition directly to Boca Manu, since she noticed an airstrip.

Max explained that this had been his and Sloan's original plan. In the absence of regular flights, however, and with the limited availability of planes and pilots for charter from Cuzco, the expedition leaders had settled on the river approach.

If he were to admit the truth, Max knew that although it would have been expensive, he would have been able to arrange it. Rachel, however, would have taken much longer to catch up with them than she had needed to reach Shintuyo. Rachel's presence was essential to the expedition, since the forests they would enter in another day or two would bring them into Yaminhua territory.

Dr. Ramón, Amasu and Tristan Sloan left the camp immediately after breakfast. Amasu knew of a nearby small settlement of Machiguenga Indians. Until about twenty years earlier, the Machiguenga had been infamous for attacks on white explorers. Visitors to the area now considered these Indians one of the "friendly" tribes.

During the mid-morning, the men returned, accompanied by two young Machiguenga men who had been hired as guides.

The expedition was equipped with two to three weeks' worth of supplies. Moreover, the team members had strapped bedrolls, tents and other equipment onto the frames of the packs. Max and Tristan had engaged most of the local men to serve as porters. Eight of these carried the heavier backpacks. Chico and another Peruvian with a machete led the way and would open the trail when needed. The rest of the expedition members, including Rachel, carried lighter packs with medical supplies, rain gear, and their personal items. Max Arnold and Tristan Sloan both carried rifles, slung over their shoulders, and Max also wore a sidearm. Two of the other hired Cuzco men at the rear of the column also carried rifles. The weapons alarmed Rachel a little, but they were entering a jungle, after all. Better to be on the safe side, she supposed.

Before their departure, an officer of the Guardia Civil checked the entry documents that Max had obtained through Dr. Ramón's help, in Cuzco. The officer warned the professor that the area into which the expedition was heading was uncharted and very dangerous. He also offered his personal view that the entire group must be crazy. The officer regretfully told Rachel that he knew nothing of a plane crash, but that he would be happy to file an official inquiry. Rachel told him that she had already done that in Cuzco.

The expedition loaded everything into two trucks that Tristan had hired in advance. One truck would have sufficed, but Tristan had warned Max that two would be safer. One might get stuck in mud or break down, even in the short distance that the group had to travel back toward Puerto Definitivo. They would be on foot soon enough and, in the jungle, even fifteen miles is an extremely long way to walk.

The ride consisted of bumping their way along for an hour or so, but the road wasn't nearly as bad as Rachel had expected. Once again, despite the convenience, it saddened Rachel to see the intrusion of the road into the rain forest.

Upon their arrival at Puerto Definitivo, the Machiguenga guides plunged directly into the forest. Amasu told Rachel that the guides claimed knowledge of two or three stone cities, deep in the jungle to their north. Max also had Amasu query the guides about ancient tunnels, and Rachel asked whether they knew anything about a crashed airplane. The Indians knew nothing of either subject.

The two Machiguenga led the way, slipping effortlessly past interwoven trees, vines and brambles. Although the two expedition members with machetes slashed a few vines to make the passage easier for the rest, the going was not that difficult at the outset. Still, the forest was uncomfortably warm and humid. Every member of the expedition, except the two Indian guides wore lightweight knee-high rubber galoshes such as those that Rachel had bought in Cuzco. Besides being needed because of the mud, these provided a measure of protection against the many species of venomous snakes that abounded in the Madre de Dios.

The Machiguenga guides soon intersected with an established trail, and for a little over an hour, the group made good progress. During the trek, Rachel occupied her mind by absorbing the surrounding sights. The forest itself was made up of many mixed layers of vegetation. The towering tree canopy above allowed little sunlight to penetrate to the ground level, so most colors were fairly muted along the trail. Even so, Rachel delighted in the patchworked play of light and shadow that splattered the jungle floor.

Despite the low light and surprisingly poor soil condition endemic to rain forests, the heavy rains, heat and humidity created an otherwise fertile environment for vegetation. Smaller trees and large bushes flourished in the spaces between the taller trees' trunks and huge buttress roots. Heavily leafed and sometimes thorny *liana* vines competed for the intervening space from the lower foliage to the branches above.

Rachel felt immersed in a myriad of emotions as the group moved deeper into the rain forest. The jungle exuded a natural power that made Rachel feel like she was only inches tall. Even Max and the massive Raóul seemed puny in the primeval setting of the Madre de Dios. Juxtaposed against this feeling was an aspect of the jungle that was pure poetry to Rachel. Around her, the calls of birds, chirping of insects and shrieking of monkeys mixed in a chorus reminiscent of *The Wizard of Oz.*

Lions, tigers and bears! thought Rachel.

Although the Indian guides never seemed to notice, the trail later disappeared altogether. Chico and Raóul, were now having to work harder to clear a path through the vines, bushes and undergrowth that snagged and caught on the group's packs and clothing.

Twice, their direction veered sharply before curving back north, as the guides skirted swampy "*varzeas,*" areas of flooded forest. Occasionally, they came to small streams where the expedition members followed the Machiguenga guides across knee-deep to waist-high water.

At one stream, however, the guides stopped and spoke with Amasu, who translated and passed a message back.

"Piranha."

Rachel still wondered how the Indians knew which streams contained piranha, and which were safe. Someone had once told her that brown water was safe, but all the streams and rivers looked brown to her.

While the rest of the expedition waited, several of the men used hatchets and machetes to fell a couple of small trees and strip most of the branches. Then Chico and a couple of the other men lashed these small timbers together and let them fall across the stream. The Indians scrambled nimbly across, followed by Raóul. Chico tossed a rope to Raóul, and both wound the ends several times around trees, so that the stretched rope might serve as a handrail.

When Rachel's turn came, she crossed slowly, but sure-footed. Max, a bit more heavy set than the other team members and less agile, faltered, but retained his balance via the rope. Tristan and Chico brought up the rear, and the group moved on.

By midday the vegetation had become so dense that Chico and Raóul began taking turns with the other men in opening a trail, while the Machiguenga waited a few yards ahead. Soon, the group was only moving forward a hundred yards in an hour's time. Now and then a snake would slither past, or an unseen animal would bound away, making a racket as it crashed through the undergrowth. Such distractions fascinated Rachel, and she thought that Tristan also seemed to take pleasure from their surroundings. She noticed that he would reach out from time to time to feel the texture of a leaf, a vine or flower, and Rachel subconsciously began to imitate this behavior. Most of the others, excluding the Indian guides, just appeared nervous. Despite the path the machetes were making, by midday, nearly all the members of the expedition had tears in their clothing and cuts from thorns on the branches or vines.

Armed with the knowledge of past experience, Rachel had smothered her body in a "backwoods strength" insect repellent. Even so, she frequently felt the sting of invisible "no-see-`em" gnats that seem to plague human intruders in jungles worldwide. Once, when they stopped to rest, she found a leech attached to her shin, apparently from one of the streams they had waded. Amasu deftly removed it for her, revealing a bloody sore. She applied some antiseptic ointment and a Band-Aid, and hoped it wouldn't get infected. Sores and infections tended to get serious in the jungle.

Along the way, Rachel frequently sneaked glances at Tristan. He moved in an almost cautious way that was unlike most men she knew, not with a swagger like Max, but with graceful hesitancy—just short of tentative—as if not fully committing an action until the last instant. Once, she tried copying it and immediately tripped on a vine. She quickly recovered, but furiously chastised herself for the lapse. She had probably spent more time in this particular terrain than he had. She knew how to make her way through a jungle. She was relieved that Tristan seemed not to have noticed the stumble.

After lunch, the group was again inching its way through the jungle, when something suddenly fell out a tree a few steps ahead of Rachel and landed around Dr. Gallagher's neck. As the professor screamed and crashed about, Rachel saw that he was entangled in a deep green-colored snake. The aggressive reptile looked to be about four to five feet long. Most of the men backed away, startled and frightened, but Sloan reached up firmly and disengaged the creature. He tossed it away, into the underbrush.

"It bit me, I think it bit me!" cried Gallagher, still tottering about, out of control.

"Calm yourself," soothed Tristan, "It was a chicotillo. They're no more dangerous than a big garden snake."

"But it bit me," insisted Gallagher. He was a little reassured by the news, but still unnerved.

"It might have gummed you, but I doubt seriously it bit you. They don't even have the same type of fangs as poisonous snakes. You're fine. Let's get moving again."

Rachel recognized what Sloan had said was true. At first, she too had been startled. Quickly, however, she also had realized that it was the same harmless species she had seen on multiple occasions at Cocha Cashu. They were aggressive, but non-poisonous, as Sloan said. Still, Sloan's coolness impressed her. He had calmly and without hesitation detached the snake, while most of the others were still scattering for safety. What a picture they must have made…the intrepid jungle expedition being attacked by the dreaded chicotillo.

When the column started forward again, Rachel noticed that several porters had begun to whisper among themselves. They looked displeased.

The farther away the group had gotten from Puerto Definitivo, the more skittish the men had started acting.

About mid-afternoon, the expedition broke through the worst of the vegetation, and entered a part of the forest where a fire had at sometime in recent years thinned the trees and vines. Despite this, the expedition's advance didn't move perceptibly faster, as mud and undergrowth had reclaimed this space and replaced one obstacle with another.

Soon after, the Indian guides came upon a trail of sorts, and changed course slightly to follow it.

"Who would have made this trail? Indians?" Dr. Gallagher asked.

"Possibly, but I don't think so," Ramón answered. "Amasu, is this an Indian trail?"

Amasu shook his head no. "Animal. Maybe tapir, maybe jaguar…maybe both."

Gallagher, embarrassed by the earlier episode with the snake, looked about nervously at the mention of jaguars, but made no comment.

After only about ten minutes following the trail, the Machiguenga left it and continued back into the heavier brush. A few minutes later they stopped and looked back at the group. One of the Indians lifted an arm and pointed into the trees. Rachel peered in the direction the guide had pointed. A small rise lay off to their right, exposing several large rocks. Atop one of the larger boulders, an incredibly large boa constrictor lay partially coiled, a hump visible in its body, beginning just behind the head and taking up about a third of the reptile's body. Jutting from the creature's mouth was a small set of antlers.

"I'll bet it's eighteen to twenty feet long," Max whispered.

"It can't hear you, Max," Tristan said. "You don't have to whisper."

"The snake will lie there, until its digestive juices dissolve the animal's body—that might take many days—and then the antlers will just fall off," Dr. Ramón explained. "An amazing sight, no, Señorita Rachel?"

"Amazing," she agreed. She hurried past. In the two years she had spent in Brazil and Peru, Rachel had only seen two such reptiles. Now, she had seen the same number in as many days. If one went by omens, Rachel figured things were shaping up darkly. She surreptitiously knocked her knuckles a couple of times on the next tree she passed.

The next time the guides stopped, it was nearly four o'clock in the afternoon. Rachel's clothes were drenched in sweat. She was exhausted and already tattooed with dozens of small scrapes and minor scratches inflicted by the jungle. She welcomed the opportunity to rest, and sat down, right in the middle of the trail. She wiped away the sweat from her forehead, and took a deep breath. The air was still refreshing, in a somewhat damp and earthy sort of way, but she wasn't enjoying the wilderness as much as before, because of her general state of discomfort. She reflected that jungles are best taken in moderation.

The Machiguenga guides now came back toward Amasu. The three of them conferenced about something, gesturing on ahead, then back in the direction the expedition had come. Rachel wasn't close enough to hear their words clearly.

Amasu then consulted with the expedition leaders, Max and Tristan.

Finally, Max came back to speak with Rachel. *Nothing like third-hand news*, she thought.

"The Machiguenga guides say that a part of the territory of the Yaminhua Indians begins here," Max told her. "They won't go further than this. I know you speak Yaminhua. How well do you know their customs and treatment of outsiders?"

"They still don't embrace us very warmly, but it's hard to say. Different tribal groups react in different ways. Can't we just go around?"

"That depends on you," Max answered. "The crash site is right in the center, about another day's march east-northeast from this spot."

"Did you have some kind of plan?" Rachel asked.

"We don't have to go in," Max said, gambling on Rachel's reaction. "We could head northwest toward where we think we'll find Gran Paititi, but that means by-passing the crash site. Or, we can take our chances and forge ahead, counting on you to do some fast talking, if we run into trouble."

Yes, she could talk, but Rachel thought the odds of the Yaminhua listening were fifty, fifty. The rule of thumb for many tribes that had small exposure to whites was to shoot first. But, if she turned back now, she might never know what happened to Kenny. Abandoning him was unthinkable.

"I'm game, if you are," she answered.

"Excellent," Max smiled. "Then we'll camp here. The Machiguenga say there's a small tributary of the Río Pinquen, less than a hundred yards ahead. Maybe the Yaminhua will come to us and we won't have to go on without an invitation."

"Anything's possible," she answered.

Tristan had paid the Machiguenga tribal chief in advance for the two guides' services. The Indians disappeared silently, back the way the expedition had come, without so much as a backward glance.

The expedition had been on the march for seven and a half hours, yet had made only twelve kilometers progress from Puerto Definitivo. The next day's progress wouldn't be nearly as easy.

Chapter Eight

The Gateway God, a.k.a. Staff God

****

Madre de Dios Jungle, Wednesday, February 18

Only after they had established the camp, set up the tents and the group had gathered back in the center of the small clearing, did Tristan notice that two of the porters were missing. In the midst of all the activity, the two men must have slipped away and followed the trail back to Puerto Definitivo.

Most of the rest of the Cuzqueño porters looked extremely restless. Max asked Chico to promise the men more money and coca leaves.

"If they leave, tell them they get nothing!" Max ordered.

Chico approached Max a few minutes later, as he and Tristan sat talking with Dr. Ramón.

"The men are not happy," Chico told Max. "They say it isn't safe to go on. These are simple men, very superstitious. They believe the forest is full of spirits, and that the Machiguenga guides knew better than to continue when the *espiritus* are angry. The men believe that's why the guides turned back. They think the chicotillo was an omen, and are also afraid of the Yaminhua. I told them you will pay more, and I gave them coca leaves. That may satisfy them for a while. It strengthens their courage. I'm not sure if *any* of them will stay, if we continue much further into Yaminhua land."

Rachel thought that Chico also looked uncomfortable with the prospect.

There had been no need to stand watch at Shintuyo. Even at Boca Manu, the men who had taken turns had treated the job lightly. Here, however, several miles inside an untamed jungle, Sloan set up a schedule with overlapping assignments. There would be two men on watch at all times. The group included enough men to do short two-hour shifts.

Rachel insisted on taking her turn along with the rest of them. Tristan scheduled her to share the first half of her shift with him and the second half with Max.

Supper consisted of dried fruits, a stew and some piranha that Amasu had caught in a nearby creek. Rachel knew that many local people ate the ridiculously easy-to-hook piranha, but she had never sampled it. She tried a tiny portion, but found the thought of eating the ferocious fish unsettling. What if it had eaten...*somebody?* She left the fish mostly untouched.

By the time they had finished eating it was already dark. Most of the group chose to turn in early—Rachel included. It had been a full day and she was exhausted.

Chico and Dr. Gallagher were on watch duty first. Tristan had scheduled experienced men to spend the overlapping shifts with the Egyptologist. Rachel was sure that Sloan had little confidence in Dr. Gallagher. She recognized he had done the same in scheduling her, but she decided it was pointless to take offense. She had never really camped in such exposed fashion in the wilderness. Both in Brazil and Peru, she had always slept inside buildings or within the confines of Indian villages. She was glad that Max and Tristan were more experienced in the open jungle.

Rachel felt like she had only been asleep a few minutes, when Gallagher woke her for her assigned shift. Tristan had replaced Chico an hour earlier, and Gallagher had just finished his two hours. Rachel noticed that there was a rifle leaning against a rock near the fire, and another propped within Tristan's reach. She sat on a folded blanket near Tristan. The warmth of the fire felt good. A cold front had moved in while she had slept, and the temperature had dropped into the mid-fifties. After the scorching ninety-plus marks earlier in the day, she now felt goose bumps as she shivered in the cool night air.

"Everything okay, I guess?" she said, just to make conversation.

"Nice and quiet," Tristan replied.

Listening to the shrill night symphony of a dozen or more mixed jungle sounds, Rachel had to smile. The jungle was anything but quiet.

Tristan regarded Rachel pensively. She was totally unaware of the captivating picture she made, crouched and shivering in the flickering glow of the campfire. He knew the young doctoral candidate was older than she looked. She was slender and dark, and even her oversized khaki shirt failed to hide the suggestion of a slim waist that flared into agilely rounded hips. She wore her hair in the short boyish-style haircut that was a fad Tristan found too "butch" on most younger women. He thought it looked attractive on Rachel. He tried to look more closely at

Rachel's arresting eyes without appearing obvious. He found the anomaly extremely alluring. Sexy or not, he still wished he'd been able to find an Indian interpreter. He had enough to worry about, without looking out for her.

Mistaking Tristan's attention, Rachel figured he was reflecting upon how much extra trouble she was causing him, having to go so far out of the way. Sloan's demeanor until now had warned "If it isn't useful, get rid of it—if it isn't relevant, shut up." Max referred to Tristan as his partner, even though Rachel understood that Max almost entirely bore the financial weight of their adventures alone.

"How long have you known Mr. Arnold?" she asked, half-expecting a lecture on minding her business. For the moment, however, the adventurer was apparently receptive to small talk. Probably needed to chat just to stay awake, Rachel figured.

"Off and on, about fourteen years. We first teamed up on a project in Thailand. He's had something going just about every year since then."

"His wife doesn't mind?"

"Max is gay."

"Oh." That was quite a surprise. Rachel wondered if Raóul knew. The Cuzqueño giant was Max's tent mate and followed him around like a pet pony. "And you are…?"

"Not."

"No, I meant married."

"Same answer…and I was just pulling your leg about Max. He's straight. Actually, he seems to like to play the field too much to settle down. I guess you'd have to ask him about that."

"Ah." Tristan's tone didn't invite further pursuit of the question. *Thailand, he said.* Rachel wondered if the men had been a Special Forces types or something like that during the war in Vietnam. *No…Tristan wouldn't be old enough, unless he hid his age extremely well.* Maybe he had been some sort of mercenary after the official conflict was over. She had learned from Max that Sloan was Canadian, but she was knowledgeable enough to know that the Canadians had also been in Southeast Asia along with American and Australian troops. She decided not to ask, lest she find out more than she wanted to know.

When Rachel asked him how far he thought they were from the crash site, Tristan didn't look at her as he answered. His expression stilled and grew serious.

"Maybe a half day, maybe more. It's hard to tell exactly how far we've come. Everything looks the same out here."

Tristan didn't look at Rachel because she had again reminded him that she was here under false pretenses. Max had not told him how Rachel had been lured to Shintuyo, until she had already been on her way, but Tristan knew that did not excuse his failure to alert her to the truth. Tristan found it inconceivable to think that Max had not even bothered trying a straightforward, truthful approach. He had just gone ahead and tricked her, as his first choice. Max had a short fuse, and Tristan knew that if he pressed the subject, it could be the end of a long and mutually beneficial relationship, just as Max had warned. Tristan had reluctantly kept quiet, and now it was souring his stomach to continue the charade. Max had cast him in the same role as the pitiful Harold Gallagher. Gallagher was also keeping his mouth shut, on account of the money Max was paying. Tristan would never have stayed for the money, alone. This was his discovery. He couldn't just walk away from an adventure like this.

"I guess it must be especially hard having your brother be missing," Tristan said. "Is being a twin like everything you hear or read? Psychic bonding and all that?" He hoped his conscience wasn't plastered all over his face.

Rachel leaned closer to the fire, hugging her knees to her. "Maybe. Sometimes it seems like it. We usually don't have to finish our sentences. He always knows what I'm going to say, and vice versa. It's funny sometimes, because people around us usually haven't got a clue as to what we're talking about. I'd say that was a stronger bond than other siblings have, but Kenny's my only real family. He's the only one I can judge by. We were like most kids, the occasional hair pulling and bit-ing...you know, kids' stuff. But we're best friends. Always have been. I suppose it's normal with twins, because there's nobody in the whole world more like you. You know?

"Not really. I have a hard time imagining that," Tristan said. "I've always valued being a sort of maverick. I think it would be a little unnerving to have someone so similar to myself."

"I thought it used to be a bit tough, too," Rachel admitted. "Looking so much alike, dressing alike, sharing so many characteristics. It's hard to set yourself apart as unique. I think that's why we went off in such separate directions in school. I haven't finished yet, and Kenny zipped straight through. He took the fewest classes he could, and then got a job doing something that has nothing to do with his degree. He plans to fly planes for the rest of his life."

"You don't approve?"

"No, it's not that, at all. Whatever makes him happy makes me happy. I guess I'm just jealous. It's all been so simple for him. So far, the elusive key to happiness has stayed just beyond my reach. There's always one more pre-requisite step that I find I'm supposed to take."

"Why do you do it, then?"

"What? You mean I should settle for being a housewife?" A defensive tone invaded Rachel's voice.

"No, I just meant...if you're not happy..."

Rachel didn't answer. All of a sudden, this was getting a little too personal. Tristan correctly interpreted the silence.

"Well, probably when you finish your studies everything will all work out."

"Maybe."

Rachel was a little surprised and a bit self-conscious about how much she had told Tristan, a virtual stranger. They chitchatted quietly and a bit awkwardly for the remaining hour of Tristan's shift. Rachel noticed that

Sloan never addressed her by name. He just asked his questions, or started talking. She, too, felt strange calling him by his first name, but even more so saying 'Mr. Sloan,' so she followed his example and used neither.

When Tristan's shift ended, he woke Max who, judging by his snores, was not losing sleep over the scam he was pulling on Rachel.

Max emerged from his tent and found a seat next to the fire.

"Everything okay?" asked Max as he rubbed the sleep from his eyes.

Rachel decided this must be a standardized question everyone asks when standing watch. "Eleven o'clock and all's well," she answered.

"When did it get so bloody cold?" Max asked, scooting closer to the fire.

"Beats me. A front must have come in before my shift. I hope it sticks around, though." She paused. "I asked Mr. Sloan about the crash site. He wasn't sure exactly how far away we are. Do you know?"

They spoke quietly, to avoid disturbing the others.

"Oh, it can't be more than another half day, I'd say. We made good progress the last part of the afternoon."

"Uh huh. For this jungle, at least. I'm not surprised though. He seems to be very competent."

"Tristan? Yeah, one of the best. In all, I bet we've done ten or eleven expeditions together. Tristan has probably saved my ass a half dozen times."

"You must have a knack for getting into trouble."

"You joke, of course, but I'm not exaggerating. Once, about ten years ago, Tristan and I were hunting for a lost temple just inside Cambodia. We accidentally stumbled into a squad of Camer Rouge guerrillas. They started shooting and I took a bullet in the thigh. All our porters and guides—local riffraff as it turned out—immediately hightailed it. Tristan had to half carry me, zigzagging through the jungle, under fire and unassisted, almost a half mile back to the Thai border. Most guys— they'd be telling a story like that at the drop of a hat, for the rest of their lives. Tristan's *never* mentioned it."

Rachel thought Max looked momentarily disconcerted as he related the story, as if acknowledging a debt that he couldn't repay, but if it bothered him, it wasn't for long. Rachel wasn't sure which part of the story impressed her most.

"You weren't exaggerating," she admitted. There was more to Tristan Sloan than met the eye, it seemed.

"I have to admit, though—ten or eleven expeditions sounds like a lot in fourteen years. That's how long Mr. Sloan said he's known you."

"Yeah, that probably does seem like a lot to someone like you. Remember, though, that in this business, most trips turn out to be false leads. That means a quick trip home."

Rachel smiled shyly. "I'm afraid that if you were to ask for my professional opinion, I'd have to tell you that the rest of this trip—that is, the part to find the lost city of Paititi—is a good candidate to fall into that false lead group."

Max almost sneered. Rachel wondered what he meant by 'someone like you.'

"You haven't seen the map," Max boasted. "Hold on just a second…I'll be right back. If any cannibals show up, tell 'em to start without me."

Max strode to his tent and ducked inside.

Rachel looked around at the close circle of trees surrounding the campsite. The clearing was very small, and the jungle resumed right at the edges of the camp. Rachel shivered, and this time it wasn't only caused by the coolness of the night. In the Madre de Dios, there were all too many things that go 'bump in the night.' Like she had told Dee, it was a lethally beautiful place that simultaneously enthralled and frightened her.

Max reappeared from the tent, carrying a small satchel. He brought it with him to the campfire, and sat next to Rachel. Opening the bag, he extracted two stone tablets, both inscribed with lines and symbols. Holding up one of the tablets, Max turned it so that the surface caught the light from the fire.

Rachel leaned closer and saw that the symbols were Egyptian hieroglyphics.

"The famous map of the golden city?" she asked.

"None other."

Rachel had to concede that the tablets looked impressively ancient. That still didn't convince her that they represented what Max believed.

Max began to show Rachel the different symbols and to repeat what Dr. Gallagher had interpreted. He concluded by pointing at the sun-shaped symbol ☼ that Gallagher had said represented the fortified city that he and Tristan believed to be Paititi.

"Is that the reason you think it says Great Tiger?" she asked, pointing out a small catlike figure among the glyphs.

"No. The city's name is this other part, ⌘⌘ , *Ah-bee Ur*. It translates as Great Panther, or Great Tiger. The little leopard symbol is just something that Dr. Gallagher says means it's a title or a name."

Max went on to explain Tristan's and Dr. Gallagher's theory about the map having east as its topside orientation, rather than north.

"I can accept at least that part of your argument," Rachel told him. "Pre-Columbian Indians in Central and South America did orient their maps in such fashion."

"There are a lot of other things, too. Like the Incas' seven Children of the Sun and the Egyptians' seven Sons of Ra."

"Coincidence."

"There's a point where you have so many coincidences that you start knowing they can't be. That's what initiated this little trip."

He lifted the other tablet and continued.

"We still don't know what this one is really for. There's a bunch of words that Gallagher can translate, but can't put together into a sensible purpose or explanation. Same goes for this thing…"

Max reached back into the bag and removed a red crystal amulet. He handed it to Rachel. "Scary looking thing, isn't it?"

"Wow!" said Rachel, admiring the intricacies. "Aren't you a little worried about carting these things all around the jungle? Shouldn't they be in a vault, somewhere? Even if the map leads nowhere, Dr. Gallagher believes them to be authentic artifacts. They ought to be worth a bundle."

"That's a risk I'm willing to take. A photo enlargement might not capture a detail that we might need when we get close. If these take us to Gran Paititi, the wealth we could find there could buy a whole museum full of such artifacts."

"But even if you do find the city," Rachel said, "…there's no guarantee that there will be any treasure. The Indians would more likely have buried it or sunk it in a lake, or just scattered it all over the country as they dispersed back into their own autonomous tribes."

"I don't think so," Max replied. "All the gold, silver and gems that the Spanish ever took back to Spain was supposed to be only a small part of the total Inca wealth. What made it to Spain is said to equal eleven billion dollars. Eleven *billion*. Let's say the Spaniards got their hands on even a fourth of the total. According to the accounts of Spanish missionaries, after Pizarro had the Inca ruler Atahualpa killed, thousands of Indians fled, carrying off inconceivable amounts of treasure into the jungle. That would leave thirty-three billion dollars sitting here waiting to be found, including a seven-hundred foot chain of solid gold that was documented by eye-witnesses, but never captured. You just don't disperse thirty-three billion dollars around here and there, and never have a trace of it show up. Are you beginning to get the picture?"

Rachel nodded. "I know about the chain. It was commissioned at Huascar's birth. Neither it nor the Sun Disk from Coricancha was ever found."

"The Christianized Indians who stayed behind claimed that the treasure was taken to the realm of the Great Tiger Lord."

"I know the legend. That still doesn't make it true."

Despite the professional and personal repugnance Rachel felt for what she considered glamorized grave robbing, the numbers Max was throwing out made it a little more understandable why Max and Tristan Sloan were chasing around the jungle. The almost unimaginable richness of the missing treasures was the reason, over four hundred and fifty years later, adventurers had still not given up the search.

Rachel returned her attention to the crystal amulet.

"It almost looks like a *relámpago* staff," she said.

"Excuse me?"

"*Relámpago*," Rachel repeated. "Spanish for lightning bolt. This one is styled a little bit like carvings of a lighting bolt that several Indian cultures depict as a staff held by the Gateway God."

"You're sure of this?" Max asked.

Rachel looked at the piece again. At one end was a figure of a hawk's or eagle's head, and two smaller caiman heads at the other end. The hawk was most likely the "*Quiquijana.*" The "Conquest Bird" was the sacred bird of the Incas. The light from the fire wasn't the best for a detailed examination. More figures on the side looked like primitive jaguar heads and other bird motifs. She had seen similar designs among the ruins excavated at Tucumé and elsewhere throughout Peru. Lines and geometric patterns decorated the entire length of the piece, a little more elaborate than usual, but still typical of the staffs held by the Gateway God.

"I could be more positive if I saw it in the daylight, but yes, I'd say there's a reasonable similarity. Did Dr. Ramón think it was something different?"

"Dr. Ramón hasn't see it."

"But why not? I'm sure he would have been fascinated by it! He's sure to be more knowledgeable about it than me."

Max looked a bit embarrassed.

"I've only worked with Dr. Ramón once before. I don't know that much about him. He signed on because we offered him a considerable amount of money, and he wants partial credit for the discovery. As your little speech in Shintuyo illustrated, professional archaeologists aren't very keen on objects like this being in anybody's hands except their own. You should have heard Harold Gallagher squawk at first. He eventually came around, but I don't know Ramón well enough."

"You mean to say that you don't know if he can be trusted, or were you thinking that he might try to confiscate the item as property of the Peruvian government?"

"I don't know. The piece certainly doesn't belong to the Peruvian government; that much is beyond question."

"You probably have good reason to be concerned about Dr. Ramón's reaction," Rachel said with a slight frown. "If this is genuine, it most certainly belongs in a museum. It's beautiful. What type of stone is it? Jasper? It's too light-colored and way too big to be garnet."

"No, it's carnelian—a semi-precious like garnet, but less valuable. In the agate family, I think. Who's this Gateway God you mentioned?"

"The principal deity of the Chavin, Huari, Aymara cultures and perhaps a few other tribes. The Inca had their own variation. They called him Illapa, the Flashing One. The Gateway of the Sun excavated at Tihuanaco bears a sculpted image of the god, so archaeologists and anthropologists dubbed it the Gateway God. He supposedly protected the Indians' cities from their enemies and other intruders. He casts thunder and lighting bolts at those who violate their premises. He's usually depicted with a staff like this one in each hand. That's why he's also called the Staff God."

"Is that right? So, the staffs represented thunder and lightning bolts?"

"Yes. Usually, one of the staffs was either a spear or a war club with which he struck thunder. The other was a sling or spear thrower, from which the god hurled lightning, or *relámpago*. Alone, like this, I imagine it is a scepter or protective amulet. Where did you find it?"

Before Max could answer, a new sound came from the jungle. Something that sounded like two short barks from a large dog. Rachel looked back over her shoulder toward the noise. Surely, no dogs roamed this far out into the jungle.

"Jaguar?" she asked Max.

Max had taken up the rifle and turned to face the direction of the sounds.

"I imagine so. I don't think there are any wolves around here," he answered. "Foxes barks, and there are birds and even monkeys that make a similar sound, but not as deep a cough like that. Put a couple more logs on the fire, won't you?"

Rachel did as Max had asked. A single bark sounded again, this time closer and off to their right. It did sound more like a cough, this time, or a low growl.

Max put the rifle to his shoulder and raised it part way.

"Stay low, beneath my line of fire, but pick up the other rifle. Find the safety and switch it off. If anything comes out of the forest at us, don't wait to see what it is. Just point the barrel and squeeze the trigger. Have you fired a rifle before?"

"Not that I can recall."

"Try not to point the barrel anywhere near me, then."

"I've never heard of one attacking a camp site."

"No…" Max acknowledged. "I doubt it will come any closer. They're very reclusive. It's probably just checking us out."

Rachel picked up the rifle, as directed, and found the safety. She held the barrel up even with her chest and pointed out at the darkness. Max might be overacting a bit for her benefit. She had never needed to worry about jaguars either time she had been in the South American jungles. Like Max had said, they did their best to avoid humans. Still, maybe this one didn't know better. Every muscle in her body was tensed. She was afraid she would jerk the trigger, if even a twig were to snap.

Five minutes passed, then ten, and a soft rain began to fall. The rifle grew heavier, and Rachel began to have trouble keeping the barrel up. The barking, or jaguar's cough, finally sounded again, but this time it was farther away. After two or three more minutes, Max told Rachel to relax.

"I think it's moved on. You can relax, now. Where were we?"

The rain began to fall a little harder, and a low rumbling sound of distant thunder came along with it.

"Huh?" Rachel asked. She was still thinking about the jaguar, and didn't follow Max's meaning.

"We were talking about the map and the crystal staff. You asked me something, before were interrupted."

"Oh. I think I was asking you where you found the staff."

Rachel had set down the carnelian piece when she had taken up the rifle. She reached over to retake the artifact now.

"Tristan bought it in Morocco. Some Arab kid in the north of Morocco apparently brought it into an antique dealer along with the Egyptian tablets. Probably found it in a cave somewhere. No trace of the boy now, of course."

As Rachel's fingers reached for the carnelian staff, a flash of lightning brightened the sky. She jumped—more than a little startled in the aftermath of the near encounter with a jaguar. A roll of thunder followed a second later. For a moment, Rachel was afraid to touch the surface of the red crystal, but then she realized she was being foolish.

Silently, she gathered up the artifact and placed it back inside the bag. She was digesting what Max had just told her. How could a native piece, like the *relámpago* staff, have wound up in Morocco? Was somebody playing a giant trick on Max, mixing the artifact with the Egyptian tablets, half a world away? She remembered what Dr. Ramón had said about the Chavin culture dating back to the same period as the Egyptian tablets. It was a little spooky to think that these men might not be as crazy as she had thought. Was their belief tilting her judgment off-center? She was fatigued. The other-worldliness of the day's events and the jungle surroundings could be playing with her sense of reality.

Max moved to the side so she could get to the tablets, as well. She picked them up and stared at the glyphs for a second without saying a word. Then she inserted the tablets inside the bag.

"What time is it?" Max asked, breaking the spell.

"A little past midnight."

"Your shift's up," he said. "Wake Dr. Ramón, will you? He's up next. We'll talk more in the morning."

"Goodnight," she gratefully replied.

Rachel found Dr. Ramón's tent and roused him from his sleep. She told him about the jaguar, and warned him that he might want his rain gear, as it was starting to come down fairly heavily now. Good advice. It had already drenched Rachel and her teeth were chattering from the chill.

Rachel returned to her tent and changed into dry clothes, but the adrenaline coursing through her body prevented her from sleeping. The day's events kept replaying themselves in her mind. Finally, over an hour later, the patter of the rain on the tent top lulled her into a restless demi-sleep. She dreamt.

In the dream, she was being chased by a jaguar. She was running as fast as she could through the jungle, but the vines and thorns tore at her skin and clothing, tripping her and slowing her down. The animal kept gaining on her. The jaguar grew so close, she was sure that she could feel its hot breath on the hairs of her neck. Suddenly, she stumbled and pitched forward into a deep pit. She landed on something hard that clinked like metal. When she looked to see what it was, she saw she had landed on a pile of gold and emeralds. Above, she heard a low cough that turned into a roar. Looking up, Rachel gazed into the yellow eyes and sharp fangs of a huge jaguar. She stared, terrified, unable to move. The jaguar transformed into a giant, muscular Indian, covered in brightly colored feathers and golden Inca armor. "Great Tiger," whispered a voice that reverberated inside the darkness of the pit. Out of the gloomy recesses of the pit, a shadowy figure stepped toward her, draped in gold chains and dripping with blood. She tried to back away, but felt a wall against her back. The Indian above raised a fist, and Rachel saw that it clutched the carnelian rélampago staff. A clap of thunder sounded as the Indian brought the fist downward, throwing the car-nelian piece into the pit. As he did so, the roar of the jaguar merged with the thunder in a deafening rumble, and a brilliant flash of lightning illuminated the bloody figure in the pit. For one heartbeat, she thought the face was Kenny's. With the next beat, she recognized it as her own!

Awakening, she bolted upright to a sitting position and realized she was covered in sweat. *It's a dream*, she realized. *It's just a dream.* The roar of the jaguar softened into a distant thunder, and the thunder dissipated into the patter of rain against the tent. Rachel slumped backward and drifted off to sleep. This time it was a dreamless slumber, born of both physical and mental exhaustion.

Chapter Nine

The Tet of Carnelian

✶✶✶✶

Madre de Dios Jungle, Thursday, February 19

Rachel awakened to an eerie, continuous clamor—not quite the roar of a lion, yet stronger than the howl of a blustery winter's wind. It took her a second to realize where she was, then an instant longer to register the sound as a troupe of howler monkeys.

She peeked through the door of the tent, and saw that it was dawn. She heard another racket as someone scrambled out of a tent, and recognized Dr. Gallagher's voice asking what was happening. Howler monkeys had been fairly common around the biological station where Rachel had stayed four years ago, and she still retained an acclimation to the sounds of the jungle. She felt sorry for Dr. Gallagher. He was beginning to look a little wimpish.

She recalled the previous night's dream and shivered. *Thank god, we should reach the crash site today,* she thought. With luck, the wreckage wouldn't be from Kenny's plane, the expedition could backtrack and she could find a way to return to Cuzco. There, maybe she could sort out what had happened.

The howler monkeys began another chorus in the treetops above and Rachel strained for a glimpse of them among the rustling leaves. She wondered if the apes were expressing pleasure or outrage. They almost seemed to be laughing at her. Perhaps they just enjoyed dawn in the rain forest, as did she. The morning air was still quite cool, and the rain had stopped. All in all, it was a beautiful morning.

Rachel wished it was possible to bathe, but she knew she'd have to wait until they came to a safe river. No lodges or mission stations out here. Soon, she could hear more of the men moving about the camp. She used one of her rubber galoshes to collect rainwater pooled on a few nearby leaves, and returned to her tent to freshen up as best she could. Afterwards, she joined the men at the campfire. She gratefully accepted a mug of coffee from one of the porters named Luis who was doubling as the expedition's cook.

"I hear I missed the excitement," Tristan greeted.

"Good morning. You mean the jaguar? Yes, I guess so, though I understand from Max that there was little danger of anything really having happened."

"That's the general rule of thumb, but I never count on it. Sounds like you did fine."

Rachel saw Tristan throw a quick glance in Dr. Gallagher's direction as he said this, and again felt a tug of sympathy for the professor. After a few moments, she went over and sat next to him.

"Max showed me the tablets and the carnelian piece, last night," she said. "Amazing stuff. You did the translations?"

"Yes. Totally mind-boggling. I wouldn't believe it if I hadn't gone over the hieroglyphics myself."

Rachel told him about her belief that the carnelian cylinder was a depiction of the lightning staff held by the Indians' Gateway God.

"I'd believe just about anything at this point," the professor replied. "Nevertheless, it's unmistakably Egyptian. The shape is traditional for a protective amulet that the Egyptians called a *Tet*. This is quite an unusual one, both in size and detail, but I'm quite certain that's what it is. There's even a Tet of Carnelian, the same type amulet and crystal as this, mentioned in the Egyptian Book of the Dead."

"I think it's a remarkable coincidence that both the Tet and the lightning staff of the Gateway God are protective symbols."

"Perhaps, but it's not altogether that uncommon a theme. You can also find a Tibetan example, Varja-Bhairava, 'Terrible Lightning,' a protective lesser deity who serves Yama, the Hindu Lord of the Underworld. One finds many such parallels in widely dispersed cultures."

"What about the other tablet? Max said that you hadn't come up with an explanation for it, yet."

"I've been spending a lot of time thinking about it. I've only been able to make out very few complete words: 'journey'…'yesterday'…'West' and a few others. Not nearly enough to go on."

"Do the two tablets refer to each other?"

"Your guess is as good as mine. I also don't know what the carnelian staff would have to do with either tablet."

"A carnelian staff?" Dr. Ramón asked. The Peruvian professor had just emerged from his tent and joined the group.

Rachel looked over at Max, not sure what to say.

"Yes," Max intervened. "I hadn't gotten around to showing you, but from what Rachel tells me, now might be an opportune time." Max retrieved the carnelian artifact from his pack.

Dr. Ramón whistled in appreciation.

"*Muy bonita*. Very beautiful. I have seen many carved objects like this, in petroglyphs and woven *tokapu* pictures, but never such a beautiful crystal staff. A lightning rod, yes, Señorita Rachel? A *relámpago* staff of carnelian. How astounding."

Rachel felt exonerated. Dr. Ramón agreed with her evaluation.

"The staff turned up in the same batch of artifacts as the map tablets," Max clarified.

"In Morocco? Extraordinary. This adventure becomes more puzzling each morning that I get up," the surprised Dr. Ramón exclaimed. "I would have been willing to swear that it was Peruvian. There may even be some connection of a staff such as this one with the so-called 'Great Tiger Lord.' The Quechua people even today fear a supernatural being called Ccoa. This being is supposed to be a vicious Jaguar God who lives up among the mountain peaks, and who causes lightning and thunder storms."

Several of the Cuzqueño men had glimpsed the crystal staff and heard Dr. Ramón mention the terms *relámpago* and *Ccoa*. The words caused most of the porters to begin murmuring about evil spirits and bad omens. Chico tried to calm the others, but with very little success. He approached Max.

"This is bad," Chico said. "The men are extremely upset that this *huaqua* is in your possession. They say that it has brought a curse upon the expedition. They believe it will bring disaster and death."

"*Relámpago* is believed to be a very deadly weapon of the Staff God, by most local people," frowned Dr. Ramón. "I'm afraid that these men believe that you are *huaqueros*, grave robbers. They think you have stolen this crystal from the ruins of some sacred place. As Chico says, they think that you have directed the wrath of the ancient gods upon the expedition. Perhaps they will listen to me."

As Dr. Ramón went over to the men and began to converse in Spanish, Max cast an accusing glance at Rachel.

Dr. Ramón remained engaged in earnest discussion with the Cuzqueños for several more minutes. Finally, the men appeared to have reached some sort of agreement. Ramón and Chico returned to the campfire.

"Regrettably, Señor Amasu will have nothing more to do with the expedition," Dr. Ramón announced. "He's leaving as soon as he can gather his personal belongings. Two more of the porters also have decided to go back with him. They'll follow the trail that we cut getting here. They want to be paid for their time through today. That only leaves us with Chico, Raóul, and three porters, Renaldo, Felipe and Luis. It might be prudent to backtrack to Puerto Definitivo and hire replacements…"

"Tristan?" Max asked.

"That would cost us two full days, and then put us right back where we are now. If we take only what is essential, and split up the rest, I think we can handle it. Amasu and the two porters that want to bail out can take three of the tents and the extra equipment we won't need back to Boca Manu. Is there a chance of finding friendly Indians, who could act as guides?"

"Perhaps," Dr. Ramón answered. "There may be Amahuaca villages in the vicinity. Señorita Rachel, you have worked near here, yes?"

"Sorry, we're already beyond the reach of my travel. I rarely left the confines of Manu National Park. You would probably know better than I, which tribes we're likely to run into past this point."

"All right then," Max said. "We'll take our chances. All the rifles stay with us, though, and nobody that leaves gets paid any more than a day's wages."

Amasu and the two other porters still were determined to turn back.

It turned out that Tristan was right. After taking only the essentials, there were enough of the remaining expedition members to split up the rest. No one had to assume too heavy a load.

Rachel walked over to where Amasu was packing his belongings.

"You think it is foolhardy to continue deeper into the jungle?" she asked him.

"Perhaps. *You* must be the one to answer that, Doña Rachel. For me, I must weigh the promised reward, compared with the expected danger. Señor Arnold was not honest about his purpose or destination. It would be foolish for me to continue, for so poor a reason as money."

"I've been thinking maybe I should also turn back."

Amasu shrugged. "Is what you seek worth the dangers of the jungle?"

"I told you. I'm looking for my brother. The risk isn't important. I have to find out whether he's okay or not."

Amasu finished his departure preparations and stood upright. He fixed his attention on Rachel.

"You just answered your own question. I am told that you have spent much time studying the story of my people. We call the part of the Four Corners where you go, 'Ayacucho,' Corner of the Dead…"

Rachel started to point out that the Ayacucho region was over a hundred miles in the opposite direction. Amasu intercepted her train of thought.

"*Arí*, yes…now this name only means a smaller area to the west. Once, however, in the days of the ancient ancestors, even before the great Inca Pachacutec, Ayacucho was the name of a larger area. Only those with a pure heart and clean soul may safely enter this forbidden land where you now go. I don't possess the advice you need. Nor does any of these men with whom you travel. You must listen closely to the different pieces of your inner soul. Because they are in conflict with one another, you have come to fear your own instincts. Yet, you carry within you a power that no man possesses. I speak of the great female soul— the goddess Pachamama. Pachamama lives not only as the earth and the jungle, but within you, as she does within all women. To co-exist with Pachamama…to cross this jungle and return, you must reclaim that which is lost within you. If you had grown up with the earth, like the women of my people, you would already know this. Find the goddess and listen to *her* advice."

Rachel opened her mouth to object, but found that she didn't know where to begin. Instead, she remained silent and lent the old Indian a hand as he slipped on his pack.

"*Tupananhiskama,*" Amasu said. Until we meet again.

"*Tupananhiskama,*" Rachel repeated, waving feebly.

Rachel watched Amasu's small group start back down the trail toward Puerto Definitivo. For a simple Indian, the old man was certainly full of many strange and disturbing ideas. The worst part was that some of it almost made sense. The faith that Amasu placed in the earth goddess Pachamama, however, was sorely overvalued. If she was going to make it out here in the jungle, the last thing she needed was to get in touch with her more feminine side. For the space of several seconds, knowing fully that Amasu might be heading in the smarter direction, she still considered leaving the expedition. She could follow Amasu back to the Alto Madre de Dios River and arrange further transport from Puerto Definitivo. But Kenny could yet be out here. One more day should help decide the answer to that question. One day, after all, was a small price to pay. If Max and the other men could continue onward, so could she.

Tristan and Max consulted a laminated paper map, onto which they had annotated the various reference points shown on the Moroccan tablet. Tristan directed Chico and Raóul to again take the point positions, and to begin slashing a trail northward into the jungle.

Thankful for the cool front that had moved in the evening before, the group again entered the inner reaches of the rain forest. They had broken camp early, before eight a.m. For the next two hours the forest was as dense as any part they had encountered so far. By ten o'clock, Rachel figured they had only moved about a half mile. To her amazement, however, the foliage began to thicken even more. An hour later, the jungle had was a nearly solid mass of trees, cane, reeds, thorny bamboo and hanging vines.

Like her companions, Rachel repeatedly slipped in the mud or tripped on briars, exposed roots and fallen branches. Now and then, they passed through areas where the ground reeked of wild pig, and once she spotted a giant sloth moving in ultra slow motion from tree to vine. Capybara or other small animals frequently scampered through the brush, giving Dr. Gallagher or one of the others a brief scare. On another occasion the group detoured to give wide berth to an enormous and deadly bushmaster serpent, coiled almost invisibly against a backdrop of dead leaves.

Many members of the team took up stout sticks to help support them as they ducked and twisted past the obstacles that Chico and Raóul missed. Rachel sank to her calves in spots where the rain had turned the mixture of loose earth and decaying foliage to a foul-smelling bog. As she waded through such spots, the mud fought to capture Rachel's galoshes and only reluctantly gave them up with loud complaints voiced as obscene sucking sounds. Rachel trudged through, with wrinkled nose and a bad temperament that improved only a little when ground was again firm beneath her feet. She dared not reach out to the trees, many of which were covered with thorns, toadstools, jelly-like fungi, or occasionally writhed with a snake or lizard. Tarantulas and other unnervingly large and wicked looking spiders crept across broad leaf surfaces, or labored to reconstruct their rain-damaged webs. Rachel began to muse about the relative merits and drawbacks of rain forests, and congratulated herself on having long ago decided that the inner jungles were best left to the animals. For just a few brief seconds, she dryly entertained the idea that maybe she might not get all that upset, if just this one stretch fell subject to "slash and burn" encroachment.

Tristan called for a rest break around half past ten, more for the benefit of Chico and Raóul than the rest of the expedition. Rachel found a relatively dry piece of ground and took a seat. She hadn't been resting long before she noticed Tristan standing extremely still and intently listening to the jungle.

Max also noticed Tristan's behavior. "What's up?" he asked.

"I think we have company. We're inside Yaminhua territory now, and I've been noticing strange movements around us for the past ten minutes."

"What's your advice?" Max asked Rachel. "These are your Indians."

"That would be very presumptuous," Rachel answered. "Each family group is autonomous from the others. The ties between different clans are pretty loose. I wouldn't rely on any past relationships that I've had with them."

"This is a hell of a time to find that out!" Max snapped.

Rachel glanced at Max. His reaction struck her as peculiar. What did Max think? That she was here as his personal ambassador to the Yaminhua? She was here to look for her brother, nothing else. He was lucky she could even speak the language. The Yaminhua were notoriously unpredictable.

"I'd recommend that everybody sit down and wait," Rachel suggested. "Act like we are expecting them. Try not to look nervous or defensive."

Tristan and Chico instructed the rest of the expedition members to comply with Rachel's advice. The entire team sat there for a few minutes more, until Rachel, too, began to sense the Indians' presence.

"*Mã mã oamẽ?*" Rachel called in greeting.

For a few moments, there was no response. Rachel repeated the greeting.

Finally, there was a rustling of foliage and a naked Indian with a bow and arrow stepped into view. He maintained a discreet distance.

"*Ejẽ, mã nõ oa,*" responded the Indian. Yes, we have come.

"*Ofe. Nono tsaoxõ ofe,*" invited Rachel. Come sit here and visit.

So far, the exchange was pure Yaminhua protocol. Rachel dared not deviate until she saw whether the Indian would accept the invitation.

She and her companions were trespassing, and were therefore on very delicate ground.

The Yaminhua Indian appeared to be considering the situation.

"*Ia,*" he spoke, after an uncomfortable delay.

The butterflies that had been fluttering in Rachel's stomach disappeared. With this simple, but positive, acknowledgment of the invitation to sit with the outsiders, the tension of the moment was broken. As long as the other expedition members did nothing stupid, Rachel knew the rest of the encounter would go well.

"*Afaa mĩ akiyimẽ?*" the naked Indian asked as he sat on the ground a few feet from Rachel. Why have you come? As he posed this question, four other Yaminhua emerged from the forest and squatted a few feet away.

"*Ẽ fanakĩ exto.*" I'm looking for my brother. She explained to the Yaminhua how her brother had come into this area by way of airplane, but had vanished. She told him that these men in the expedition were helping her, and would quickly pass through the Yaminhua territory, if they would be so permitted.

"*Ẽ oĩmisma afẽ exto. Nanime?*" I never saw your brother. Did he die?

Rachel paled at the reminder of that possibility, but answered confidently. "*Nanima.*" He didn't die.

"*Rakikiã poomanã afẽ exto.*" Perhaps a jaguar carried off your brother, insisted the Indian.

"*Maa...Tãpiama,*" Rachel politely replied. No...well, I don't know.

The gruesome possibility posed by this Yaminhua would normally be a shocking question to anyone of Rachel's background. Her prior exposure and study of these Indians, however, had exposed her to a different reality here among nature. While not routine, the snatching of a young child by a puma or jaguar was an occupational hazard of life for Indians such as these. There was little point explaining that her brother was a grown man. It would only confuse the Yaminhua. Better to keep it simple.

So far, so good, Rachel noticed. The other expedition members were all sitting quietly—a little skittish, but doing nothing to alarm their

Yaminhua hosts. Rachel quickly summarized the exchange of dialogue up to that point for Max and Tristan. "Do you want me to see if we can get an escort past the rest of their territory?" she asked.

"Definitely," Tristan nodded.

"Ask whether they know of any very old tunnels beyond this area," directed Max.

Rachel posed Max's question first.

"*Mẽ oinĩ,*" answered the Indian. I saw one a long time ago.

"*Fania?*"

Past the mountain, near the Amahuaca land, the Yaminhua answered, pointing northward.

Rachel told the Indian that this was where she and her companions were going. She asked if one of them would come along to guide them safely to this tunnel.

"*Ẽ mefe kaima. Fepaikanima. Sharama. Ono ichapa chakakoĩ.*" This was the longest and most animated stream of dialogue the man had spoken the whole time. Max and the others waited expectantly for Rachel's translation.

"He's seen a tunnel. He said it's beyond that mountain, near Amahuaca territory. But when I asked him to guide us, he said he doesn't want to go there. None of them will. There is 'much very bad there,' to use his exact words."

Tristan had Rachel ascertain whether the Yaminhua would permit the expedition to cross their territory. To show his thanks for this concession, Tristan presented the Indian a handful of small trinkets like mirrors, copper wire, and a pocketknife.

The Indian accepted Tristan's gifts with curiosity, but without much show of emotion. He told Rachel that there was a river not far ahead. That would mark the end of Yaminhua land.

"*Aicho,*" Rachel thanked the Indian. She rose slowly and told Tristan it was okay for the others to rise, as well. As the Yaminhua began to depart, the expedition members turned and slowly began to resume their northerly course into the dense forest. When Rachel glanced back over her shoulder a few moments later, the Indians were nowhere to be seen.

"That went well," Tristan commented. "There's no telling how a group like that might have reacted, without your intervention."

Rachel shrugged. Except for a nervous moment at the outset, the encounter was no big deal to her. "I'm just glad I haven't forgotten everything I learned about their language."

About a half-hour before noon, the group came to a small valley. At the bottom, a small river ran into and past six natural pools of varying size. Tiny cascading falls of water poured over a boulder-laden overhang running half the length of the valley. More water also emptied from small forest brooks and streams into the river. The water looked extremely inviting to Rachel.

Tristan consulted the laminated map and concluded that the river was either the Río Pinquen or yet another of its tributaries. Tristan must have read Rachel's thoughts, because he immediately suggested the group take advantage of the site to catch their first real bath of the two-day trek.

Getting down to the river proved more difficult than it looked. To maintain their footing, Raóul and Chico mostly had to hang onto vines with one hand as they hacked at others with their machetes. Without exception, the expedition members slipped and fell many times on the treacherously slick mud or moss-covered ground, stopping only as they crashed, cursing in English and Spanish, into bushes, trees, or one another.

When they reached the water, Chico cut off a piece of raw sausage and tossed it in to check for piranha. Soaring high above the valley were what she thought might have been condors. Tristan told her, however, that the birds were Giant Harpy Eagles, the dominant birds of the Amazon rain forest. Along the opposite bank, orchids and hibiscus bloomed, six-inch iridescent dragonflies hovered, and beautiful large blue butterflies fluttered over emerald green elephant leaves and corkscrew vines. The entire valley had the idyllic appearance of a lost paradise, the end effect of which was the immediate improvement of the mood of every member of the group.

Rachel retrieved a small towel, a spare set of clothes and a small bottle of shampoo from her knapsack. She shed her boots and removed her socks, but entered the river fully clothed, a discreet distance upstream from the men. The change of clothes and towel she balanced on a boulder that could serve as a dressing partition. The water was quite cool, but her body became accustomed to it quickly. Once she was in the water she slipped out of her shirt and pants and scrubbed away the mud she had gathered sliding down the hillside. Swimming to the boulder she draped the clothes over the side to dry. The water felt great, as did the opportunity to wash the dirt and sweat from her hair. She had started wearing her hair short during her first Amazon field trip, because it made a less inviting nest for like spiders and bats. She had later kept it that way, because she thought it made her look taller. A few yards away the men laughed and splashed like boys at a neighborhood swimming-hole. Rachel dove beneath the surface and relished the caress of the cool water across the dozens of small cuts and scratches that the jungle had thus far inflicted. Finally, she swam up behind the boulder and emerged into the cool air. A breeze brought goose bumps all across the surface of her naked skin.

The men couldn't discipline themselves not to glance in her direction, as Rachel toweled dry behind the boulder. The shelter was high enough to provide an adequate amount of privacy, but the men looked, anyway—Rachel's bare shoulders and wet hair visible over the top. The men's imagination filled in what their eyes couldn't see. Rachel didn't much care, so happy was she to have the chance to clean up.

Half of the group had already emerged from the water, when Rachel caught a glimpse of movement on the other side of the river. She looked up just as a jaguar stepped from the heavy foliage lining the opposite bank. Rachel instantly froze. She had seen a few of these savagely beautiful animals before, but mostly in primitive community "zoos" in Brazil.

The one watching Rachel was a large male. The jungle cat's ebony and gold pelt draped magnificently over its tightly coiled and heavily muscled frame.

The river was only twenty or thirty feet across at Rachel's location. She suddenly remembered having read somewhere that jaguars are excellent swimmers. Rachel remained motionless, ready to dive beneath the water and swim toward the others, should the animal show signs of entering the river. She could feel her heart pounding, yet she was entranced by the combined auras of primitive savage power and elegance that emanated from the large jungle cat. She was close enough that she could clearly see the cat's eyes. As she stared back into them, she could almost read the indecision in the animal's demeanor. The jaguar's mouth opened in a snarl. A deep rumbling roar emanated from the beast. The sound seemed to Rachel as if it penetrated to her very soul. Her muscles felt momentarily paralyzed. Had the jaguar chosen to attack at that moment, she doubted she would have been able to move. The jaguar continued its piercing stare for another moment. Then, as if Rachel was not even there, the animal lapped up a few sips from the water's edge and, without a backward glance, turned and vanished into the foliage on the opposite bank.

The adrenaline racing through Rachel's body soon reached her brain and she found that her control over her muscles had returned. Turning, she saw Tristan and Chico lower rifles from their shoulders. For a moment she just stood there, then it occurred to Rachel that she should wave to let them know she was all right. She did so, then quickly finished getting dressed. Frightened as she had been, and even still tense and trembling, Rachel instantly classified the face-to-face encounter as one of the most sublime she had ever experienced.

****

Lima, Peru, Sunday, February 22

Kenny Aguila chased down three false leads before locating the type of craft he needed. By some miracle, he was even able to bluff the aircraft owners into adding the lease onto an account that Max Arnold had earlier set up. Prior to their arrival, the expedition leaders had hired a plane to fly an aerial reconnaissance of the targeted part of the Madre de Dios. Max had left the account open, in case an aircraft was later needed. Kenny leased the seaplane for a week and then also charged a full tank of fuel to Max's account. Next, he prepared a flight plan to Shintuyo and presented it, as required, at the airport control tower. After picking up a few emergency supplies in the city, he returned to the airport and got under way.

****

Pinquina River, Peru, Sunday, February 22

After their swim, everyone agreed to make an early lunch on the banks of the Río Pinquen. The climb up the opposite side of the small valley was easier than their descent had been, because of rocks and boulders that they were able to use as steps.

Such luck didn't last long. A few feet past the beauty of the riverside beach, the jungle on resumed its former savagery and stalwart resistance to their advance.

The ten expedition members worked their way north for another twenty minutes, then momentarily came to a halt while Chico and Raóul attacked a thick network of *lianas* and thorned vines that barred their way. Rachel was watching an inch and a half long soldier ant crawl up the side of a tree with pale bark. As the ant reached face level, Rachel found herself staring into the unblinking eyes of a painted face, which all but blended into the shadows of surrounding foliage. As she moved her eyes to the left and right, she glimpsed the vague outlines of five or six more faces! Tristan Sloan was standing about a foot away from Rachel, looking in the opposite direction.

"Tristan," she said in voice that was almost a whisper. It was the first time she had used his first name.

"I see them," he answered softly. "Nobody make any sudden moves. More Indians. Chico, Raóul, hold up a second…let your machetes hang loosely at your sides."

Rachel spoke softly in Yaminhua, repeating the greeting she had in the earlier encounter. The faces in the foliage showed no reaction.

"Chico," Tristan murmured, "See if they speak Quechua."

"*Napaykullayki!*" greeted Chico. "*Nuqayku qasi kawsayniykuwanmi hamuyku.*" he added, telling the faces in the shadows that the expedition members came in peace. There was no answer.

"*Holá, amigos! Hablan Español?*" Chico tried.

There was still no response, other than the normal sounds of the jungle.

"None of the Indians this deep into the jungle are likely to speak Spanish," advised Rachel.

"More Yaminhua?" Max asked quietly.

"I don't think so," Rachel answered. "They didn't respond to my greeting, and the other ones said that Yaminhua territory ended at the river. Whoever they are, it's a good sign that none of us is lying around stuck full of arrows."

Rachel called out again in Yaminhua, repeating Chico's greeting.

A moment passed, then the leaves parted, and a naked figure emerged from the shadows. This Indian carried a bow, already fitted it with an arrow that was pointed it directly at Rachel's chest.

The native's forehead and shoulders were painted with a reddish dye. The lower part of his face and other areas of his body were covered or striped with a contrasting bluish black pigment.

The Indian spoke to Rachel in a language none of her companions understood.

"Ah-oh," Max muttered.

"That wasn't Yaminhua," Rachel said. "It sounded like a dialect of Huni Kui."

"You *speak* a language called Huni Kui?" an astonished Max asked.

"A little. It's their name for Amahuaca."

"Oh, well *that* explains it…"

"Be quiet for a moment."

Rachel spoke again to the Indian pointing the bow, this time using a few words of the Amahuaca language.

The Indian lowered his bow and said something over his shoulder to the other Indians still hidden in the surrounding foliage.

"Everybody smile," Rachel ordered. "They're Amahuaca, all right, but they haven't had much contact with the outer world. See this one's nasal disks and the feather holes in his ears? That's been an abandoned practice for at least two or three generations among all the Amahuaca clans I've ever seen. We don't want to make them nervous. Just smile."

The rest of the expedition fixed nervous grins on their faces that no doubt would have frightened small children, but this small gesture had an immediate positive effect on the Indians. Figure after figure materialized from the jungle and formed a crowd surrounding the expedition. Like the first native, these had similarly streaked their bodies with red *achiote* dye and the other blackish paint that Rachel now remembered as a pigment the Amahuaca called *huito*. The Indians spoke incessantly to Rachel and the uncomprehending men, all the while pawing at their hair, faces, hands, backpacks and clothing. One of them would have removed Rachel's silver necklace and eagle, had she not gently stopped him, telling him it was a sacred gift from her deceased father.

One of the Indians pointed at Rachel's short hair, murmuring "*Nawa?*" and unexpectedly stuck a hand between her legs, groping at her crotch.

Rachel instinctively let out a short shriek and hopped backward, nearly falling, but two other Indians caught her, laughing hysterically.

Rachel spoke again, and the Indians, still smiling, stopped to listen. She asked which of the Huni Kui was the "*Iria,*" the leader. The one who had aimed the bow at Rachel pointed to himself. She told him that they were looking for her brother, whom they believed had fallen from the sky in a "*owapaxaoni xuri,*" a tremendous bird. This was the closest translation she could come up with in their language for airplane.

The Indian shook his head, no. They sometimes see the "*owapaxaoni xuri*" from a clearing, but none had fallen into their forest, and they were "*tiwa,*" the first white people that these Huni Kui had seen in many months.

Rachel's face showed her disappointment. She translated for the others.

"We're probably still too far away," Max lied. "The jungle has slowed us down a lot more than I had expected. But listen—maybe the Amahuaca can help us out. The map tablet showed a tunnel that had an entrance on the other side of what Tristan and I think could be the Alto Madre de Dios river. The underground passage we're looking for could lead as far as forty kilometers. If we could find that tunnel, we could move over twice as fast to the crash site than if we have to fight the jungle the rest of the way. Can you ask if these 'Hooney-Cooey' fellows know of such tunnel?"

"I'll try." Rachel posed the question to the Amahuaca leader. She described the tunnel as an underground trail of stone, built by the ancient ones, which led to the Río Pinquina. She didn't know the Indian's name for the river, so she translated as the local Indians often refer to larger rivers, "*honi diri ra,*" River of Rapids.

The smiles left the faces of all the Amahuaca.

Rachel had learned that the leader of this group of Indians called himself Xoko Doto, meaning the Crocodile Killer. Xoko now solemnly told her yes, the Huni Kui knew of such an underground road. But it was a place of "*iuxibo,*" evil spirits. The Huni Kui would not go there.

"Tell the chief that I'll pay them well to guide us to the tunnel," Max replied.

"With what?" an incredulous Rachel asked. "Money doesn't mean a thing to these Indians."

"Hmmm. I suppose you're right. But we must have something they would want."

Tristan removed his pack and placed it on the ground. He poked around in a side compartment for a few seconds and removed a small plastic bag containing a dozen fishhooks.

"Try these."

Rachel showed Xoko the hooks.

The holes in the end of the fishhooks, through which the hooks could be securely fastened, greatly impressed the Indian leader. The Huni Kui's hooks were primitively simple, and they lost many that came untied.

Xoko told Rachel that none of his people would go near the tunnel, although the fishhooks were "*maxi,*" which meant very nice. Perhaps, he told her, if he had a powerful amulet such as her sacred silver "*nawatoto,*" he might be brave enough to bring the strangers to a nearby animal trail. That trail passed close to the entrance of the tunnel. They would know they were near the entrance, Xoko explained, when they came to many "*bakahua nixi,*" flowered vines. The entrance was to the right of the trail. He told her that it would be much better to go past the entrance, and keep an eye out for her brother from the trail, rather than risk the anger of the evil spirits.

Rachel translated none of this last exchange for Max. Instead, she told Xoko that her brother, in all likelihood, lay injured or dead at some place along the tunnel of the ancient ones. The eagle amulet would protect her alone, since it derived its power from her dead father, who had given it to her. Did not the Huni Kui honor the spirits of their fathers, and take care of their wounded or dying?

Xoko thought about this for a moment, then answered that he would accept the fishhooks as a tribute to the Huni Kui for leading the white people to the animal trail. In exchange for the fish hooks and the bright red cloth that "the fat one" wore around his neck. As an afterthought, Xoko added one machete as a part of the expected tribute.

Rachel quickly accepted the deal before Xoko could add anything else he wanted. She told Max what she had negotiated. She translated "red cloth worn by the fat one" as "the large man's red bandanna."

Max removed the bandanna he had tied around his neck, and handed it to the chief. He directed Chico to surrender his machete, as well. They still had spares in the packs. One didn't enter a jungle like the Madre de Dios with only two machetes.

Rachel was glad that Xoko apparently wasn't familiar with firearms, lest he had asked for one of the rifles or Max's pistol.

Satisfied with the payment, Xoko motioned for Rachel and the others to follow. The rest of the Amahuaca melted back into the forest, as Rachel and the others did their best to keep up with Xoko Doto.

Chapter Ten

"Ankh-em-fentu"

Third of the nine snakes infesting the way between
this world and the next, according to the Papyrus of Iuaa.
(Also the name of the keeper of the fifth Arit).

****

Madre de Dios Jungle, Thursday, February 19

Xoko led them, as promised, to a trail of sorts. "*Txaxo*," he said pointing at the trail.

"He says it's a deer trail," Rachel told the others. She turned to thank Xoko, but the Amahuaca chief had already silently vanished.

The trail was better than nothing, Rachel supposed. By stooping low, they were able to proceed a little easier. Max retrieved another machete from one of the packs to replace the one given to Xoko. Chico and Raóul again moved forward, ahead of the rest of the group.

They followed the deer trail for about twenty minutes. Sometimes the trail disappeared, but then Tristan or Chico would pick it back up a few feet farther along.

Finally, Chico called out that there was a vine with large purple flowers, just ahead. More of the vines were visible a bit farther down the trail. When the party reached a place where the purple flowers were most abundant, Tristan ordered everyone to spread out to the right of the trail.

"Look for anything that could be an entrance to a tunnel," he added. "...an odd-shaped boulder, a sinkhole...anything that might be a clue."

The group had only just begun their search, when there was a shout from Dr. Ramón. Rachel was surprised it had been so easy to find the entrance. As she headed toward Dr. Ramón, he warned her to stay back.

"A snake attacked me. I didn't get a good look, but it wasn't a chicotillo. It bit me on the leg. Be careful."

Most of the eight other expedition members were also converging toward Ramón, thinking like Rachel, that the professor had found the tunnel entrance. Ramón's warning came as Rachel was in mid-step, and she too another stride forward before the warning registered.

As misfortune would have it, the snake had turned to the new and next closest intruder. That happened to be Rachel. Unlike most pit vipers, this species fearlessly attacks anything that approaches, with or without provocation. The viper hurled itself with lightning reflex at Rachel's left leg.

Rachel saw the blur of motion only a blink before the snake struck. She felt a slight stinging on the inside of her left leg, just above the top of her boot.

Another blur followed, even before Rachel had reacted. This time, however, the movement was the blade of Raóul's machete, which moments too late, decapitated the upper seven inches of the serpent's body. Both parts continued to move, the upper part rocking and twitching ineffectively for only a few moments. The lower half continued to writhe and coil upon itself, as blood spurted from the exposed end. The snake was huge, about nine feet long.

"Where were you a half second ago?" Rachel gasped.

"*Señorita?*"

"Never mind. *Nada,*" she told the confused Raóul.

Tristan reached Rachel first, closely followed by Max and Dr. Gallagher. Tristan looked down at the snake's body in silence, then at Rachel and Dr. Ramón.

"Poisonous?" Max asked.

Tristan nodded. "Fer-de-lance. Not my choice of snakes to be bitten by. Gallagher, see if you can find a red plastic box in Chico's pack. It's about the size of a paperback book."

"I'll get it," Max said. "I know what it looks like."

"Keep your eyes open and watch where you step! There might be a den around here somewhere."

"*Now* you tell us!" Rachel mocked.

"Are you certain it bit you?" Tristan asked.

"I don't know," Rachel answered. "I think I might have felt a small twinge, but then again it could just be my imagination. It happened so fast."

Tristan had Rachel sit, as Chico and Raóul searched the area for more snakes. Dr. Gallagher moved to check Dr. Ramón's bite.

Tristan used his knife to cut open Rachel's trousers leg. Two small red pinpricks were visible, just where she thought the fer-de-lance had struck.

"Damn!" Tristan exclaimed.

"These were new pants," said Rachel with false bravado. Her understanding of poisonous snakebites was that less than two percent were fatal. Still, she too had recognized the viper species and knew that the venom of the fer-de-lance was far more toxic than that of rattlesnakes or any other poisonous North American snakes. Treatment, especially in the field, was also less successful. This snake had also been a large one, which meant that it would have more venom.

Dr. Ramón, too, had now found the telltale evidence. Two small red marks were displayed about three inches above his right ankle, where the viper's fangs had penetrated the thin rubber boot.

Max had located the firstaid kit and was about to start back, when a thought occurred to him. Dr. Ramón could prove to be a serious problem. If Paititi turned out to contain the riches they all hoped to find, and if Ramón elected to report the find, there's no telling how much of the treasure would be lost.

Max opened the case and looked at the vials of serum in the kit. Glancing around to make sure he wasn't observed, Max switched the caps on two of the vials, then quickly returned to Sloan's side.

"This one?" asked Max, handing one of the vials to Tristan.

Tristan nodded, and also removed a syringe from the red case.

"Are either of you allergic to horses?" he asked.

Puzzled by the strange question, both Dr. Ramón and Rachel shook their heads no.

"The poison must be making me delirious," Rachel wisecracked. "I could have sworn it was a snake, rather than a horse that bit me."

"This is an antivenin for the fer-de-lance's poison. They make it by injecting the poison into horses, then collecting the resulting immune serum. If you were allergic to horses, the antivenin could put you into shock, and that could be lethal. The antivenin should keep the effects of the poisoning from becoming life threatening, but you're probably going to be sick for a while. You should stay off your feet."

Tristan frowned. "Preferably, we should get you to a hospital. But the nearest one is three days away, under nearly impossible conditions. We'll just have to wait it out."

Without real warning, Tristan injected the syringe into Rachel's leg right at the point of the bite. Rachel cringed and stiffened, but it was over just as quick.

"Ouch! I hope you have malpractice insurance! Where did get your bedside manner?" she asked.

"Sorry, no time to chit-chat, I've got another patient."

Tristan moved to Dr. Ramón, and prepared a second syringe. Max handed him the second vial.

"You are using a clean needle, I hope?" Dr. Ramón admonished.

"Everybody's a comedian," Tristan responded. "We'll see how funny you think is it in about four to five hours."

"Hey," Rachel said. "We're just trying to make the best of things. You know what they say…laughter is the best medicine?"

"Yeah? Rodriguez used to say that too. You remember Rodriguez, Max?"

"You mean that Colombian guide, a couple of years back, who died from a coral snake's venom?"

"Aren't you supposed to be reassuring us?" Rachel asked.

The area around the bite was already beginning to redden and cause a sharp and painful burning sensation. Despite his jocular remarks, Sloan's furrowed brows and grim facial demeanor were so serious that he was beginning to frighten Rachel.

"Don't worry, you'll be fine. If we have to amputate, we have plenty of big strong guys to hold you down."

Rachel blanched at the mention of amputation, even though she was sure that Sloan must be kidding.

Tristan saw her go pale, and quickly apologized.

"That was stupid of me. I was just teasing. We've already taken the most important step, that being the antivenin. We just need to cleanse the wound and apply an antiseptic, to treat for possible contamination and head off infection."

Tristan eased Rachel's left boot from her foot, then removed her sock.

"Aren't you going to suck out the venom?"

"You kidding? You think I want a mouth full of poison? Listen. Drawing out the venom is an old wives tale. Sucking on a snakebite just further contaminates it. It's potentially more harmful than helpful. The same goes for a tourniquet. Besides, there's a possibility that the bite wasn't even envenomated. We may not know that for another six hours or so. We'll leave your boot off so that it doesn't constrict your circulation."

"En-veno-mated...," Rachel slowly repeated. "Is that a real word? I don't like the sound of it...I'd rather you had said: 'You may feel some mild discomfort...'"

Chico interrupted their banter.

"Señor Tristan, we've found the entrance to the tunnel! It's over here, about seven meters away. And you were right about another thing...we also found a snake pit. You want to guess where it is?

****

Three large stone rectangles rested in a U-shape around the tunnel entrance. Each was about a foot high and two feet long and partially covered by bushes and vines. Moss-covered stone steps led into the tunnel. On the lower steps and floor, two and a half meters below, slithered three more fer-de-lance vipers.

"Great. How do we get rid of those?" Max asked.

"If we use your pistol," Tristan cracked. "the bullets will ricochet off the stone floor and walls and could hit one of us. On the other hand, I wouldn't recommend getting close enough to use a machete, either. Maybe we could cut long poles with forked ends."

"What if we dropped one of these stones on top of them?" Dr. Gallagher asked.

"That's not such a bad idea. I can't think of a better one. Want to give it a try?"

Chico cut away a few vines to make a better opening. Four of the men then lifted one of the stones, which must have weighed over two hundred pounds. On the count of three, they heaved it toward the floor of the entrance.

Miraculously, the stone landed on top of all three snakes, crushing or pinning them down.

"I wouldn't count on that holding them forever, unless it killed one or two of them," Tristan cautioned.

"Somebody needs to go down there with a machete and finish them off, just to be safe," Max agreed. "Chico?"

"Not me. You think I'm crazy?"

"You afraid of snakes?" Max bullied.

"Even other snakes are afraid of *these* snakes," Chico replied. "Raóul will go. He is very good with the machete."

With extreme caution, Raóul ventured down the steps, taking a bright headlight-size lamp with him. After ensuring that no more vipers were in the immediate vicinity, he used the machete to finish off each of the three snakes pinned by the stone.

"*No mas,*" he called.

"All clear. All right then, what do you say to moving Rachel and Jorgé inside the tunnel?" Max suggested. "It will be dark soon. I'd feel more comfortable getting out of the forest, and inside the tunnel. We can set up a couple of Coleman lanterns and keep watch for other snakes. At the same time we'll reduce the likelihood of running into more Indians."

Tristan agreed with the plan. When he had finished cleansing and covering Dr. Ramón's and Rachel's wounds, the group moved from the jungle into the tunnel entrance.

Tristan and a few of the other men helped Rachel and Dr. Ramón as they made their way down the dark passageway. Raóul led, illuminating the way several meters ahead with the bright lamp.

The tunnel was damp, dark and stank as if something had died there—a place of bones and shriveled snakeskins.

"Maybe we should rethink this…" Rachel suggested.

Small creatures of indeterminate origin scurried into cracks as the lamp beam flashed back and forth across the stone floor. Tristan and Max, however, still thought moving into the tunnel was a grand idea and trudged straight ahead.

"It's safer," Tristan promised.

"Did you see that?" Rachel protested. "That big black thing that just scampered into that crack? I think it was a scorpion. There's too many yucky…"

"I thought you were used to living in jungles, for crissakes," Max said.

"I lived in research shacks…Indian huts…not holes in the ground."

"Would you *please* keep quiet?" Max asked, a bit testily.

"Bugs, bugs, bugs!" Rachel griped, in a voice just above a whisper.

After Max thought they had come far enough, he ordered the group to set up camp on the tunnel floor.

While there was still a bit of daylight, Tristan decided to return to the forest and try and catch a fish or two from a stream that had paralleled the animal trail. All the Cuzqueño men, except one named Felipe, were ill at ease in the ancient tunnel and volunteered to accompany Tristan. Even Chico whispered to Tristan that a devil called *Purun Machu* lived in such tunnels. The bad luck of the snakebites was an obvious warning. Felipe boasted that his fellow Peruvians were superstitious fools, whereas he, an educated man, had no fear of the tunnel or its supposed demon spirit. Felipe had attended one term at the university in Cuzco.

Max decided he and Dr. Gallagher would remain with the two injured members of the expedition, along with Felipe and an unhappy Raóul, whose quick eyes and faster machete would provide protection from snakes or other dangers. Tristan and Chico took two of the rifles, a pack of fishhooks, and a spool of fishing filament that they would cut into hand lines. Luis and Renaldo, two of the porters, followed them back to the deer trail.

"Be careful," Max warned. "We've used half of our antivenin serum already."

Rachel propped her back against one of the supply packs and tried to keep her mind off the creepy-crawlers and the snakebite wound, which was becoming increasingly uncomfortable. Dr. Ramón was also starting to feel the effects of the poison.

"A fine rescue this is turning out to be," Rachel commented to Max. "I'm turning into one of the victims."

"Everything will all turn out just fine. Tristan came well prepared, as usual. The antivenin ought to control the poison."

Max paused and masked his face in sympathetic concern.

"Dr. Ramón and you are obviously in no shape to travel for at least a day or two. I may leave Tristan and the other men here with you, come tomorrow morning, and explore on ahead with Raóul. I'm impatient to see just where this tunnel goes."

"And you'd check on the crash site, along the way?"

"Oh, certainly. I'll bet I find it before mid-morning."

Max reflected silently that this was the perfect opportunity to wrap up that charade. He could hear himself reporting back. "*Good news! It wasn't your brother's plane! It turned out to be an old wreckage...Probably been there for years!*" If the tunnel led all the way to the Río Pinquina, he wouldn't really need the young woman's language skill any longer. If the tunnel led to Paititi, he'd rather Rachel not know its exact location, anyway.

"I'm astonished the tunnel really exists," Rachel said. "Mind you, I'm not saying I buy the entire story that your tablet is an Egyptian map of South America. I will admit, though—finding this kind of evidence of an advanced culture so far into the jungle is extraordinary. What an argument for anthropologists who believe that the Incas might have had their origins here."

"How's the knee doing?" Dr. Gallagher interrupted.

"It's hurting more. I think my leg is starting to swell a little. I've got a headache, too."

"And you, Dr. Ramón?" the Egyptologist asked.

Ramón pulled up his pant's leg a bit. His swelling was worse than Rachel's was, and his facial coloring had taken on an odd hue.

"I'm afraid I am not feeling all that well," he answered. The Peruvian looked quite worried. He had good cause to be. He, too, knew that the venom was life threatening and the serum wasn't one hundred percent effective.

The four of them talked about different things for another hour or so, trying to shift attention away from the disturbing turn of events. Raóul and Felipe kept watch.

****

"That should be plenty," Tristan announced to Chico and the two porters. The three Peruvians had caught eight fish in about fifteen minutes, not counting those that had gotten away. Tristan had kept watch, holding his rifle ready, while the other men fished for the group's supper. Chico retrieved the other rifle, and the four men began making their way back to join Max and the rest of the expedition at the tunnel. Tristan, in the lead, was just about to step back out onto the deer trail when he experienced the uncanny sensation that they were being watched. He motioned for the others to stop, and stood still, listening to the jungle noises around them. He couldn't detect anything out of the ordinary, but he still had an uneasy feeling. He motioned the others forward and stepped onto the trail, followed by Chico and the two Cuzqueño porters, Renaldo and Luis.

Tristan set a brisk pace and the flowering vines were soon in sight. Luis, who was bringing up the rear, suddenly gave a surprised yelp. Tristan turned around in time to see Luis' face twist into a mask of agony. The Peruvian pitched forward onto the ground, an Indian *virote* blowdart sticking up from beneath his left shoulder blade, and a pair of arrows in his back! Tristan pointed the rifle blindly into the jungle and fired a shot.

"Head for the tunnel!" he shouted, then turned and sprinted down the path. He hadn't seen the Indians, but hoped the noise of the gunshot might startle them enough that he and the remaining two men might reach shelter in the tunnel. Chico and Renaldo followed Tristan at once, neither stopping to check Luis for signs of life. All three of the men knew that the *virote* darts, dipped in a deadly poisonous *cuare* mixture, produced a lingering and painful death. Every moment that they remained in the open increased the likelihood that a dart or arrow would strike another of them. The Indians must have only found the group seconds before the attack. Otherwise, Tristan knew that the natives would have already cut off their escape from the opposite direction. He left the trail at the flowering vines and sped toward the tunnel entrance. He heard a howl and saw Renaldo flail wildly, as he became the second victim of the deadly accurate *pucuna* blowguns and poison-tipped arrows! Tristan swung his weapon around and fired again. Chico also shot a couple of rounds from his rifle into the trees, then raced after Tristan. A dart whizzed by Tristan's neck close enough for him to feel the breeze from its passage. He leapt forward toward the tunnel opening, and nearly broke his ankle as he landed on the stone slab they earlier dropped onto the snakes. Chico tumbled on top of Tristan a half second later. Both men quickly found shelter behind the slab and began firing toward the tunnel entrance.

✳✳✳✳

About the time that Gallagher was wondering aloud about Tristan and the rest of their group, the silence of the tunnel was shattered by several sharp popping sounds coming from the tunnel entrance.

Raóul stood and moved in that direction with the flashlight. The sounds came again.

"That's gun fire!" Max exclaimed. "Felipe, Gallagher—you two stay here. Raóul, *vamos!*"

The two men ran toward the tunnel entrance.

As he drew nearer, Max could see Chico and Tristan's silhouettes against the opening. They had backed inside a short distance and were in crouched defensive positions, aiming their rifles toward the jungle. Raóul reached them first, with Max close behind.

"Indians?" Max asked.

"Hivitos, Achuara or some other poison dart tribe," Tristan acknowledged. "All I know is they were shooting at us with blowguns. We'd just started back, when Luis was hit. They got Renaldo a few seconds later."

"You two are okay?"

"Yes, barely. One of those darts missed me by inches. There hasn't been a sign of them, though, since we entered the tunnel."

"Let's move a bit back toward the others," Max suggested. "They won't be able to see us in the dark, and for a little while, we'll be able to tell if anyone comes through the entrance. Any possibility that Luis or Renaldo might still be alive?"

Tristan grimly shook his head no. "No chance. The poison wouldn't kill them instantly, but the Indians would. It's just as well—cuare poison can take hours. It's supposed to be extremely agonizing." Tristan shifted uneasily with the sudden realization that any of the dozen new scratches on his body might be from one of the darts, rather than the jungle.

The four men retreated a distance into the tunnel, as Max had suggested, and waited. After about ten minutes and nothing new, Tristan spoke.

"It could be that they're afraid of the '*Purun Machu*' demon, and won't enter the tunnel. On the other hand, there might be an entrance on the other side of Ramón and the others. You and Raóul had better head back. Lend your pistol to Felipe or Gallagher, whoever is the better shot. Stay there. Chico and I will watch this end."

"Right," Max agreed. He moved back along the passage, feeling his way along the wall, until he saw the glow of the lanterns. The others were fine, but Dr. Ramón was looking even worse. Max quickly summarized the bad news.

"If they *are* Hivitos, they won't attack until tomorrow morning," Rachel told Max.

"What makes you so sure about that?"

"Their sacred rituals. Hivitos believe they have to periodically change souls. Before attacking, the warriors have a ritual ceremony wherein each man tries to glimpse his soul. Each of the warriors must then describe what the soul looked like to the others. The ceremony lasts until dawn. Then they attack. If they kill an enemy, his soul is released and the Hivito warrior is able to capture that soul for himself."

"Fine," Max said. "We'll keep watch, anyway. You might be wrong, or they might be a different tribe." Max unholstered his pistol, an old Army Colt .45, and gave it to Felipe. They moved the lanterns another twenty feet away from Rachel, Dr. Ramón and Gallagher, then Max Felipe and Raóul retreated into the relative darkness and waited.

Chapter Eleven

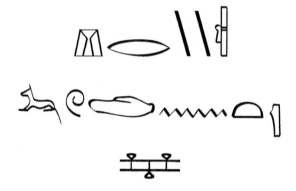

underground way, tunnel

✳✳✳✳

Ancient Tunnel, Madre de Dios Jungle, Thursday night, February 19

The men stood watch in pairs through the night. Whichever four were guarding against an attack traded turns napping, or tended to Dr. Ramón and Rachel.

Dr. Ramón's ankle and lower leg had already swollen to a gruesome size, and he grew increasingly feverish as the hours passed.

In addition to increasing pain and swelling, Rachel found that she was having difficulty following the discussions that went on around her.

She felt nauseous and dizzy, and her skin felt clammy, despite the coolness of the tunnel.

She understood only a part of Tristan's explanation to Gallagher that Dr. Ramón had undoubtedly received a greater amount of the snake's poison. When the fer-de-lance had bitten Rachel, it was after having emptied most of the poison in its venom glands into Dr. Ramón, and much too soon to have created more venom. Had the snake been a smaller, younger viper, Tristan believed Rachel might not even have experienced much discomfort. The older vipers learn to ration their poison, and Rachel had been the unluckily beneficiary of that wisdom.

"Jou tink snakes hab dat mush intelligenz?" Rachel slurred. She was having difficulty sleeping.

"What's wrong with your tongue?" Tristan asked.

"Nuffing. My lebs ar tingwing."

"Your legs?"

Rachel shook her head feebly. "No, my lebs," she said, bringing a hand up to touch her lips.

"Oh. Yes, that's not an uncommon complaint. Your scalp, fingers and toes may start to tingle, as well." He left out that some survivors of the fer-de-lance's poison experience permanent paralysis or tissue damage, sometimes bad enough to require amputation. Rachel was holding up quite well, under the circumstances. Dr. Ramón's condition worried him more. The professor's pulse was much too fast, and he was running a dangerously high fever.

Tristan turned the lanterns down lower and resumed his position. At one point, he heard unmistakable movement. He moved one of the larger backpacks to shield his body from the poison darts, but nothing happened. A few moments later, there was a low rumbling growl, and he thought his sharp ears caught the sound of padded footsteps fading back into the darkness.

As Rachel grew more tired, she drifted into a feverish sleep, again visited by the dream where she was in the pit. This time a blurry Inca warrior opened his mouth and an obscenely long tongue darted in and out, like a snake's. The Inca then became Tristan, and finally Trish, the tongue still darting in and out. Rachel pitched and turned in her sleep, mumbling in an incoherent mixture of Yaminhua, English and other languages. Eventually the antivenin gained an upper hand, her fever broke, and Rachel slept peacefully.

****

Rachel woke into darkness. She could hear the breathing of the men not on watch, and saw the dim and distant glow of the lanterns. Her left foot felt funny, and her big toe tingled. Tristan had splinted both Rachel's and Dr. Ramón's legs to immobilize them as much as possible. Fatigue overcame her discomfort and she soon fell back to sleep.

The next time she woke, it was to the sound of Max's voice. He and Tristan were quietly arguing about something. She thought she heard Tristan mention the Pinquina and Manu rivers, but she couldn't make out the rest. Max was telling Tristan something like "no choice, but to wait in the tunnel." She could just barely make out their outlines in the darkness, even when they had rejoined the rest of the group.

"What time is it?" she asked.

"About six in the morning," Max answered. "How are you feeling?"

"Better. Less nauseous, but my leg still burns. The pain has reached my foot now, too."

"Let's take a look," Tristan said. He fumbled around for a few moments until he found a small flashlight and switched it on.

Rachel blinked as the light blinded her for a second, then stared in horror and bewilderment at her left foot. Instead of her bare instep and toes, she was looking at something black and misshapen…She felt violently ill.

"What the hell?" Max exclaimed.

"Bat," Tristan said. He grabbed a blanket and quickly dropped it over Rachel's foot. The blanket began to flutter and throb, and before Tristan could seize the source, something black and about ten inches long escaped, screeching, from under one edge. Dr. Gallagher also awoke and bolted upright. The bat flopped around once or twice, and as Tristan rushed toward it, it extended wings each over a foot long. The bat flew off into the darkness, past Raóul and into the tunnel.

Rachel fainted.

When she came to, Tristan, Max and Gallagher were all gathered around her.

"Wh…What…?" was all that she could manage.

Tristan grimaced. "Vampire bat. Sorry about that. I guess we should have left one of the lanterns closer to the group. I already cleansed the bite area on your toe and treated it with an antiseptic. So long as it doesn't get infected and the bat didn't have rabies, you should be just fine."

Rachel rolled her eyes. "Rabies? Vampire Bat?"

"You're going to be fine," Tristan repeated. "Your fever has broken, and the swelling is going down in your leg. You should be able to travel in a day or two."

"Poor thing. If you want to hear the bright side, just think…" Dr. Gallagher offered, "…the Chinese word for bat is the same word as for 'blessing.' This could be symbolic. Maybe the worst of our troubles are behind us."

Rachel exhaled heavily.

"Yeah, and Mesoamerican cultures treat the bat as a symbol of enlightenment, because of how a bat awakens in darkness. You know what? I would just as soon have passed on both the blessing and the enlightenment." She looked over at Dr. Ramón. His eyes looked half-open, but red and watery, and he was breathing with much difficulty.

"He's not doing too well," Dr. Gallagher said. "…but he's nearly twice your age. Tristan thinks he got over twice as much of the poison as you.

The antivenin should've taken care of it, even so. We think he may be experiencing some sort of an arrhythmia problem, or has had a stroke."

"I'm afraid he's going into shock," Tristan said. "He's past the point that we can safely move him...even if there was anywhere we could take him. The best treatment for shock is to keep him calm and reassure him, but I don't think he can still understand us. I've done everything I can."

Rachel nodded , then remembered the bat and shuddered.

"I hate 'em. Bats, I mean. Even the little ones. I got one caught in my hair when I was only about three years old. I used to get nightmares about it. The one when I was three was only a tiny thing. I saw vampire bats once or twice when I was here before. I *never* liked the look of them. This one was...what?....the size of a goose?"

"More like a pigeon. We already checked your teeth while you were unconscious, and they're still normal," teased Tristan. "I'm keeping a sharp stake handy, just the same."

"Bastard," moaned Rachel.

"For someone who's spent an extended period of time in the jungle, you sure seem prone to have a knack for getting into trouble with the local wildlife," Max noted dryly.

Rachel shot him a withering glance.

"I'm an anthropologist, not a zoologist."

"It could have been worse," Tristan replied. "I've heard of men waking up to find a vampire bat sucking the blood out of their nose or chin. Can you imagine opening your eyes and..."

"Hey! Can we change subjects?" Rachel admonished. The mood turned more appropriately somber as talk returned to their situation. Tristan hated to just leave Luis' and Renaldo's bodies lying in the forest.

"The Indians probably already moved them," Max said. "Are Hivitos or Achuara cannibals?"

"The Hivitos, possibly," Rachel, answered shuddering again at the thought. "...but I doubt that they were Achuara or Hivitos. Like I told you, either tribe would have attacked at dawn. This is also a long way from either ones' known territory. It could easily have been some other tribe who use blowguns. Nobody really knows which Indians live out here, for sure. Most of the jungle, for about a hundred miles northwest and the same to our southeast, hasn't been explored at all."

The men decided that Max would take Raóul and see what lay farther down the tunnel. If they came to an exit, they would only check it out if it was far enough from the group's present location to make it unlikely that the Indians would be lying in ambush. Depending on how far the tunnel was passable, Max and Raóul would only go as far as left time to return by six p.m.

By Tristan's calculations, the Río Pinquina could not be much over twenty kilometers, twelve to thirteen miles, in the direction the tunnel was leading. Figuring on about three miles an hour, with two or three hours to poke around outside any exits they might find, that only gave a maximum of about four hours for Max to explore.

Of the four rifles the expedition had brought, one had been in Luis' possession. Circumstances made it impossible to try to recover that one. The poison dart Indians would undoubtedly leave at least one warrior to watch the entrance. Such sentries would remain for as long as the Indians might think the expedition was still there. That could mean days.

Max took one rifle and his pistol and left the other two weapons with Tristan and Felipe. The group was now down to eight members. Two of these were totally or partially incapacitated. Rachel wondered, as they disappeared into the blackness of the tunnel, if Max and Raóul would be the next casualties.

* * * *

Shintuyo, Friday, February 20

Kenny landed at Shintuyo in the early afternoon. At the mission station, he was able to verify that Max's expedition had camped there. No one present knew if a young American female had been with the group or not. The group had set up their camp down on the riverbanks, away from the mission. The padre was out visiting an Indian village, and didn't return to the mission until just before dark. He confirmed that a young lady fitting Rachel's description had been with Max's group. The Señorita had made a small financial contribution to use the mission's shower on the morning of the expedition's departure. The padre did not know the details of the expedition's itinerary. He speculated that the boats on which the group had departed would almost certainly have stopped in Boca Manu, the last semblance of civilization for many miles in any direction.

Because it was growing dark, Kenny accepted the padre's offer to overnight at the mission station. He would follow the river toward Boca Manu in the morning, and try to get more information there.

****

Madre de Dios Jungle, Friday, February 20

Tristan stacked the backpacks and bedrolls to form a circular barricade around the six of them. The visibility from the direction of the entrance was limited, but enough that they ought to have ample notice of anyone trying to sneak up. In the other direction, he fashioned a makeshift alarm with fishing line, metal pots and other utensils.

To help pass the time, Rachel asked to see the map tablet again. Dr. Gallagher reviewed the translations of the hieroglyphics and the presumed locations with Rachel, while Tristan, Chico and Felipe kept watch.

"I'm sorry for the way things have turned out," Gallagher apologized. "When I first decided that this tablet was authentic, all I could think of was getting it to my colleagues and exposing the significance of its discovery to the rest of the world. Max wouldn't hear of that. I had hoped you would join me in pressing that argument. The real reason I

came along, despite the money Max offered, was to keep the tablets in
sight so that nothing would happen to them. Whether we had found the
lost city or not, even the discovery of the map would have been a discovery of huge historic significance. To think that the ancients even
knew about this continent! Now, ever since we left Cuzco, all I have
been able to think about has been survival. I have a wife and three kids
at home, for heaven's sake. I keep wondering if I'm ever going to see
them again. I'm afraid my fieldwork in the Nile Valley has been an
extremely poor preparation for this type of expedition. I'm useless here.
I'm so sorry that I've involved you."

"I'm afraid I did that all by myself," Rachel answered. "How could
you possibly be responsible? By telling Max that I wrote a paper on
some native jungle tribes? How absurd! Max is just an opportunist who
capitalized on the coincidence of my coming here to look for my
brother. If it wasn't that I keep getting bitten by wild animals, it would
be a symbiotic arrangement. This was the only timely means I had of
getting to the crash site." Realizing that it had been nine days since
Kenny was reported missed, Rachel bit her lower lip and tears threatened
at the corners of her eyes. Things were not going well at all.

Felipe and Chico were standing watch, but Tristan still sat apart,
apparently relieved to be released from the conversation.

Rachel could also tell that Dr. Gallagher was holding something
back, but she didn't feel up to pressing the subject. Instead, she changed
the topic of conversation back to the tablets.

"Tell me more about the map, where we are now…and the tunnels,"
she said.

"Well, as you can see, we're located right here on the modern
map…between the Alto Madre de Dios and the Río Pinquina. The
Egyptian tablet doesn't accurately reflect all the same rivers—obviously
not the Spanish names for the rivers. We believe, however, that the
Manu, Pinquina and Madre de Dios rivers all might have existed that
far back, and are represented by these lines on the Egyptian tablet."

Dr. Gallagher pointed at the river lines on the tablet.

"This is our tunnel here…leading all the way over to the Río Pinquina. Somewhere just to the north side of that river is the indicated location for the fortified city that Max believes is Gran Paititi. The exact distance is unknown. As you can see, the continent is only a crude representation. The scale is also too small to say whether the ruins would be, say ten kilometers from the river, or forty. Assuming a deviation of forty kilometers south to north, and perhaps ten east to west, we would be trying to locate the city within an area roughly equal to 150 square miles."

"All of which is dense jungle filled with poisonous snakes, hostile Indians and vampire bats. Is every person on this expedition out of their minds?" Rachel asked.

"I suppose it might appear that way. If, however, we can follow the tunnel all the way, it's supposed to lead right up to the lost city. As you must be aware, there are similar tunnels all around the world, near major archaeological sites in Giza, Thebes, Jerusalem, Mexico, Guatemala, the Orient and, of course, here in Peru. In every case, such tunnels exit underneath or within eyesight of the ruins of a pyramid or a temple. Max is just counting on staying along the same line as the tunnel, until we spot such ruins. As big as he believes they must be, they should be hard to miss."

"It all sounds like fiction to me," Rachel said. "I never thought the Egyptians spread their empire much beyond what we think of as present day Egypt."

"That's mostly correct," Dr. Gallagher answered. "But there were exceptions. The warrior kings Amenhotep III and Ramses III spread their empires to more distant locations. One of their armies must have reached Morocco."

Rachel turned the professor's attention once again to the map. "What are these three smaller circles to the south of the Paititi location?"

"Smaller fortified outposts, set up in an arc around Gran Paititi. They would protect the approach from the south or the west. The English names would translate to something like One Thousand, The-Leopard-Comes-Here and Daybreak. We believe this line represents the Pinquina River. Along with the jungle itself, the river apparently was thought to be enough protection to Paititi's north."

"Either that, or the other half of the perimeter hadn't been created when the tablet was carved," Rachel suggested. "Hmmm, that's interesting. One of the outposts is called One Thousand?"

"Yes. Maybe it meant the number of warriors assigned to defend it. Why? Is there something important about that number?"

"Not the number itself...just the Quechua translation, *Waranka*. There's a few obscure references I've come across before to another lost city in Peru or Bolivia called *Oreganka or Huareganka*. *Waranka* is close enough to be another variation."

"You may just come to believe in this map, yet" Dr. Gallagher chuckled.

"I'll admit I'm intrigued, but it still seems more likely it's just a fraud."

"Of course, that's possible. Based upon my personal experiences of the past few days, though, I find that explanation improbable. An Egyptologist would have had to spend sufficient time in this jungle to have accurately found this lost tunnel, and to have learned the native tongue of the Inca. Then he would've had to painstakingly carve and artificially age a tablet like this, and then top it all off by losing it somewhere in Morocco. The forgery would also have to be relatively recent. The discovery of the Rosetta Stone wasn't until 1799. The subsequent knowledge we now have of hieroglyphic meaning was only in its infancy even by the mid-1800's."

"But *Egyptians* in pre-Columbian Peru?"

Dr. Gallagher sighed. "Your skepticism is shared by archaeologists and anthropologists, worldwide. You may be aware, however, that a small fringe element within academia believes that transatlantic voyages were quite common in the period of the Egyptians. Or the Greeks, Sumerians, Phoenicians...you name it, somebody has tried to prove that they were here. The distance from the west coast of Morocco to the mouth of the Amazon is actually shorter than the length of the Mediterranean. There is always some small amount of concrete evidence to support claims of such visits, but never sufficient to prove it. That doesn't even include the New Age nuts who believe that Atlantis was America."

"Do you believe in such stories? The ones about ancient civilizations reaching the Americas?" Rachel asked.

"The tablet and this tunnel have caused me to question much of what I thought I believed. But, after all, this is what an archaeologist does. He or she goes out looking to prove or disprove a theory. It's not just what we have already proved that is important—such as the knowledge that Columbus or the Vikings made it here. It's also important to study why it has to be so certain that they were the *only* ones?"

Rachel was silent. There was some sense in what the professor was saying. Perhaps the pursuit of knowledge justified his and Dr. Ramón's participation in this wild trek across the jungle. Maybe Tristan Sloan had an equally valid reason for being here.

It wasn't quite eleven o'clock in the morning. Gallagher went over to check on Dr. Ramón again. The swelling was about the same, but a blackish discoloration had begun to appear around his ankle.

A noise echoed from the dark end of the tunnel—the direction that Max had gone with Raóul. Tristan turned to listen. More sounds followed. Someone or something was hurrying down the tunnel toward them

Chico and Tristan trained their weapons toward the darkness, as Rachel and the others crouched behind the makeshift barricade.

"Hello?" a distant voice echoed. "Hello, it's us!"

"Max?" called Tristan.

"Yeah. Don't shoot. It's us."

A few minutes later, Max and Raóul emerged from the darkness. Max was huffing and puffing and clearly was excited. The more athletic Raóul had hardly broken a sweat.

"Tristan, you're going to have to see it to believe it. There's a large underground room up ahead, a little less than two hours away. Less, if you move as fast as we did getting back here. The tunnel's open all the way, but dead-ends into this big room. Gallagher, you're going to piss your pants. The walls are covered in the same kind of hieroglyphics as the tablet. We need to move everybody down there."

"Not possible. Ramón is worse," Tristan said, "…and Rachel's still on the mend. The only way Dr. Ramón is going anywhere is if we improvise some sort of litter. Did you come across any other exits from the tunnel along the way?"

"Three of them," Max nodded. "At about thirty minute intervals. We didn't risk the first one, in case it was too near the Indians. If they know the tunnel, they'd expect us to try to escape through the first exit we came to. We checked out the next one quickly. I didn't see anything. The last one we spent a little time looking around."

Max turned to Rachel.

"Good news. I saw a reflection from something in the treetops and went to investigate. It was a plane wreckage, all right, but it looked like an old Cessna. Certainly not the Cherokee Piper your brother was flying. Looks like our luck is turning around, after all."

"See?" Dr. Gallagher said, "I told you that bat was a good omen."

"Thank God!" Rachel sighed. "There's a good chance he's all right then."

"Hey, I'd bet on it, Honey," grinned Max. "Probably some damned communication equipment failure. That stuff is down about as often as it is up, if you ask me."

Max acted as happy as a little boy with a new room full of toys. He turned back to address Tristan.

"How soon do you think Rachel could move?"

Rachel was feeling uplifted because the wreckage was not Kenny's, but she thought it inappropriate for Max to act this way. Indians had killed two of his men only the evening before. Poor Dr. Ramón was deathly ill from the snakebite. Only six able-bodied men remained from the original group of fifteen. Yet, it sounded like Max was planning to forge ahead with the expedition.

"Shouldn't Dr. Ramón be our first priority?" she asked. Somebody needed to call attention to the question of getting out of this jungle, not deeper into it. It might as well be her.

"I agree with Rachel," Tristan said. "Ramón needs a real doctor, and very soon. Follow me?"

"Absolutely," Max agreed. "But see here—we're miles from nowhere. There's no question of returning back the way we came. We'd all probably die in a matter of hours. Does anyone here doubt that? If we continue to follow the tunnel and the map, it will lead us to the Río Pinquina. The closest known settlement, once we got there, would be Boca Manu. We'll have to fashion a raft or a dugout, and float down to the Manu River to Boca Manu. We can hire a plane out from there and take Dr. Ramón on to Cuzco, or better yet to a larger hospital in Lima."

The rest of the group was silent. Then they all begin to nod in agreement. There simply wasn't another option.

"Tomorrow morning. No earlier," Tristan admonished

Max was disappointed, but accepted Tristan's decision.

"Tomorrow morning," he agreed. "Excellent."

Good luck or not, that night as a precaution against the bats, Rachel pulled her sleeping bag all the way up and over her head, leaving only a golf ball sized opening for air.

Chapter Twelve

Anubis, Judge of the Dead

****

Ancient Tunnel, Madre de Dios Jungle, Saturday, February 21

With the deaths of Luis and Renaldo, transporting the added contents of the two dead men's packs would be out of the question. Tristan had already redistributed the provisions left behind by Amasu and the two porters who had returned to Boca Manu. The group also had to worry about carrying Dr. Ramón, and assisting Rachel. Chico and Tristan fashioned a stretcher from two of the backpacks and one of the remaining tents. Tristan now discarded three of the bedrolls, the dead Peruvians' clothes and more of the supplies. Raóul traded the lighter knapsack he had worn as he had slashed the trail through the jungle for one of the larger packs. Each of the other men all assumed slightly heavier loads as well. Still, it was necessary for the group to abandon several personal items. Because much of the weight of the packs came from food supplies and water bottles, these also comprised a good part of what the group was leaving behind. From here on, it would be necessary to obtain at least a part of their sustenance from the forest, and to purify their water from whatever natural sources they found.

Morning arrived, without improvement in Dr. Ramón's condition. Rachel's leg was still sore and discolored, but most of the swelling had disappeared.

As the group started down the tunnel, Tristan led the way, followed by Felipe and Raóul carrying Dr. Ramón on the makeshift stretcher. Max and Dr. Gallagher helped Rachel walk along behind, each lending her an arm for support. Chico brought up the rear, keeping an eye out in case they were followed. Tristan had fastened the bright beam flashlight onto one of the backpack poles used on the stretcher. The four able men all wore packs, while Rachel retained her much lighter knapsack.

Moving the injured Dr. Ramón and Rachel through the tunnel was much slower than Max and Raóul had traveled the prior morning. It took an hour to reach the first exit. No one suggested looking around outside. Even Rachel sped up as they passed the dim rays of light that heralded the opening to the jungle.

Once the exit was a safe distance behind them, Max and Dr. Gallagher took over as litter bearers from Raóul and Felipe. The group had just resumed its way, when Rachel saw that the tunnel no longer had a uniform height. There was also a distinct odor. Raóul noticed it, too.

"*Huano,*" he said.

"Bat dung. Hold up just a second, guys," Max warned in a voice just above a whisper. "Just up ahead is where we passed beneath a bunch of bats. More of that vampire variety."

"You're not seriously considering going this way, are you?" Rachel gulped. "How do we detour around them?"

"We don't," Max answered irritably. "We switch to a penlight and move very quietly. There must be two or three thousand, but they're all collected in an area that runs about a hundred yards. Raóul and I passed them going and returning yesterday, without rousting them. You just have to keep quiet and creep by."

"I'd *really* rather not do that."

"I'm afraid there's no other way," Tristan said. "You're going to have deal with it."

"This tunnel is already too claustrophobic. Maybe the Indians don't know about the other exit. I could…"

She let the sentence die. What was the use? She knew as well as the men that they were right. There was no other way. She was going to have to crawl underneath hundreds of these horrible monsters, her sanity already in tatters, for a distance the length a football field. This was a nightmare. She couldn't wait to see how her dream about the pit would turn out tonight.

"In the unlikely event that I ever get back home," Rachel muttered, "I bet I have to start seeing a psychiatrist."

Tristan took one of the blankets covering Dr. Ramón.

"Here. Put this over your head and just keep concentrating on taking the next step."

Rachel mused that the suggestion was overly condescending, but on second thought decided that the blanket would at least keep the beastly vermin out of her hair. She silently accepted the blanket.

Tristan turned on a small penlight like the ones the group used at night to find things in their packs, or when they were inside their tents. He switched off the bright beam lamp.

That helped a little. At least she couldn't really see the bats.

The group moved forward slowly. Perversely, this reminded Rachel of tip-toeing out of the sleeping infant Tyler's room, when she had tried baby-sitting a couple of times for Dee.

Even though the bats were sleeping, occasionally one or two would stir, fly off, or make a high pitched peep. Rachel cringed each time. *Left foot forward. Right foot forward.* Try as she might, it was impossible not to think about what was covering the ceiling above her head. Maybe if she counted steps. She was taking small strides, so she figured there were maybe six hundred steps until they passed the bats. She probably had taken fifty or sixty, so that only left what? Five hundred fifty, five hundred forty more steps? *Bad idea.* She was so tense that she started feeling nauseous. She tried to find something pleasant to think about, and her brother came to mind. Kenny probably was okay! She kept running the thought through her mind and that helped.

After what Rachel thought must at least be half of the distance past the bats, nothing bad had yet happened. She started thinking this was going to work, after all.

Then, somebody tripped.

Either Max or Gallagher stepped in a hole or on a rock and stumbled forward. This caused the two men carrying Dr. Ramón to lose their grip on the stretcher, dumping the professor unceremoniously onto the ground.

Several bats sensed a disturbance and awoke. First four or five, then fifteen to twenty dropped from the ceiling and took wing.

"Down!" Tristan ordered, but Rachel was already curled in a fetal position on the floor with the blanket clutched tightly around her head and body.

The flutter of the bats' wings filled the tunnel, rising from a mild racket, as more of the bats filled the tunnel, to a thunderous roar as the entire horde swept overhead.

Rachel didn't know how long it lasted, and wasn't sure she really heard Tristan when he first announced that the bats were gone. When she finally got up, somebody had turned on the bright beam flashlight. She looked around, ready to dive for the floor at an instant's notice.

"You okay?" Tristan asked.

"I feel like punching somebody. Let's not *ever* do that again."

"Sorry," Max chuckled. "I tripped."

Tristan checked on the ailing professor and then helped ease him back onto the stretcher, and Max and Gallagher picked it up again.

Tristan did his best to brush away as much of the guano as was possible from Dr. Ramón's face and clothing.

"All right, break's over," Max announced, nonplused by the incident. "Let's get moving before the bats come home to roost."

Rachel hated the darkness did not allow her to read the expression on Max's face. She wondered whether she might have detected any trace of a smirk.

An hour and a half later they reached the second exit. Tristan didn't think that the Indians would lie in wait this far from the original site where the attack had occurred. Even so, all agreed that it would be safer to press on. There was still another exit to come. With the group not yet low on water, there was no reason to take unnecessary risks.

The tunnel was too narrow for four to carry the stretcher, so the six able men had to take frequent stops to trade off carrying Dr. Ramón. By the time they made it to the third exit, it was past noon.

"Could we stop here for a break?" Rachel asked. "I could really use some fresh air and a rest."

"It would be best to move on along to the chamber," Max suggested. "We're still less than ten miles from where we were attacked. That could easily lie within the same hostile territory."

"But you and Raóul already checked the area out. This is the exit where you hunted for and found the wreckage, isn't it?"

"That's right," Max answered cautiously.

For someone who had already been here once, Max was strangely reluctant to venture outside. She supposed he must be extremely eager to have Dr. Gallagher take a look at the hieroglyphics. Still, Rachel had not seen the light of day in nearly sixty hours. She needed a break from the tunnel, even if was a very short one.

"If there is a tunnel version of cabin fever, then I've got it. I just want to sit in the open air for few minutes. I think it's a safe enough distance."

"I don't," Max answered curtly.

"I thought you were relying on my knowledge of the local Indians. Even more so, now that Dr. Ramón is delirious."

Max turned to Tristan, hoping to pass the buck.

"Tristan?"

"You're the one who scouted the area, yesterday. You tell me."

"We weren't out there all that long. Oh, all right. Not long, though. Five minutes. We don't want to attract attention."

Tristan had Raóul and Chico exit first, then helped Rachel through the opening. Max and Felipe came behind them.

"Will Jorgé be all right down here alone?" Dr. Gallagher asked.

"No better or worse, one way or another," Max answered. "Come on out, if you want. He's not going to wander off."

The Egyptologist climbed out to join the others.

After very tentatively checking around the entrance for snakes, Rachel sat on one of the stones marking the opening to the tunnel. She was able to hobble around now, but the leg was still sore. She pulled aside the cut cloth of her pant leg to get a better look at her knee. The skin looked bruised around the snakebite area, and a bit more swollen than the last time she had checked. Tristan told her that wasn't unusual, given the distance she had covered on it during the day.

"Max, where exactly was the crash site?" she asked.

"You can't see it from here. Over in that general direction, I think." Max waved his hand ambiguously toward about a third of the forest.

"Do you think I could take a look? I mean…I know you saw it, and it was a different kind of plane and all…but, still, I've come so far. I'd just like to see it with my own eyes, you know?"

"I'm not sure I could find it again. I stumbled across it by accident. Another search would be silly. What point would there be? I've already told you it wasn't your brother's plane. Besides, we've already spent our five minutes. We really ought to be getting back inside the tunnel."

Rachel didn't like the explanation she was getting. Max was being far too evasive about checking the area out. This was the whole reason for deterring out of their way, and for her being here in the first place. She wondered if he was hiding something from her. The more she thought about it, the more she became convinced that it was so.

"What aren't you telling me?"

"What do you mean?"

"These trees must be two hundred feet high. The branches are so close together that if a light plane like Kenny's crashed into them, most of the wreckage would still be really far up. So far, in fact, that I don't see how you could be so positive that it wasn't the same plane. I'm not going a step farther until I see it."

Max glared at her for a second.

Every curve of Rachel's body spoke defiance. At this point she was well beyond intimidation.

"Suit yourself. The rest of us are heading back inside the tunnel. Get the picture? Let's move it."

Max wheeled around and stepped into the opening. Raóul, Felipe and Chico moved to follow, but Gallagher and Tristan remained where they stood.

"Sloan! Gallagher! I said let's get moving."

Gallagher's conscience had finally got the better of him. Perhaps, he had just needed someone else to stand up to Max so that he wouldn't have to do it alone. A room full of hieroglyphics awaited only minutes away, and he was the only member of the group who would be able to make sense of it. To be truthful, he could barely wait get there. Yet, he rarely held such an advantage in confronting Max. He relished the moment.

"How's your ancient Egyptian, Max?"

"What?"

"I think I'll stay here with Rachel. That means you'll have to read the hieroglyphics yourself.

Tristan had also reached his limit.

"Tell her, or I will."

"Jesus, Tristan! Don't be an utter fool."

"I have been, but this is where it stops. This isn't right. I should have stepped in a long time ago."

"Tell me what?" Rachel demanded, fearful of what the truth might be. *Please don't let it be Kenny.*

Max looked from Sloan to Gallagher, and then directly at Rachel. The expression on his face made it obvious that he intended to make the two men pay for their mutinous behavior.

"All right. You want the truth? Here it is: I never saw a plane wreckage. I don't know that there ever was one. I even suggested it might be just a communications lapse, if you'll recall."

Rachel stared at Max in disbelief. There was no trace of guilt in his tone or facial expression. He spoke like this was all a mundane matter.

"I jumped the gun in telling you about the wreckage...that's all. By the time I figured out that it was all most likely a break in communications, you were already in Shintuyo. Nobody forced you to come along on this expedition, remember? I thought it might even interest you, because of the location, and your being an anthropologist and all." Max reflected that he might placate Rachel to an extent by telling her that her twin was safe, but stranded on the Bolivian border. He decided against it. Neither Tristan nor Gallagher knew the whole story. Better to leave as much in the dark as possible.

Rachel was thunderstruck. She kept looking at Max, her mouth agape, thinking of all the things that had befallen her since she had arrived in Peru.

"You sorry bastard. You dragged me out here under false pretenses? You made up the entire story about my brother crashing his plane?"

"I tried to tell you in Shintuyo, that the other pilot said it looked like a different kind of plane wreckage..."

"Liar! There was no wreckage at all. You already admitted that."

"Whatever. At that point, I was even suggesting you might want to return to Cuzco, and let the local authorities check things out. I haven't done anything wrong here. All I've done is be a good Samaritan, letting you tag along."

"You haven't done a thing but lie to me day after day, about how close we were getting to the crash site. You son of a bitch. And *you…*" she said, whirling to face Tristan. "You said if he didn't tell me, you would. You were in on this?"

"By keeping quiet…yes, I suppose so. I suspected something like this. I'm really sorry…"

"Oh, I just bet you are! You aren't sorry about anything except having your stupid treasure hunt go awry. I don't get it, though. Why did you need me? You had Dr. Ramón. He has a lot more experience than me."

Rachel was angry enough that neither Gallagher nor Tristan was feeling brave enough to tell her the real reason Max had lured her along. To some extent, they were indeed accomplices. Max, however, was happy to further implicate the two for their moment of defiance.

"You speak Yaminhua. Dr. Gallagher remembered that from when you were at U.C.L.A. He volunteered you, after you ran into each other at the Libertador. As for Tristan, he's the one who insisted we needed your Yaminhua language skills. You wouldn't be here except for these two gallant heroes."

Max was seriously twisting the facts, but neither Tristan nor Gallagher tried to contradict him. There was, after all, an element of truth in what Max was saying.

Rachel stared at the men like they all had horns and three heads.

"Dr. Gallagher knew too? And Dr. Ramón?"

"Not Ramón," Tristan replied. "Listen. This is a lousy thing we've done to you. I should've said something in Shintuyo. I don't know what got into me. But Max is right about a couple of things. The only way out is forward, and we *have* been out here in the open too long. We're risking some very unwelcome attention. Maybe the room that Max found can give us some clues about the best way out of here. Regardless, we have to move back inside."

Rachel hesitated. She was now suspicious of every suggestion that the others might make. Yet, it was clear she still had no other recourse but to depend on them to help her make it back to Boca Manu, where she could find more trustworthy assistance.

She pushed herself to her feet. Shaking off Tristan's attempt to help her back through the opening, she re-entered the tunnel.

As Max had said, the room of hieroglyphics was another ten to fifteen minutes away. Despite her anger, Rachel was soon forced to take Dr. Gallagher's and Felipe's arms for support. Only in that way could she keep enough weight off her wounded leg to manage her way down the tunnel as they continued onward.

When the group reached the chamber and deposited Dr. Ramón's stretcher on the floor, Rachel could at first see only shadowed glimpses of the wall. Egyptian symbols covered every part that was visible. She hobbled a couple of steps closer to make sure, but there was little question that the carvings could be anything else. The chamber flabbergasted her. She had seen pictures of the La Jalca statue found in the seventies-a stone figure with a pharaoh's beard. Like all but an extremely small and radical minority of archaeologists and anthropologists, she had put that off to an interesting but insignificant coincidence. This room was beyond the realm of coincidence. Preposterous; yet she was viewing it with her own two eyes.

Max unpacked and illuminated one of the Coleman lanterns. The chamber was about fifteen square feet. The ceiling and the floor were devoid of the ancient writing. At the center of the floor was a square stone slab, also unadorned.

"Isn't it fantastic? What does all this say?" Max asked.

The Egyptologist looked at Max with an incredulous expression.

"Ancient hieroglyphics aren't exactly the equivalent of Freshman French, you know. This could take a while. You might as well make yourself comfortable."

Dr. Gallagher stared at the walls for four or five minutes, then retrieved a large paperback book from his pack. He returned to his perusal of the hieroglyphics. Occasionally, he would consult the book, or flip a few pages and make some notes. Every now and then, a "Hmmm" or an "Ah!" would escape his lips. Max waited impatiently. Even Rachel momentarily set aside her outrage at the fraud that the men had perpetuated. She too was swept into the spell of the moment. They were standing in a pre-Columbian Indian tunnel that had dead-ended at a room filled with Egyptian hieroglyphics. Rachel shook her head to make sure she wasn't dreaming.

Finally, Dr. Gallagher cleared his throat and made a pronouncement. "*Ankh-em-fentu*," he said, with an unmistakable air of triumph.

"Ankhf-em-what...?" Max asked.

"The fifth Arit set by Anubis to guard the dead body of Osiris. This is his name, over here on this wall, ⚱〰◉🦅〰⚰...Ankhf-em-fentu."

"Oh yeah? Is that important?" Max asked.

"Very. I didn't put all the pieces together at first. In fact, despite several obvious clues that should have tipped me off, I only began to suspect the truth yesterday. Then a few more symbols on the second tablet started making sense."

"Mind filling the rest of us in on your little secret?" Max asked. "I know that Anubis is the jackal-headed figure at the tombs of pharaohs, but what's an Arit, and what have you've got all figured out?"

"Arits are guardian spirits. In the Egyptian Book of the Dead, Anubis is the judge of the dead." Dr. Gallagher reached up and touched a symbol carved in the wall 𓁢 . Anubis appoints seven of these Arits, or spirit entities, to guard the approach to the underworld. Ankhf-em-fentu was the fifth of these. Here on the wall are the carvings of three guardians. They bear the faces of a hawk, a man and a lion, just as it describes in the Book of the Dead."

"Where the hell are you going with all this?" asked Max.

"Actually, your question includes the answer. I'm talking about going to the underworld. Tristan's map tablet names two oceans. One is called '*heh*,' Millions of Years, and the other called '*Uadj Ur*,' the Great Green. In the Egyptian Book of the Dead, the question is asked, 'What is the double nest?' The answer was the Million of Years and the Great Green. The double nest question related to the location of the underworld, which is called *Tuat*."

"Dense forest," Rachel murmured.

"Come again?" Gallagher asked.

"*Tuat*," explained Rachel. "In the Achuara Indian language, '*Tuat*' or '*Tsuat*' means dense forest."

"No kidding?" Dr. Gallagher asked. He seemed genuinely impressed. "That fits perfectly. The Tuat is the land of the dead…the underworld of Egyptian mythology. *That's* what I figured out. I think the Egyptians' Tuat was here. In Peru. Not in the spiritual sense of an afterlife, but as a physical location for the safekeeping of their remains! The Tuat is described as lying in a distant land to the west of Egypt, between the great 'Double Nest.' It was also supposed to be near a 'domain of fire,' in a region called '*Manu*,' meaning fortress. As I recall, the Andes are the most active geologic mountains in the world, thus the domain of volcanic activity, or fire. On Tristan's map, the Manu River cuts the Madre de Dios nearly in half."

"Intriguing…" Rachel admitted. "The Inca called a large area just a hundred miles southwest of here by the name '*Ayacucho*' That translates as 'Corner of the Dead.' Amasu tried to tell me that this area used to be part of the Ayacucho, centuries ago."

"Perfect," Gallagher agreed. "There's also the matter of our carnelian Tet. I think it's *the* Tet.

This revelation met with blank expressions, all around.

"In the Book of the Dead," explained the Egyptologist, "…Osiris is presented with two amulets. One of gold, the other of carnelian. The Tet of

Carnelian was presented to Osiris by his sister/wife, Isis. The reddish color of the Tet was said to have come from the tears of blood shed by Isis upon Osiris' death. The Tet of Carnelian supposedly possessed magical powers to protect Osiris from whoever might harm him or otherwise disturb his remains during the passage into the underworld.

"What are you trying to say?" Rachel asked. "That Osiris and Isis were real entities?"

"Not as gods, of course. But yes, there's a school of thought that Osiris was a very early king, long before even the pyramids existed."

"And this talisman is the same sort as in this Osiris story?" Max asked.

"Technically, the Tet isn't a talisman," answered the professor. "It's an amulet. Although, both are meant to ward off evil…"

"Who gives a flying &%4#?" Max. said

Dr. Gallagher ignored Max's derision and continued his explanation. "I wasn't just suggesting this amulet was the same sort as the one given to Osiris. I think that this is the *actual* Tet of Carnelian mentioned in the Book of the Dead. It must be a special key or a map of some sort, not just an amulet. If this is the fifth door, then we must be getting very close to the end of the journey into the Tuat-underworld."

"Closer for some of us than others," announced Tristan, who had been checking Dr. Ramón for the past couple of minutes. "I'm afraid that Dr. Ramón is no longer with us."

As the others looked toward Tristan with mixed expressions of incomprehension and surprise, he put it more bluntly. "He's dead."

Chapter Thirteen

sbai: door, gateway

****

Boca Manu, Saturday, February 21

Kenny had already refueled and talked to the people who operated the nearby Manu Lodge. There, he learned about the guides and porters Tristan and Max had hired to accompany the expedition into the jungle. At least one of the expedition members had already returned and was said to be in Boca Manu. After a few hours of asking questions and searching, Kenny succeeded in identifying and finding this man, an Indian named Amasu.

What Amasu had to say did not make Kenny happy. The expedition had lost several porters to desertion, but nevertheless had plunged even deeper to a dangerous part of the jungle. Amasu was able to confirm the direction and distance that the expedition had traveled. Kenny wasn't about to try to follow by land. He lacked that kind of experience, and Amasu had already shown an unwillingness to follow in the expedition's footsteps. Instead, Kenny managed to hire the old Indian to accompany him in the seaplane. Amasu would be able to help translate, if they met anyone along the way, and would be far more knowledgeable about the geography of the area than Kenny. The old Indian was willing to start the next morning. The Manu Lodge would serve as their base. From here, Kenny and Amasu would scour the area by air during the day, trying to catch sight of the expedition, their tents or evidence of their location. He arranged for overnight space at the lodge for the next five evenings.

****

Madre de Dios, same day

The silence following Tristan's announcement lasted an uncomfortably long time. Rachel was the first to break it.

"You're sure? He's not just in a coma or something?"

Though she was doing her best to hide it, the professor's demise from the snake venom both shocked and scared Rachel. Her hand went instinctively to her own wound. Dr. Ramón was now dead from the same poison that coursed through her body. All of a sudden, her vulnerability was much more obvious. Back home, she had been dreading her approaching thirtieth birthday. Now, she vowed that she would have a really big celebration, if she survived to observe it.

"I'm sure," Tristan replied. "There's no pulse. He's gone. The professor was much older than you are. He must have had some other health problems, besides fighting a much higher dose of the venom than you. If that's what is causing you to turn white, don't worry about it. You're recovering fine. A couple more days and you won't even have any signs of having been bitten."

"We have to bury him," Rachel asserted, somewhat reassured by Tristan's comforting remarks, but still shaken.

"After we get everything set up here, one of the men and I will take care of that. We'll backtrack to that last exit from the tunnel. I think it might be best for Raóul and I to scout around outside, and see if we can find the quickest route to the Río Pinquina. We can travel a lot faster and quieter alone, than if we have to cut a trail for the whole group."

Max didn't object. He obviously found it exciting to be back at the chamber, and thrilled at Dr. Gallagher's revelations. He had already shrugged off Dr. Ramón's death. "If this is the fifth door," he asked, "...where are the previous four?"

Dr. Gallagher allowed Max to distract his attention from the depressing news of Dr. Ramón's death. He lowered his gaze for a few seconds before answering. When the Egyptologist looked up and answered, his tone was a bit less excited than before, but he seemed to have accepted that there was nothing more to be done for his friend.

"I'd only be guessing. From what I can get out of the Papyrus of Ani, the first must be somewhere in Memphis, near the Nile Delta. Sometime around 1300 BC, Egypt began experiencing a serious decline in power. At that same time, the priests of ancient Egypt started having more difficulty concealing and protecting the burial sites of the Pharaohs." Dr. Gallagher glanced again at the body of Dr. Ramón as he mentioned the word burial. "We believe looters vandalized even the great Ramses II's tomb and removed its treasure not long after Ramses' death. The first Arit was probably a secret exit that the priests used to move the Pharaohs' mummified remains and accompanying treasures out of the temple complex at Tanis."

"What's the Papyrus of Ani?" Max asked.

"The name of one version of the Book of the Dead. Ani is the scribe who narrates the rituals in those ancient Egyptian funerary texts. I think the second door may have been in northern Morocco. That could explain why the maps and the carnelian staff were found there. Morocco would have been the ideal embarkation point for a transat-lantic sea voyage. As Tristan pointed out when I first translated the map for you, the Amazon River is only about a thousand miles from the Moroccan coast."

"All seven of these secret doors are all described in those papyrus texts?" Tristan asked.

Gallagher nodded. "This is a translation from the Book of the Dead..." The Egyptologist held up the tattered paperback.

"You just happened to have brought that with you for casual reading?" Tristan scoffed.

"No. Not just happened to; I brought it along on purpose. There is, as I have mentioned before, a very small fringe element in Egyptian Anthropology, which has expressed belief in an ancient Egyptian presence in the Americas. After the discovery that the Moroccan tablet was a map of South America, I researched the reasons for those claims. The book was an obvious resource to bring along. Do you want to hear what it says about the third door, or not?"

Tristan nodded.

Gallagher opened the paperback to a dog-eared page and began to read. "*I am he who is hidden in the great deep...I tie firmly upon the place where he resteth, coming forth from the Urt.*"

He lowered the book to explain.

"That was a reference to Osiris. Just as the Pharaohs thought of themselves as the god Horus incarnate during their life, so they believed they became the god Osiris, after death. That would also help explain why the Tet wound up in Morocco. It was waiting for the next dead Pharaoh. The bearers of the dead Pharaoh then transported the body past the seven Arits into the land of Tuat. Tuat was here in the double nest, between the two oceans. At any rate, the third door or Arit-spirit's place of abode would be somewhere along the Amazon River."

Rachel was following the discussion closely, but remained angry with the men and unsettled by Dr. Ramón's death. She sat apart from the others in stony silence.

"The fourth door, I think was in Cuzco," Dr. Gallagher continued, "beneath the Temple of the Sun that you described. That is also pure speculation, but it fits with the Book of the Dead."

"So, you're saying that there is some kind of secret door in this chamber?" Max asked. "And this book provides clues on how to find and open it?"

"That's my opinion, yes. If so, it would also provide the safest route to the Pinquina River."

"Then what are the directions for opening this door?" Tristan asked.

"I'm afraid I haven't worked that out."

"What about this slab?" Max suggested, indicating the altar stone in the center of the chamber. "Maybe it covers an opening?"

Max bent and tried to budge the stone, without success. The other men added their muscles to the effort, but the slab didn't move a millimeter.

"Read more about what it says about the fifth door," Tristan said.

"*The name of the doorkeeper is Ankhf-em-fentu. The name of the one that watches is Shabu. The name of the herald is Teb-her-ka-keft. Osiris-Ani shall say truthfully, upon approaching the Arit: I have brought the jawbone in Ra-stau. I have brought the backbone in Anu. I have gathered together the many members, and forced back the Aapep. I have spit upon the wounds. I have made myself a path. I am the Elder of the gods. I have made offerings to Osiris. I have defended him with the word of truth. I have gathered his bones and his members.*"

"That's it?" Max asked.

"That's it."

"A lot of nonsense about bones," Max murmured. "Jawbones, backbones, gathering bones…"

"With the slab so prominently placed, it's almost like it was put there for sacrificial offerings," Rachel noted. She was still angry, but was now irresistibly drawn into the mystery with the rest of the group.

"A human sacrifice? Very possibly," Gallagher said.

"We've already had our quota of those, haven't we?" Rachel mumbled.

Max raised his eyebrows and looked over at the body of Dr. Ramón. Tristan and Gallagher followed his glance.

"Help me move Ramón," Max said. "Maybe the slab is counter-weighted or something, from underneath the floor. A sacrifice, placed on the altar slab, might trigger a door-release."

"I don't believe this," Rachel gasped. "Don't any of you have any respect for the dead?"

"I respected him when he was alive," Max lied. "But he's dead, now, and more useful for this."

Max's voice was absolutely emotionless, and it chilled Rachel.

"Why not just stand on the slab, yourself?" she asked.

"What if it's a trap door, with a pool of piranha or something underneath?"

"Well then, better yet, trick Raóul over there into doing it. That's more your style, isn't it?"

"Raóul, give me a hand," Max ordered, gesturing at the big Cuzqueño.

For a minute, the confused Raóul thought Max meant to use him to do just that: test for a trap door. Max, however, moved to one end of the stretcher beneath Dr. Ramón's dead body. Raóul comprehended and picked up the other end.

The two men moved the professor's corpse over the stone slab, and laid it on top. Nothing happened. Rachel stared at Max with contempt.

"Why is it that you keep saying there's no going back?" she asked Tristan. "At least we have the benefit of knowing what the dangers are. If we continue toward the Río Pinquina, we could be headed directly into worse conditions than we've already encountered. Maybe the best thing would still be to turn back."

"We're a whole lot closer to the Río Pinquina than we are to the Alto Madre de Dios. We're closer to civilization if we continue going forward. There's less likely to be as many hostile Indians and other dangers, the closer we get to cultivated, cleared areas."

"This Book of the Dead...it says you're supposed to recite that stuff when you come to the fifth door?" Max asked, ignoring Rachel's and Tristan's conversation.

"Yes," Dr. Gallagher said, "...but I don't see how that would change anything unless some sort of human guard was on duty."

"What if there is one, and he's hidden...watching us even now? Didn't you say something about the one who watches?"

"*Shabu*," Dr. Gallagher affirmed. "But since I already read the password out loud, that addresses that theory." He obviously regarded Max's idea as ludicrous.

"Maybe it has to be said in ancient Egyptian," Max suggested. "Or that Achuara language?" He looked at Rachel, who promptly gave him the finger.

"Have you read enough of the other hieroglyphics to see if there might be useful information right here on the wall?" Tristan asked.

"Some of it. Most of it consists of hymns of praise to Osiris and Ra," Gallagher answered.

"What about the jawbone and backbone stuff?" Felipe asked. "What did that mean?"

"Osiris and his brother Set had this big battle. According to the story, Set later triumphed and killed Osiris, cutting his body in several pieces and throwing it in the Nile. Osiris' sister-wife, Isis, gathered up all of the pieces and put them back together. Well...all but one piece, that is. A crocodile had already swallowed the penis. Anyway...the jawbone and backbone had to be collected from different locations in the Nile, before Osiris was put back together."

"Maybe that's the problem," Rachel suggested, addressing Max. "Maybe somebody has to cut your off *your* penis and feed it to the crocodiles before the magic door will open. After all, it is in the Book of the Dead..."

"Just remember who'll be watching your back the next time we get out there in the jungle," said Max, not bothering to disguise the malice in his tone.

"Are there symbols on the walls meaning a jawbone or a backbone?" Tristan asked, scowling at Max.

Gallagher began to search the symbols on the wall, looking for either word.

Silence again fell over the room. Finally, Gallagher stopped and pointed.

"Here," he announced. "Here's the symbol for backbone ⚹, 'Pesd,' on this stone. The symbols containing it say the same thing as the translation I read to you from the Book of the Dead. Just the one phrase, about bringing the backbone from Anu."

Tristan moved to Gallagher's side. The stone the Egyptologist pointed at was at chest level. Tristan reached out and tried to work his fingers between it and the adjacent stones. There wasn't enough space.

"Perhaps, if you pushed on it…" Gallagher said.

Tristan placed his palm on the surface and pushed. The stone slid back. Tristan instinctively retreated, as did Dr. Gallagher.

When nothing more happened, the others gathered behind Tristan and the professor.

"Maybe they all move," Chico said. "Maybe it's hollow behind that spot. There could be a secret door right there."

Tristan pushed six or seven other stones. None budged.

"Can you find one that says jawbone?" Tristan asked.

Gallagher began to look above, below and to the sides of the sentence about the backbone.

"You said something about the jawbone being found in another direction," Rachel said.

"You're right!" Gallagher exclaimed. He moved quickly to the opposite side of the chamber and began scanning for the phrase about the jawbone. He quickly found it at the same chest level location, directly across from the other stone.

"Here it is. The symbol 'Art, ⟆ .'"

He hesitated only a moment before placing his palm over the appropriate symbol and pressed as Tristan had done. This stone now slid back like the other.

From the center of the room, the grating sound of stone on stone drew the attention of the group back to the altar slab, on top of which rested the body of Dr. Ramón. One end of the slab was rapidly sinking downward, creating a steep enough angle for the body to begin to slide off. Felipe reacted first, but before he was able to reach it, the slab angled another foot downward and the professor's body disappeared into a black void below. Rachel ran to the opening, joined immediately by Tristan and the others. There was no visible bottom to the pit.

As the slab came to a stop, hanging down from one end in a vertical position, there was another grating noise. Rachel spun around with the others to see that a part of one of the chamber walls also began to sink into the floor. The top edge moved down to rest even with the floor level, revealing a new stretch of tunnel leading out of the chamber and into darkness. Tristan whistled in appreciation, as most of the other men stared wide-eyed and apprehensively at the new opening.

"Now we're cooking," Max said.

Rachel looked from Max to the new tunnel and then back to the pit through which Ramón's body had vanished. Obviously, there was no point in trying to recover the body. Not that the men would have thought it important, anyway.

"Shall we?" Max invited. He hefted one of the packs onto his back and waited expectantly.

"Can't we rest a little longer?" Rachel asked.

"The door may not stay open but a few minutes. Do you plan on being the next human sacrifice on that slab? Because it may be that the weight of a human body is a part of the combination needed to reopen the door."

"Are you up to it?" Tristan asked.

"Playing human sacrifice, or continuing on? I have to ask, you understand? I know how you don't always tell me what my part in the plan is."

"I probably had that coming, but Max is right. This opening may close at any moment. Do you want to get out of here or not?"

Tristan's pained expression reflected genuine concern, enough so that Rachel regretted her jibe. She picked up her small knapsack, but purposely took her time strolling past Max and through the secret doorway.

Raóul, Chico and the rest of the men quickly donned their packs and followed her through the opening. Tristan carried one of the lanterns to illuminate the way. Lamentably, the bright beam light had still been attached to the stretcher when Dr. Ramón's body had disappeared into the pit. Rachel wondered which of the two Max considered the biggest loss.

Chapter Fourteen

magic square

****

Madre de Dios Jungle, Saturday, February 21

Kenny used the afternoon to fly along the route that Amasu had described. From there, he began a grid search northeast from the approximate point where Amasu had left the expedition. There was no sign of the group. Kenny didn't find this too surprising. If he was going to spot them, it would have to be along one of the rivers—either during a crossing or encampment. The forest was just too dense to permit a view of anything beneath the jungle canopy.

When Kenny returned to Boca Manu that evening, he enlisted the help of the Guardia Civil. The officer-in-charge used his station's short wave radio to check with Guardia headquarters for confirmation that Rachel had not resurfaced in Cuzco or elsewhere.

He decided to repeat the procedure the following day and hope, with Amasu's more experienced eyes, for a change of fortune.

✶✶✶✶

Ancient tunnel, Madre de Dios Jungle, Saturday, February 21

The group was still within hearing distance when the secret door closed to the chamber. To Rachel, the echoing sound of the stone door thudding shut was an ominous and eerie reminder that the possibility of retracing their steps was now removed.

The expedition spent most of the rest of the day following the new tunnel another seven to eight miles. Never having been very conversant with the *Norte Americanos* to begin with, the three remaining Peruvians were now as silent as the Egyptian stone guardians who had stared impassively as the corpse of Dr. Ramón dropped to an ignominious oblivion. Max chatted every once in a while with Tristan, or asked an occasional question of Dr. Gallagher. Except to stop briefly for lunch and rest breaks, the journey was uneventful. Tristan flashed the light frequently back and forth across the walls of the passage as the group filed onward. No further hieroglyphics were visible, nor did they pass any new openings to the jungles.

By six o'clock in the evening, they had found nothing new. Even Max was about to call it a day, when Tristan called out from ahead that it looked like they were coming up on another room.

Upon first glance, when the group entered the second chamber, it was nearly identical with the other. The room's size was similar and also covered in Egyptian hieroglyphics. Two noticeable deviations were distinguishable. The first and most obvious was the absence of a stone slab in the center of the room. The second difference was beneath their feet.

A three-foot wide, cross-shaped walkway divided the floor in four equal parts. Several large triangular stone tiles filled each of these quadrants. The tiles measured roughly three feet to a side and were also inscribed with hieroglyphics. The floor of the other room had been bare, except for the altar slab. As in the previous chamber, three stone guardians occupied prominent niches on the wall facing the entry from the tunnel. These three statues bore the heads of a jackal, a crocodile and some sort of dog or wolf.

"Door number six?" Max asked.

Dr. Gallagher had already started examining the hieroglyphics and found, in a similar location, the appropriate inscription. He nodded yes.

"*Atek-ta-kehak-qeru*, the sixth Arit."

"It's the obvious place to stop for the evening," Tristan sighed. "Let's set up camp."

Max grunted his agreement. Tristan, Rachel and the Peruvians began to open the packs and sort out the items the group would need. Max stood examining the walls. Gallagher retrieved the paperback and read aloud from the Papyrus of Ani.

"*Osiris-Ani shall say…I have arrived each day, making for myself a path. I have passed by that which was made by Anubis. I am the Lord of the crown of Urt. I hold the words of magical power. I am the one who avenges according to the law. I have avenged his eye. I have defended Osiris. I have ended the journey. Osiris-Ani goes with you, with the word which is truth.*"

"Hmmm," Max said. "Nothing about bones this time. Any bright ideas, professor?"

"Your guess is as good as mine. Words of magical power? There's more about that here, but it will take some sorting out. I haven't a clue, at the moment. The stuff about vengeance and the eye refers to the battle between Set and Osiris. During the fight, Set was supposed to have temporarily blinded Osiris in one eye. Set was later defeated and banished.

The argument has been made that the story of Lucifer is a close parallel, and that the name Satan is derived from Set."

Gallagher and Max continued to trade theories about the language describing the sixth portal in the Book of the Dead. They tried different interpretations and pressed on stones that contained the relevant words, but no new doorway opened.

Felipe tried to offer his help to Dr. Gallagher, but was mostly a nuisance. Raóul and Chico sat alone. Their demeanor was not necessarily calm, but nor were they as jittery as they had been above ground in the jungle. Rachel wondered at this, since there were now only three surviving Peruvians accompanying the group. She mentioned this to Tristan.

"Raóul said something about that, earlier. Apparently, the men now think that as long as Max has the carnelian staff on his person, anyone staying close to Max will be all right. They've gone from thinking it's cursed to believing it's a protective amulet. Raóul thinks it's the only thing that's keeping the rest of us alive."

"Fascinating," remarked Max, who had been eavesdropping. "*Muy bueno observación acerca del relámpago, Raóul.* Now, who would figure, him coming up with an idea like that? That's exactly the sort of amulet that Dr. Gallagher has described."

"We're going to need all the ideas, including Raóul's, that we can come up with, if we're going to find the secret of this chamber," Dr. Gallagher said.

Try as they might, no one came up with a suggestion that produced results. When Rachel finally dozed off for the evening, the Egyptologist was still poring over the script and his footnotes from the Book of the Dead, trying to solve the riddle of the sixth Arit.

✳✳✳✳

Ancient Chamber, Madre de Dios, Sunday, February 22

Rachel awakened to the echo of voices. Sitting up, she saw that she was the last to rise. "What time is it?" she moaned.

"About a quarter of eight," Tristan answered. "Go back to sleep, if you want. It doesn't look like we're going anywhere soon."

"No big brainstorms, yet?" she asked, stifling a yawn.

"Nothing that opens any secret doors. Dr. Gallagher has a few ideas, but we haven't found a way to apply them."

"What gives, Professor?" Rachel pushed her way out of the sleeping bag and crawled closer. Her leg was still a bit tender and swollen, but much better than the previous day. This improvement relieved much of the heightened anxiety she had experienced since Dr. Ramón's death.

"The main theme of this room seems to be the word *Maat*, meaning Truth," Dr. Gallagher answered. "Several phrases mention it: *'I am the avenger according to the Law'*...Law is the same word as Truth in ancient Egyptian. Then the last line says...*'the word is truth.'* Possibly, there is an intended reference to the earlier phrase: *'I am the one with the words of magical power.'* There's even a potentially cryptic clue in the sentence *'I have avenged his eye.' His eye* is pronounced *Maat-f* in ancient Egyptian. That could be an intentional use...or not."

"We've already pressed on about every stone in the room, but that hasn't worked this time," Max added. "If the magic word is *Maat*, we just need to determine how to use it."

"I wouldn't really think it would be so easy to open every secret doorway as it was with the last one," Rachel noted. She bit her lip as soon as the words had left her mouth, embarrassed that her remark might be taken as a casual dismissal of the loss of Dr. Ramón. None of the others took note of the slip.

"I did some more research after you went to sleep," Dr. Gallagher said. "Listen to this later chapter: *'Come then, pass in over this door of this hall of Maat. Not will I let enter those past me, saith the bolt of the door, except those who sayeth my name. Weight of the Place of Right and Truth is thy name.'* It goes on to give other passwords that are supposed to be given."

"No doubt, Max has already tried shouting the name *Maat*, at each of the four walls?" Rachel goaded.

Tristan grinned, and Rachel guessed that something to that effect had indeed taken place. Something had been nagging at her subconscious mind, however, during the conversation. *Something about the floor.* Now, she remembered. The triangular shape of the stones and their arrangement reminded her of another pattern she had seen in Peru. She asked Dr. Gallagher about it.

"What about the floor in this room, versus the other? Have you attributed any significance to that?"

"We were discussing it earlier, but nobody's come up with an explanation," Gallagher replied. "Why? Did you have an idea?"

"Possibly. It has to do with the pattern of the tiles. Sets of four triangles are used to make up a square, you see? Not so unusual, but it reminds me of certain petroglyphs and *tokapu* fabric designs that you see here in Peru. They're called magic squares."

"I know of the concept," Gallagher said. "I didn't realize that they were used in Pre-Columbian cultures."

"Yes, yes," Max acknowledged, impatiently. "Another name for them is 'kamea.' A Rubic's Cube puzzle is one type. More traditionally, the horizontal row of numbers has to add up to equal the vertical sum of a column of different numbers. The magic number is the sum produced by both additions, right? But a magic square requires at least three rows and three columns."

"Not the Indian squares. They contain four triangles, like these. The numbers in the top and bottom two triangles just have to equal the numbers in the two side triangles. The ancient Peruvians usually used simple dots instead of hieroglyphics. Along with the system of khipu knots and petroglyphs, the squares are the closest thing anyone's ever found to writing among the Incas."

"So what?" Max asked. "What's all that have to do with us?"

"One of these sets of four adjacent stones could be one of these magic squares?" Tristan asked.

Rachel nodded.

"I suppose it's as good an idea as any," Gallagher noted, pensively. "It would tie in with the papyrus' mention of a magic word. The Egyptians were master mathematicians. They would certainly have been familiar with magic squares."

Rachel's observation set Gallagher to the task of searching the stones for words that might translate as numbers. Felipe counted sixty-four triangular stones in the floor. Gallagher would have to look at each one for possible numerical content.

The Egyptologist needed the next hour and a half to conclude his search, resulting in only four possible magic squares out of a possible sixteen. The arithmetic didn't produce matching sums on two of these, which narrowed their choice to only two squares.

The first potential candidate contained a symbol, $\mathcal{H}$ which Dr. Gallagher pronounced 'Ua,' and described as meaning "magical knot," within the context of its use with the other surrounding symbols.

"*Ua*," the Egyptologist explained, "…was also the pronunciation of the Egyptian numeral one."

The opposite triangle included one glyph that resembled an oblong teardrop. "This symbol is *met*, representing a dagger or weapon. The Egyptians number ten, also pronounced '*met*,' would normally be represented by an arch or horseshoe symbol. But the meanings inscribed in these tiles were most likely intended to be cryptic. Whoever designed the room probably would have avoided using the normal hash marks and other numerical symbols to represent the magic numbers."

"The two vertical triangles would equal eleven," Rachel said. "Does it work out horizontally?"

"Yes. The left triangle contains the symbol $\mathring{\downarrow}$ for the word *sen*, which means both brother and the number two. We would therefore be looking for the number nine in the opposite triangle. Nine is the word *Pesd*, which you might remember means backbone, which is the symbol used in the right triangle. That makes the magic number eleven, which would be *Met-Ua* or *Ua-Met*."

"Which means…?" Tristan asked.

"In numerology, eleven is equated with the Egyptian Tuat, but I can't think of anything new that tells us. There's the possibility that it might mean the word *metu*, which could mean either the verb 'to speak,' or the noun 'speech.' That could be the second half of 'magical words.' The best match I can think of is '*Ua-meti*.' That's another name for a monster usually called *Aapep*. He causes lightning, thunder, hurricanes, storms…much like the Gateway God you've described, Rachel."

"Gateway God! Excellent. That sounds like our doorway," Max said.

"I don't know. In Egyptology, we view *Aapep* as more evil, than protective. Eleven is also the number associated with magic and sorcery."

"If the meaning really is *Ua-meti*, then if this square was a doorway, it could even be some type of trap," Tristan noted. "What about the next square?"

Gallagher explained the numerical possibilities.

"The upper triangle contains both the backbone symbol, *Pesd*, equal to nine, and the normal horseshoe symbol for number ten, *met*, ⌒𝔐. That adds to nineteen. The lower triangle contains the word *Up-ua-ut*, which is another name for Anubis. *Up-ua-ut* translates 'opener of the way.'"

"That's encouraging," agreed Max. "Anything tricky about Anubis?"

"Depends on how you look at it," Dr. Gallagher answered. "He's a guardian and judge of the dead in the underworld. *Up-ua-ut* doesn't have a numerical equivalent, but its middle syllable, Ua is the same as the number one. One plus nineteen gives us twenty for the vertical sum. Twenty is pronounced *Tuat*."

"The same as the first square…and the name you've said means the underworld," Rachel remarked.

"Correct," Gallagher said. 'Then, here in the right triangle is the hieroglyphic representation for the same word—*Tuat*," He pointed to a symbol that resembled a sand dollar—a star with a circle around it.

"But that already makes twenty," Tristan said. "To qualify as one of these magic squares, there couldn't be any number on the left side except zero."

"Exactly," Gallagher replied. "And what we have is the symbol for an ostrich feather. That's also how the goddess Maat is symbolically represented. Maat is the wife of Ani, and is the goddess of the scales of right and truth in the underworld. According to legend, she weighs the heart of the dead against the ostrich feather, to test who had led a pure and honest life. If the heart outweighs the feather, the dead could not enter the Tuat."

"So you're saying that a pure heart is weightless, and therefore the feather means zero?" Max asked.

"That's my theory. If correct, both the vertical and horizontal values equal twenty. Twenty would therefore be the magic number."

"Which would mean the magic word is *Tuat*, rather than *Maat*," Rachel added. "That goes along perfectly with what you read a while ago about 'the weight of the *place* of truth and right is my name,' especially if we read weight as meaning numerical value. *Tuat*, the underworld, would be both the weight and the place for *Maat*, who is truth and right."

"So what do we do, now that we know this?" Max asked. "According to that same passage, the bolt of the door isn't going to be opened, unless we somehow use the magic word."

"Maybe that's it…we have to use the magic square, the one on which the Tuat solution to the puzzle is written. Perhaps it opens like the one in the first chamber."

Max and Gallagher began a closer examination of the stone tiles of the two squares in question. The two men could not find a way to cause any of the tiles to open or otherwise move. Because of the negative connotations of the *Ua-Meti* square, they concentrated their efforts on the other.

While Max and the professor looked for a way of opening the square, Tristan and Chico turned their attention to scrounging up something for the others to eat. In leaving behind many of their provisions, they had severely limited their choices. "Breakfast?" interrupted Tristan. He handed Rachel a couple of granola bars and a canteen.

"We're starting to run low on supplies. There's some Tang mixed up in the canteen."

"Lovely. Nothing with a little caffeine?"

"Sorry."

Rachel munched on the granola bars. Although she wasn't forgiving them, she had decided to ease up a bit on blaming Dr. Gallagher and Tristan Sloan for their roles in Max's deception. As for Max, he could catch fire and she wouldn't spit on him to put out the flames.

Another idea came to her as she took a swallow from the canteen.

"Dr. Gallagher? If this is the Hall of Maat that you were reading about, then this is also where the heart is supposed to be weighed against the feather. Am I right?"

"Figuratively speaking, yes."

"Well then, where are the scales…figurative or otherwise?"

Dr. Gallagher stared at her for a moment, and then a look of enlightenment came over his face.

"You're right…the triangle with the ostrich plume. Perhaps it's a scale of some sort. Who wants to stand on it?" Gallagher asked. He was thinking of the pit in the chamber where they had lost Dr. Ramón's body.

No one volunteered. Tristan took Max's pack and stood it upright on the Maat stone. Nothing happened.

"Maybe it has to be about the same weight as a human," Rachel suggested.

Tristan removed the pack, opened it and retrieved a coil of nylon climbing rope. This he unwound and tied around his waist.

"There's no telling how fast it might open," he said. "Max, you and Raóul take the other end."

The two men braced themselves to support Tristan's weight, in case the floor was to suddenly open beneath him. Tristan stepped onto the relevant stone triangle. Again, nothing happened. After much frowning, they tried the same thing on the Tuat stone, again with no effect.

"A scale has to have two sides, doesn't it," Gallagher asked. "Maybe, we need to have someone stand on both the Maat stone and the Tuat stone. Do you have more rope?"

Tristan found more of the nylon climbing rope and tied it securely around Gallagher. Tristan moved onto his spot, then Gallagher stepped onto the other stone. Max and Raóul each held onto the end of one of the ropes. Still no result. A half-hour passed, with several other ideas discussed. They tried one person standing in each of the four triangles of the magic square. Following the suggestion that since the Maat feather had no weight, and the scale might be the Tuat stone alone, everyone but Tristan moved out of the chamber. They watched from the tunnel, along with their packs, so that no weight would be elsewhere on the floor of the room. They tried pressing different stones on the wall, while Tristan stood alternatively on the Maat, and then the Tuat stones.

"*Tal vez*…you need both?" Felipe suggested, pointing at the second *Ua-meti* square.

The group next tried a combination of actions involving both squares without success. Finally, Dr. Gallagher sighed in resignation.

"We're still overlooking something. Otherwise, the magic square idea is the wrong approach altogether. Maybe we should try something else."

"Do you have anything in mind?" Max asked.

Dr. Gallagher flipped through the paperback, shaking his head no.

"There's more passwords mentioned, but they're the same symbols as the stones we've already been pressing on the walls. There's one other relevant passage, as I recall."

The professor paged through the paperback, looking for the specific reference.

"Here it is…it was back earlier in the text. It reads like this: '*The following are the words which the heart of truth shall speak when he comes with the word of truth into the Hall of Maat…*' Then there's bunch of other stuff that doesn't apply…but later it continues with a question: '*What do they give unto thee?*' The answer is: '*A torch and a scepter-amulet of crystal.*'"

"The Tet of Carnelian?" Rachel asked.

"Perhaps. The papyrus goes on to say that the torch and crystal scepter are to be buried '*on the furrow of M'naat, as things for the night.*' Then apparently the door is opened, because one of the next things is the phrase: '*Come ye now hither, pass over the threshold of this the door of the Hall of Maat.*' Again it makes sense…Pesd is one of the four parts of the magic square. There's an amulet called '*Djed,*' which is a symbolic representation of the backbone, or '*Pesd*' of Osiris. Just as we've decided we somehow had to use the stone called Pesd and these squares…it might mean we have to use the Tet amulet in the way described for the scepter of crystal."

"What does *M'naat* mean?" Rachel asked.

"And what does a furrow have to do with this?" Max asked. "You mean like a wrinkle in someone's forehead?"

"Sort of. A furrow is a groove. A wrinkle would be one type, but I think this means a groove in the ground, or on the floor. M'naat is a bit of a question mark. The word could just be a hieroglyphic variation on Maat. There's another word, *M'nit,* that can mean either a type of necklace or a mooring post."

"A grooved mooring post would make sense for holding a torch, wouldn't it?" Tristan asked. Has anyone seen any kind of groove or hole for a torch?"

The members of the group spread out around the room, to make sure they hadn't missed anything that might act as a torch holder. Searching outside the entrance to the chamber, Max located two stone torch slots. These had been carved upon the tunnel walls, just above head level and on opposite sides of the entrance to the chamber.

Max retrieved the Tet and tried inserting it in one of these openings, but neither end would insert. He then tried the Tet in the opposite slot, which easily accepted the smaller end of the staff. As he stepped back a look of surprise appeared on his face.

"Here! Come listen to this!"

A gurgling sound of running water came from the slot with the crystal staff. Max removed the staff and the sound stopped. Water dripped out of the holes in the bottom and the middle of the Tet. He replaced the crystal in the slot and the water sounds resumed.

"Could it be a key of some sort?" Rachel suggested. "It acts like inserting it either interrupts or initiates a stream of water."

"Maybe if the tiles *are* some sort of scales, they work on a system of hydraulics," Dr. Gallagher said.

They re-enacted the various scenarios they had already tried, standing on one stone or another, but no doors opened.

"What comes after the stuff you read about the crystal staff?" Tristan asked.

Gallagher consulted the paperback. "That's where it says '*Come ye now hither…*' The next part goes on to the various other passwords. The first one is *Tekk bu maa.*"

Gallagher pressed the appropriate wall stone bearing that inscription. The stone didn't budge.

"Try again," Tristan said, stepping onto the Maat triangle..

This time when Gallagher pressed, the stone slid back, as had happened in the other room!

A chorus of cheers and mutual congratulations followed the discovery.

Gallagher set about pressing the next stones in the sequence from the Book of the Dead. Dr. Gallagher and the others recessed each of eleven other password-bearing stones around the room, in turn. Still no door opened.

Max moved to the Tuat stone, but there was still no result.

"I should think it would be obvious what's wrong," Rachel said, taking another verbal jab at Max. "Dr. Gallagher already pointed it out in the Book of the Dead. A person has to have led a pure and honest life to enter the Egyptian underworld. Max's life is obviously too laden with lies and trickery."

Gallagher looked startled. "You just might be onto something!"

"I beg your pardon?" Max growled.

"I just mean that Max is heavier than Tristan. In the legend, the heart being weighed may not be heavier than the ostrich plume. The Maat side of the scale would need the heavier weight. Switch places."

A split second after they had done so, the Tuat stone began to sink into the floor. Tristan, still tethered to the line being held by Raóul, Chico and Felipe, began to sink along with the stone, as the Peruvians allowed the line some slack.

"Hurrah!" Gallagher shouted.

"Listen, somebody hand me a flashlight, quick!"

Rachel raced to retrieve one and placed it in Tristan's hand at the last second, just before he sank out of sight.

Chapter Fifteen

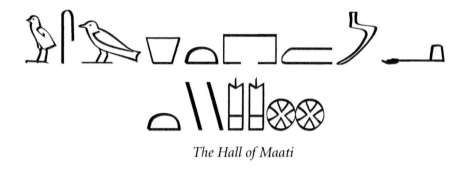

The Hall of Maati

✶✶✶✶

Egyptian chamber, Madre de Dios Tunnel, Sunday, February 22

Max leaned forward slightly from his perch on the Maat stone. "Can you see anything?" he called.

"Yeah," Tristan answered. "There's a very short tunnel leading one direction only. It looks like it goes to an exit above ground. I can see daylight from here. Better send Chico next with a couple of the rifles. I'd say it was only a fifteen foot drop. Raóul could let the rest of you down by rope, then he could drop down."

As Tristan moved away from the Tuat triangle, below , the stone suddenly began to rise back out of the ground, forming a triangular pillar that pushed up from the tunnel floor.

"That's okay; we'll just repeat the sequence," Max called.

"I hope it works more than once," came the worried reply from below.

Chico successfully descended to join Tristan, followed by Felipe. With three of them now below, Tristan sent Chico to scout the exit.

"Go ahead and drop down the packs," Tristan shouted to his companions above.

Raóul and Dr. Gallagher dropped the six packs, one by one, to Tristan, who set them to the side.

"You're next," Max ordered Rachel.

"I need to gather the rest of my things. Let Dr. Gallagher go."

"Go ahead," Max told the professor.

After the ascending pillar closed back in its triangular slot at the chamber level, Gallagher took up the position on the Tuat side. Max remained on the opposite triangle. As the stone started downward, Rachel continued to hurriedly stuff things into her knapsack.

"All right," Max said, once the professor was below and the pillar had started to rise. "Raóul is heavier than me. I'll go ahead. Rachel can follow whenever she gets her act together. *Aqui, Raóul!*"

Raóul took the position on the Maat triangle as directed, and Max stepped onto the other, triggering the descent.

With only he and Rachel remaining, Raóul suddenly came to a realization. As the heavier of the two, once Rachel descended, he alone would remain in the chamber. There would be no one to act as counter weight for the Maat side of the scales. No one had yet bothered to explain to him about Tristan's suggestion that he drop through the opening after the rest had safely descended.

"*No quiero restar aqui sin el amuleto!*"

"You don't want to stay here without the amulet? But…"

Before she could react, Raóul had lowered himself through the opening, and was hanging by his hands. As the Tuat pillar reached the half way point in its rise to the chamber, he dropped first to it, then jumped the remaining seven or eight feet to the tunnel floor. Rachel heard the men cursing below.

The pillar continued to rise. Rachel realized she had to act fast. She moved to the opening in the floor. The pillar was nearly all the way to the opening! She wouldn't be able to repeat Raóul's stunt; not with her injured leg. Besides there wasn't time! She'd be caught between the pillar and the floor and be crushed.

The amulet.

In their excitement, everyone had forgotten that the crystal staff was no longer with Max, but rested instead in the groove near the entrance of the chamber.

Rachel limped as fast as she could on her injured leg to the entrance of the room and withdrew the Tet of Carnelian. She whirled around to see if the rising pillar had come to a stop. It had not. With a sinking feeling, she watched the triangular opening close the final few inches.

"Great!" she exclaimed, throwing up her hands in despair. "Now what am I supposed to do?" Rachel looked around the room. There was nothing left except her knapsack, a lantern and the machete. She replaced the Tet in the slot by the door, and moved the lantern on top of the Maat stone. She took the required position across from it and waited. When nothing happened, she retrieved the machete and the carnelian Tet. She laid them next to the lantern and tried again. Finally she sat, defeated and depressed.

She banged the machete against the floor.

"Can you hear me?" she shouted. "Hey, down there! Can you hear me?" She put her ear against the cold stone. She could hear no sound coming from below. Rachel couldn't help laughing aloud at the total implausibility of her predicament. As her laugh echoed in the chamber, she wondered if there wasn't a touch of hysteria in her voice.

✳✳✳✳

Max held the flashlight beam on Raóul's ankle while Tristan examined it.

"Nothing broken. Just a sprained ankle." He didn't bother chastising Raóul. The man had instinctively acted in the interest of self-preservation. He only wished that the stunt hadn't occurred to the Cuzqueño, until after Rachel had been on her way down. He cursed silently for not having made sure Raóul understood the plan. No one had expected the man to panic. Too late now.

"There's got to be some way to open the doorway from down here," Tristan mused.

"That pillar could weigh a couple of tons," Max said. "We could never do it by ourselves. The only thing to do is…"

"…find a different way in," Tristan completed.

Dr. Gallagher had unpacked the remaining lantern and lit it. The tunnel was unimposing, except in its uniformity. The entire length ran only about two hundred feet to an opening, through which sunlight poured.

"Amazing, isn't it?" Max asked. "The walls and ceiling and floor of this tunnel are perfectly straight and smooth."

"Too smooth," agreed Dr. Gallagher. This is bound to be some sort of stucco or adobe—pasted and smoothed on top of the rock beneath. Remember the sound of flowing water near the doorway slot up in the chamber? Whatever kind of hydraulic mechanisms control the scales must be behind the walls of this tunnel."

"You're right," Tristan said. "There can't be any other explanation. We're going to have to break through one of these walls to get at them. It's the only way we can figure out how to rescue Rachel. We can't just leave her."

Oh really? Max thought.

Dr. Gallagher nodded sadly. "If there was just some other way. It's unquestionably the only thing to do. It's not that I would even think of leaving Rachel…but the of idea of tearing into all this is just so…"

"Don't worry," Tristan said. "I understand. The rest of us can take care of this."

"No. This is a question of priorities...I'll help. Let's get to it."

They still had two remaining machetes and a couple of small rock-climbing hammers in the equipment packs. While Chico stood guard at the opening, the other five men started tapping the walls for hollow-sounding spots and soon were chipping away at the walls of the tunnel.

****

The Hidden Place, Madre de Dios Jungle

From the jungles near the Río Pinquina, up to the *Chinkana,* and now to the king's ears, drums and word of mouth had passed an alarming message. Their Tchacha allies were reporting strange outsiders in the forest near their village of Shabu. Three of the trespassers were dead, but at least one had escaped inside the forbidden tunnel. The news had not concerned Olca Capac too much. It was a very rare occurrence for anyone to make it past the Tchacha, and only once in Olca's life had intruders penetrated the ancient tunnels. Only those with the secret knowledge of the gods might safely and successfully pass into the Hidden Place.

With considerable surprise, Olca now listened to newer reports of intruders in the sacred cave on the Anhuar side of the Amentet River. Although the gorge was passable by the secret and sacred routes known only to the shamans, the Indian ruler would not risk sending his warriors into the valley to investigate. For anyone uninitiated to the dangers, a successful descent to the canyon floor was improbable. If they did, the Terrible One would surely deal with the intruders with merciless efficiency. In *all* the centuries Olca's ancestors had lived in the Hidden Place, there was no record of an outsider ever having penetrated past the valley.

****

Rachel understood she had few options but to wait in the chamber. The tunnel leading to this chamber would only take her back to the doorway beneath the other room, and she had heard the heavy thud of the chamber door closing. She would have no more luck opening that door than this one.

Would the men just abandon her? Would they have a choice?

Rachel studied the stones in the walls and floor. They would be heavy enough that if she could dislodge one and somehow push it on top of the triangle bearing the ostrich plume symbol, there might be a chance of activating the scales. These stones, however, fit next to each other so exactly that there was no hope of dislodging one. The stones in the tunnel, however, were less exact and held in place by dried earth or mortar of some sort. She moved the lantern and her knapsack into the tunnel, just outside the chamber. The stones were huge. It was almost laughable to imagine that she might be able to dislodge one of these. She sank to the floor and stared for a long period at the tunnel wall. She was all alone. The situation was hopeless. From her pack, Rachel extracted a small knife. The predicament was admittedly unique, yet the gambit of emotions she was experiencing was all too familiar. Alone, abandoned, trapped. And this time, she didn't have Kenny to cheer her up. That thought made her feel even worse. Who really knew *what* had happened to her twin? Her earlier relief might be completely unfounded. Max was too full of lies for her to know what to believe.

There was really only one resort, she decided. With a heavy sigh of resignation, Rachel grasped the knife firmly and leaned forward. Dragging the blade along the joint between two of the smaller boulders making up the tunnel wall, Rachel began the impossible task of loosening one of the stones.

****

Rachel slumped back against the tunnel wall and regarded her work. She had been at it for a couple of hours, and her hands were sore and blistered. She wasn't giving up. She had made enough progress to be able to move one stone back and forth. When the knife blade would reach no deeper in the joint, she had retrieved the machete and used it. The stubborn rock had still shown no sign of being ready to budge. If it did…*When* it did, she corrected, she only hoped she wouldn't precipitate a cave-in. The idea might work. She would surely be able to trigger the pillar release, once she had enough weight placed on the Maat stone. For the moment, however, Rachel had to take a break. Besides the sad state of her hands, she could barely force her arm muscles to continue the arduous work.

When the grating sound first began, the noise startled Rachel, and she looked all around for its source. Then from the corner of her eye she caught a glimpse of movement. The Tuat stone was sinking.

The Tet of Carnelian was still inserted in the M'naat groove. She retrieved it and stuck it in her waistband, then gathering the lantern, machete and knapsack, she limped back toward the triangle.

The stone had sunk only about three inches. She tentatively stepped one foot onto it and shifted part of her weight over the triangle. The stone sank a little faster. She moved all the way onto the stone. The movement downward continued…not as fast as when the others had descended, but she wasn't complaining.

When Rachel's boots became visible in the tunnel below, the men called out to her. Soon she could make out their faces in the light from the lantern. When the pillar had sunk low enough, Tristan and Felipe stepped forward and lowered her to the floor. "Sorry for the delay," Tristan said. "It took us a while to figure out the plumbing."

Rachel glared accusingly at Raóul. He looked uncomfortably abashed.

"Welcome across the threshold of the Tuat!" Dr. Gallagher smiled.

"Thank you…I think."

"Ah, good," Max said. "I see you remembered the Tet."

"Nice to see you again too, asshole."

Rachel looked around at the walls. The men had punched gaping holes in the sides of the tunnel. She could see the stones behind a layer of adobe. Behind the demolished wall, there was an area with several rock slabs set up like teeter-totters, lying across pivot stones and each other.

"The whole thing is really an ingenuous design," Dr. Gallagher said. "Levers and counter weights are tied into a hydraulic system using these cisterns at both ends. When all the 'switches' are set, the water in one cistern is gradually released and a monumental lever beneath the pillar allows it to sink into its housing below this tunnel's floor. When the weight is taken off the doorway pillar, water flows backs into the cistern. As the cistern begins to again outweigh the pillar, the pillar rises back up!"

"We couldn't uncover everything, but we kept experimenting," Tristan explained. "Finally, we discovered that we could shortcut a few levers, by propping rocks beneath one end. We also clogged up a conduit that lets water into one of the cisterns, and were able to slow the flow enough that the water was going out faster than what was coming in. That allowed the pillar to descend."

Rachel told them how she had been trying to dislodge one of the tunnel rocks, when the sound had attracted her attention. Her hands were covered with blisters, scrapes and cuts. Tristan retrieved the first-aid kit. He cleaned up and covered the worst of them with antiseptic ointment and bandages. Rachel thought he worked with a very gentle touch. She watched his face closely, but looked away abruptly when his eyes met hers.

"What's outside?" she asked.

Max described it for her. The tunnel opened out onto a very narrow canyon with sharply vertical walls. Less than a hundred feet separated one side from the other. The forest canopy stretched out from the opposing precipices above, filling much of that gap. A very narrow pathway led downward from the tunnel, but it was impossible to tell if it went all the way to the canyon floor. Max didn't think the path looked like it received much use, on account of an abundance of vegetation.

Max asked Rachel to return the Tet to him, but Tristan suggested he let her hang onto it, and after a brief discussion, Max agreed. Tristan's presumption was that Raóul would therefore stay close to Rachel, and there wouldn't be re-occurrences of his unfortunate earlier lapse in judgment.

The group took advantage of the cisterns to refresh themselves and to boil water for their canteens. They also used the opportunity to prepare as much of a lunch as was possible from their dwindling provisions. Chico and Tristan both were confident that they could replenish their food supplies once they made it to the base of the canyon.

"Where on the map is this canyon?" Rachel asked.

"We can't tell. The gorge was obviously cut into the earth over thousands of years," Tristan said. "The small river that's left probably hasn't ever been charted. Apparently, the location must not be very noticeable from the air. There's nothing that shows a canyon on the modern maps. Still, I think it can't be far from the Río Pinquina."

Once everyone was ready to begin the descent into the canyon, they moved out onto the ledge. High above their heads, a half dozen condors soared against a backdrop of gathering storm clouds. The height of the path from the canyon floor was dizzying, but provided a spectacular view of the valley and a breathtakingly beautiful waterfall on the opposite side of the gorge. The falls dropped perhaps fifteen hundred feet to a pool of pale turquoise green. Just beyond the falls, the canyon turned sharply toward the east.

"A lost Eden," Dr. Gallagher marveled.

His observation voiced the mirrored opinion of each of the others.

The seven survivors began their descent down the narrow path.

Chapter Sixteen

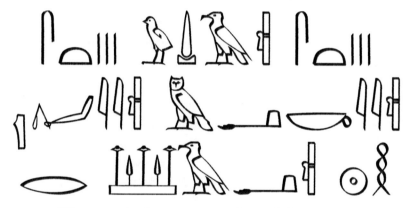

"*They are safe, they are protected, guarded until eternity*"
-*Papyrus of Ani*

****

Ucupacha Valley, Madre de Dios Jungle, Sunday, February 22

The contour of the canyon wall curved and wound. At the second such bend, the group came upon a human figure sculpted in red granite. Rachel was ecstatic at the discovery.

"This is the staff god I was telling you about—the one that holds the thunder and lightning rods like our carnelian piece. What a fantastic specimen! See? Here are the two staffs. Not as detailed as the Tet, but there's no telling how long this statue has endured the rain and wind, out here. I wish I had a camera."

Max pulled a tiny, spy-type camera from a side compartment on his pack, and handed it to Rachel. "We only have a few rolls of film, so use it sparingly."

"Is it my imagination," asked Dr. Gallagher, "…or is the gorge wider across here than it was where we exited the tunnel?"

"It's wider," acknowledged Tristan. "Looks like it broadens even more, below."

After a brief rest, they resumed the descent. Around the next bend was a rock formation that took everyone by surprise. The path continued, but the ledge separated from the side of the canyon. Immense fissures spread downward between the wall and the path. The ledge soon deteriorated into little more than a row of enormous freestanding rock columns. The columns were wedged into a larger ledge made up of a colossal pile of loose rocks below. Several extremely jagged and sharp-edged boulders that had fallen from above had collected around the base of the rock columns. It didn't look like the columns were far enough apart from one another to create an impassable obstacle. Nevertheless, caution would be needed. A slip would send the unfortunate victim to a grisly death on the rocks below.

Tristan went first, the rope attached around his waist. As he moved onto the first column, it rocked forward, and as the other four gasped, Tristan lost his footing and barely kept from falling.

On all fours, Tristan continued cautiously from the first column to the second. The columns rocked again, but this time Tristan expected it and maintained a steady grip. He moved in similar fashion across the subsequent columns, to where the ledge reattached to the canyon wall.

Rachel breathed a sigh of relief.

Safely across, Tristan secured his end of the rope around a tree and took a hold of the line to help steady it.

Max hooked a lanyard and safety line to Gallagher, then took hold of the rope along with Raóul and the two other Peruvians. Wearing one of the smaller packs on his back, the professor eased his way out and crossed, without undo difficulty, to the other side of the columns.

Determined not to be again left behind, Rachel attached her safety line to the rope next and crossed next. With the aid of the rope to steady her, it was not as bad as she expected. Max followed, pushing one pack ahead and pulling another behind. Chico, then Felipe followed, bringing across the remaining backpacks.

Without a tree or large boulder for securing his end of the rope, Raóul had to cross in the same fashion as Tristan—on hands and knees. The big Peruvian fastened the rope around his waist while Max, Chico and Tristan took up the slack on the other side.

"Just take it nice and easy, Raóul...*despacio*..." Tristan called. "The first four columns are the most dangerous."

From those first columns the distance of the fall to the jagged rocks below was less than the length of the rope to the other side. Once Raóul had passed the fourth column, if he fell off, the shortened length of rope ought to save him.

"*Entiendo*," Raóul answered, signifying that he understood.

Despite his size, the Cuzqueño moved nimbly. When he made it safely to the fourth column, the others began to relax.

"*No problema*," Raóul called. He made to the next to last column. Then, with the end in sight, he hastened his crossing too much.

"Watch out!" Tristan cautioned.

The warning came too late. The column rocked violently and Raóul teetered dangerously off balance. For a moment he clawed wildly at empty air. Finding nothing to grab onto, he fell backward and plunged toward the jagged rocks!

The accident caught Tristan and the others holding the rope off guard. They were jerked forward as Raóul's weight hit the end of the rope. The rope was now looped only loosely around the tree, because

Tristan had steadily been taking up the slack. The three men continued to slip forward several more feet without regaining their footing.

"Quick! Give us a hand!" Tristan grunted. Felipe, Dr. Gallagher and Rachel all rushed to help. With their help, Raóul was hauled slowly back up. The Peruvian had bumped up against the side of the last rock column and was bleeding slightly, but otherwise had escaped serious injury.

When Raóul was safe, everyone collapsed on the ground to catch his breath. Soon, however, Dr. Gallagher pulled out his trusty paperback version of the Book of the Dead. He turned to an earmarked page and began to study it. As he read, a concerned look appeared on his face.

"Something else we should know about, Gallagher?" Max panted.

"I think we may be about to encounter a few more obstacles," the professor replied. "I'm just checking something it says about that in the Papyrus of Ani."

"*More* obstacles? I thought there were only seven Arits," Rachel said. "Shouldn't this have been the last one?"

"There *are* only seven Arits, but this wasn't one of them. I think this is what remains of the first '*Sebxet*,' or in English, Pylon."

"Pylon?" Max asked. "What's that?"

"Just following the part of the Papyrus of Ani that describe the Arits, comes a section that describes the Pylons of the House of Osiris. For the first one it reads: '*Queen of tremors, high-walled, queen of destruction who saith the words that drives back those who come to destroy, and who delivers he that comes, from destruction.*'"

"Possible, I guess," Tristan said. "These columns have probably stood here a long, long time; maybe thousands of years. Did I hear right, though? Did you say the first Pylon? Do you mean there are six more of these, too?"

"I'm afraid not," the professor answered. "The papyrus translations describe a total of *twenty-one* Pylons!"

****

None of the group was thrilled with the prospect of dealing with twenty-one new obstacles—least of all, Rachel. Tristan and Max, however, were not convinced that Gallagher was correct in his analysis. Placated by Tristan's assurance that, if a second and worse pylon turned up, they would look for another way out, Rachel reluctantly followed the men's lead.

Armed with the clues from the Book of the Dead, the expedition proceeded cautiously, but the second pylon did not materialize. Dr. Gallagher reasoned that the description 'devourer by fire' must have described magna vents from an earlier age. Such vents had apparently long since cooled. This theory was supported by large deposits of lava rock along the way.

Next, they found a weathered pedestal that might have signaled the proximity of the third pylon. None of the group was able to uncover what significance or dangers might be heralded by the papyrus' description of an altar and sacrificial offerings, unless there were hostile Indians waiting in ambush. They proceeded cautiously, even though there was no place for such Indians to hide.

When it became obvious that the third pylon's threat was equally idle, Rachel began feeling optimistic that the remaining obstacles had not survived the centuries and forces of nature. Just about that time, however, they came to another of the stone pylons in a relatively wide area along the ledge. Here, there was soil, bushes and several trees.

"*Prevailer with knives, Mistress of the two lands, destroyer of the enemies of the Still Heart,*" read the professor.

"Knives…" Tristan mused. "That's just dandy."

Tristan went ahead of the rest of the group, moving in the same tentative manner that Rachel had noticed in the rain forest.

They continued about a hundred feet farther. Tristan had just taken a step, but sensed something wrong. There was a whooshing sound and Tristan reacted instantly and instinctively, lunging backward. This undoubtedly saved his life. A pair of wooden slabs embedded with spikes shot up from beneath a thin covering of sand. A second's delay and the spikes would have impaled Tristan.

"Whew!" Max whistled. "That was too close!" He carefully approached the trap. "Look at this thing. It's like a cross between a bear trap and Iron Maiden. It couldn't be too old. The wood would have rotted in a few years. Somebody's been maintaining this."

Pale and grim-faced, Tristan took a better look at the spring mechanism. He saw that when his foot had placed enough weight on a triggering plank a few inches beneath the sand, he had released a locking pin. The downward pressure of two wooden pistons onto a fitted lever pushed upward on two other pistons, driving the planks upright and toward each other and the victim in between. The trap was primitive, but effective.

"I wonder how many more of these there are." Tristan took his time, cautiously probing the path as the group continued.

As it turned out, the trail was clear of traps the rest of the way up to the next Pylon marker, a few hundred yards ahead.

The fifth Pylon was another describing fire, and like the earlier one, extinct. The sixth turned out to be a snake pit filled with dozens of deadly snakes. This hazard was poorly camouflaged and easily detected in the daylight. Tristan hoped they could reach the floor of the canyon before dark. Many of the dangers might be difficult to detect at night. Again, it was obvious that Indians had to be maintaining some of these traps. Tristan wondered why they hadn't just waited in ambush at the third pylon. Perhaps it was a very boring job. How many visitors could the canyon ever have had from the outside, given what the expedition had been through to get this far?

Following the marker for the seventh Pylon, the path led briefly into and then back out of a cave. For this Pylon, the Book of the Dead described a 'garment which envelops the helpless one.' The meaning became clearer after Tristan became entangled in a giant spider web. A monstrous spider the size of a Pekingnese came scurrying forward! Raóul's quick reflexes and sharp machete intervened, slicing the creature neatly in half before it got a chance to try out its fangs. Rachel shuddered and wondered that she didn't faint at the sight, but she reasoned that after what she had been through, she was just about ready for anything. Chico and Tristan found and steered the others clear of several more webs, before the path led back outside and onto the ledge. At this lower level into the canyon, the gorge now looked to Rachel to be about a hundred yards across.

Two of the next six pylons were extinct lava hazards. Two others, halfway to the canyon floor, were now home to families of howler monkeys. The monkeys made a frightening racket, amplified by an echo inside the canyon, but posed little threat. Of the Pylons Eight through Thirteen, only the Ninth was disastrous.

The Ninth Pylon made mention of a guardian '...*of great strength, clothed as in green feldspar, who bound up, enveloped and devoured the helpless one.*' When the path led to a small cave, the floor of which sloped into a pool of water forty feet across, the group produced several ideas about the possible danger. Chico tested the water for piranha, but found none. Max thought it could be caimans, but the others quickly produced compelling arguments against that, too. Tristan suggested quicksand. He decided to cross the pool, tethered to a rope so that he could be pulled back to safety if it turned out there really was quicksand or something worse.

Rachel had already decided that Tristan must have nerves of steel, and held her breath as Tristan waded across the murky pool. The water rose chest-high, but once again he encountered no danger.

"The bottom is sandy, but solid. I didn't have any problem," Tristan called. Try to cross in the same line as I did, in case it isn't as safe elsewhere."

Chico crossed next, a fearful expression on his face as he waded toward Tristan. Felipe taunted his fellow Cuzqueño until Chico reached the other side, then brashly splashed into the pool with a wide grin on his face to show how easy it was. Two thirds of the way across, the grin vanished and Felipe staggered. He tried to use his arms to swim forward, but he was unable to move. Felipe's expression changed to one of panic.

"Madre de Dios! Something is wrapped around my legs!"

Tristan tossed the end of the rope toward Felipe and started back into the water from the other side. Raóul, too, headed into the pool carrying one of the machetes. Felipe was suddenly pulled under the water, then fought his way back to the surface. A glistening greenish-brown and black shape was entwined around the struggling Peruvian.

"Help me!" Felipe screamed.

"Do something!" pleaded Rachel.

"I can't shoot without hitting Felipe or Raóul," Max snapped.

It was too late. There was more turbulence and splashing, but Felipe failed to resurface.

"I never had a shot," Max said.

"Raóul, get out of the water. Now!" Tristan ordered. Raóul stared only a moment longer at the spot where Felipe had disappeared, then hurriedly rejoined Max and the others on the near side of the pool. The others stared at the murky pool in silence for several more minutes but there was nothing more to evidence what had occurred. Neither the serpent nor Felipe reappeared.

Expectedly, it was Max who first emerged from the aftershock produced by the drowning. His voice was almost an affront to the silence.

"Time to get tough," he growled. To illustrate his meaning, he produced a small bundle of dynamite from his backpack.

On each side of the pool the expedition members backed away a safe distance, Tristan and Chico on the far side, Rachel and the others on the near side. Max prepared, lighted, then tossed a short-fused half-stick of dynamite into the pool. A few rocks broke loose from the ceiling when the stick exploded in the water, but otherwise the dynamite caused only the intended harm. The concussed anaconda, an immense creature of indeterminable size, floated dead or stunned to the surface. Felipe's drowned body, still weighted by his pack, stayed below. Chico pumped six rounds of gunfire into the serpent just to be on the safe side. Afterwards, the rest of the silent and solemn group waded across to where Chico and Tristan waited. Raóul, joined by Chico, briefly searched for the body, but gave it up when Max called to them.

"There could be hidden access holes under the water where more of those things are holed up. The dynamite blast would only have stunned or killed any that were in this pool. No sense in losing anybody else. Felipe is beyond our help."

Dr. Gallagher insisted that someone should at least say a few words, so as the others stood silently the professor recited what part he could recall of the twenty-third Psalm. Raóul and Chico made the sign of the cross, but Rachel wished the Egyptologist had picked a different passage. Her imagination needed no reminder that they were entering a gorge that had all the makings of the Valley of the Shadow of Death.

The group was markedly more somber and cautious as they continued their march. They were now down to only six of the original team of fifteen. Four of the ten who had continued had since met unnatural deaths. The five who had deserted were beginning to look increasingly wise. Even Max was momentarily tamed by their latest misadventure.

Pylons Fourteen and Fifteen led them past hidden pits, one with snakes that even Tristan almost missed, and another that was empty.

One of the other pylons included a surprise torrent of water that nearly swept Rachel over the edge. Another hazard was a device similar to the earlier 'iron maiden,' but used a swinging blade. This later device malfunctioned, otherwise Tristan would have also become a casualty. Two more fire hazards surprised them by forcing the five survivors to tread their way gingerly across narrow spans of rock ledge, flanked by semi-molten lava.

One of the final obstacles required the group to inch their way forward. The path into the canyon had suddenly narrowed to a mere ten inches. As they negotiated the ledge, strategically placed mirrors of polished copper or tin reflected the sun's bright glare directly onto the rock face of the canyon wall. The glare blinded them as they made their way across the pre-carious stretch. Rachel was thankful that they were making the crossing without anyone in pursuit.

The final Twenty-first Pylon took them again inside a small cave, where apparently a pool of lava had long ago poised the last obstacle. Now it was just an empty cave.

The next ten minutes were a relatively easy descent down a comfort-able grade, and into the river valley. The descent had taken nearly six hours. Without the hazards and their cautious pace, Tristan figured they could have otherwise reached the canyon floor in less than two hours.

"I'm almost afraid to ask, but what does the papyrus say we can expect after the twenty-one Pylons?" Max asked.

"We still haven't found the seventh Arit," Dr. Gallagher replied. "There's also a couple of guardians mentioned as living within the Domain of Manu and the Domain of Fire. The Princes of Tchacha are one. That might be Indian allies enlisted by the Egyptian visitors. If they've continued the practice...incorporated it into their religious beliefs...that could explain who maintains and replenishes the animal traps along the descent to the canyon."

"It could also have been the Indians who killed Luis and Renaldo," Rachel ventured. "I wonder why they don't just come after us? There's no question now that know we're here, after the gun shots and the dynamite."

"That sort of makes you worry, doesn't it," Dr. Gallagher agreed. "I wonder if it has anything to do with the second guardian protecting the entry to the Tuat."

"What guardian?" Tristan asked testily.

"The 'Keeper of the Bend' of the River Amentet, the beast *Am-mit*. Like most Egyptian deities, this one has other names: *Baabi, Biba,* and *Herisepef*...to name a few. I expect to find some sort of monolithic statue, with a ferocious countenance meant to scare away intruders. According to the papyrus, Am-mit is supposed to have the head of a crocodile, the foreparts and claws of a lion, and the hind quarters of a hippopotamus."

"That doesn't sound very intimidating to me," Max said. "I think I'd be more inclined to laugh, than run away from it. Hind quarters of a hippo?"

"I wouldn't be laughing at anything, if I were in your shoes," the professor replied. "And for what it's worth, the Egyptians apparently didn't agree with your assessment."

"It's not worth much, I assure you," Max snapped.

Gallagher continued, ignoring Max's remark. "They called this beast-god by descriptions like Devourer of Men, Everlasting Devourer, Lord of Terror and the Terrible One. They wrote that he feeds on the intestines of men. The Indians probably performed human sacrifices to this idol. If we can find the statue, we'll be near the seventh and final Arit. The Book of the Dead says that this Am-mit lives in the Domain of Fire, near a chamber called '*Sheniu.*'. We must be close. Domain of Fire undoubtedly refers to the molten lava vents of this valley."

"Wherever threat the statue represents, we'd better get going," Tristan said. "We need to find a suitable place to set up camp. It'll be dark soon, but the river didn't look like more than a quarter of a mile away."

The group set off in that direction. The appearance of the valley amazed Rachel. The undergrowth was much easier to traverse, but what flora there was resembled a scene from some prehistoric era. The air was extremely humid, and the ground somewhat marsh-like. Steam rose in places, and many plant leaves were larger than she was. Rachel felt like she was a character in a Jules Verne novel.

Raóul and Tristan led the way, but there wasn't nearly as much need for the machetes here. The group had not moved along very far, when they stopped in their tracks. An unearthly roar bellowed and echoed throughout the narrow canyon from somewhere in the distance.

"What the hell was that!" Max exclaimed.

"Jaguar?" Tristan suggested. "The echo from the canyon must amplify and distort the roar. Remember how much noise there was back there with the monkeys?"

"That's no monkey and it damn sure didn't sound like a jaguar," Max responded.

"What else it could be? C'mon, let's get moving." Despite his outward demeanor, even Tristan didn't want to be around when whatever was making the chilling noise showed up.

They continued but the roar froze them all again, moments later. This time, it sounded closer. Rachel's fear grew. What if it *was* some sort of Great Tiger? Who really knew what kind of unknown animals lived in the more remote reaches of these jungles? Scientists were finding new species all the time.

By now, even Tristan and Max were nervous. What they could see of the sky between the high canyon walls was already dappled with pink-tinted clouds. Tristan figured they had less than thirty minutes before it would be dark.

"Screw it," Tristan announced. "Let's turn around and go back to the wall. I'm getting a real bad feeling about this place. We can spend the night in that last cave. The lava pit there was extinct, and I'd feel a whole lot better being inside than camped next to the river."

"No argument here," Max replied, and there was hasty endorsement for the plan from each of the others.

Hastened by the frightful roar, the pace of the trip back to the canyon wall was near twice as fast as before.

As had become their custom since the attack by the poison dart Indians, Tristan led the way while Chico trailed behind the others, acting as the rear guard. As they moved quickly back toward the cave, Chico began to check more frequently over his shoulder. The last few minutes, his experienced ears had detected what might be movement through the brush behind them. Because of their rush and the noise that the six expedition members were making, it was impossible to be sure. He halted for a moment and let the others continue. If this was a jaguar, it was not acting like one. Neither jaguars nor pumas would dare to pursue or attack a group of this size. Yet, his hair bristled in apprehension, and Chico held his breath so that he might listen as closely as possible. It had now turned early evening, and only the final remnants of dusk illuminated the forest. All was quiet, except for the fading noises of his companions. Even the air was still.

It was Rachel who first noticed that he was no longer behind them. She had looked backward, more in trepidation of what she might see than in anticipation of Chico's absence. She called out in fright to the others.

"What's wrong?" Tristan asked, as he jogged back toward Rachel. "Where's Chico?"

"I just now looked back and he was gone," Rachel panted. "That's why I called out."

Tristan hesitated, trying to decide whether he should send the others on to the cave, or keep everyone together. If this was a jaguar, it would be less likely to attack a larger group, he reasoned. Yet, it would be foolish to jeopardize more lives by going back to look for Chico.

The question was cut short by the paralyzing roar of the creature along with a simultaneous human scream. Tristan raced toward the sound, followed by Max and Raóul, then more tentatively by the frightened Rachel and Dr. Gallagher.

The first three arrived only in time see a flash of something huge tearing off into the darkened shadows of the forest, dragging Chico's limp and bloodied body into the brush. Tristan and Max fired their rifles repeatedly at the spot where the creature had disappeared. "Missed it," Max muttered.

"Chico was already dead," Tristan said, shaking his head from side to side. "Or if he wasn't, he is now."

"Wh…What was it?" stammered Dr. Gallagher, who had caught only the briefest glimpse of the beast.

"A huge jaguar, or something like it. Didn't you see the spots?" Tristan said.

"Jaguar, my ass!" Max exclaimed. "It was as big as a polar bear...and what about the head and teeth? Like a mixture of a crocodile and a saber-tooth tiger! A bear of some type?"

"I didn't get a very good look at it," Tristan admitted. "But whatever it was; it's still out there. Let's get to the cave...and quick."

No one had to suggest that twice. Rachel hadn't really seen a thing, but her imagination was supplying plenty of terrifying ideas. She wished she could limp along faster than her still healing leg would allow. Chico's shocking and horrible fate, coming so close on the heels of the other fatalities, had triggered a chilling question—was an inescapable death sentence already ordained for the rest of them?

The beast bellowed twice more during the race back to the cave, a little closer the second time than the first. It was returning.

By the time the group started back up the canyon path all six were jogging—Rachel being half-carried between Tristan and Raóul. Everyone was relieved when they finally reached the cave.

Tristan and Max positioned themselves at the cave entrance with the two rifles, while the other huddled together quietly in the garish, light of one of the lanterns. Tristan suddenly realized that besides the loss of Chico, they now were also minus one more rifle. It would be useless and callous to mention this, so he did not. When the roar came again, it sounded more distant and less frightening from the shelter of the cave.

The mood remained somber and tense. For supper, they shared the last of the packaged provisions. Max vowed that he and Tristan would find something for the group to eat the next day, even if they had to trek a bit farther back up the canyon wall and shoot one of the howler monkeys.

Rachel shuddered inwardly at the thought.

"I can hardly wait," she said, thinking that there must be more appealing fare below in the valley. Having spoken, she immediately wished that she had kept her mouth shut. They all knew now that the valley was not the Eden it had appeared from the ledge. Two more of their companions had come to ghastly ends here in just a few short hours. *Valley of the Shadow of Death...*

Each of the remaining five took turns standing watch during the night. Rachel took the last slot, from five to eight a.m., knowing that Tristan was usually awake by then, anyway. The chilling roar shattered the silence of the night and everyone's restless sleep, on four more occasions, but the hours of darkness passed without further incident.

Chapter Seventeen

"Am-mit" (a.k.a. Biba, Baabi, Herisepef, Mates)

****

Ucupacha Valley, Madre de Dios Jungle, Monday, February 23

Rachel's turn on watch was only half over when the sun came up, and a couple of the men began stirring. Even though the others were only a few feet away and she knew Tristan had only been half-asleep, Rachel had remained apprehensive throughout her lonely vigil, twisting and untwisting her necklace, and biting her nails. She started remembering how lions and leopards often hunt just around dawn. She didn't know if the beast that had killed Chico was in the cat family or not, but she was unforgettably aware that, unlike lions and leopards, this creature did not try to avoid human beings. To make matters worse, whenever she forced her mind away from the present danger, Rachel's mind kept returning to her missing twin.

Tristan pulled on his boots and came over to sit with Rachel. To say she welcomed his company would be putting it lightly. Dr. Gallagher woke next, and quietly occupied himself with going back through the notes on the Book of the Dead, and studying the two stone tablets.

"I thought I'd go see what I can find for breakfast," Tristan said.

Rachel looked at him, aghast. "Do you think that's safe? Shouldn't you take Raóul to watch your back?"

"I won't go far. That thing had the advantage of darkness, last night. It won't be so bold in the daylight. I don't suppose you've noticed anything unusual, since it started getting light outside?" His eyes darted across the treetops below, then stopped on Rachel, who blinked nervously under their scrutiny.

"No, thank God. But then, I'm not as experienced as you at knowing what ought to be considered unusual."

"Oh, you'd know, if you saw anything. Something would attract your attention, or startle you. You'd say to yourself, 'I wonder why those birds suddenly flew off?'"

Rachel smiled back. "Well, I guess it's okay then. I haven't asked myself anything like that all morning."

"You have a nice smile. It's good to see it again. For a few days, I was afraid you had lost it."

"I think I've had more than enough reason to be upset, don't you? I'm surprised I can smile at all, after yesterday."

Tristan nodded. He picked up one of the rifles and stood. "I haven't heard the roar since two a.m. Hopefully there's deer in the canyon. I'm not too fond of monkey meat."

"I never tried it. I'm sure it takes just like chicken, but I'd rather not find out. Do you remember seeing some trees with small, bright red roots down in the valley?" Rachel had noticed these the previous evening.

"Yeah, why? Are they edible?"

"Uh huh. They're called *huasai*. They won't provide much of anything in nourishment, but they cause anyone who chews them to feel more or less satiated."

She reached out and touched his arm. "Be careful. We're all very dependent on you, you know?"

Tristan placed a hand over Rachel's and patted it a couple of times.

"I don't know about that, but don't worry. I won't be gone long."

He turned and left. Rachel watched him disappear down the path. She was growing very fond of Tristan, despite his earlier lapse in character. He had warmed up quite a bit, since they had first met, and now seemed to like her too. She wondered what he was like in a normal setting. Was he as confident and relaxed? Or did the jungle and the challenges of adventure bring out the best in him? She felt a little confused. What was she thinking? The last thing she needed in her life right now was a romantic entanglement. Wasn't it? Besides, all she *really* knew about Tristan was that he wasn't married and had collaborated with a power-crazed bully for the past twelve years.

Max woke soon after Tristan had left. He guessed where Tristan had gone, and Rachel confirmed it. Dr. Gallagher called Max to his side. He had something he wanted to show him on the map tablet.

"This is very puzzling," the professor said. "I find it difficult to imagine that a canyon such as this doesn't show up on either the Egyptian map or the modern one. By all indications, we should nearly be on top of the location for ?-bee Ur, which you believe to be Gran Paititi. There is an indication of a valley ⟦𓀭𓏤⟧ near the fortified city symbol, but it ought to be on the other side of the Río Pinquina. There's also something I hadn't noticed about the other tablet, before now. One of the words that's obscured begins with the glyph for 'S-'. The word might be Sheniu, the chamber I mentioned, or possibly 'Sekhemmetenusen,' the name of the seventh doorkeeper. The sentence containing it says that this S-something is the gate, which is at the pillars or columns..., or something like that. The glyphs are too worn away to be sure. This gate is located at the 'bend of the river.' The same bend which is supposed to be protected by the Am-mit statue."

"And so...?" Max prompted. "What does that tell us?"

"Not much more than we already knew," Dr. Gallagher admitted. "Unless we're already *past* the Río Pinquina. From the ledge of the canyon, do you remember how the canyon bends sharply just beyond the waterfall?"

Max nodded.

"If that were the bend of the river that the second tablet and the Book of the Dead mention, then the waterfall itself might be the pillars. The gate could be behind the waterfall...a cave or even a man-made tunnel. What could be a better hiding place?"

"But we're *not* past the Río Pinquina," Max said. "We must be very close, but it's a large river. The one in this canyon is too small. There's no possibility that we could have missed it. Even through the tunnels, we would have known had we gone underneath. The tunnel walls are too porous to hold out the volumes of water that we are talking about."

"Here comes Tristan, already," Rachel called. "It looks like he's found something for breakfast. I hope you're not too hungry, though. Doesn't look like a whole lot."

As he got closer, Tristan looked grim. The friendliness of only a few minutes earlier, when he had been chatting with Rachel, had vanished.

"No meat?" asked Max, as Tristan spilled a cloth sack of fruits and gourds and some of the red huasai roots onto one of the sleeping bags. Rachel recognized the gourds as Brazil nut pods. Each pod would contain about eight nuts.

"I saw deer tracks, but I was afraid to use the rifle."

"Afraid of attracting attention ? Of what? I thought you said it was just a big jaguar."

"All right, I was wrong. It wasn't a jaguar. I found some other tracks besides the deer's. Bigger ones. Much bigger."

"How much bigger?" Max asked, growing more serious.

"Did you ever see hippopotamus tracks?"

"Jesus!"

"The forepaws were smaller, but still bigger than a tiger's. Clawed, but not identifiable. The back prints were the larger ones. Those were more ambiguous. It could be anything—some sort of bear...cat...who knows?"

"You're not suggesting that this creature could be that part-crocodile, part-lion, part-hippo thing Gallagher was describing?" Max asked, incredulously.

Tristan ignored the question. "There was something else about the tracks too. I found them all along the exact route we took last evening getting back to this cave, wherever the ground was muddy or marsh-like. It tracked us. Right up to the base of the canyon wall."

"Why didn't it come to the cave?" Dr. Gallagher asked. "What if this is *its* cave?"

"I don't think it can climb that well. From what little I saw last night, it was very bulky in the hindquarters, like the description Gallagher gave. The path is only about a foot wide near the canyon floor, less in places, remember? Too narrow for a creature of that size. The wall of the canyon is nearly vertical. There was probably no way for it to reach us."

"Thank God for that!" Rachel said.

"I wonder why nobody has ever reported sighting something like this," wondered Tristan. "Surely, at least some local stories would have surfaced."

"There are some Amazon-based stories of huge mysterious creatures," interjected Rachel. "The dinosaurs in Arthur Conan Doyle's novel, Lost *World*, were inspired by rumors from the Roirama plateau, in Brazil."

"And the Egyptian Am-mit legend, of course," Gallagher added. "This has to be the source of that myth."

"Didn't anyone else see its teeth?" Max asked. "It had extra long canines, like a saber-tooth tiger. Maybe that's what it really is—some sort of dinosaur. Maybe it survived the last ice age."

"It might look like a saber-tooth tiger in the teeth, but there were other species that had that same characteristic, Max," Rachel said. "Saber-tooth tigers have been extinct for too long a time. There was a much more recent species of saber-tooth marsupial that was indigenous to this part of South America."

"Marsupial?" Max scoffed. "You mean like a kangaroo? Or an opossum? Are you saying this thing that dragged off Chico was just some sort of big 'possum? How do you know it wasn't a saber-tooth tiger, *Doctor* Aguila? You're a linguist, not a paleontologist."

"I'm only saying none of us really have a clue what it is," Rachel glared.

"Whatever," Max said. "Who cares what it is? It's dangerous—we know that. Even so, it's mostly irrelevant. All we're interested in doing is continuing with the next leg of the journey out of here. This is a long valley, but a narrow one. We only have a short distance to cross. If there are any of these things still around, they could be miles away. We're not here to capture one. All we have to do is get across the canyon to the waterfall. For all we know, this big mutant 'marsupial' is off hunting at the other end of the valley."

"Why just to the waterfall?" Tristan asked.

Max told Tristan about Dr. Gallagher's theory on the bend of the river and the presumed secret entrance behind the falls.

"So you've changed your mind? You now agree that this probably is the same place that's described in the Book of the Dead and the second tablet?" Gallagher asked.

Max nodded. "If it's supposed to be guarded by this Am-mit beast, we must be close. Where else could these things live without somebody knowing about them? How many big hippo-lion-crocodile monsters could there be?"

"More than one, that much is likely," Rachel said.

"How do you arrive at that conclusion?" Max asked.

"Unless the life span of one beast is three thousand years…" Rachel started.

"Longer," interrupted Dr. Gallagher. "The Osiris story and Am-mit myth are at least five to six thousand years old."

"What I was going to say was:..unless it lives several thousand years, then, there *has* to be more than one. Where did this one come from? It had to have a mama and papa. To have survived this long there must be a sizable enough population to sustain reproduction of the species."

"That's an unpleasant thought," Tristan said, "…that there might be dozens of those monsters roaming around this canyon. Doc, you didn't find anything about a secret tunnels, running *under* the canyon that would get us safely to the other side?"

"No. Nothing like that. All it really says in the Book of the Dead about the next phase of the journey is that a person needs to have a pure heart," the professor answered.

"I imagine a pure heart tastes about the same as any other kind to that creature out there," Tristan said. "At some point, we're going to have to make a run for it."

"We still have two rifles and a pistol. Do we have other options?" Max asked.

"We could go back," Rachel suggested.

"Back through the Hivitos territory? I'd much rather take our chances against *any* animal, than risk that again," Tristan said. "Max and Raóul nodded their endorsement.

Rachel and Dr. Gallagher reluctantly agreed that forward was the better plan. It was just an animal, after all. Everything was less intimidating by the light of day.

The group started sorting through all the packs, trying to decide if there was anything else they might discard. Tristan had earlier discarded most of the cooking utensils. He now tossed out all those, which remained, except for a couple of lightweight pots for boiling water or cooking a stew. Everyone dumped all but a change of clothes and a jacket, for when it turned cool again. Except for a few ropes, the machetes, rock hammers, sleeping bags and first aid kit, that was about it. Max insisted that they still needed the stone tablets, bulky though they were. Rachel still had the Tet. She had blushed only slightly when Tristan upturned her pack and two of her thong panties tumbled out along with the rest of her clothes.

Tristan made light of it. "You can take those; they won't slow us down much."

Once everything was ready to go, they sat outside on the path and watched the condors flying overhead. It was a nice day for a race with a mythological beast, thought Rachel. Not a cloud in sight.

After the morning had passed ten a.m., and there still had been no roar, everyone started getting impatient.

"Maybe it's out of hearing range," Max said. "We should have heard it by now if it was still nearby."

"Or maybe it's smarter than we think," Dr. Gallagher said, "and it's patiently hidden down there in the edge of the trees waiting for us."

"I won't pretend I'm an expert on this creature, whatever it is," Tristan said, "…but I do know a fair amount about present-day carnivores. I would think this animal's general habits are similar. By its behavior last night and from its prints, it's clearly a carnivore. Most carnivores are mainly nocturnal; they hunt at night and sleep during the day. If so, there's a good chance we wouldn't encounter it at all."

Tristan polled the four others. Everybody was in favor of going at once. They would retreat to the cave if they heard the roar before they got halfway to the falls.

Max and Tristan carried the three rifles. Max gave the pistol to Dr. Gallagher. Raóul carried one of the machetes, and since Rachel was the only one unarmed, she asked for the other machete. She knew it wouldn't be of much use against something the size and temperament of a what had killed Chico, but it made her feel better to have a weapon in her hand.

After they reached the canyon floor and moved into the marsh, Tristan stopped to show them the tracks. Rachel stood back a bit, not wanting the others to see how badly she was trembling, but she need not have been concerned; even Raóul was petrified.

"From the spacing and size of the tracks, I'd have to say this creature is at least twelve feet long!" Tristan said.

"How big are opossums in Oklahoma?" Max baited.

"Why don't you go off and find this one, just to prove me wrong?" Rachel suggested.

With the "reassuring" image of a carnivore the size of a Buick, the small group moved as quickly and quietly as they could across the canyon. In twenty minutes, they had traversed roughly two thirds of the distance and emerged from the more troublesome undergrowth. When they neared the banks of the river, the trees and heavier ground cover rapidly dissipated. Nothing much was able to take root here, since the ground was mostly rock and small pebbles. The waterfall was clearly visible beyond the other side of the river, perhaps a hundred yards away. The plunging column of white water was just as impressive from the river as it had been from across the valley and the canyon wall. For a moment, Rachel forgot the danger. The water in the stream was so clear, she could see the hundreds of stones lying submerged almost all the way across the forty feet or so, to the other side. The stream was no more than three feet deep. With the bend in the canyon allowing a view of both high canyon walls and the waterfall in the immediate background, it was as scenic a postcard quality view as Rachel had ever seen. She was about to pause to take a photo when Max shouted.

"Tristan. Come take a look at this! My God, it's humongous!"

Rachel turned, her heart beating a staccato rhythm against her chest and her mind prepared to see some monstrous creature rising out of the stream…

Instead, Max was standing knee deep in the river, looking at something in his hand. He was holding a fist-sized rock that shone metallic yellow.

"Gold, Tristan! Look at the size of this."

Tristan had started walking toward Max to take a look at the nugget, but suddenly stopped halfway. He bent to look at something else at the water's edge.

"Here's another one of that creature's footprints, right in the mud at the water line. This can't be an hour old. The current from the stream hasn't even blurred the edges. This thing is still somewhere nearby…"

Hardly had the words escaped his lips, when a small flock of birds fluttered from the treetops less than a hundred yards to their left. The commotion was on the same side of the stream as Rachel and the other four. Tristan quickly glanced back at the forest.

"Oh, oh," Rachel said, remembering their earlier conversation.

"Damn!" Tristan swore. "Head for the trees on the other side. Right now. Run!" He leapt forward into the stream before the last words had left his mouth.

Rachel didn't stop to look. She ran into the stream and then, slowed by the water, hopped forward from one foot to the next as fast as she was able.

A deafening roar came as the beast lunged from the jungle. Rachel dared not stop to look back. She heard gunshots and another bellow, then felt the earth tremble under the strides of the giant creature. More shots rang out as she struggled to reach the opposite bank.

"Raóul! Run!" Rachel heard Tristan shout.

This time she couldn't help it, and chanced a glance backward. She stopped, in horror. Whatever the creature was, it was quickly bearing down on them. Even in the daylight, she couldn't tell much about the beast—only that it was huge and terrifying. As Max had described, she saw rows of large gnashing teeth and long curving canines. As much like a Tyrannosaurus as a saber-tooth tiger, it bore large black splotches across an orange colored back. As she stood paralyzed in frightened fascination, the gigantic beast thundered toward her.

Max and Dr. Gallagher also now began shouting at Raóul who hadn't even made it half way across the stream. He had turned and faced the beast, like Rachel, frozen in either terror or awe. The monster was almost on top of the Peruvian before he suddenly broke free of the spell. Perhaps realizing it was too late to run, Raóul chose to die fighting. With a blood-curdling scream and raised machete he charged insanely toward the Am-mit beast. The three other men who had made it most of the way across were alternately shouting at their companion to run, and firing shots. Rachel heard a voice screaming as the creature opened its colossal jaws, then snapped them shut around Raóul's head and shoulders. For a moment she thought the screams came from the doomed Peruvian. Then she realized it was her voice. She quit screaming, turned and ran the last few feet out of the stream and into the trees in the direction of the waterfall. More shots sounded behind her, followed by another terrible roar.

Rachel ran on, not waiting to see what was happening. She ran straight over small saplings that whipped back in her face, and ducked under limbs without breaking her stride. She bumped into trees, and stumbled repeatedly. Somewhere in her mind she realized that this scene was all too familiar. The dream. The same jaguar nightmare she had dreamed twice before, only this time it was something more terrifying chasing her!

Wake up! she commanded, but this time it was no dream.

She charged straight into something stringy and sticky, accidentally dropping the machete as she struggled to get free. Horrified, Rachel saw that it was another of the giant webs, like Tristan had tangled with in the cave. In utter terror, she watched as one of the huge spiders scampered out onto the web in response to her struggles. She only succeeded in getting more entangled. The spider crept forward. She screamed again and kicked viciously toward the spider.

Suddenly, Tristan was at her side, snatching up the machete and slashing at the web. He cut her free and yanked her forward. Dr. Gallagher and Max ran up right behind Tristan, and passed without stopping. Dr. Gallagher and Tristan had both dumped their packs. Max had stubbornly clung to his, which contained the tablets. Tristan grabbed Rachel's arm and pulled her back into a sprint. She didn't dare slow down enough to discard her small knapsack.

Max shouted back at them. "It's still coming! I'm out of ammunition."

"Me too," Tristan. exclaimed "No time to stop and reload. Head for the falls."

"Right," Max panted.

Rachel could hear the heavy crash of the creature through the saplings and undergrowth not far behind, and ran with all the strength she could muster.

Suddenly, Rachel and Tristan broke free of the trees. The waterfall was straight ahead—only a few more strides. Rachel felt like her lungs were going to explode, and that Tristan was about to jerk her arm from its socket, but still she ran. Max and Dr. Gallagher were just a few steps ahead. The explosive roar again filled the air around them. The creature had finished with Raóul and had almost caught up with the rest of them! Max and Gallagher plunged into the shallow pool at the base of the falls, and disappeared behind the curtain of water. Tristan and Rachel followed a second later. Max and Gallagher were standing there, knee deep in water, drenched and dumbfounded. As Rachel wiped the water out of her eyes, frantically peering into the background for the expected opening, she experienced one of the worst moments of her life.

There was no opening.

"Shit! You were wrong," Max wheezed "Gallagher, you…idiot! You were wrong. There's no cave. Nothing!"

The professor waded away from the others toward the far side of the waterfall, searching in desperation for some sign of a secret doorway. The water deepened as he took a few steps and he struggled to maintain his footing against a small whirlpool created by the waterfall.

"Godzilla is going be on top of us in about two seconds," Tristan huffed. "There's no place else to hide. Everybody move as deep in the pool as possible, and up against the back of the wall. Get down in the water as much as possible. I'll try to draw it away…"

Tristan started to wade back out. "No!" Rachel shouted, grabbing his arm and pulling Tristan off balance. Both of them stumbled backward into deeper water and were at once caught in an undertow. At the same moment, a huge mass burst through the curtain of water and Rachel stared momentarily into the gaping jaws of the creature. Then she was sucked under water. She tried to find the bottom, but found that the whirlpool motion created by the waterfall water was too strong for her to swim against. In panic, she felt herself being pulled sideways. The current rolled her against the bottom and bumped her up against a submerged ledge. She fought wildly to get a hold on the slippery algae-covered rock surface, but was drawn under the ledge.

The undertow suddenly let up as she was swept past the ledge. Unable to hold her breath any longer, Rachel kicked frantically to the surface. Gasping for air and fully expecting to have her head bitten off the moment she popped up, she was surprised to discover she was inside an underground chamber. She was still wearing her jacket and knapsack, and she was having a lot of trouble treading water. Her boots hindered her, and she knew she would have to remove them or drown.

The only illumination came from a small amount of daylight that diffused inward from beneath the ledge.

"Who made it?" sputtered a voice that Rachel recognized as Max. She choked out a reply and heard her answer chorused by Tristan's and Dr. Gallagher's voices.

"Unbelievable!" Max exclaimed. "Was that something to tell your grandkids or what?"

Chapter Eighteen

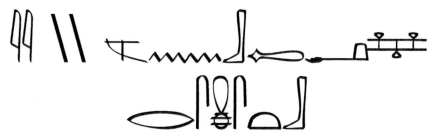

ina aa er semat: "I come advancing to the examination."

****

Ucupacha Valley, Madre de Dios Jungle, Monday afternoon,
February 23

"I think I can touch the bottom over here," Max called.

Rachel had been struggling to remove a boot as she treaded water for three or four minutes in the darkness. She swam in the direction of Max's voice.

"It's still over my head…" she sputtered, after reaching the others. Rachel was almost a foot shorter than any of the three men.

"I'm standing now," Tristan said. "Hang onto me."

Rachel grasped for Tristan in the darkness and, finding him, gratefully clutched his shoulders.

"There was a flashlight in my backpack," Max said. "...but I lost the pack in the undertow. I don't know if it got swept in here or not."

"I have a small dive-light in mine," Rachel said. Her small knapsack had stayed on when the current had washed her under the ledge. She had brought along the dive-light from home, precisely because it was so compact and watertight.

"Hold still a moment," Tristan said. "Let me see if I can find it."

"I can't hold still," objected Rachel, "I'm treading water. I'll sink."

"Let go of my arm a second."

Tristan waded behind Rachel, and she stiffened slightly as his arm encircled her waist. An unexpected and half-forgotten sensation surged through her as he pulled her back against him in the water, and began to fumble through the knapsack with his free hand. She hoped he could not feel how badly she was trembling, but he showed no reaction if he had.

After a few seconds digging, Tristan found the light.

"Twist the bottom," Rachel sputtered as Tristan fidgeted with the small device.

"Just a second, I'm busy with the flashlight."

"I *meant* the flashlight," Rachel blushed.

The small light came on, and Rachel could see the dimly illuminated, garish faces of the three men around her.

"Not much of a light," complained Max.

"Better than nothing," Tristan said.

"Is everybody else all right?" Dr. Gallagher asked. "Poor Raóul..."

Everyone except Tristan reported nothing but scratches and scrapes from the ledge.

"I think my shin must have gotten raked by a claw or that thing's teeth," Tristan said. "I felt something sharp across my leg just as I was going under. It hurts like hell!"

Tristan shined the small light around the cavern.

"I think it keeps going back in that direction," Rachel said, letting go of Tristan long enough to point.

The three men and Rachel swam in the direction that she had indicated. Soon they were able to distinguish a shape against one side of the cavern. As they got closer and Tristan shined the light directly at it, they could begin to see what it was.

"A pier. It even has mooring posts," Max said.

"But no boat..." Tristan noted.

"A boat probably would have rotted, ages ago," Gallagher said. "Whoever is maintaining the traps in the canyon probably doesn't even know about this cavern."

They made it to the pier, which was just a flattened rock ledge. Someone had chipped, drilled or ground holes, and inset oblong stones to serve as the mooring posts. Rachel crawled on top of the ledge and just lay there.

Safe for the moment, the image came back of the Am-mit creature closing its giant jaws onto Raóul. That sight had been the most horrifying thing Rachel had ever witnessed. She hadn't even watched the whole gruesome event. Instinct and pure terror had caused her to turn away and start running, as soon as she had seen the beast clamp its jaws onto Raóul. Still, she could not rid her mind of the image. Her head reeled and she knew she was about to be sick. She crawled to the edge of the pier, just in time to vomit what little there was in her stomach.

None of the men spoke or moved to comfort Rachel. Each was also replaying the terror of the chase and Raóul's grisly death in his head, and fighting a similar urge. Finally Tristan broke the silence.

"Are you okay?"

"I don't think I'll ever be okay again." Her teeth chattered and her body trembled. At the moment, she wasn't up to coping.

"Max," Tristan said. "The first-aid kit was in Raóul's pack. Do you think you could find anything in Rachel's knapsack that you could use to bind up my shin?"

Tristan shined the light on his leg. Blood had started flowing freely from the wounds. Rachel looked away, feeling sick again.

Max came over and helped Rachel remove her knapsack. Inside he found a shirt, which he took back over to Tristan and began to tear into wide strips to bandage the shin. As she watched him tend to the wounds, it occurred to Rachel that she should offer to help. Still feeling nauseous, she crawled over near Tristan and held the small flashlight until he had finished tearing the strips. She avoided looking directly at the wounds. When he was done, Max took the light from her and examined Tristan's injury.

"There are a couple of nasty cuts. I think I had a tube of antiseptic ointment in my backpack."

You think you could find it with that dive-light, if it's inside the cavern?" Tristan asked.

"The water out in the pool was crystal clear…I imagine it's the same in here. The pack might not be too hard to find. The tablets were in there, too."

Rachel couldn't believe that the stupid tablets still concerned him. One catastrophe after another, and Max didn't feel any remorse. Nothing was important to him but the lost treasure.

"I just can't believe it," Dr. Gallagher exclaimed. "Am-mit, Lord of Terror. Still inclined to laugh?"

Max glanced at Dr. Gallagher. "No; not at the Egyptians; only at the bumbling idiot who told us to expect a door behind the waterfall. It's just dumb luck we wound up in here, at all. And since you brought it up, that monster damn sure wasn't any statue."

"I still don't see how there hasn't been some prior sighting of that thing," Tristan wondered.

"I think it's probably isolated to the canyon," Rachel said. "There may not be a way out for an animal that size. As for not finding others, it may have evolved entirely within the small pocket represented by the gorge. That happens on islands and in isolated land areas. We call such evolutionary pockets *refugia*. The theory is that *refugia* are the way nature permits the development of biological diversity between species."

"Too damn much diversity, this time," Max said.

"Everything is too unreal," Rachel admitted. "I keep thinking it must be a bad dream, and I can't believe I'm unable to wake up."

"Somehow, I'm not having that problem," Tristan said. "Having these mythological teeth marks across my shin makes it real enough for me."

Rachel grimaced again as she glanced at the wounds, and was grateful that the cavern was too dark to discern all the gory detail. It embarrassed her that it was Max who had taken the lead in dressing Tristan's wounds. Biting her lip, she looked away. Max seemed to notice this. Rachel could swear through the darkness that he was wearing the smallest of sardonic smiles.

Max finished making a temporary compress of a few of the cloth strips to retard the bleeding from Tristan's shin, then started removing his shoes so he could swim easier.

"Do you want some help looking for the pack?" Dr. Gallagher asked.

"This little thing won't shed enough light for more than the person holding it," Max replied. "I might need some help hauling the pack back here, though, if I do find it. It's sure to be waterlogged. Sure, come along if you want."

Max and Gallagher slipped back into the water and swam back toward the hidden entrance.

"Max!" Tristan called. "Don't do anything stupid, like trying to go back outside and find more of those nuggets." He wasn't really joking. The idea was something Max might be capable of entertaining.

"Don't worry. I have no intention of ever setting eyes on that beast again."

The small light grew dimmer as Max and Dr. Gallagher swam farther away.

Rachel retrieved a small PentaPur cup from her knapsack, and dipped up a cup full of water. She let the water drain through the iodine and resin filter to kill the bacteria and other microorganisms, then rinsed out her mouth. She refilled the cup for Tristan and offered him a drink.

He thanked her and sipped at the water. Neither of them spoke for several minutes. Rachel soon began to find this silence uncomfortable.

"I haven't ever asked why you thought the Moroccan map was real," she said.

"Blind luck, I suppose. It turned out the kid who found it lived near the town of Volubilis. That's an old Roman site with a lot of partially intact mosaics, forums, columns and the like. I did a little research and found out the local inhabitants call the town by a different name: Ksar Faraoun, 'Pharaoh's Palace.' Berber legend has it that the original site was constructed by an Egyptian Pharaoh. That was enough to intrigue me. Local kids bring in a lot of fakes to the antique dealers, but real artifacts turn up, now and then, too. I knew it wasn't a botched map of Egypt, like the dealer thought. Gallagher's translations helped fill in a lot of details."

"The three of you seem such odd companions."

"It's a marriage of convenience. This is the first time I've worked with Gallagher. Max continues to be a necessary evil."

"I believe the evil part."

Tristan didn't respond. A few more moments passed, and the silence again became awkward.

"I was surprised to learn that you were from Quebec," Rachel said, lamely. She was just making conversation, to break the awkwardness and to keep her mind off the events of the past half-hour. "I can hear a bit of an accent, but it sounds more British than French."

"I grew up in Kenya, near the Aberdares. My grandparents were British Kenyans. After independence, my father feared a black backlash against white landowners, so he sold his farm to the government and moved us all to Canada."

"How old were you?"

"About nineteen or twenty, I guess. Few people notice an accent."

"I have a knack for that kind of thing. And now? Do you still live in Canada?"

"When I'm not on one of these little excursions I spend a lot of time in New York, Los Angeles, Toronto…but home is a little cottage in a place called Neuville. Ever heard of it?"

Rachel shook her head apologetically.

"It's a small city on the St. Lawrence, between Trois Rivieres and Quebec. I don't spend much time there. I'm out on one expedition after another, whenever I can arrange it that way."

"That's hard for me to imagine, based on what I've experienced during this one. How much worse has this been than normal? Aside from almost being bitten in half."

"No, that part hardly ever happens," he admitted. "Max and I have been snake-bit and had spears chucked at us a few times. This was a first for poison darts. Mutinous porters are fairly common. That's why we started with so many men, and why we still were able to carry most of what we really needed without much trouble after the desertions. I always count on a few drop outs."

"Six dead. Is that very routine?"

The smile vanished. "No. We've had a couple of casualties here and there, over the years. It's part of the trade-off, but nothing like this. I should have known better. This isn't the first team to disappear in these parts."

"What do you mean?"

"There was a combined French and American expedition into a valley not twenty or thirty miles south of here, back in 1972. They disappeared. Without a trace. Later, a story developed that Machiguenga Indians killed them all. Most of them were still very unfriendly to outsiders back then. Now, I'm not so sure that's what really happened."

"I'm sorry. I didn't mean to imply that it was your fault…"

"No, that's all right. I am to blame, at least in part, for the two killed by the poison darts. I should have known better than to have so many of us collected together out in the open like sitting ducks. I knew we were in a territory where the Indians tend to be hostile. I shouldn't have let you wade around in the underbrush looking for the tunnel, either. Everybody else came here willingly and was paid a price to take risks. I almost got you killed, too."

"I knew about the Indians and the other dangers, beforehand. My brother is more important than any of that. Anyway, you've saved my life at least twice. You make a decent enough knight in gleaming armor for an old bachelor."

"I'm 41, and I *was* married...just not anymore."

"Oh...I'm sorry...I hope that wasn't insensitive." *You just had to ask, didn't you?*

"It was a long time ago. I was too young...back before I knew what I was really looking for in life. By the time I found out, I had a disillusioned wife who didn't understand, and who wouldn't put up with my frequent absences. Besides, I suppose it all worked out for the best."

"Because it leaves you free to pursue lost treasures?"

"No, because it leaves me free to be *alive*. Working with Max is just one way of going about it. This is what I do...what I *like* to do. It's not really the lure or the reward of the treasure, for me. The adventure along the way is what grabs me. I could never live in a big house, stacked full of the kind of expensive stuff Max collects, and I'm uncomfortable around crowds. My little cottage is simple and isolated. I like that. There's not that much I really need, but I have to depend on Max to finance these expeditions. My part of the bargain is to try to sniff out the dangers and avoid them. As long as I can avoid any bloodletting, a little blood stirring is what keeps me going. This time, things just came unraveled."

"It doesn't bother you that Max is robbing a culture of its ancient heritage, whenever he takes an artifact out of a country?"

"You mean rather than having a corrupt local governmental official sell it to him? Or perhaps having it safely wind up catalogued in a protective box, in a museum warehouse somewhere? I can't begin to tell you how many really beautiful artifacts I've helped find that nobody except a couple of professors will ever see again. Sorry. I just can't subscribe to that crusade. I see it from both sides, so I mostly keep a neutral position."

Rachel thought Tristan's voice changed as he spoke the last few sentences. Like he was embarrassed. *My God,* she realized. *He keeps some of the artifacts, too.* Her question had been little more than a condemnation in disguise. She probably wasn't going to change Tristan's mind, and it hadn't been her intent to accuse him, so she decided to drop the subject altogether. He probably thought she was blaming him for everything. Max probably deserved that kind of blame, but Tristan was largely responsible for the rest of them still being alive.

"Up there on the canyon wall, you were very brave, going out ahead as the fall guy for all those traps. That and the…Am-mit, or whatever we're supposed to call it. I imagine that stirred your blood enough for this trip."

Rachel grimaced as Tristan frowned and shifted uneasily.

"Your leg is hurting badly?"

"Yes, but that wasn't what caused me to squirm. Suddenly, it just got a little uncomfortable up there on that pedestal you created. There's a fine line between being brave and being foolish. My problem is that I've never been able to tell where that line is. What little I know about surviving out here has been learned as the result of mistakes I've made during earlier expeditions. Sometimes at quite a cost—like this time. You're the one who's shown a lot of courage. You've had a bow and arrow aimed straight at your heart, been bitten by a poisonous snake, vampire bat and leeches. You were left behind and sealed up in the tunnels, and now as you've already pointed out, nearly eaten by a creature that nobody even thought was real! You never bargained for any of this."

"What can I say? It's a jungle out there."

Tristan smiled. "It is. Many men I've known wouldn't have held up as well as you have out here."

"You're sweet to say so, but I don't feel like I've been holding up. Besides, what's an old snake bite or bat bite, compared to yours? It looks awful!"

"Just a flesh wound."

"Well, it'll make some pretty impressive scars to show off in the locker room."

It suddenly dawned on Rachel that she had no idea of what Tristan did when not on an expedition. "Surely, you must have some other means of supporting yourself, besides running around jungles with Max?"

"Yeah. When I'm able to, I work as a literary agent."

"You review books?"

"No, no. I represent writers who are trying to get their books published."

"Don't you have to be in an office on a regular basis to do something that?"

Tristan hesitated, as if exploring the question for the first time. "Well…I have an assistant," he replied. "Most of the work is easy. She just opens the mail, trashes queries or submissions that don't have return postage, and stamps and returns most of the rest of it as 'not interested.' Follow me?"

"Yeah, but I don't see how you can make any money at that."

"Well…she holds the good stuff until I get back. That's rarely more than six to eight weeks. That's when the real work starts. I guess I probably don't spend enough time at it to be very successful."

"Oh," Rachel said. Some of her disappointment must have crept into her voice. She'd imagined him doing something different. She couldn't say what, exactly…

"It's not like it's sleazy or anything."

"Oh, no…I didn't mean that it was…"

"What about you?" Tristan asked. He was suddenly anxious to change the topic.

"Oh, I'm fine. Just a few scratches and bruises. My leg's much better…"

"No, I meant I've been telling you my life's story. It's your turn. What's Rachel Aguila like when she isn't off frolicking in the underworld? How is it, for instance, that you haven't married and started a family?"

"Oh, I've been way too busy for that," Rachel answered, a bit uncomfortable with the question. She'd scarcely even dated since the death of her fiancé. "I've been working on one degree after another for about the past ten years. It hasn't left much time for socializing."

Rachel paused for a moment. She didn't often reveal much about her life, but something about the mood and the moment compelled her to continue.

"When I was living in California, there was this guy. Doug was his name. We dated all through high school and into college. We probably would've gotten married. He was killed in a car accident."

"Sorry," Tristan murmured.

"It was a long time ago. Ironic, though. I'm the one who was always the risk-taker, the one who scuba-dived and traveled to far-off developing countries where freakish accidents happen too often, and terrorists run amuck. Doug was just going for pizza. Somebody ran a stop sign."

That had been the year before Rachel's first field study trip to the Brazilian Amazon. Her father's death had been the primary catalyst that had shifted Rachel's objectives and career plans. Doug's death had been the clincher.

"Besides, I was mostly a tomboy growing up, I guess. I've never been altogether comfortable with the thought of settling into the traditional feminine roles of wife and mother. I've always been full of far too much curiosity to settle for that."

"I suppose it's not for everybody. So, instead, you started your climb up the academic ladder?"

Rachel nodded. "My father was an anthropologist. He was always extremely proud that I was following in his footsteps. After he died, I made myself a promise that I'd finish my Ph.D. Lately, however, I've started to wonder if I haven't 'leaned my ladder against the wrong wall.'"

"Joseph Campbell?"

"Yeah," she replied, a little surprised that Tristan had recognized the quote. *I don't even know who I really am, myself*, she thought,…*much less be able to describe it for you.* The previous semester, Rachel had been asked by an instructor to describe the one most important thing people should know about her. After fumbling around for an appropriate response, she had finally answered "I'm very conscientious." That simple question, and her subsequent failure to produce a satisfying answer, produced a state of depression that still lingered. *Who am I supposed to be?* thought Rachel. She wondered if she wore the question externally, like some sort of garment. She was glad it was dark enough that Tristan couldn't see her face too well.

Tristan mistook Rachel's introspection, and instead thought she was waiting for a comment. "I've never cared much for climbing any of those ladders, myself," he said.

The remark took Rachel a bit by surprise. It occurred to her that she had never really stopped to think whether the professional career model might not be working that well for men. Kenny was an obvious exception to that model, but most men sure seemed to spend a lot of time talking wistfully about retirement. Had her father been happy with his career?

Tristan must be a lot like her Carson-namesake, reflected Rachel. Full of an adventurous spirit, confident, rugged, brave…and quiet. Quiet like a panther, graceful and deadly, all in one. In the darkness of the cavern, she suddenly became aware of how close she was sitting to Tristan. He was silent again; only inches away and seemingly lost in an intense scrutiny of Rachel's shadowed silhouette. For a brief instant, she thought he might be about to reach out or kiss her, but just as suddenly, the spell was broken.

The distraction was the splashing of water as Max and Dr. Gallagher made their way back toward the ledge.

"Any luck?" Tristan called.

"You betcha," Max's reply echoed. "We found the pack. It got washed inside, just like us."

When the two men reached the ledge, Tristan helped them haul the heavy water-soaked pack up onto the ledge. Max removed several items, among them the stone tablets, before locating the antiseptic ointment. This he applied liberally to the wounds. Max wrapped the leg more thoroughly this time, and tied off the ends of the cloth to keep it from coming off.

"That will have to do for now, pal."

"Thanks," Tristan said. "So, Dr. Gallagher...you think this cavern leads to a Seventh Door?"

"Where else could it lead? With the pier here, and a mention in the translation of the *Sektet* funerary barge, it would seem to make sense. I'm afraid the book with Sir Wallis' translation is outside in the canyon stream...still inside my backpack. Besides, I know it fairly well. Just not all the fine details."

"I hope you remember enough. No one's likely to volunteer to go back for it," Tristan said.

"Maybe we should rest up here a while, then I could swim on ahead with the light and find out what's up ahead?" Max suggested.

Gallagher volunteered to accompany Max again, when the time came. For the next couple of hours the group alternately catnapped and brainstormed. No one suggested a better plan than Max's original idea.

Max and Gallagher slipped back into the water. They waded away from the pier and began to make their way farther into the cavern. The light was still barely visible, when Max shouted back to Tristan and Rachel.

"There's another pier. This one has a boat!"

Rachel peered into the gloomy darkness in their direction anxiously, as Max and the professor loosened the vessel from the second pier.

"It even has oars," Dr. Gallagher called.

The light slowly returned toward Rachel and Tristan. Dr. Gallagher tossed a rope to Rachel, when they were close enough, and Rachel helped guide the boat alongside the pier. The carved bow resembled a serpent's head. The sides bore a wavy pattern apparently intended to resemble an anaconda.

"Maybe it's my imagination, but this boat doesn't look very old," Tristan noted.

"It's creepy," Rachel said, shivering as she thought of the giant reptilian creatures they had already seen, and Felipe's watery death.

"It's hard to tell how old a vessel like this is, in this light," Dr. Gallagher said. "The style is reminiscent of the barges found buried in the canals near the Giza pyramids, only smaller. I can't say without better light. I still think a wooden boat like this would rot within a hundred years. A leak would have sprung in the hull in much less time than that. I agree with Tristan. This one is in much too good a condition."

"Time for a new plan," Max announced. "I say we get moving in case whoever left it here is still alive. Better not stick around to find out. The boat's big enough for all four of us. What do you say to all of us heading up the other direction and seeing what we find? If nothing else, we can sleep in the boat."

All four of them agreed on the new plan. They loaded Max's and Rachel's waterlogged packs onto the boat, then helped Tristan on board. When everyone was settled, Max and Gallagher took the oars and started to row. The boat glided slowly away from the first pier, and up to the second one. As they approached, Max picked up the small divelight and shined the light so the others could see the pier more clearly.

"Get a look at the statues in the wall," Max said.

Three more of the stone figures, like those from the two Arit chambers, stared blindly toward the underground river. All had human bodies, but each with a different representation for the head.

"The one with the two stalks coming from the head is supposed to be a hare," Dr. Gallagher explained. "The others are a lion and a man. They're described in the Papyrus of Ani. This is the seventh Arit."

The statues faded back into the blackness as the boat drifted farther along, down into the belly of the subterranean cavern and its dark, Stygian river.

Chapter Nineteen

ufa arek, maketu sma ?a: "Come forth then, verily hast thou been examined"

✶✶✶✶

Ucupacha Valley, Madre de Dios Jungle, Monday afternoon,
February 23

A slight current drew the boat deeper into the cavern. Max and Dr. Gallagher made an occasional sweep with the oars, but mostly allowed the boat to drift silently in the darkness. Max's pack contained one of the lanterns and a cigarette lighter, but both the lantern's mantle and the lighter's flint were too wet to be of use. The remaining flashlight in the backpack had a watertight seal and was still in working order.

Max had lost one of the rifles in the current beneath the falls, and the remaining firearms were all useless. Gallagher and Tristan had held onto the pistol and other rifle, but both weapons would require disassembly and drying before they would fire again. That wouldn't be possible until they were outside in the sunlight. That left them with one machete, which had also been in the pack, and two hunting knives that hung from Tristan's and Max's belts.

Never was gloom a more fitting name than for the murky obscurity and stillness that had enveloped the four drifting survivors. With no outward distraction to draw Rachel's eye, her attention turned inward and her connection to the moment waned. She began worrying again about what might have really happened to Kenny. Rachel didn't realize she had dozed off until the sound of the men's voices woke her.

"There's another pier coming up," Dr. Gallagher explained, "with two small canoes and another boat like this one."

Max and Tristan were trying to decide what to do. The underground cavern continued past the pier. A stone staircase was visible in the wall behind the pier. The steps spiraled upward into the wall of the cavern and out of sight.

Their choices were simple. They could float on past and find out where the river led. The "up" side of that option was that the underground river might flow from the cavern and empty into the Río Pinquina. The "down" side was that there might not be a visible or usable exit, besides this stairway. There was the high probability that the cavern might just lead back to a different location in the same canyon, or into a deadly whirlpool. An unknown factor for the stairway option was the tribe of Indians who inhabited the area above. Circumstances suggested that they did not welcome visitors. Alternatively, they could give them some much-needed help. Max and Tristan decided to explore the stairway first, and see where it led. Rowing back to this pier would be difficult against the current, so now was the best opportunity.

The men moved the boat alongside the others and tied it to a mooring post. They left most of the items on the boat, but took the lantern, antiseptic ointment for Tristan's leg and a machete. Max hid the Moroccan tablets in the bow of the boat. Rachel stuck the Tet of Carnelian into an inside pocket of her still damp jacket and discarded her knapsack. The amulet had acted as a sort of key, once already. It was worth taking along, just in case. The guns were still useless, so they were left behind.

Max discovered a second set of steps at the opposite end of the pier. The two stairways appeared to spiral, one within the other, upward through the rock wall. Rachel thought that this looked familiar, like a DNA helix model, but it was Dr. Gallagher who remembered that a similar double spiral had been designed by Leonardo da Vinci into the staircase of the Chateau Chambord. Rachel then remembered having seen the same staircase. As she recalled, a person who headed up one set of the steps could avoid encountering anyone who was descending the opposite set. For some reason, she was still unable to dispel her sense of déja-vu.

Max suggested that Tristan could stay behind on account of the wounds to his leg. Tristan didn't think much of that idea. He said that the wounds were superficial and wouldn't hinder him. If they ran into trouble, the group would need all the help they could get.

Which of the twin staircases they picked didn't seem to matter, so Max chose the nearest, and the four battered survivors began the climb.

****

Madre de Dios Jungle, Monday, February 23

Kenny turned the plane in the direction of the Manu River. He was becoming doubtful that he would be able to spot the expedition. The only signs he ever saw of human presence were on the rivers. Whenever he spotted more than one canoe in the same place, he brought the plane in as low as he dared over the water to get a better view of the occupants. All that he had done so far was to confuse or startle an occasional group of Indians moving up or downstream. None of the canoes carried anyone who slightly resembled a white-skinned explorer, male or female.

He realized that there was a point where he would have to give up the search. Amasu was content to give it a few more days. Kenny was paying the old man well, and asking for little in return. He decided to stick it out until the following Wednesday or Thursday.

****

"Doesn't this just beat everything?" Max marveled. "Somebody has gone to a hell of a lot of trouble tunneling around down here."

The four had climbed about the equivalent of three stories when the stairway terminated in a chamber. Rachel was having a problem with her sense of orientation. Sometimes it had almost felt like the group was descending, even though the steps led upward. At other times, the steps sloped perceptibly to one side. This sensation began to upset Rachel's balance, and by the time they came to the next chamber, she was starting to feel a little nauseous again. Three new stairwells exited from this chamber. Two spiraled upward. The other led down.

"That must be the other stairway from the pier," Max noted, indicating the other set that went down. He chose the upward leading opening to their right and they resumed their climb.

After a while, Tristan commented on the same phenomenon that Rachel was experiencing. Gallagher and Max had felt the same thing, but had thought it was just exhaustion and dizziness from winding around inside the stairway.

After another short while they exit to another chamber. This one was identical with the first. They took a short break to let the dizziness wear off, before continuing.

Rachel wondered exactly how long it would be before they would emerge into the open. Did the steps lead all the way to the top of the canyon wall?

When the stairway ended, they were all in for a surprise. The exit led back out onto a stone wharf, much like the one where they had started!

"Do you think this river spirals inside the mountain?" Dr. Gallagher asked.

"Maybe. Everything looks the same as the other pier," Max replied.

Tristan walked across the rock pier to the boats. "That's because it is. There's our stuff in the boat. We're back to the exact place where we started."

"But how?" Dr. Gallagher asked. "We must have climbed those steps for nearly an hour. We came out of the same stairwell that we went into, and at the same level?"

"The stairs must lead through a maze, and use some sort of optical illusion," Tristan suggested. "They must lead down sometimes when it *seems* to be heading up. Follow me?"

"If it's a maze anything like the one beneath Cuzco, then we might as well give up on it," Rachel said. "Before it was sealed off, almost everyone who entered wound up hopelessly lost and never made it back out."

"I'm inclined to agree," Tristan said. "I think we should go ahead and follow the river. We gave this option a shot, and it doesn't look promising. Let's see where the river leads."

"I'm afraid we might not have that choice anymore," Max said, quietly.

"Why's that?" Rachel challenged.

"Because we have company." Max was looking toward the stairways. His three companions now also turned in that direction.

Facing them from the foot of the nearer stairs were seven Indians, some armed with poised spears, others with bows and arrows. As they watched, five more warriors appeared from the second stairway.

Rachel stared at the Indians in fascination. They were lighter-skinned than most of the Indians in Peru and, unlike the naked forest tribes, these wore colorful tunics and thin metal shin, wrist and breastplates. In addition, most wore brightly colored, feathered necklaces, and large spools through pierced openings in their ears. While their outward appearance was far more civilized than the forest Indians, their demeanor and postures were no less menacing. This was no friendly welcoming committee.

One of the warriors stepped forward. The only thing distinguishing him from the others was his bronze-tipped spear. The spearhead bore elaborately incised iconographic design motifs.

"*¿Mayqentaq hamawt'aykichisri?*" the warrior asked.

Rachel understood the question as a dialect of Quechua. She pointed at Max. "*Paymi*," she replied. "He asked who was the leader. They're speaking Quechua. That should be a good sign."

"*¿Maymantan hamurqankichis?*" asked the warrior, directing the question to Max.

"*Manan pipas runasimita rimanchu. Nuqayku chinchaymantan hamuyku. Nuquayku khumpaykichismi kayku,*" Rachel answered. "He asked where we come from. I told him none of you speak their language, and that we come from the North, and are friends."

"*Manan qankuna khumpaskunachu kankichis. ¡Qankumaqa mana riqsisqa mistikuna kankichis, qhamiyaqmi!*"

"I guess I'm going to have to eat my words. He says we're not friends. He says we're outsiders...spies."

"*¡Patapataman siqaykichis!*" ordered the warrior, pointing toward the stairs.

"Better do as they say, for now," Max said. "I'm sure we can straighten it all out, once they see we mean no harm."

"*¡Utqhay!*" the warrior ordered, this time brandishing his spear.

The rest of the group didn't need to hear the translation to understand that the Indian meant for them to get moving immediately. Rachel and the three men started toward the door. Two of the other Indians stepped forward and removed the knives from the scabbards hanging at Max's and Tristan's belt. Another took the machete from Max.

The group again started up the stairwell, this time as prisoners. An Indian warrior with a spear flanked each one of the captives. Escape was out of the question.

The Indians were obviously familiar with which sets of steps to take. Sometimes they appeared to head downward, but then wound up in another room where the leader would choose a set that led upward. For a while Rachel tried to remember the way. Soon, however, she gave it up, as the details became hopelessly confusing. She wondered how the Indians could possibly keep it straight. Perhaps some small markings above the correct openings provided a clue. If so, it wasn't at all obvious unless one knew what to look for. She looked closely, but could see nothing.

At some point in the next hour, they went through a chamber that served as a guard post. Several other Indians of similar appearance were present in this room. A couple of these carried identical bronze-tipped spears as the leader of the group escorting the captives. It wasn't until a half-hour later, after finishing a climb to yet another guardroom, that Rachel paid closer attention to the bronze spearheads. Each bore a grooved design motif that was vaguely familiar.

Suddenly, Rachel realized why she recognized the design. The Tet of Carnelian, inside her jacket pocket, was carved in an almost identical fashion. She would very much have liked to take it out and compare the markings, but didn't dare. Thinking about the Tet's curvilinear patterns also made Rachel realize what had caused her earlier sense of déja-vu. The patterns spiraled around the carnelian cylinder with parallel grooves that never intersected, much in the same way as the staircases. Might the Tet serve as a map of this underground maze? The carved piece of carnelian had already proved to unlock one of the previous puzzles the expedition had encountered in this "*Tuat*" underworld. Were the markings on the bronze spearheads also maps? She waited to see if the leader glanced at the markings the next time they came to a choice of openings.

When the opportunity next arose, Rachel was nearly certain that the Indian hesitated for a brief second to study the spearhead, before choosing the next staircase. She could be wrong, but if the occasion presented itself to make a getaway, she planned to make sure one of the expedition members got their hands on one of those spears. The Tet's markings might be different.

All this climbing caused Rachel to remember how it used to be possible to reach the top of the Eiffel Tower by way of the steps. Only the young and stalwart had an inclination to do so, as the top level is roughly a thousand feet in height. Rachel had once done this with Kenny, and remembered how tiring the climb had been. In comparison, the top of the canyon wall had been roughly fifteen hundred feet above the valley floor. With all the winding detours that the maze forced the group to follow, Rachel noted that the climb took a little less than two hours. By the time the Indians brought them to a halt, Rachel felt like she had climbed the Eiffel Tower twice. She hoped they were at the top. Her leg had mostly healed, but the stairway ascent had punished her muscles to the point that she could hardly remain standing.

"*Qankuna Kayllapi suyaykichis.*"

"We're supposed to wait here," Rachel translated.

The four exhausted captives slumped to the stone floor. The climb had taken them through four separate guardrooms, and ended at this larger chamber. The Indian leader exited by another door. The other Indians remained to guard the captives.

"Can you tell what tribe they are?" Max asked.

"No. As I said, they speak Quechua. Occasionally, I think I also heard them use some Aymara words."

"Could they be an isolated and forgotten branch of the Inca?" Tristan wondered. "Maybe they've remained cut off from the rest of the world for all these centuries. Look at their clothing and weapons. That would also explain why they speak Quechua."

"I'm ready to agree with anything, at this point," Rachel answered. The same thought had already occurred to her, but she wasn't ready to jump to conclusions. "I wouldn't go by the language alone, though. Quechua is still spoken by over eight million people in South America."

One of the Indians spoke sharply and brandished a spear in their direction.

"No more talking," Rachel whispered.

The four sat in silence, until the Indian with the bronze-tipped spear returned. He gestured for the captives to come with him.

They followed the Indian through the door and down a corridor. The guards accompanied them. The group entered through a doorway and found themselves in another large chamber.

As Rachel stepped inside, she glanced around in awe. The entire room was furnished with resplendent objects of all sorts, the predominant material being gold. The floor covering was made of dozens of overlapping jaguar pelts. Pitchers and goblets of gold and silver rested on circular wooden tables, inlaid with lapis lazuli and other colored semi-precious materials. Trees, plated in gold, down to the individual leaves, stood in each corner. Their branches were host to sculpted birds of silver and copper. Platters, tubs, wall decorations, statues and other objects of precious metals or gemstones rested in various places about the room. Against the far wall, upon a foot-high platform covered with the furs of rare black panthers, rested a relatively simple throne. Over the armrests were draped multi-colored fabrics onto which hundreds of small feathers had been sewn, arranged by color in dazzling rows of red, green, yellow, and blue. Two windows flanked the throne, allowing sunlight and a slight breeze to drift through the room.

Seated upon the throne was an elderly Indian. He was adorned in a multi-colored tunic, richly decorated with gold and jeweled platelets. Around his neck, hung a pendant fashioned in the shape of a stylized puma or jaguar's head, with curling fangs typical of Inca artwork. Golden ear spools, ringed by small down feathers of every hue, hung in the pierced and stretched lobes of his ears. At his waist, attached to a wrapped fabric cloth, Rachel noted a "*khipu*," a sort of Inca abacus, made of knotted cords. Finally, around the old Indian's forehead was a cloth-covered ring. At the front of the ring, hanging directly over the man's forehead and eyes, were dozens of strands of red string.

Rachel immediately recognized the headpiece as the Scarlet Fringe, the traditional Inca crown.

The Indian warrior who had guided them to this room told them to kneel. Rachel numbly complied. This was overwhelming. Here was a group of Inca Indians, possibly including a direct descendant of one of the great Inca emperors, still living in total isolation in the middle of the Madre de Dios jungle. The expedition had come looking for ruins. Never had any of them expected an inhabited Inca city.

"*¿Runasimita rimankichu?*" Apparently, one of the guards had already had told him that only Rachel spoke their language. The Inca directed the question to her.

"*Arí. Pisichallatan,*" Rachel answered.

"*¿Maymantan hamurqankichis? ¿Qankuna sapallaykichischu kankichis?*"

Rachel confirmed, in response to the Inca's question, that there were only the four of them, and that they came from the far North.

"*¿Mayman qankuna rishanki? ¿Imaynan qankuna mach'ayman hamurqankichis?*"

The Inca was naturally very curious about his captives. Now, he asked her where they were heading, how they had come to be in the cavern.

"*Nuqayku wayq'u mantan lluqsimuyku.*" We came out from the canyon. Rachel continued to speak in Quechua. She told the Inca ruler that they were looking for her brother, or "*turay,*" who had become lost in the jungle. She told him how the expedition had started with more men...how five had turned back, and how a tribe of unknown Indians had killed two members of their group along the way. They had entered the cavern by accident from behind the waterfall as they were trying to escape the *runa mikjuj,* the man-eater that had killed two more of their companions.

"*Biba,*" the Inca nodded. "*Biba nisqan Chinkanata qhawan.*"

"He calls the creature 'Biba,'" Rachel explained to the others. "He says Biba guards the hidden place."

"Biba is one of the names for Am-mit," Dr. Gallagher confirmed.

"*Payqan ch'irwayun. ¿Imanarqunmi chakanta?*" Olca asked, pointing at Tristan's bloodied and bandaged leg.

"*Biba nisqanmi chakantaqa kachurqun,*" Rachel replied, telling him that the beast called Biba had bitten Tristan's leg and that was why he was limping. The Inca ruler looked almost amused at the news. Rachel decided to ask the Inca what city this was.

Olca waved off the question impatiently, answering curtly that it was the home of the Inca. Rachel saw from his expression that she should not press her luck. The old ruler examined the four captives for several moments in silence, ending with a prolonged study of Rachel.

The Inca then directed a question, not to Rachel, but to the Indian guards.

"He asked who accuses us," Rachel translated. "That doesn't sound good…"

The warrior who had led the captives up from the subterranean cavern stepped forward. He was holding the two Moroccan tablets, which he held aloft. Rachel thought about the Tet stuck inside her jacket pocket. None of the guards had bothered to search her.

"*¡Mana riqsisqa mistikunatan huchachani! ¡Paykunaqa qhamiyaqmi! Mana riqsisqa mistikunaqa pistakun kanku. Rumi sunquyuqkunaqa runakumatan wañuchinku, laqq'u chinku. Mana riqsisqa mistikunaqa unaymantapachan runakunata ñak'arichinku.*"

"This fellow either *really* doesn't like us, or is playing out some sort of role," Rachel explained. "He says we are all spies, demon predators. He says that we are cruel hearts who murder and deceive the Inca people. He says that outsiders have made the people suffer since the beginning of time."

"*Ayllu kamachiqcha paykunaata kuskachanqa,*" the Inca ruler said, standing. "*¡Ch'ankana wasipi paykunata wisq'anqa!*"

"We're to be judged by a council of some sort," Rachel said. "Meanwhile, he's told the guards to take us away and to keep us under guard"

Chapter Twenty

aria nek xut setat em nutk p?wt titi:
"I have made for thee a hidden horizon in the city of thy primeval image."
-Unexplained inscription from the second tablet

****

"The Hidden Place," Monday night, February 23

Rachel had intended to appeal to the Inca ruler, to explain that this was all some sort of colossal mistake. She took a step forward. A dozen guards immediately surrounded her and the three other captives. Rachel was suddenly staring at three spearheads, inches from her face.

"Talk to them, Rachel," Max ordered. "Explain things. These Indians are obviously more civilized than the Yaminhua and Hooney-Kooies. They'll listen to reason."

Rachel tried to address the Inca king, but he rose and left by another door without looking back.

The Indian guards marched the captives out of the room and back up the corridor from which they had entered. The guards led them down the spiral staircase and through another door that exited to the outside.

The sun was just beginning to set in the western sky, and narrow shafts of rose-tinted light reflected downward through the tall canopy of the treetops above. Though the light was already quite dim, Rachel was able to discern much of their surroundings. What she saw caused her and the other three captives to stop short in their tracks. They had exited onto an immense courtyard. As large as a principal plaza of many a modern city, the courtyard was paved in its entirety, except around the base of each tree that rose from the courtyard. The treetops thoroughly hid the city from aerial view. Elephant-eared plants, ferns and beautiful flowers that prospered in low-light conditions grew alongside the buttress roots of each tree. Masterfully carved stone benches sat near many of these. Many large rectangular buildings, erratically splashed with a soft pinkish glow from the waning sun, were partially visible at the edges of the plaza. There were also several smaller circular structures. Rachel believed it to be one of the most beautiful places she had ever seen.

Rachel was jerked back to reality by the sharp prod of a spear between her shoulder blades. The guard forced her to resume her way across the plaza. Rachel estimated that over a hundred people moved about the great tree-canopied square. Some were crossing, others entering or exiting buildings, and still others collected here and there in small conversational groups. All who spotted the captives being escorted across the plaza stopped to gawk in fascination. It was difficult to tell who was more astonished—the captives or the jungle city's inhabitants.

Near the center of the square, an incredibly huge egg-shaped white boulder drew Rachel's attention. Resting in the heart of the plaza was a ceremonial "*ushnu*," a large rectangular platform constructed of many square-cut stones. The huge boulder rested on top of, or more accurately, nestled inside this platform. She recognized the boulder as a "*huancauri*" or "*yuraq rumi*" stone. The Incas of old had treated such boulders as sacred. They were common at Inca ruins around Peru, but this one was immense. Rachel wondered at how in the world it had come to be located atop this isolated jungle plateau. On the sides of the ushnu platform were large petroglyphs of panthers or jaguars.

Max and Tristan also saw the carved designs and glanced at each other in acknowledgment. Gran Paititi!

The guards led the four captives into one of the rectangular buildings and down a flight of stairs. Upon entering a room guarded by two more warriors, the men were directed to descend a ladder to a subterranean cell. Once Dr. Gallagher, Tristan and Max were all below, the guards removed the ladder.

"Don't worry," Tristan called. "We'll get another chance to talk to their chief. If they were going to kill us, they'd have already done it." Tristan knew this to be little more than hopeful thinking, but such was all that he could offer.

The remaining Indians then led Rachel to another nearby room. Except for one guard posted at the one exit, the Indians withdrew, leaving Rachel alone. A narrow slot high upon one wall served as a window, and a small bench stood in the center of the room; otherwise the room was empty. Rachel looked up at the window, through which the fleeting light of the day was barely visible. Even if she had anywhere she could go, the window was much too small to permit an escape. Dejectedly, Rachel sat on the bench and awaited fate's next blow.

****

In the men's cell, the three captives spoke excitedly in hushed tones.

"This *has* to be Paititi!" Max avowed. "Did you see the jaguars carved out there in the square? And the jaguar face on the king's necklace? There must have been a million dollars' worth of treasure in that one chamber alone. There's no telling how much more is in the rest of the palace or in these other buildings. This is it. The big one…the mother of all jackpots!"

"Are you completely insane?" Tristan asked. "Haven't you noticed how outnumbered we are? We'll be extraordinarily lucky to get out of this alive. Even if we could overpower the guards and make a run for it, we'd have to cross the plaza in plain sight to get back to the stairs. Even then, we don't know how to find our way back down the maze to the cavern. The guards would have all the time they need to recapture us. There can't be any question of stacking even more cards against us by anyone, including you, trying to steal anything!"

"I didn't mean *now*. I'm talking about returning, when the odds are more in our favor. You're right. For the moment, we have to play this extremely cool. But if we can convince these primitives that we're harmless, we're home free. We must be nearly sitting on top of the Río Pinquina. We can follow it back to Boca Manu. Now that we know the secret of how to get here, we can come back for the treasure. We'll get good men…as many as we need. We'll bring a bazooka…better yet a missile launcher! We'll blow that saber-tooth Am-mit thing, or whatever it was, straight to hell…along with anything else that gets in our way."

"You *have* lost your mind. You sound like you're planning a small war!" exclaimed Tristan. "Count me out. First, we don't know this jungle a fraction as well as the Indians do. We can't hide in these forests, like they can. Second, have you even thought about what you're describing? This isn't the Wild West. You can't just come in here, guns blazing, taking whatever you feel like. Even if that scenario doesn't bother you, the Peruvian government isn't about to let you enter the Madre de Dios equipped like that. They'd be extremely interested in what you were up to. Finally, things aren't looking all that optimistic for you even getting the chance. I don't speak Quechua like Rachel does, but I know a few words and phrases. From what I could pick up, and what Rachel translated, we're in a whole lot of trouble."

"We'll see…I've been waiting for something like this my whole life. I'm not getting this close, just to be thwarted by a group of savages. Damn it! If only the phone was still operational."

"What phone?" Tristan asked.

"He had an iridium telephone the whole time," Dr. Gallagher answered. "That's the first thing he checked when we swam back and fished out his pack in the cavern. The phone was ruined, of course."

Tristan's blue eyes widened in accusation.

"You sorry son of a bitch! Why didn't you tell me earlier that you had one of those things with you? We might have been able to arrange an evacuation for Dr. Ramón and Rachel."

"Be realistic," Max said. "There wasn't anywhere a rescue plane or chopper could have landed. There wasn't any point in trying. I also didn't want Rachel to see it. She would've been nagging me every five minutes to call the Guardia Civil and check on her brother. The battery would have gone dead, the first day. What difference does it make? The phone's useless now, like Gallagher says. Ruined. We need a plan. We've probably only seen a fraction of the wealth here. They must hide the rest of the treasure underground."

"Screw the treasure," Dr. Gallagher murmured. He had his wallet out, and had been drooped over a soggy photo of his wife and children. "I just want out of this alive."

"That's what we all want," Tristan replied, looking dubiously at Max. He just hoped his partner wouldn't do anything to endanger that priority. Tristan decided something. If they got out of this alive, he'd never join Max on another expedition. The man was dangerously without conscience.

****

With the advent of darkness, another guard arrived with a torch. The flickering flame from the guards' antechamber allowed only a sliver of light into Rachel's cell. She was grateful, nonetheless, that she wasn't sitting in total darkness. She was also glad that she still had her jacket. Alone in the cell, Rachel was abnormally aware of the coolness of the night. She realized she hadn't eaten anything except some nuts and a mango in almost twenty-four hours.

She called out to the guard.

"*¿Munanki?*" he asked, leaning in through the doorway.

Rachel told the guard she was hungry. She heard him call out to someone else. After a while an Indian woman brought some food. After she had eaten, Rachel again sat in the darkness waiting. She hoped it was a good sign that it was taking so long for the Inca council to decide. At least, she hoped they were still deciding. What if the Inca ruler had made his ruling mere minutes after she entered this cell? Was the king just waiting until the next day to make his announcement? The decision would ultimately be the wish of the ruler. Councils were meaningless in cultures such as the Inca's. At the time of the Spanish conquest, the Inca Indians even considered their ruler to be a god.

Before long, Rachel had an answer. Two more warriors came to fetch her and provide an escort back to the Inca's chamber. When she entered, she saw that she was the first of the captives to arrive.

The Inca told her to come closer.

Rachel complied, approaching to within a few feet of the older man.

Olca Capac once more studied Rachel, before speaking. He stared unblinkingly at Rachel's mismatched irises. Rachel held his gaze, aware of the power of "evil eyes" in most primitive cultures. Maybe she could put this to her advantage.

Finally, the Inca spoke again, asking her who she was.

"*Sutiymi Rachel.*" She knew better than to ask the Inca's name. Although the members of the ruler's family could use it, others were forbidden to speak the Inca's name aloud.

"*Rachel...*" repeated the Inca. "*Rachel, ama llulla.*" The Inca ruler told her not to lie. He again asked where she was going, why the outsiders had come searching for him. Was she a spy?

Rachel again explained that she had come looking for her brother, but that now she was trying to return to Cuzco. She had known nothing of the Inca king. She certainly had not come as a spy, nor had her companions.

"*¿Tarirqunkiñachu turaykita?*" The Inca asked if she had found her brother yet.

Rachel told him she was still looking.

Just then, the other three captives arrived in the Inca's chamber. In addition to the guards, a younger Indian couple also entered the room. From their rich attire, Rachel gathered that they were of some importance. These two moved to the front of the room and sat at the Inca's feet.

The three captives looked no worse than normal. Tristan was limping a bit more, and Rachel noticed that their captors had not bothered to change the dressing on his wounded leg. "Are you all right?" Tristan asked her.

"I'm fine..." she answered, and was about to ask about his leg, when the Inca ruler interrupted.

Olca Capac addressed Rachel, telling her to interpret what he was about to say to the three other captives.

"*Unaymantapacahn runakunaqa chay Chinkanapin tiyanku...,*" he began, and continued on as Rachel translated.

"Since the beginning of time, the People have lived here in the Hidden Place. The first Inca, Ayar Manco Capac, came here with his brothers and sisters to find a safe haven for the '*panacas*,' the remains of many ancient ancestors. These remains were transported here from across the Great Green. To protect these deceased ancestors from those who would abominate the horizons of their burial, a great city was built upon the Chinkana. Here in the sheltered region above the gorge, the People still watch over these ancient ancestors. The surrounding territories are protected by our allies, the princes of Tchacha, and by the

Terrible One who lives below in 'Ucupacha,' the nether region. For two thousand years the People have remained hidden here in the Corner of the Dead. The Amaru descendants of the Seven, with the help of the Tchacha, spread their domain across the Manu and past the Tuat. A few remained here with the shamans. By the time of the Inca Pachacutec, the People had created a great empire. Many had lost all knowledge of the Hidden Place. This plateau became mere legend, the 'Hanan Pacha,' the place of heaven."

"Hinamanta Tayta Intiqa phiñakurqa..." continued the Inca.

"But then the sun god Inti became angry...," translated Rachel. "He sent into the Four Corners the Viracochas, a group of sorcerers who had harnessed the powers of the sun god.

The Inca ruler had resumed speaking, and Rachel hastened to keep up. "For many centuries, no outsider has set foot upon these grounds. You are the first."

With this the Inca paused and looked hard at each of the captives.

"Ayllu kamachiqqan kuskacharqan. ¡Yaw runakuna, ñuñupa hinan kankichis! ¡Viracocha!"

"The council has made its judgment. He says we are a brood of vipers. White demons." Rachel translated, her heart sinking at these ominous words.

"Qankuna paqarin phankipin wañunkichis, manataq warmiqa. Warmiqa kay Chinkanapin qhipanqa. Payqa runan kanqa."

All color left Rachel's face, and her expression as she turned to the three captives forewarned them that what she was about to translate was disastrous news.

"You will all die at the dawn of the new day...except for the woman. The woman will remain here in the Hidden Place. She will become one of the People."

Max gasped. "What the devil is he talking about? Didn't you explain things to this stupid savage? We haven't done anything to harm these

Indians. We just stumbled in here by accident. If there was ever a time for you get eloquent with that language ability of yours, now is it!"

Rachel hardly heard Max speak. She was already churning through alternatives in her mind, searching for some piece of trivia from her academic knowledge of the Inca that she could turn to their advantage. "Humane One, I beseech you," she implored. "*¡Paykunaqa mana huchayuqnmi kanku!*" They are innocent!

Olca Capac shrugged, as if to both acknowledge and dismiss Rachel's pleas.

"*Qankuna Chinkanamanta yachankichismi. Manan kawsayta atin-kichu.*"

"He's says it is impossible for us to live. We know the secret of the Hidden Place."

Max was turning red with impatience and anger. "Oh yeah? Impossible, my ass…"

"*¡Upallay!*" Olca Capac thundered. Silence! The guards swarmed onto Max, as he attempted to resist. One Indian struck Max with a curved wooden club, felling him to his knees. Several more seized Tristan as he moved instinctively to help, while others leveled spears at the befuddled Gallagher. There was nothing they could do; the Indians outnumbered them four to one in this room alone.

The Inca ruler ordered the guards to tie up the men. The guards swarmed over Rachel's companions at once in compliance, binding the three men's arms to their sides.

"Why?" Rachel protested. "For what reason?"

Olca Capac put up a hand to quiet her entreaties. It was not a request.

Rachel watched helplessly as Tristan, Max and Dr. Gallagher were again led out of the king's chamber. With the odds so great against them, resistance was useless. Even if the men had fought back successfully and escaped the guards, the captives didn't even know where within the city they were, or where to flee. Rachel tried to force her confused emotions into order, but could only remain frozen in limbo—*any* decision or action was impossible. Whatever she did would be wrong.

She listened, stunned and powerless, as Olca Capac told her not to concern herself with the fate of her three companions. She absently acknowledged the younger Inca man and woman, now introduced by the Inca king as his son and daughter. Rachel learned that Olca intended for her to become the newest bride of this son. The Inca's words barely registered on Rachel's dizzied senses. Torn between conflicting emotions of stress, she had an urgent wish to scream in frustration and anguish at the extremity of the group's current life-and-death crisis. At the same time, she felt like exploding in hysterical laughter at the implausibility of the Inca's announcement.

Even Olca Capac seemed to realize that the tide of events must be overwhelming for Rachel.

"The hour is already dark and you are tired," he told her. "You will sleep, now.

Sleep? Rachel thought. How could she sleep? She desperately needed a plan long before tomorrow arrived. Tristan, Dr. Gallagher and Max were all scheduled to die at the dawn's first light!

Entranced by the surreal surroundings and reeling from the dizzying whirl of one peril after another, Rachel followed the young Inca princess from the room.

Chapter Twenty-one

Inca pictograph: meaning unknown

Egyptian glyph Herui: Horus and Set, duality

****

"The Hidden Place," Monday night, February 23

"Sutiymi T'ika," the young Indian woman said.

"T'ika...," repeated Rachel. Flower. "What a pretty name," she added in Quechua, drawing a smile from her companion. *"Sutiymi Rachel."* T'ika led Rachel through the unfamiliar corridors to a connected building. Rachel wondered a little that only one guard accompanied them, but realized almost immediately that the Inca ruler must believe that she would not have anywhere to go. The solitary guard preceded the women, bearing a flickering torch to illuminate their way.

Rachel glanced at the walls lining the halls of the new building. These walls contained panel after panel of petroglyphs. Although several symbols were of typical Pre-Columbian appearance, those had evidently been added after the bulk of the other inscriptions. The majority of symbols bore an unmistakable resemblance to Egyptian hieroglyphics. Rachel asked T'ika who had made these inscriptions.

"Ñawpa ayllukuna," T'ika replied. The ancient ancestors.

When they arrived at the princess' apartments, Rachel saw that they were decorated much like the Inca's audience hall. In T'ika's chambers, however, were several murals that strongly resembled Egyptian artwork. In response to Rachel's further inquiries, T'ika explained that the city's artisans periodically retouched the murals as the colors deteriorated.

The young Indian princess frowned at her guest's tattered appearance. Rachel's clothes were badly torn and soiled from the flight through the forest from the Am-mit beast. Rachel caught a glimpse of her face in a polished copper mirror and realized how unkempt she must look. Her appearance was by far the least of her worries. T'ika, nonetheless, decided to remedy this situation as her most immediate task. Although Rachel believed she was alone with the princess, T'ika called out as if there was someone else present. Instantly, four young Indian maidens materialized at the recesses of the room, and Rachel realized they must have been there all along, waiting until summoned. T'ika instructed the maidens to prepare a bath.

Rachel removed her light leather jacket and placed it on the floor, in a darkened corner of the room. As in the king's audience chamber, utensils and decorative items of gold and silver were present in T'ika's quarters in abundance. Woven reed mats covered the floor here, however, rather than furs. Only a few jaguar and puma furs were visible. While the attendants prepared the bath in some other room, she looked more closely at the murals. Despite the discussions of the past week with Dr. Gallagher, she found the pictographs indecipherable. All she saw or understood in looking at them was the illustration itself. The pictures contained several human and anthropomorphic figures. One of the murals showed a group of seven people. She guessed that it was a mythological representation of the original Children of the Sun. Another showed a woman handing two wands to a man. As she looked closer, she was shocked to recognize that one of the wands was an unmistakable match with the Tet of Carnelian zipped inside her jacket.

Rachel began to spin different schemes through her mind, wherein she might offer the Tet in trade for the lives of her three companions. Nothing she came up with made much sense. The Inca ruler would just confiscate the Tet, once he knew it was in her possession. She couldn't count on his gratitude or astonishment at recovering the object. He might already possess a dozen such amulets. After what she had seen so far, it would not surprise her if he had one made of the world's largest ruby. Rachel realized that if she was going to figure out a way to stop the executions, she needed to know more.

She asked T'ika to explain the history of the murals, which the young woman did without hesitation. She was right about the Children of the Sun mural. Another turned out to show the journey across the Great Green. A third showed the weighing of the heart of someone T'ika called 'Awsar.' Rachel listened attentively to all the stories, especially when T'ika told the history behind the mural containing the Tet of Carnelian.

T'ika described how one of the sisters of Awsar presented him with two powerful amulets. Generations upon generations of the Incas had passed one of these, a staff of gold, along to their successors.

"How many cities are in the Chinkana?"

"Four," T'ika answered. "Three smaller outposts, and the main city. The Chinkana is an eye-shaped plateau, bounded by Ucupacha—the great gorge, and the home of Biba."

Rachel told T'ika that she had seen this terrible Biba. She described for the princess how the group had fled from the beast after it had killed two of their companions. This greatly impressed T'ika. She had never seen the beast. Only special warriors ever went into the gorge. The Terrible Ones killed most of their own cubs that made it to adolescence. According to the verbal history of the People, never more than four or five of the creatures co-existed at a time. T'ika explained that the People controlled the number of these animals by poisoned offerings. Occasionally, the Inca supplied the creature a human sacrifice. Usually, the victim was an Indian captured by their Tchacha allies from a nearby tribe. Other times, the sacrificial victim was chosen from the People themselves.

No wonder the creature wasn't afraid of people, thought Rachel. *It's been conditioned to view us as meals.*

Rachel asked T'ika to continue the story about the wands. T'ika told her that the golden wand that her father possessed was the same one that the great Ayar Manco had sunk into the ground at Cuzco. According to Inca legend, after the Children of the Sun emerged from the cave at Tamputocco, they traveled north. They stopped when their leader, Ayar Manco, had been able to press the golden rod a foot into the earth. Here the seven Children of the Sun built the Temple of the Sun, around which grew the city of Cuzco.

The other wand was a red crystal amulet that had the power to protect the bearer from all dangers, T'ika said. Rachel didn't volunteer the information that such power didn't apparently extend to those around the bearer, or keep one from being taken captive. T'ika explained that Ayar Manco had also brought this amulet with him. The staff had later accompanied one of the ancient ancestors back across the Great Green over three thousand years ago. An ancient prophecy foretold that the scepter would only return when the time came for the rebirth of the empire. With the disappearance of the second scepter, the cousins of the People across the Great Green had also stopped sending the remains of their kings through the secret routes into the Corner of the Dead.

The handmaidens again emerged from the shadows and signaled that the bath was ready. Rachel followed T'ika through two more richly decorated rooms, and into a small bathing chamber.

Despite the late hour and the location in the middle of a primitive jungle *tepui*, or isolated plateau, the People of Paititi did not lack some comforts, marveled Rachel. The floor of the bath chamber comprised four adjoining sets of stone steps descending to an enclosed pool of steaming water. Rachel couldn't tell if servants had brought in the water, or if a large bed of coals heated the pool from beneath the floor, as in ancient Turkish and Roman bathhouses.

Rachel allowed two of the handmaidens to help her remove her tattered clothing. She noticed that the others attended likewise to T'ika, who apparently intended to join her in the bath. Whatever the source, the method was perfect. The temperature felt wonderful and Rachel sank blissfully into the heated water.

As had happened so frequently during the past eight or nine days, Rachel became entranced by the other-worldliness of her surroundings. Here she was in an ancient bath chamber, illuminated by torchlight, attended by servants, naked and soaking next to an Inca princess in a lost city in the Amazon jungle! Rachel momentarily succeeded in suspending the more sinister aspects of her situation from her thoughts. She needed this opportunity to first clear her head, before she could think of some plan to save her companions. T'ika interrupted the trance with a question.

"*¿Chaypa iman sutin?*"

The princess had glided up next to Rachel in the water. She reached out and touched the small eagle pendant that Rachel wore around her neck. Now the four handmaidens disrobed and came into the bath with Rachel and T'ika. One began to gently scrub the dirt from Rachel's body and hair, as another dipped and rinsed water using a large golden urn. The other two did the same for T'ika. Rachel wryly reflected that this was the most crowded bath she had ever taken. She imagined how delicious her friend Trish would have found the moment. If not for the severity of her companions' plight, Rachel might have laughed.

"*Ankan*," Rachel said, answering that the small silver pendant on her necklace was an eagle. She explained that her family name was Aguila, which itself meant eagle. She told T'ika about the necklace being a gift from her father, and how her twin brother was now her only real family. She explained how her three traveling companions were helping to find her brother, but had experienced many accidents, and were now only trying to return to Cuzco.

"What am I going to do?" she asked. Perhaps if she was able to win the friendship of the princess, the young woman might intercede with her father, the Inca.

T'ika seemed to be able to relate to the situation. T'ika's brother, Atoq, was her only sibling. Rachel's misfortune saddened her, the princess said, but she was nonetheless delighted that she would soon have a new sister.

Rachel had still not given this part of her circumstances much thought. She was still far too preoccupied with the executions scheduled for the next morning.

"*¿Yanaparquwankimanchu?*" she asked T'ika. Can you help me?

The princess shook her head from side to side, and cautioned Rachel that it would be impossible to flee.

Rachel studied the Inca princess as she spoke. The young woman was probably five or six years younger than she was and exceptionally pretty. Her jet-black hair had been meticulously cared for, and cut at sharp angles that framed the delicate, yet regal features of her face. Rachel had a trim, athletic build, but she was instantly envious of the sensuous figure the princess revealed when she stepped naked into the bath. Rachel suddenly felt like she needed to go on a diet, and sank a little lower into the water. T'ika's skin color was unusually pale for a Quechua Indian. Rachel knew from her anthropological research that the Spaniards too had been surprised at the light skin of the Inca royalty. Most anthropologists agreed that the original Quechua Indians, rather than the Inca themselves, had been the indigenous inhabitants of the Cuzco Valley. No one really even knew what had been the native language of the Inca Indians. One of the kings had simply ordained Quechua as the required dialect of the entire Inca empire, and so it soon became. Rachel's first-hand experience was now pushing her to accept the Egyptian-Inca link as fact.

T'ika continued to explain the lack of Rachel's options. T'ika dared not risk her father's anger. Even the family of the ruling god-king must not question his judgments.

Rachel's face betrayed her disappointment. T'ika's sympathetic eyes mirrored some of this back to her. The princess might yet prove to be a valuable ally.

After the two women had finished their bath, Rachel followed the princess up the stone steps. There, the handmaidens toweled T'ika and Rachel dry. T'ika then led Rachel into another room where the servants had piled furs upon the floor. From one of these piles T'ika took a simple tunic that had openings for the head and arms. Handing the tunic to Rachel, the princess then donned an identical garment and reclined upon one of the piles of furs. She indicated that the other bed was for Rachel.

"*Qan sayk'usqan kashanki. Kunan puñukusunchis.*" You are tired, she told Rachel. Let us now sleep. The handmaidens began putting out the torches that illuminated the rooms and total darkness soon immersed the sleeping quarters.

Rachel did not believe for a moment that she would be able to rest. She began searching her mind once again for some piece of information or strategy that might stop the morning's executions. Despite the crisis, fatigue soon won out and she quickly drifted off to sleep.

Chapter Twenty-two

The blood of Isis, the spells of Isis, the magical powers of Isis
shall make this shining one strong, and shall be an amulet of protection
against he that would do to him the things which he abominateth...
This chapter shall be said over...

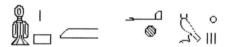

...a Tet of Carnelian
...placed on the neck of this "Shining One"
-excerpts from the Egyptian Book of the Dead

****

"The Hidden Place," Tuesday, February 24

No matter which direction Rachel went, she kept returning to the same room. She tried a different door, or a different direction up or down a stairway each time, but she always returned to the same spot! She had worked herself into a state of panic. It was urgent that she find the way out! Where was the Tet of Carnelian? Might it serve as a map of the maze? Had she forgotten it? Someone must be in pursuit by now! She was hopelessly lost! How many different doors were there? Weren't there only four exits from the room? How many times had she repeated her steps? Twenty? Thirty? Something about this line of logic, or lack thereof, caused her to realize that the situation was too unreal to be true. A sense of relief flooded across her mind as she awoke. Another dream! For a moment, she lay there re-orienting herself. Was it all a dream? The jungle, the Am-mit creature? The Inca Indians?

She groped at her sides, feeling the furs that comprised her bed. The sense of relief evaporated, and was immediately replaced by a feeling of despair. It was morning. The king had scheduled the other three captives to die at first light! She sprang to her feet. The room was still dark, and she could barely make out the other pile of furs. She didn't see T'ika. Making her way out of the room, she heard voices from another part of the princess' quarters and ran toward the sounds.

T'ika saw Rachel as she rushed up to the entry of the other room. The princess had apparently just finished her breakfast. Her face lit up with a friendly smile. "*Haykumuy. ¿Munankiñanchu ñaupaq mikunaikita?*"

Rachel ignored the offer of breakfast, and instead asked what time it was.

"*Ñan yaqa illarimuyashan panay.*" Sister, it is already almost dawn. She was surprised at her guest's sense of urgency.

"*¿Paykuna wañusqañachu kashan?* They are already dead? Rachel gasped.

"*Manaraqmi. Manan wañunqachu, inti lliphipimunkama, llapa runakuna qayllanpin.*" T'ika answered. The men still lived. They would not die until sunrise, and then in the sight of all the people.

The princess again urged her to have something to eat.

"There is still time before the execution," she explained innocently.

Rachel took a few bites from some fruit to placate the princess. How could she eat at a time like this? She plied the young Inca woman with questions about where the men were being held, and what type of execution was to occur. She had to find out anything that she could use to delay the killings until she could somehow persuade the Inca to set her companions free.

She tried to explain to T'ika that her father, the king, was using poor judgment concerning Tristan and the other two men.

"*¡Paykunaqa mana huchayuqnmi kanku!*" she repeated. They are innocent!

T'ika glanced around in alarm, worried that one of the serving women would hear the heretic remarks. She shushed Rachel and warned her that she must not say such things. Rachel too might end up a victim of the executions, if anyone heard her criticizing the rulings of her father. T'ika then announced that it was time to get dressed. She led her into a chamber that served as a wardrobe, and retrieved a garment for Rachel.

"*Churakay kay musuq yuraq p'achata. ¿Allinchu?*".

Rachel nodded impatiently. Yes, the garment was fine. She would go out to the square with T'ika, and then find some way to make the Inca ruler understand that he had to stop the executions. He would have to listen to her. She would find some way to make him listen.

"*Suyaykaway, p'achallikuyniyta p'achakusqaykama. Nuqanchis kuskachikmi lluqsisun.*" T'ika told her. "Just a minute, while I dress. We will go out together." The princess then left to find her handmaidens, taking a similar garment with her.

Rachel removed the sleeping gown and changed into the white tunic that T'ika had handed her. T'ika had also provided a sash. She had seen from the other women's attire that it was to be worn around the waist, like a belt. She remembered the picture of the goddess in the mural holding the Tet. The garment worn by the goddess was much the same style. Thinking of the mural reminded Rachel of the crystal amulet. She found her way back to the room where thankfully her jacket still lay against the wall. She retrieved the Tet from the inner pocket and tucked it inside a fold of the tunic and beneath the sash. The amulet was her only hope. She had to at least try to use it as a bargaining tool, regardless of the consequences.

Rachel made it back to the wardrobe room before T'ika returned. When the princess arrived a minute later, she was wearing not only the white tunic and sash, but an enveloping cloak of cloth and multi-hued feathers. Atop her raven black tresses, she wore a golden crown, which itself was fanned by a rainbow arc of plumes. Rachel was again struck by the young woman's extraordinary beauty.

The Inca princess looked at Rachel, and nodded her approval. Escorted by her company of handmaidens, T'ika ushered her back through the living quarters and out into the great plaza. A huge crowd of Indians had already filled the square, leaving a passage lined by the Inca's warriors from the structures that housed the king's chambers and the princess' quarters. T'ika motioned for Rachel to wait at the edge of the square with her until her father arrived to lead the procession to the *huancauri* stone at the center of the plaza. Before long the king made his entrance, heralded by the haunting note of a conch or other instrument that echoed from the stone structures lining the plaza. A roar of support rose from the crowded plaza. "*¡Kawaschun Inka! ¡Wawa Intimanta! ¡Kanki churita punchaymanta!*" the Indians shouted in ceremonious unison. Long live the Inca! Child of the Sun! You who are the offspring of the Day!

Olca Capac was bedecked in a similar finery to that of T'ika, but wore the added accouterments of his position, including his badges of authority, the Scarlet Fringe, an ax-shaped scepter and a shield. A company of some twenty men and women accompanied the king's retinue. They too wore colorful finery, and a few related royalty sported gold or silver-plated belts, breastplates, and feathered headdresses. These preceded or followed the ruler, including the young prince, Atoq. Neither Olca nor the son glanced at her as they processed past, followed by the king's wives, honor guard and retainers. T'ika joined the procession with her attendants, and whispered that Rachel should follow a few steps behind her. Rachel decided she would have to wait until the procession reached the plaza center to get the ruler's attention.

The crowd had left a space three to four meters wide next to the platform supporting the huancauri stone. A small dais now rested next to the stone, a simple throne at its center. Only the Inca ruler and his two children mounted the dais. T'ika motioned for her to stay behind with the servants. As Rachel stood at the forefront of the throng of Indians, she realized there must be between four and five thousand men, women and children jammed into the plaza, or standing on the rooftops of the adjacent structures. Most of these people were talking or shouting, and she saw that it was going to be very difficult to make herself heard, and to get the Inca's attention.

With horror, she also noticed a stone bench-like object that stood directly in front of the Inca's dais. The bench was almost certainly a sacrificial altar, much like the Chacmool altars of the Mayan culture. This stone bench had the shape of a stylized jaguar, with somewhat larger hindquarters, and curved fangs to give the face a more frightening countenance. It was an obvious representation of the Biba creature. Four large Indians stood apart from the other warriors, and she could see that they carried what must be the equivalent of the executioner's ax. These weapons looked more like a Sioux war club. Rachel knew from her studies that the Incas did not normally behead their victims. Instead, the Incas of old massacred their victims with clubs, then often flayed them. These human skins were then stretched and dried for use as drumheads. From her conversations with T'ika, Rachel imagined the Indians were planning to first bludgeon her companions to death, then drop them over the edge of the plateau as a sacrifice to Biba.

A stir from the crowd alerted her to the arrival of her three companions. Still bound, and tattered, her three companions understandably looked like none of them had slept a wink. As the men half stumbled, and were half dragged toward the center of the Plaza, the crowd reacted raucously, shouting insults and jeers at the captives. Rachel stepped forward, but one of the guards held her back. At least twenty warriors formed a perimeter around the huancauri platform. She called out to the Inca ruler, trying to get his attention, but her voice could not carry over the din of the crowd. After the shouts died out, Rachel saw that the Inca ruler had raised his hands for silence, and had begun to speak. He repeated much the same pronouncements of the evening before, and ended with the order to go ahead with the execution.

She again shouted out to the Inca, but the crowd had simultaneously begun to hoot and holler in approval of the sentence of death. Their clamor again drowned out her voice. She tried to force her way toward the dais, but the guards roughly shoved her back.

As she watched, two of the guards separated a wild-eyed Dr. Gallagher from Max and Tristan, and led the struggling professor forward toward the executioners. Max and Tristan were both bound and held back by several guards.

What can I do? Rachel wondered in desperation. *What was it Amasu had said? "Pachamama lives within you, as within all women." What could the Earth goddess do? Command lightning to strike down from the sky?*

She suddenly experienced a flash of inspiration, triggered by the memory of Amasu's words and the thought of lightning: *rélampago.*

"No!" she screamed. "*¡Suyay!*" Wait!

Rachel quickly pulled the Tet from the folds of her clothing and held it aloft, shouting at the top of her lungs for the Inca ruler's attention.

At first, no one noticed her at all. Then someone saw the Tet and cried out, pointing at the crystal scepter in her raised arm. A few more noticed and began to retreat backward, obviously frightened or deterred by the recognition of the ancient symbol. As more of the Indians reacted to the carnelian scepter, the king's attention switched from the impending execution to the disturbance nearby.

"*¡Suyay!*" Rachel shouted again, as the guards forced Dr. Gallagher's body across the stone bench. This time as she stepped forward, the guards stepped away in astonishment, even fearfully.

"*Manaraqmi,*" the Inca ordered. The executioners and guards stepped a pace or two back from Dr. Gallagher.

"*¿Imatataq ruwashanki?*" asked the Inca. He was directing the question at Rachel, and had not yet noticed the Tet of Carnelian. He was asking her what she was doing. He did not look at all pleased by the disturbance and interruption. T'ika looked like she was beside herself with embarrassment and fear for her sister-to-be.

"*¡Paykunaqa mana huchayuqnmi kanku!*" Rachel shouted. By this time the crowd had fallen deathly quiet, spellbound by the sudden drama of this evil-eyed outsider who wielded the ancient amulet of their ancestors. Word filtered through the crowd, like a wave upon the ocean, and now not another person stood within twenty feet of her. "They are innocent!" she repeated.

Olca had now seen the reddish crystal staff in Rachel's upraised hand, and heard the murmur of "*¡Layqa!*" Sorceress! He motioned for her to approach closer.

Rachel strode to within a few feet of the dais. She glanced quickly at Dr. Gallagher. He was understandably shaken, but still unharmed. From the professor, she switched her attention to Max and Tristan who were bound and helpless. Both men's faces were gradually changing from displays of shock and anger, to new expressions of curiosity and fearful hope. The moment was Rachel's. She prayed fervently that it might include a happy ending.

Olca Capac looked closely at the Tet of Carnelian. Although the sight of the amulet equally astonished the king, his face betrayed no emotion. "Hand it to me!" he commanded. "*¡Haywamuway chayta!*"

Rachel stood her ground, offering the Tet in exchange, instead. "*Chay kamachiq tawnata qusayki kinsa qhari chhalayninta.*"

"*¡Waw!*" exclaimed Olca in disgust. "*¿Qan kamachiwanykipaq?*" You are giving me orders? "*¿Manachu yachanki Inka kasqayta?*" Don't you know that I am the Inca?

Olca gestured at the guard nearest Rachel. "*¡Punkukamayuq! ¡Apamuy kamachiq qispi tawnata!*" he said, ordering the guard to bring him the crystal staff.

"*¡Ama kaychu mana allin yuyayniyuq!*" she warned the guard, who had started toward her. Don't be stupid! "*¿Manachu yachanki ima qispiqa kasqanta?*" Don't you know what type of crystal this is?

The guard obviously was afraid of the Tet of Carnelian. He froze in his tracks at these words.

"*¡Phiñakusani! ¿Manachu uyariwanki? ¡Hap'imuy chay kamachiq qispi tawnata!*" growled the Inca, again ordering the poor, terrified guard to confiscate the crystal staff.

The guard was torn between his fear of the unknown magic of the ancient amulet and his knowledge of the swift death that the Inca, Olca Capac, could deliver with a word. He took a hesitant step forward.

Rachel knew that if the guard reached her, not only were the lives of her three companions forfeited, but hers as well. She pointed the Tet toward the guard as if it was a weapon. She brought all the drama she could muster into her act. She hoped that she might still frighten the Inca's men enough to force a stalemate. Above the canopy of trees, Rachel thought she heard the faint whine of an airplane. For an instant, the incongruity of this hidden city under the very nose of modern civilization distracted her. No time for such thoughts now! Her attention quickly returned to the crisis at hand.

The Indian guard again froze in mid-step. He was close enough that Rachel could see the man's eyes. They reflected the terror the native carried for the ancient magic that he feared be cast at any minute. Rachel saw, with astonishment, that the man was utterly panicked. A few more steps, however, and the warrior might be able to detect the doubt and desperation hidden in her own eyes. Hoping to avail herself of the man's terror and put him over the edge, she established direct eye contact with the frightened guard, blessing the contrasting irises for perhaps the first time in her life, and shouted a single word.

"*¡Ñak'akuy!*"

She had hoped the guard might treat the pronouncement as a curse and back away, raising more doubt in the minds of the other guards.

Soon, the Inca king would be sure to order more guards to overwhelm her. At least one was bound to be less superstitious than the others, and would prove the threat of the crystal amulet as idle as Rachel herself knew it to be.

What Rachel did not count on was how much the "curse" would affect the guard. Upon looking directly into Rachel's eyes, one blue, one brown, and hearing her pronounce the word "suffer," the poor man crumpled to the ground. He began to shriek and writhe like his blood was boiling! By good fortune, the plane that was passing overhead was flying fairly low over the treetops, and happened to pass very nearly above their location at exactly this moment. The crowd treated the sound from the sky above like it too was something caused by the magical crystal amulet. A chorus of sounds of awe arose from the crowd, and even the Inca ruler rose to his feet.

"*¡Hark'ay!*" he commanded. Stop!

She again pointed the Tet of Carnelian at the shrieking Indian guard, and commanded him to be healed. She hoped his faith in her ability to remove a curse was as strong as his fear of the curse itself. Apparently it was. The man stopped writhing and became quiet. He rose to his feet and quickly tripped backward into the crowd. The whole front row of the crowd also retreated. Not one native wanted to be the closest person to this powerful white sorceress and her magic amulet. Rachel heard a few of the closer Indians uttering the word "*¡Viracocha!*"

Rachel now saw that one thing was certain. She had to retain the Tet. She faced the Inca ruler squarely and took one step forward. She spoke loudly so that the crowd of Indians would hear what she said to the king.

"*Tayta, ñan chay qispiq qhapaqminta riqsinki.*" Sire, now you remember the power of the crystal staff. "*Qanta walikusqayki, tayta.*" I wish to ask you a favor, Sir. "*Paskay chay qharikunata. Kachariy paykunata.*" Untie the men. Release them to me.

For a long and disquieting moment, the Inca ruler studied Rachel and the Tet she brandished.

"*Paykunaqa qanpan,*" said the Inca, finally. They are yours. He signaled to the guards to set the three men free. "*Kawsanaykikamallapas,*" he added in a lower voice that only Rachel was close enough to hear.

She paled momentarily at the Inca's words, but then realized she probably was misinterpreting the context of the Inca's words. She swallowed hard, lifted her chin and met the Inca's gaze.

"*Yasulpayki.*" I thank you. She added that she would remember the king's compassion and his noble heart.

At his father's directions, Prince Atoq made an announcement to the crowd, dismissing them. The god Illapa had sent these events as a sign to show that he did not wish for the sacrifice of the outsiders' lives, at the present time. Rachel thought this wording was somewhat ominous. The crowd of Indians began to disperse from the plaza, looking back fearfully over their shoulders at her as they went.

Tristan, Max and Dr. Gallagher all quickly moved to her side, whispering congratulations. Rachel saw that Tristan and Max looked nearly as shaken as the professor. Tristan was as white as a sheet and even Max was trembling, if she could believe her eyes. More likely, she thought, it was she who was doing the trembling.

"Fantastic!" Tristan exclaimed.

"You just earned your keep, kiddo," Max muttered.

"I'm as relieved as any of you. For God's sake, stay on your best behavior, though," Rachel warned. "I'm not sure this is over yet, and I don't think I can bluff my way through something like that again."

The words that Olca Capac had uttered, as he released the three men, had startled her. Had she misunderstood the Inca's meaning? Had he intended to mean that the men were now under her perpetual guardianship? Or had there been an intentional malice behind the Inca's words?

"They are yours," he had said "…for as long as you are alive."

Chapter Twenty-three

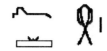

setep sa: worker of magic

****

"The Hidden Place," Tuesday, February 24

"How is it that you happen to have the Tet?" Max asked. "I figured it was still in your pack, and the Indians had found it, along with the tablets and our gear."

"I put it inside my jacket before we went into the staircase maze," Rachel replied. "I just thought that since it had already been one of the keys to a previous puzzle, why not keep it handy?"

"No one is happier than me that you did," Dr. Gallagher said, rubbing his arms where the ropes had bound them. "But how did you know that it would be so effective in frightening the Indians?"

"I didn't. That wasn't even on my mind. I wasn't having any luck getting to talk to the king. I hid the Tet in my clothes when the princess left me alone for a few minutes this morning. I was going to try to trade it for your lives, but when things took a different turn, I had no choice but to go with the flow."

"Well, it worked like a charm—no pun intended," Tristan said. "What was it you did to cause that guard to go nuts?"

"Nothing more than what each of you witnessed. I guess he went into some sort of psychosomatic shock. Many the Indians here are unquestioning in their belief of the powers of their gods and the stories of divine ancestors. I saw some incredible Egyptian murals in Princess T'ika's quarters, including one which shows this amulet. They must be so impressionable about their myths, that the guard believed he was feeling some horrific magical pain."

"Is there any chance that we could leverage that fear, and get them to help us reach the Río Pinquina?" Tristan asked. "Or at least return the things we left in the cavern?"

"I'd be afraid to try," she shuddered. "Are you sure it's even wise to ask for our stuff back?"

"If we're going to get out of here, I think we have to," Tristan said. "It would be suicide to try to make it out of the jungle without the machetes and medical kit."

Rachel looked around the plaza. A few of the Indians still hovered at the outer edges, watching the four white outsiders. Most had already slipped into the narrow alleys leading off the plaza, or into the surrounding buildings. Olca Capac and his retinue, including the prince Atoq, had disappeared back to the chambers of the great stone palace. Only T'ika remained, unsure and at a safe distance with her four handmaidens and two warriors as an escort. A few more warriors, apparently assigned to keep an eye on the outsiders, also watched, warily, from a hundred yards away.

"If anyone can help answer the question about our belongings, it would have to be the princess," she told Tristan.

Rachel lifted a hand to wave at T'ika. She walked casually toward the princess and her servants, hoping that they would not flee.

All the Indians except T'ika averted their eyes as Rachel approached with the men. The servants even took a few steps backward. T'ika's face showed fear and indecision.

"*Ama manchakuychu khumpay, nuqan kani,*" Rachel said. Don't be afraid, my friend. It's only I.

"*¿Ichaqa manachu layqa utaq supay kanki?*" But are you not a sorceress or a demon spirit? "*Puka qispimanta kamachiq tawna utinkayninta qhawarqanin.*" I have seen the magic of the red crystal staff.

"*¡Manan riki!*" Of course not. "*Runa sipiyta hark'aytan munarqani.*" I only wanted to stop the execution. *¿Ñaupaqri? ¿Manachu nuqa khumpayki kani?*" And before that? Was I not your friend?

T'ika, nodded uncertainly.

Rachel explained to the princess that her only wish was to depart peacefully with her three companions. She asked about the equipment that her group had left in the boat. Obviously the warriors had found everything. They had already seen the tablets being held aloft by one of the Indians in Olca Capac's audience chamber. The king now had those. She asked T'ika if she knew anything about the whereabouts of the other items. The princess did not know. She asked the two warriors, but they too knew nothing.

"I'd feel safer if we could move inside," Max suggested.

Rachel asked the princess if she was still able to stay in the princess' lodging

"*¿Qurpa wasiykipichu qurpachasunchis?*" She motioned to include that she meant the men now, as well. T'ika looked a little doubtful, but was agreeable to this request. It was improbable that the Inca's daughter was accustomed to hosting guests. Rachel had undoubtedly been a special exception, but there was no one else to whom she could turn. T'ika told her that she would do what she could to find out anything about their belongings. The princess led the group back to her quarters. Once inside she set the handmaidens to the task of gathering food for the men, and preparing bath water for them. Rachel doubted that the men would do anything stupid, but just to be on the safe side, she suggested to T'ika that the men bathe without help from the handmaidens.

T'ika left to see what she could find out about their equipment.

****

Madre de Dios Jungle, Tuesday, February 24

Kenny banked the sea plane back around to the west. Once again, he passed as low as he dared over the canopy of trees. A slight variation in the endless foliage below had caught his attention. An oblong elevation in the carpet of green below, about two to three miles in diameter, lifted ever so slightly from the rest of the forest. Amasu peered closely as the plane flew over one of the boundaries, and agreed that it looked like the section of jungle was an area surrounded by two very narrow, river gorges. The jungle canopy reached out from both sides of the gorge to nearly mask the canyon in between. Kenny contemplated trying to fly into the narrow valley, but wasn't sure if the risk was worth the effort. The probability was low that any expedition would have entered the gorge, if it was avoidable. Plus, it might be very difficult to maneuver the aircraft, once inside the narrow canyon. He turned the plane back around and continued the morning's surveillance, onward to the west. If time permitted later in the day, or maybe tomorrow, perhaps he'd chance entering the canyon as a last ditch effort before discontinuing the search.

****

Olca Capac was simultaneously pleased and furious. This made for a very unpredictable mood. Even his son Atoq tried to avoid words and acts that might draw the Inca's attention.

Olca was angry that the pale-skinned female outsider had been able to overshadow his authority and position. He had very nearly seized a sword and jumped from the dais to strike the young white witch. Only his astute grasp of politics had restrained him. Many among those of the royal blood felt that he was growing too old and domineering. If the crowd believed that the witch was in alliance with the sun god, his political foes would have been able to use her execution or even those of the three men against him. Even a small disaster of some sort during the next year might serve as "proof" of the Inca's poor judgment. If any of the priestly *kura* was in league with his enemies, astronomical events such as comets or an eclipse might be "foretold" as a sign of the gods' displeasure with the king. His loyal *amautas* normally predicted such celestial events. These were put to such use as would advance the general welfare of the People.

Yet, one aspect of the morning's events had brought the Inca ruler great pleasure. Surely, the unexpected appearance of the red crystal staff of Illapa was a sign for which he had been waiting. He had been close enough to the crystal to see that it was a perfect match with the carved or painted images left behind by the ancient ancestors. Would the Viracocha be clever enough to be able to fabricate such a match? He did not believe so. After all, he had seen the white witch use the crystal's magic not an hour earlier. There was also the news conveyed to him from T'ika through his son Atoq, that the witch wore a silver amulet around her neck. This amulet was shaped as an eagle. The outsider had also told T'ika that her family name meant eagle. T'ika also claimed that the white woman was searching for her twin. Olca knew that such duplicity in nature was a mark of the supernatural, of godly intervention. The white witch bearing the lightning staff must be an earthly manifestation of the goddess Piquerao, twin of the thunder god Apocatequil. All this fit perfectly with the ancient prophecy of the Inca Huayna Capac, centuries ago. The prophecy said, "When the Condor of the South joins the Eagle of the North, the spirit of the Mother Earth,

Pachamama, will awake…and with her the spirits of millions of her children." These Viracocha had claimed to come from the North. This woman was the fulfillment of the prophecy. Now, he would reunite the two staffs of Illapa for the first time in three thousand years!

The Viracocha, however, knew of the amulet's power. Getting his hands on the carnelian staff, while the witch lived, would be difficult. Olca believed that Rachel had completed her part in the prophecy. Whether she lived or died was now irrelevant. He was the Inca. Was not the Inca a god?

His original plan to have the young woman become a wife for his son was discarded. The only thing that mattered was the red scepter of lightning possessed by the white witch. As long as she held the staff on her person, Olca knew she would be as invulnerable as the legend said. But at some point, the Inca knew the young woman would put down the amulet, and momentarily take her eyes from it. At that moment, he would have his spies at hand. They would have orders to seize it and bring it to him. Then his guards would kill all four of the outsiders. He bore no personal malice toward the strangers, but it was his responsibility to protect the secrets of the Hidden Place. If any of the four strangers was to leave here alive, that person could dangerously breach the security of the Chinkana. This was, of course, impermissible.

If the Viracocha strangers tried to escape, he would wait until they were outside the city, but adopt the same plan. The men would be killed at once, and the woman as soon as his warriors had recovered the staff. Either way, the crystal scepter of the eagle would join the golden scepter of the condor. Again, the Inca kings would rise to assume their rightful domination over all the earth.

****

From her brother, the prince Atoq, T'ika was able to discover the location of the outsiders' belongings. The Indians had broken apart most of the items, rendering them useless. This included the rifle, pistol, lantern and Max's flashlight. What remained were mainly articles of clothing. The knives were missing, but surprisingly the machete was still there. T'ika returned with two Indian men who brought what was left back to her quarters. Tristan, Max and Dr. Gallagher had slept for about four hours following their baths. With the arrival of their belongings, they were able to dress in the rumpled, but otherwise undamaged clothing. Rachel's spare shirt had been used to make bandages for Tristan's shin, but T'ika's servants had washed and mended Rachel's clothing during the night, and she changed from the Indian tunic back to her own garments.

The Moroccan tablets were still in the possession of the king. Because of the consensus of the three men, Rachel reluctantly agreed to ask for the return of the tablets if an opportunity presented itself. She would have to choose her moment. She was still doubtful that the Tet was sufficient protection from the king's anger, should she rouse him sufficiently.

T'ika, by now, had mostly returned to her normal self. She had stopped acting like Rachel might, at any moment, turn her into a toad or worse. In response to their questions, the princess told the four outsiders that it would be impossible for any of the city's inhabitants to guide the group anywhere. Royal decree forbade that any of the People ever venture into or past the gorge that surrounded the Hidden Place. Olca had also given orders that the four outsiders could move freely within the city itself, but might not leave until he granted permission.

Dr. Gallagher wanted very much to view the murals Rachel had described, and the petroglyphs that she had seen in the corridor en route to T'ika's quarters. The four agreed that they should all stick together for the time being. They spent an hour or more asking T'ika more questions about the history of the Hidden Place. Rachel translated as T'ika retold the stories she had heard the night before, as well as a few new ones.

Rachel and the others learned that the people, whom T'ika called the ancient ancestors, had built the city over three thousand years ago. The creatures called Biba apparently had always lived in the gorge along with many other animal upon which they fed. After the ancient ancestors had discovered the valley and the plateau that it surrounded, they had extended local caverns and built tunnels. The one that Rachel and the expedition had used, T'ika claimed, at one time stretched from the Temple of the Sun, in Cuzco, all the way to the gorge.

The primitive Indians who already lived in the surrounding forests received the ancient ancestors as gods. These Indians later became the loyal subjects of the People. Among these other Indians were the Amaru, or serpent people. These allied themselves and intermarried with the Tchacha. The Tchacha, who called themselves Amaz'ika were a separate race from the People, but had accompanied the ancient ones across the Great Green. The Amaru and other Indians claimed that in the beginnings of time there was only one valley in the region, through which ran a great river. Then the gods had hurled three great eggs down upon the Earth. One of these was the sacred boulder of the Hidden Place that rested in the central plaza.

From such boulders, the creator, Kon Tiki Viracocha, had made the first men, T'ika said. Now, the *huancauri* also held the spirits of her ancestors. To T'ika's story, Rachel added a condensed version of anthropologists' theory of a prehistoric meteorite storm. According to the anthropologists, this storm had precipitated floods and volcanoes and left these giant boulders strewn about Central and South America. The timing of the meteorites fit with a period of geologic upheaval in the region. The myth of the three eggs from heaven was a parallel theme among the Inca, Mayan and Aztec cultures.

T'ika went on to explain that the Tchacha legend told that the impact of the egg was so great that it had created a bowl-shaped depression on the earth. It even caused the course of the nearby rivers to change. Only a small tributary of the former river now flowed through one of the few breaks in the rim of this crater. This source supplied the People with water. The tributary emptied through another break as the waterfall that dropped into the Ucupacha. The crater and the twin gorges cut off the Hidden Place from the rest of the jungle.

When the ancient ancestors arrived in the jungle, they built the four cities within the crater on the protected plateau. From the Chinkana, the People had spread out into the jungle, subduing the native tribes with the help of their Tchacha allies. T'ika told how the Inca alliance had expanded their area of influence into the montañas, defeating the fierce Chanca Indians. Their territory became known as "*Ayacucho*," the Corner of the Dead. Later, after even the mighty Chachapoyas fell to the Incas, the territory became the empire of "The Four Corners." Once again, the Hidden Place of the jungle became the domain of only priests and shamans who protected the remains of their ancestors and their funerary treasures—"the Place of Heaven". Following the arrival of Pizarro and his hated Viracocha warriors, the secret location and perilous access allowed the Hidden Place to remain as the only intact part of the once great Inca Empire.

After the princess finished her stories, Rachel reviewed her personal situation. Her main objectives were to get back to civilization and to find Kenny. The Inca city was, for the moment, however, a welcome oasis. With the immediate danger past, and the Tet as their protective shield, she was content to stay in the city until she could persuade the Inca king to grant them the help they needed. She hoped that T'ika would help in these negotiations. Rachel also recognized that it was inevitable that the Tet of Carnelian would be the pivotal item of focus in obtaining the king's help. She hoped this would not create too much of a problem with Max, who would, of course, want to take the crystal back with him.

Meanwhile, the hidden city was an anthropologist's dream come true. Max's small camera had been flooded in the pool beneath the waterfall. This was a terrible loss, since now there was no way to record the splendid images that filled the city. She didn't even have a pencil and sketch pad.

Rachel learned that food had always been a problem for the inhabitants of the Hidden Place. Unlike the Incas of antiquity who terraced and cultivated crops on the slopes of the montañas around Cuzco, the People of the Chinkana had become hunter-gatherers. T'ika claimed that the four cities supported almost seven thousand people. Although the people had learned to take from nature only what they needed, the jungle between the two gorges could not alone support the combined population of the four cities. Special warriors entrusted with the knowledge of secret accesses to and from the Ucupacha constantly forayed into the domain of the frightful guardian and beyond. These hunters brought back more food for the inhabitants of the cities on the plateau.

After an ascetically meager lunch, T'ika took them on an expanded tour of the city. The princess guided the four appreciative outsiders through dozens of covered galleries, underground chambers and corridors, and multi-storied buildings. They passed through inner and outer courtyards, over quaint stone bridges, across small canals, and down narrow, cobbled alleys. Rachel reveled at viewing multiple fountains, friezes and carved bas-reliefs of both Inca and Egyptian styled figures. Bordering many of these were inlaid decorative design motifs of amethyst, lapis lazuli, malachite and other colored stones. Some walls of the buildings were made of irregularly shaped rocks, meticulously fit together like a huge jigsaw puzzle. Adobe stucco and painted murals covered a few of these. Still other walls fit incredibly precise blocks of quarried stone, one beside another, without even the slightest gap. T'ika showed Rachel and the three men her favorite gardens. These were filled with exotic flowers, elephant ears, ferns and beautiful soft emerald-colored moss that bored Max, but delighted the others. Hundreds of brilliantly colored macaws and pastel-colored parakeets squawked high in the trees above. From those heights, thin shafts of sunlight also sketched broken designs upon the shadowed and aged stone face of the hidden Inca city.

Throughout T'ika's tour, Rachel was sure that Max was continuing to mentally catalogue the many riches they saw inside the buildings. His one-track mind irritated her, but even she was astonished at the almost casually abundant gold, silver and jeweled treasures gracing the residences and bodies of the royalty. Still, Max had been far too extravagant in his assessment of the Incas' wealth. The thirty billion dollars worth of gold and gems far exceeded the treasures that these Indians seemed to possess. If Max noticed this, he didn't show it.

At the edge of one part of the city, Rachel noticed a stone paved road that led into the surrounding jungle. She asked T'ika about it. The princess explained that there were also two other such roads, built centuries earlier by the ancient ancestors.

By the time T'ika led them back to her private quarters, the grandeur of all they had witnessed had left an indelible impression. They were also extremely fatigued.

No sooner had T'ika taken them into the room with the murals, than one of her attendants brought a message that the Prince Atoq wished to see her. The princess left her four guests under the care of her servants and the most recent contingent of two guards. Since the freeing of the three men, earlier in the day, at least two of the Inca warriors shadowed the group's footsteps. Rachel supposed this was an appropriate measure of security, considering the three alien men in the quarters of the daughter of the Inca.

With a sigh, Rachel sank to a sitting position on the floor and pulled the Tet from beneath her belt. As she laid it on the floor next her leg, she noticed that the eyes of the guards and servants followed the gesture. With a small shiver down her spine, she picked the Tet back up and placed it in her lap.

"So, what now?" Dr. Gallagher asked.

"Now we wait," Tristan answered. "There's not much else we can do. We keep asking questions and being as friendly as possible, until Rachel gets us some more help from either the king or this princess."

Dr. Gallagher lowered his voice as he asked the next question, even though none of the Indians could conceivably understand English. "Is there a chance that the princess could get us the provisions we need and a map of the maze—without the king's knowledge? She seems to be have become friends with Rachel."

"I can't imagine that T'ika would disobey her father," Rachel answered. "As far as a map goes, I have a theory." She told her three companions about her observations of the iconographic designs on the spearheads when they were in the maze. She showed them how the same designs were on the Tet, and formed a sort of maze themselves, which included the intertwining spirals that might represent the twin staircases.

"I wouldn't want to test that without some sort of confirmation," Tristan said. "Maybe we could somehow get T'ika to show us just a little of the maze, under the pretense of our fascination with their ancestors' ingenuity. And maybe get one of those spearheads."

"I can ask," Rachel answered, dubiously, "but I'd be surprised if they'd let us have any sort of a weapon, even temporarily."

"What about other ways out?" Max asked. "The princess' story mentioned breaks in the rim of the crater surrounding this place. Apparently, that's where their river enters and flows out. That must mean that the gorge doesn't surround us, after all. A river couldn't originate within a small self-contained area like this, so it can't be a true plateau. It has to be some sort of geologic rift. Wherever the river flows onto it, there must be a land bridge to the outside. If we can find that bridge, it would give us an escape route that avoids that saber-tooth monster."

"I still have a compass that works," Tristan said. "If we knew better where the other hidden cities lay, that plan might have a shot. Otherwise, we probably couldn't hope to sneak past, even with the princess' help."

"We're not in any immediate danger," Rachel said. "I want to get back to Cuzco as much as anyone, but I vote that we continue to look around and become their friends, until a convenient chance to escape presents itself."

"This is an opportunity of a lifetime…" agreed Dr. Gallagher, who had almost recovered from his morning's close encounter and last-second stay of execution.

"Sounds okay to me, for the time-being," Max said. As far as he was concerned, the longer he stayed, the more he learned about the place that would be useful when he returned.

"All right, then," Tristan sighed. An annoyed look on his face betrayed his frustration at the sense of futility they were all experiencing. "It's a pathetic plan, but I guess for the moment, we'll just wait to see what happens."

Chapter Twenty-four

Sacrificial "Tumi" knife

****

"The Hidden Place," Wednesday, February 25

One instant Rachel was asleep, dimly aware of an uncomfortable pressure against her ribcage. The next she was on her feet, alert and analyzing her surroundings. Between the two moments had blinked the semi-conscious question—*Where am I?*

Max and Dr. Gallagher were still sound asleep when Rachel's jack-in-the box rendition stirred them to equally instant states of alacrity. Tristan, awake and on guard, reassured them that there was no cause for alarm. Paititi still slumbered, and whatever plans the lost city might next unfold had not yet seen the light of day.

She guessed correctly that her left side was, or would soon be, badly bruised from sleeping on top of the carnelian amulet. The evening before, Max had suggested that he retake possession of the Tet, especially now that Rachel had so ably demonstrated its protective influence. Dr. Gallagher argued that the Indians had accepted the amulet as wielded by Rachel, because she could use the Quechua language and knowledge of their customs along with it. Tristan thought it unwise to test that acceptance by recasting roles with the drama already under way. Max begrudgingly gave in. She had therefore replaced the Tet in the zippered inner pocket of her jacket, and spent the night with the hard crystal indented in her side.

T'ika had intended for Rachel to sleep in her room again, apart from the three men. Rachel insisted that it was appropriate for her to stay with her companions, and the distressed princess had finally acquiesced. Tristan suggested that he would sleep easier if they rotated standing watch through the night, just as they had done in the jungle. Each member of the group had taken a two-hour stint.

The new day was accompanied by a familiar myriad of doubt, fear and hope. Dr. Gallagher, who from the outset had been the most jittery of the group, was still somewhat rattled by the previous day's events. He planned to spend the day etching notes with a small bronze knife he had gotten from T'ika. The princess had also provided some clay tiles that the professor hoped to take with him whenever the king might let them depart. Now that things had calmed down, Rachel's inner anthropologist self reminded her that she should also try to record some account of her incredible surroundings. She vowed to do so as soon as she got the chance.

Tristan, however, was uneasy with the quietness of their current state of captivity. He, too, was very much in awe of the Indians' civilization and their ability to hide four such cities for five centuries, but knew that such secrecy did not come cheap. Despite his fascination with the city, he was more eager to discover what might be their best chance of getting away as soon as the opportunity arose. Through Rachel, Tristan enlisted the princess' help in arranging a visit to once again view the uppermost levels of the spiraled maze. Rachel told T'ika that they did not expect the princess to reveal any of the double stairwell's secrets. She claimed that Tristan just wanted another look, because of his admiration for its ingenious design. She felt bad about lying to T'ika. Since she could not, however, expect the princess to betray her people, Rachel reasoned that this deception was unavoidable.

Despite everything that had happened, Max refused to allow the surrounding dangers to overwhelm his sense of greed. There was little doubt in his mind that he would somehow emerge from this expedition invulnerable and in control of the most fantastic lost treasure of all time. The thing that nagged him was having lost direct control of the Tet and the map tablets. The Tet was the lesser of the two problems. He knew he would be able to take it from Rachel, whenever he wanted. She could not stop him, and Tristan would not. By law of the jungle, the strongest survived, and he was by far the strongest of the group. To avoid a premature confrontation, he had thought it wise not to force the issue last night. Nonetheless, if the roof caved in on this little period of "détente" with the Inca, Max planned to be the one holding the protective amulet. Hell, maybe the Tet of Carnelian didn't have any magic whatsoever! As long as these Indians thought it did, he was going to get his hands on it…one way or the other. In the meantime, he planned to see if he might find any emeralds that he could surreptitiously pry loose, or small items of gold lying around that the Indians wouldn't miss. If he were going to recruit top-notch soldiers of fortune to follow him back into this jungle, it would be "worth its weight in gold" to be able to show the prospective recruits a small proof of the treasure. He would keep this little plan to himself. What the others didn't know wouldn't hurt them.

Rachel decided that the best way to occupy her time would be to seek another audience with the Inca king. T'ika said this would not be possible. The princess told her that her father was away, busy with other responsibilities.

"He will return this morning?" Rachel asked.

The princess shook her head no. *"Uj ratum antaraj ichá."* A bit later perhaps. She told Rachel that the prince was still here. Perhaps in the absence of the Inca, Atoq would be able to answer her questions.

"¡Uj allin yachay rimay!" Good idea! Perhaps she could enlist the prince's help in finding a way out of the jungle.

After breakfast, T'ika sent one of the women servants along with Rachel to find Prince Atoq. The servant led her to the same audience chamber where she had been twice before. She hoped that things went better with the son, than with the father. Both times before, when she had left the chamber, somebody wound up in a jail cell.

The servant spoke to one of the guards who left to find the prince. Atoq entered the room a few minutes later, less adorned than she had seen him before, but still wearing a collar and cuffs of beautifully tooled gold. Rachel thought the prince looked even a year or two younger than T'ika, but when she looked into the prince's veiled and unblinking dark eyes, she wasn't so sure. The prince's face and manner revealed no hint of either friendliness or enmity—only a scrutinizing and impersonal expression similar to those that she had often seen on the faces of men accustomed to the exercise of power. This demeanor muddled whatever youthful outward attributes might be more immediately noticeable.

"¿Nuqawan rimaytachu munarqanki?" he asked. You wished to speak to me?

"Napaykullayki" she began. Greetings. *"Yusulpayki rikuyki."* Thank you for seeing me.

"Imamanta," the prince answered, noncommittally.

"We wish to leave the Hidden Place, but we need help."

"¿Imanaqtintaq saqiyta munaki?" For what reason do you want to leave? You can remain here and become a wife of a great prince. You will learn to be happy here.

Rachel tried to explain that she was from another place very far away, and to be happy, she must return there.

"*Mana atina.*" Impossible, replied the prince, shaking his head. "*Taytallaymi kamchiqniyuq.*" Only my father has this authority.

"Even though I am able to give you the crystal staff?"

"*¿Munankichu chay kamachiq qispi tawnamanta willanayta?*" Would you like for me to tell you about this staff? My father the Inca king will recover it by force, if you do not relinquish it willingly.

"*¿Imanawanmanmi, nuqa hina layqata?*" What can he do to a sorceress like me?

Atoq smiled wryly and went on to explain the innumerable "accidents" that might befall Rachel and the others. No one could blame the Inca for such bad luck. Rachel might drink of contaminated water, or eat a bad piece of fruit. She might accidentally fall into a stream, which contained piranha, or perhaps be bitten by a poisonous snake that somehow found its way into her bed…

Rachel asked the prince if he did not believe that the magic of the Tet would protect her and her companions.

"*Kanki chaypa p'ajpaku, niy kay qan, ujkuna pichichukuna tukunanpaq, nispa.*" If you are a charlatan, then transform yourself and the others into birds and fly away. "*Reqsiykin pichus kasqaykita. Manan utinkayniyuqchu kanki.*" I know who you are. You are no magician.

Rachel tried to maintain a passive expression on her face as she thanked the prince for speaking with her. She bade him farewell. Although she was not heading to a jail cell, this time, the meeting had done nothing to improve her situation. The prince had warned her point-blank, that if she did not turn over the carnelian amulet to his father, some sort of fatal accident was probable. Any doubt that she had earlier felt about the king's intentions was now gone. When he had told her that he was releasing the men to her "…as long as she was alive," he had not used the phrase to mean "in perpetuity." He had meant it was a *temporary* solution.

It was time to get the hell out of Paititi.

Chapter Twenty-five

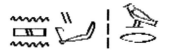

neshen: a calamity, terrible storm, great eclipse, fury
"If you gaze long enough into the abyss, it will begin to look back into you."
—*Anonymous*

****

"The Hidden Place," Thursday, February 26

Rachel hid behind a tree. She could hear the distant growl of the jaguar. It was tracking her; she was sure of that now. If she broke cover and ran, the animal would hear her and quickly close the distance. If she remained hidden, the jaguar would use Rachel's scent to find her hiding place. What choice was left? Anything she did would be wrong! What weapon did she have that could possibly be effective against a jaguar? The Tet? A jaguar had no silly superstitions. The guns were equally useless. She no longer even had the machete.

Only Amasu's peculiar advice answered. *Seek the gold in the shadow…* *What gold?*

You carry a power that none of these others possess—Pachamama...the great female soul...lost, repressed within you.

Pachamama? What could she do? What power might the earth goddess offer that could fend off a fearsome jaguar?

The goddess dwells within...

Could not the earth goddess assume any form she wanted? Why not another jaguar? A female jaguar. Even though the males of the species might be larger, Rachel knew that even the males would give a female jaguar wide berth.

From that fear—through its transformation—you are capable of drawing great strength.

Rachel quietly stole outward, away from the sheltering tree, placing one forepaw silently upon the soft jungle floor. Now unafraid, she lifted the other paw and moved forward. She crept onward, transformed from prey to predator. With her enhanced animal senses, she noiselessly closed the space to the other jaguar. When she glimpsed the male ahead, through the heavy foliage, Rachel slowed. Coiled and tensed, she extended her claws and inched undetected through the last few feet of cover. The male, suddenly sensing her presence, whirled and snarled, exposing its daunting fangs.

But what was this? No male jaguar, after all. Like her, it was female. The jaguar roared at Rachel, fixing her with its primal stare, but Rachel had already claimed her inner power.

I too have claws and fangs! Mustering her courage and bravado, she unleashed a roar that reverberated like thunder through the still recesses of the shadowy jungle.

The other jaguar continued to glare at Rachel. With a start, she realized that the irises of the other jaguar were mismatched. One brown, one blue. Rachel held the stare.

The other jaguar's gaze flickered, then lowered. Uttering a low rumbling growl, the jaguar turned and vanished back into the darkness.

Rachel awoke and glanced about the room, gradually separating the dream from her troubled reality. Tristan and Dr. Gallagher slept on, nearby. Max sat with his back against the wall, facing the doorway. Rachel could dimly discern the outline of one of the Inca guards resting outside the doorway, awake but seemingly disinterested. She tried to reassemble the dream, which as dreams will, was already fading from her conscious memory. Fear? Loss? Was that what she had been dreaming about? *Losing Kenny?* After Max's deception had been revealed, she had been furious, but she had also jumped to the conclusion that Kenny was okay. True, Max's story had been a complete fabrication. Yet, she had no basis for the belief that Kenny had not crashed. The message from Peru had been real. Kenny *was* missing. That was what frightened her most. She had already lost her father, then Doug. Even her mother, in a different way. Kenny would be the hardest of all. He was so very much like her. It would be like losing not just her brother, but...*herself.*

That was it, wasn't it? After Doug's death she had set out to recreate herself in a stronger, less vulnerable image—one able to compete and survive in a male-oriented society. In the process, she had begun to discard or and suppress small pieces of her being—bit by bit. What remained or had taken the place of those missing pieces was someone different, not a new Rachel, but an incomplete substitute—as if the rest of her real self was longing for the pieces she had hidden away, somewhere within. She stared out into the black abyss of night. It was nearly an hour before she slept again.

Much later, a shadowy figure crept silently across the darkened room.

****

Rachel woke, this time, to an unfamiliar rasping noise and the sound of the men's voices.

"Oh, sorry. We didn't mean to wake you," Tristan said. "We were just brainstorming again."

Rachel rubbed her eyes and saw that the rasping sound had come from Tristan etching some lines into one of Dr. Gallagher's clay tiles. Max and the professor sat on the floor next to Tristan, both poring over the scratched drawing.

"I think we may have found out something useful about the maze after all," Tristan said.

After everyone had returned to the princess' quarters the previous afternoon, they had discussed quietly what each other had discovered. They had waited to discuss the maze until T'ika had gone off on some personal errand. Tristan had then reported what observations he had made, and compared them to the Tet's grooves. Based upon what little that T'ika and the guards had permitted Tristan to see, none of the group saw how the designs on the Tet could match what they collectively remembered about the route from the cavern.

That the Tet mapped a maze of some location was probable. Parts of the pattern resembled the uppermost portion of the maze.

"I wonder if it's possible," Tristan told the others, "that the Tet could show the same maze, but a different route? Perhaps an escape route to which only the king, or whoever possesses the Tet, would be privy. Could we see the Tet again?"

"Yeah, just a second…" Rachel said.

"I still say there's a better way," Max interrupted, taking the clay tile from Tristan and turning it over. He began to scratch a drawing of his own onto the tile. "Remember how the location of Paititi was shown as the bigger circle with spikes coming out of it…with Pinquina River protecting its north side? Flanking it to the south was an arc of the three smaller outposts. If we could just make it to the river, we could float down far enough to crawl ashore and lash together a crude raft. That would be enough for us to float as far as Boca Manu. From there, we could arrange for a boat, or maybe even an airplane."

"Let's say you're right," Dr. Gallagher said. "We have Tristan's compass to point us in the proper direction back west from Paititi to the river.

But what about the gorge? Supposedly, it almost entirely circles Paititi. That's the impression T'ika gave us. The only way past is the tributary she said flows through a couple of breaks in the rim. We don't even know where it lies in relation to Paititi. East or west? If we make a run for it through the jungle, we could find ourselves right against the cliffs with the Indians at our backs."

"The tributary must be nearby," Max insisted. "We've seen these Indians returning with water from outside the city. Once we find the tributary, it will lead us directly to the Río Pinquina."

"But how far?" Tristan asked. "We don't know the scale that was used on the stone map. The distance could be a quarter mile or forty miles. I think it's worth spending a little more time with the patterns on the Tet. Rachel…?"

"Oh, sorry, here it…" Rachel reached inside the inner pocket of her jacket. Her face paled.

"That's odd. I'm sure I zipped it back. It must have slid out…" Rachel felt around in the furs for the Tet, but it was not there. "I…I can't seem to find it. I'm positive I zipped it back up, last night." Her voice broke, and she studied the faces of her three companions, searching, wondering.

"I know you did," Tristan said. "I was watching when you put it away."

"Then, it must be here. We took turns standing watch. Even if I slept through it, no one could have come in and taken it, could they? Not without whoever was on watch having seen them."

The others helped her search through the bedding, but the Tet was just not there. The commotion had caused the guards to re-approach the doorway and look inside.

"This just doesn't make sense," Tristan said. "How could it have just disappeared?"

"A trap door beneath the floor? Remember the room in the tunnel where we lost Ramón's body? T'ika chose the room," Max pointed out."

There was, of course, *one* other explanation. The same thought occurred to each of them at the same time just as Max made the statement to the contrary. One of *them* might have taken it. An embarrassing silence descended upon the room, finally broken by the professor.

"Perhaps, one of us might have fallen asleep during his or her watch."

Everyone looked at Dr. Gallagher. Tristan, in particular, examined the Egyptologist suspiciously.

"I didn't mean me! I was awake the whole time. I swear it."

If any of them had fallen asleep while on watch, no one was admitting it.

"Now what?" Rachel asked.

"Now we use *my* plan. That's what," Max said.

"How convenient," Dr. Gallagher remarked.

"You pansy little fart! I ought to break your neck," Max snarled.

"This isn't helping anything," Tristan said. "If it's gone, it's gone. Max is right. Without the Tet, we're going to have to head toward the river the first good chance we get. There won't be anything to hold them back now."

T'ika had now come to see what all the noise had been about. The guards spoke to her as she reached the room, describing the search they had just witnessed.

"¿Qispi tawanata…?" she asked.

"¡Manan kaypichu kashan!" Rachel told her. It's not here.

"Maybe telling her that isn't such a good idea," Tristan said. "If they know we don't have the Tet anymore, what's to keep them from locking us up back up, or worse?"

"Ask her if she took it," Max said. "Maybe we can work a private deal with the princess, if she still has it…"

"I've already confirmed the Tet is missing," Rachel answered. "She guessed from what the guards told her, that it was what we were looking for."

"Or she already knew," Max said. "Go ahead, ask her."

"Your sense of diplomacy leaves a lot to be desired, Max," Rachel responded. "She's the only friend we have here. What if one of the guards took it? If it's believed to be so powerful, how do we know they'll go straight to the king with it? Somebody might want it for their own use."

"Maybe..." Tristan mused. "They haven't had this Tet for at least three thousand years. There's no telling how it might affect the balance of power, if it's suddenly up for grabs..."

"I say we hold off on doing anything drastic, until we see what happens this morning," Rachel suggested. "I think I can still stall them."

"Without the Tet?" Tristan asked.

"They think I'm a sorceress. The Indians won't lose that conviction right away. I guess it's just your turn to trust *me*."

****

Olca Capac had returned. The upcoming events of this day required that the king appear briefly in each city of the Hidden Place. He had met with his viceroys and spoken to the assembled people of each city. He had debated moving the captives from this location, but had hesitated. Escape was unlikely, but he was a very cautious man. The Inca kings had successfully maintained the safety of the Hidden Place for centuries. While they still lived, the less the outsiders saw, the better. They had been clever enough to make it here. That proved they were too dangerous to let live.

Olca was confident that, by the end of this day, the danger would be removed. The king planned to demonstrate today to his people that his divine power was far greater than that of the white witch. Months ago, the Inca's shamans had provided him with a prediction that, a bit later in the day, he would use to his advantage. It was fortuitous that he would be able to use this knowledge to order the execution of the captives. The sun god demanded it. At least, that is what Olca would tell his people. Indeed, the sun god must have provided this chain of events to allow him to recover the carnelian scepter. He would now be able to do this without causing the People to be fearful of the consequences of his opposition against the Viracocha sorceress.

There was a hitch, however. He had learned, only moments ago, that Rachel no longer held the Tet. This was as yet a mystery. True, his guards had their orders to seize the amulet as soon as the opportunity presented itself. Instead, the guards had brought only the message that the Tet was missing. None of them admitted to having taken it. His daughter's servants had also been questioned, but to no avail. They were all in such fear of the king's power that he could not believe one of them might be withholding the amulet. His daughter T'ika had befriended the outsiders. She had even appealed to him to spare the life of the woman, Rachel. Could it be that his daughter had taken the Tet and hidden it for some plan of her own? Olca could not believe this! One of the Viracochas must be hiding the amulet. Perhaps the whole story that it was missing was some sort of a ruse.

Atoq had recounted the circumstances of Rachel's visit. His son, lamentably, was too young and inexperienced to realize that he may have erred through the information he had allowed the white witch to gain. Now, Olca did not know where the Tet was. Were the Viracochas clever enough to have construed this story for that purpose? If one of them was hiding the amulet on his person, the king would face another embarrassing stalemate if it were suddenly produced just as he ordered the Viracocha seized. And what if the Tet was very well hidden somewhere within the city? Or even spirited into the woods by a traitor, and secretly buried. There was the possibility that if he executed the outsiders, the amulet might forever remain hidden. If that happened, the fulfillment of the ancient prophecy might never come to pass.

After thoughtful consideration, He decided to go ahead with his original plan. If one of the outsiders possessed it, the Inca king was confident that this person would have to reveal it in self-defense as the day's events progressed. To no avail. The outsiders would still die.

✳✳✳✳

T'ika arrived to tell Rachel that everyone in the Inca city, including the four white outsiders, were to gather in the great plaza a half-hour before midday. The four captives received this news with much consternation.

"Damn it, he's got it!" Max swore. "He's got the Tet. I told you the princess must have been the one who swiped it. A half-hour before midday? It's clear he's planning an execution for when the sun is at its peak. We have to make a break for it, now."

"Don't jump to conclusions," Rachel protested. "There could be some other explanation. If he had the Tet, why didn't he send guards to take us away and have us locked up as soon as he got his hands on it?"

"But what other explanation could there be?" Dr. Gallagher asked.

"Every moment we wait puts us in more danger," Max warned. "There'll be guards here soon enough to make sure that we show up on schedule. If we're going to make a break for it, we have to do it now. There are only two guards here in the princess' quarters at the moment, and we'll have the element of surprise. Tristan, I can take one of them, and I know you can overwhelm the other."

"What you're planning is suicidal," Rachel objected. "The princess or one of her servants is sure to hear the commotion or notice us leaving. We'd be lucky to even make it to the forest. Even if we did, think how fast they'd catch up. You saw how easily the Machiguenga guides and Amahuaca Indians glided through the brush, while we stumbled along and entangled ourselves on nearly every thorn or vine we came upon..."

"The question is—do we have a choice?" Tristan asked.

"We can take the princess with us as a hostage," Max suggested. "The king will trade us safe passage for the life of his daughter..."

"That's the worst plan you've had yet," Rachel said. "This is a patriarchal culture; the king wouldn't hesitate to call your bluff. If any harm came to her, he'd just inflict some extraordinarily slow and painful death as retribution."

"Besides, dragging a hostage along would slow us down way too much," Tristan said. "I'm afraid I'm inclined to agree with Max, though,

Rachel. The situation has changed. There's been nothing new to suggest that the king has anything but harm planned for us. From what the prince told you yesterday, I'd say it looks like they're making their move at noon, like Max says. I say we have to make a run for it. Doc? What about you?"

Dr. Gallagher looked uncomfortably toward Rachel.

"I'm sorry, Rachel, I have to go along with Max this time, too. They were just about to kill me, before. I can't go through that again. At least I'll have a chance this way…"

Rachel frowned and examined her options. This turn of events thwarted her own hastily devised plan entirely, but what the men had in mind was even more ill advised! There was no way the group could just take off and expect to make it to the river in broad daylight. The men were not thinking clearly. They were acting out of desperation. She knew she still had one un-revealed ace, and she was tired of following Max's lead. Playing the weak little victim was all that any of them seemed to expect of her. Even Tristan.

That was about to change. Trust her feminine instincts, Amasu had told her. Well…she could hardly mess things up worse than they already were. She had tried things the men's way, and look where they were, now. They had found the lost city, but they lost over a third of the expedition to violent deaths in the process. Even Tristan's skill hadn't kept them from being taken prisoner. Her contributions thus far had helped to solve the puzzles of the tunnels and kept them alive, once the Indians had taken them captive. If she went with the men, they would all die. There might, however, be another way.

Despite the loss of her father and fiancé, or perhaps *because* of that, Rachel had never truly confronted death. Not in person. In retrospect, she knew she had been close to it on many occasions during the past few days. Yet, even after the fer-de-lance had bitten her or when the Biba creature was chasing them Rachel had always believed there would be a way out. She searched for such belief now, but could not find it. Escape was improbable if she chose the plan she had in mind. She found it curious how still her mind went—how silent all her inner voices fell, once she accepted that. So this was what being scared to death felt like— not terrified, so much as…*empty. Did inner demons then, like rats, abandon sinking ships?*

It would have to be her, she knew. That part was already cast. She was the only one who might convince the Indians that they *must* listen, must do as she commanded. The three men had already been presented and accepted as powerless. It was inevitable that her charade would also soon fade. She had no magic. Even the Tet had just been a bluff. When she was unmasked, she would also be undone. The Inca king would quickly see to that.

All, or one? Again experiencing that strange calmness, Rachel made up her mind. The time was now.

"Look," she lied. "I think my chances are best staying put and trying to deal with whatever the king is planning. If you three are determined to make a run for it, I'm sure I can buy you some extra time. I can create a disturbance here in another part of the princess' quarters that will draw the guards. I'll try to keep it up for as long as I can, while you slip out. With so many people massing in the plaza, it will be harder for the guards outside to keep track of the three of you. You'll be able to travel faster without me, anyway."

All three of the men fell silent.

More demons, she reflected. They stared at her with various expressions on their faces.

Dr. Gallagher looked shocked and confused. Abandoning the damsel in distress didn't fit well at all with his sense of chivalry, but what was *he* to do?

Max, however, was entertaining the merits of the idea. He began to nod after a minute, indicating that he liked the plan.

Tristan looked lost. He didn't know how to handle this situation. He could see that Rachel's idea might buy them a few minutes…minutes that might make all the difference. He still felt at blame for Rachel being here to begin with, and like Dr. Gallagher, he could not realistically consider abandoning her. He could take her place, but it was her, not him, that the Indians feared.

"It's my choice," Rachel said. "I elect to stay. You have to go."

"No, I don't," Tristan answered. "If you stay, I'm staying too. Max and Dr. Gallagher will make their escape, and send help back for us."

"If you stay, the king will kill you," Max objected, spacing the words evenly and deliberately. "It's that simple. Plus, what kind of chance do you think we'd have getting out of the jungle without you? If you're dead, we're all dead. There won't be anyone left to help Rachel."

"I can't believe I'm saying this, but for once I have to agree with Max," Rachel added. "So, are you going to add to my problems by staying here?"

Tristan hesitated, as his mind argued with his heart whether to stay or flee with the other two men. He searched Rachel's face, attempting to reach into her thoughts. He sought her eyes—full of life, pain and unquenchable warmth, but Rachel kept her long dark lashes downcast. Finally, he reached a decision. He took a step closer to Rachel and started to place his hands on her shoulders. She stiffened in response.

Don't touch me, Rachel thought. *I can barely do this, as it is.*

Tristan mistook her reaction. He paled and let his hands drop to his sides.

"I know you have every reason to hate me for getting you messed up in this, but this isn't over. I'll figure out a way to get you out of here. I'll be back. I promise."

Rachel nodded. Even as she pushed him to leave, a very small voice was silently pleading that he might refuse. Afraid to meet Tristan's eyes, she looked instead at Max. There was no trace of a smile on his face, but there was that gleam in his eyes again. *You see, he's coming with ME,* he seemed to be thinking. For a moment Rachel felt sorry for him. People weren't just born that way, were they?

"I'll create a distraction, as soon as you're ready," she said, careful to keep any rancor or emotion from her voice.

"They were already going to spare you..." Tristan stalled. "Whether the three of us make it out or not, it wouldn't make any sense for them to kill you."

"I'll be fine." *Stay!*

"You don't have the Tet anymore, so it wouldn't buy them anything to harm you. I can't imagine they would be worried about you making it out of here alone...no offense intended. They'll probably go back to their original plan to marry you off to Prince Atoq."

"Hey, there you go...you guys get away, and I get a rich prince as a husband. Things weren't looking all that good at finding one back in Norman..." *He's going...*

"I hate to break this up," Max said. "But the clock is ticking."

"Right," Tristan said. He looked at Rachel. "I'll be back."

Rachel sighed. "Yes, and in chains, unless you get going *now*. Go! Good luck." *Gone.*

"Thanks for the head start," murmured Dr. Gallagher. "I'll, that is, w-we'll..."

"Go!" Rachel repeated. "Let me see what kind of ruckus I can create." She exited quickly, before she could chicken out.

The men gathered up their few remaining essentials as Rachel moved back through the other rooms of the princess' apartments. She made sure the guards saw her passing by.

"¿*Kaypichu T'ika kashan?*" she asked. When she was out of their sight, she removed her eagle necklace and placed it in a pocket.

When she found the princess, Rachel began to act agitated and angry. She invoked the pretext of suspecting one of the guards having stolen her necklace, claiming that she had seen one of them looking at something that resembled it a few minutes earlier. She raised her voice and began to accuse the guards of having stolen the crystal amulet and the eagle amulet while she and her companions had slept. Rachel allowed the racket she was making to get threateningly loud. Her heart went out to T'ika, who immediately looked mortified, and a little frightened. Rachel kept up the act, nonetheless. As hoped, the guards rushed back into the room where Rachel ranted before the princess. T'ika sternly questioned the guards. They, of course, stuttered confused denials. Whenever T'ika let up, Rachel launched into another series of accusations, turning her wrath onto the guards.

It felt good. Much of the frustration and anger she had stored inside was unleashed. She told T'ika how the guards had constantly appeared at the doorway of the sleeping chamber during the night. Rachel accused them of checking to see if she and the three men were all asleep, so that one of the guards might steal the amulet and necklace. This much, of course, was true. Even while launching a new verbal attack, Rachel wondered whether the lives she might be saving mitigated whatever action might be taken against the guards. She doubted that any real punishment would befall them, in any case. Rachel figured she kept the guards thus occupied for somewhere between ten and fifteen minutes. So far, there had not been any others rushing in to alert the princess to the news of the escaping outsiders. Finally, Rachel quit talking and waited to see what the princess would do.

T'ika apologized profusely, almost tearfully, but suggested that perhaps the necklace's delicate chain had broken and was lost somewhere in the room. Rachel shook her head and pretended to pout. One of the handmaidens then arrived to tell the princess that the time was drawing near for the assembly in the plaza. The three men had left just in time.

The princess told Rachel that she would have her servants search the sleeping chamber very closely, following the assembly. She asked her to gather her three companions. The princess's other handmaidens arrived with her ceremonial finery, and Rachel brushed past the guards and headed for the sleeping chamber.

The two guards followed a few steps behind. When she neared the chamber, she turned and stuck out her palm, indicating that the guards should come no further. Somewhat cowed by the princess' interrogation and the tantrum that Rachel had just thrown, the two Indians held back a discreet distance from the doorway.

Rachel waited until a servant arrived to announce that the princess awaited, then walked from the room to join T'ika. The two guards stepped into the room to collect the three others, then hurried to search the rest of the quarters. Finding no one except Rachel, the guards rushed back to tell the princess that the three men were gone.

"*¿Maypin huqkunaqa?*" the alarmed T'ika asked, as she whisked into the room. "Where are the others?"

Rachel told her that she had followed the advice of the Prince Atoq, and used her magic to turn the three men into birds, so that they could fly away unharmed. From the wide-eyed expressions on T'ika's and her retinue's faces, Rachel could tell that their doubt did not necessarily outweigh their belief in her pronouncement. The princess sent one of the guards to carry the alarm to her father.

Entranced by the simultaneous fantasy and mad reality of her actions, Rachel followed the princess outside to the plaza.

Chapter Twenty-six

It is not that the light element alone does the healing;
the place where light and dark begin to touch is where miracles arise

—*Robert A. Johnson*

✶✶✶✶

"The Hidden Place," Thursday, February 26

Max, Tristan and Dr. Gallagher used the commotion that Rachel had created to slip away unnoticed. Tristan's compass provided them with the correct orientation needed for their northerly direction of travel toward the river. T'ika's quarters were located on the northeast corner of the plaza. A few warriors were visible around the square, but these were busy directing the throng of inhabitants already making their way into the plaza. The three captives were able to slip unnoticed into a narrow street that led off to the north. Hundreds of Indians passed them en route to the plaza, but these were older men and women, children and the laboring class of the city. A few of these Indians stopped and spoke to the men, pointing back toward the plaza. Max and Dr. Gallagher just nodded and continued on their way, as Tristan called back in his marginal Quechua, "*Arí...¡Utqhay!*" Yes...Hurry.

By the time Rachel was finishing her diversionary tactics, the men had reached the outskirts of the city and entered the forest. They adjusted their direction to try to intercept the tributary, and were surprised to burst forth from the trees, only a few minutes later, onto one of the stone roads that led out of the city.

Here, Tristan stopped short.

"I can't do this," he said. "You're going to have to make it from here without me, Max. I'm going back for Rachel."

"Oh, piss on it, for crying out loud!" Max exclaimed. "It was her decision. This is no time for a guilty conscience. We're out of here—free and clear. Get a grip, man! We've gotta get moving."

"Can't do it. You'll make good time on this road. You won't need me. Good luck." He didn't wait to argue more. He spun around and sprinted back the way they had come.

"If that the way it has to be…" whispered Max, tightening his grasp on his bundle of stolen trinkets, and tracing a finger along the grooves of one of the items inside. *Insurance.* He hadn't dared examine it in the daylight—not with the others present. He left the piece hidden inside the bundle, where he had stashed it after taking it from Rachel's jacket during the night. He spat on the ground and glared a warning at Gallagher, in case the Egyptologist also was reconsidering. "Come on," he growled.

The two men headed down the road as fast as they could travel, with Max alternately cursing Tristan, and blessing the good fortune that had presented him with such an easy escape route.

✳✳✳✳

In the grand plaza, Rachel once again waited for the arrival of the Inca king. It seemed like a week ago that she had stood here trying desperately to come up with an idea that would delay her companions' executions. *How long had it been? Only two days?* That had been Tuesday morning, the twenty-fourth. Today was Thursday, February twenty-sixth. She had now been in Peru twelve days, and ten since she had headed into the jungles east of Boca Manu. She wondered how the king would react when he saw that the three men were missing. If things got rough, at least she still had the Tet.

Ah, yes, the scepter rested safely inside her zippered inner pocket. In the early hours of the morning, she had bound it to her shin, and with it hidden beneath her pant's leg, played out the charade of having the Tet turn up missing.

It hadn't been difficult to look surprised or suspicious. Just before everyone had retired for the evening, T'ika had brought her one of the grooved spearheads, as requested. After hiding the Tet, Rachel had put the spearhead in its place inside the zippered pocket. After the meeting with Prince Atoq, she had begun to worry about having set herself up as a target. If the king really was planning to have her poisoned or set up for some other fatal "accident," she figured it would prolong all the captives' lives if the Inca ruler was unsure of the Tet's whereabouts. When none of his subjects brought it forward, he wouldn't know for certain if one of the captives was hiding the amulet, or one of his own people. If the crystal staff was as treasured as it appeared to be, she had thought the Inca would not dare kill any of the captives; not while its location remained a secret. Maybe it had been a poor plan, naïve and a gamble, but at least she had taken charge of her own fate. Whichever of her companions stolen the spearhead, believing it to be the Tet, had unknowingly abetted her plan. How, wondered Rachel, would the Inca react when she again produced the Tet? Or the thief, when he discovered the switch?

In deciding to hide the amulet, there had also been Max's impetuous nature to consider. Rachel could tell that Max was likely to take matters, including the Tet, into his hands at any time. By deceiving the others, Rachel had figured she was buying a few more days to plan an escape. She had nearly confessed when it had appeared that she would have to reveal the deception, to keep the men from leaving. Then, T'ika had brought word about the noon gathering in the plaza. As Max was bullying Tristan and Dr. Gallagher into following his escape plan, she had been forced into this lamentably poor alternate choice. Her masquerade had run its course. Now, even without the Tet, the Inca was about to act.

Rachel sighed. What had happened to the levelheaded young graduate assistant of two weeks ago? At least she had succeeded in the first half of her plan—the diversion and escape by the men. Unfortunately, there wasn't a second half. All she could do was once again wave the amulet around. You need a miracle, she told herself. *Got any?*

There wasn't, of course, anyone else to ask. She was alone. *Well, not completely.* There was Pachamama, of course. *Good ol' Mother Nature,* Rachel thought. *Supposed to be my special magical power. Got any tricks up your sleeve today, Pachamama?*

The question half-triggered a memory. Something important and connected to Pachamama. Unable to remember, Rachel pushed the thought aside. As she waited and puzzled, she again marveled at the incredible beauty of the hidden city, co-existing amid the wilderness of the dense and merciless surrounding forest. The rays of light through the trees overhead formed nearly vertical columns. *The king should be along any moment. The time must be almost noon,* Rachel thought. She could see the sun through one of the openings in the canopy of leaves and branches above, and it had nearly reached its midday zenith.

Today. What did Pachamama have up her sleeve, *today?*

February twenty-sixth! The date of the solar eclipse! Mother Nature does have a trick. Is that the reason for this gathering?

Of course. The Inca Indians worshipped the sun and had been excellent astronomers. The priests or shamans would have been sure to have told the king about the eclipse.

Rachel suddenly thought of Mark Twain's *Connecticut Yankee in King Arthur's Court.* Twain's hero had used a solar eclipse to frighten the medieval inhabitants of Camelot into believing that he was blotting out the sun.

What if the Inca ruler is planning to use the eclipse to denounce me as an evil influence? What if he tells the people that I must die to restore the sunlight? He must think the eclipse will overshadow the magic of the white witch, regardless of whether or not I have the Tet. These thoughts frightened her enough that she began thinking about another possibility. What if she stole the king's show and used the eclipse to awe the natives, like Twain's hero had done? *A way out?*

If I wait, any longer, she thought,…*the king will use the eclipse to bolster the guards' confidence. He'll claim his stronger magic will protect them from the Tet of Carnelian. Go with the flow. Trust your instincts. It worked before, didn't it?* She certainly would not get such an opportunity again.

Rachel stepped into the corridor that the crowd had left open for the Inca's procession. She drew a deep breath and forbade herself to tremble. Reaching inside her jacket, she unzipped the inner pocket. A trio of guards moved toward her with the intent of forcing her back into the crowd, but she removed the Tet of Carnelian and thrust it in their direction. The three Indians stopped immediately, just as if they had unexpectedly come to the brink of a bottomless abyss. She hastened toward the center of the square, holding the Tet aloft for all to see. As before, the crowd retreated several steps as she approached. It was as if an invisible wave preceded her toward the *ushnu* platform. Uncertain how much time she had, she began to speak even as she walked.

"*¡Uyariy!*" Hear me. Rachel looked toward the palace and saw that the Inca king had not yet emerged with his retinue. She quickly continued.

"This day I will show how great is the power of my magic. This will be a sign to you: I will cause the sun itself to darken in the sky. Unless I am allowed to return to my own land, I will blot out the sun forever!"

T'ika approached the dais, puzzled. "*Ichapis kay tukunqa,*" she said. "*Tayta Intiqa kutimunqa. Kayqa hatun inti wañuymi…*" But this will pass. The sun will return. It is only an eclipse…

T'ika's reassurance confused the guards and others nearby. They had seen eclipses before; predicted and explained by the shamans. Rachel had expected mass hysteria, pandemonium when the eclipse began. What she had failed to consider was that these were not the primitive savages of cinematic adventures.

*Whoops...*Not only the king and his shamans knew about eclipses, but even the guards and workers. The best use she could make of the eclipse was going to be this very brief period of confusion, while the Indians tried to sort out whether she had any connection to it, or not. A commotion near the king's palace alerted Rachel that the king's retinue entered the plaza. The time to act was now—as the moon began its brief ascendance over the sun.

Rachel tried to guess how much of a head start the men had toward the river. She still might have a slim chance to escape. *Might the men have waited at the river? Not likely!* she admitted. Still, she could surely create a crude raft, and almost certainly catch up with them while they were still recuperating in Boca Manu, couldn't she?

In surrendering to her instincts, Rachel's confidence had risen dramatically. The mantle of empowerment that this provided, added to the as yet unchallenged protection of the Tet, produced the surge of courage she needed for the moment at hand.

Rachel descended from the dais, and began her way toward the northern edge of the plaza. T'ika alone stood in her path. Rachel stopped in front of the princess. How would her young friend react? Would T'ika denounce her as a false magician and call upon the guards to seize her, or would she let Rachel pass?

Rachel looked for a brief moment into T'ika's eyes. There was no enmity there, only a questioning look, but still the princess barred the way. Rachel wished she could somehow show her young friend how much she now needed her help. An idea occurred to her. Rachel hesitated. Then she reached into her pocket and withdrew the silver eagle necklace. It had been a gift from her father and was one of the few personal items she truly treasured. It would be a painful sacrifice. T'ika would know this.

Rachel took T'ika's hand and wrapped the princess' fingers around the charm. She continued to look directly into her friend's eyes, but attempted to convey an unspoken apology for having deceived her, and for what she now asked. The princess looked down for a moment at the charm, and when she again looked up again, Rachel saw that T'ika's eyes had misted. Almost imperceptibly, the princess nodded.

"*Yusulpayki*," Rachel whispered. Thank you.

Rachel started to leave, then hesitated. "Paititi," she said, gesturing at the city. "This isn't it, is it?"

The princess smiled softly. "You already know the answer to that," she answered in her native language. "You alone, among your group, know the nature of Paititi and her treasures. Our people have an ancient prophecy that says when the eagle of the north is reunited with the condor of the south, the spirit of Pachamama will awaken. I do not understand all that has happened, or why, but I believe this prophecy is somehow being fulfilled through you, my sister. It is our lives that you hold in your hands. Go, but guard our secret carefully. You must never return here."

"*Tupananhiskama. Qasilla kay*," T'ika ended. Goodbye. Live in peace.

There was a potent and regal aura about Rachel as she left the princess' side. Rachel halted an approaching guard in his tracks with only a commanding glance from her contrasting irises. In the center of the plaza, the king began to speak, telling the people of the great event at hand. T'ika's messengers had not yet delivered the message of the escape. Olca was too occupied in his oratory to the crowd to have yet noticed Rachel's departure. T'ika, however, watched Rachel as she passed through the gap that opened before the white "*layqa*" with the magic amulet of carnelian. As Rachel disappeared down one of the widest streets that would lead to the outskirts of the city, the princess wondered and worried why her frightening new friend would choose to go north, directly into the heart of the Hidden Place?

As Rachel slipped from the plaza, she glanced upward. The shadow of the moon had begun its overlap of the sun. The eclipse had begun.

The jungle began inches from where the city left off. Rachel fought her way through the vines and brush as best she could, realizing that her advantage would disappear along with the eclipse. In a matter of minutes she was disoriented—unable even to discern if she was still heading in the same direction she had started. Suddenly, something brown and the size of a dog darted in front of her. Instinctively, she screamed, but then became aware of a familiar and pungent odor. It had only been a peccary. A wild pig. She marshaled her courage and took another hesitant step forward, then gasped as a much larger shape moved toward her from the foliage. It was...

It was Tristan.

Rachel tried to hide her pleasure, but unsuccessfully. "You came back for me!" she beamed.

"I had to. Listen..."

"It better wait," warned Rachel. "I just muffed my grand exit. These woods are going to be swarming with warriors any minute, if I'm not mistaken. Where are Max and Dr. Gallagher?"

"This way. Hang on to me and don't let go."

"You can count on that," Rachel murmured as the two plunged deeper into the trees.

****

"Get down!" Max ordered suddenly. Get off the road into the trees."

"What's wrong?" stammered Gallagher, as the two men slipped into the cover of the forest.

"Indians on the road ahead. Maybe even some more buildings. Look closely."

Sure enough, as Dr. Gallagher studied the scene ahead, the road vanished into the forest. Upon examining small areas of the forest ahead of them, however, he began to discern what might be the outlines of large stone structures.

"Must be one of the smaller outposts," Max surmised. "I thought all three outposts should have been to the south of Paititi…"

"That was what I was trying to tell you before. Something doesn't fit right on the map," Dr. Gallagher said.

"We don't have the map, but regardless, we can't stay on this road," Max said.

"What if it leads directly to the river? Where else would it go? Couldn't we try to parallel it from a distance?" Gallagher asked.

"We could spend an entire day trying to do that without using the machete. If we stayed very close to the road, they'd almost certainly detect us, as we tried to hack our way past. They're bound to have missed us back in Paititi by now, and are probably already in pursuit."

"This road couldn't have led us around to another part of the city?" Gallagher asked.

"I don't think so."

"My eyes must be playing tricks on me," Dr. Gallagher commented. "It almost looks like there's a big structure, like a pyramid, hidden in there."

"Yeah, and that's why we brought you along—on account of your wilderness experience," sneered Max. "Don't mess your pants over it. When I start seeing pyramids, then you can start to worry. I can't tell anything about directions by the sun right now, because it looks like it's straight up noon. We should have plenty of daylight left. Maybe we should backtrack a little bit. If we can see their movement, they might to be able to see us, too. We'll make a small adjustment to the south, and see if we can pick up that tributary. We should have followed it to begin with. I knew this road was too good to be true."

"I really *must* be starting to hallucinate," Dr. Gallagher said. "If it's noon then why is it getting so dark?"

Max sighed in exasperation. "Trust me. You're imagining the pyramid." He paused and looked up. "But you're right about the sunlight, it *is* getting darker. Must be heavy cloud cover. C'mon. Let's move back a couple hundred yards and see if there's any thinner part of the forest we can slip through."

The two men kept to the trees for a distance. In minutes, however, they had re-worked their way out onto the road and were heading back in the direction they believed to be south. The eclipse had already begun to wane.

As they hurried back up the road, they spotted two figures running toward them.

"Quick…into the trees," Max ordered.

"No, wait. That's Tristan and Rachel!" Dr. Gallagher exclaimed.

Chapter Twenty-seven

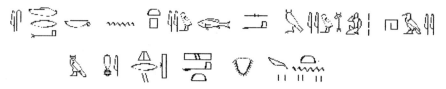

ás der-k em tepiu samiu hai em ma xeri sat-ten
"Behold, thou destroyest by voracious fish, consuming that one who enters,
as if by slaughtering knives"
-indecipherable inscription on the second tablet

****

"The Hidden Place," Thursday, February 26

"What happened? How did you get away?" Dr. Gallagher asked.

"I've been asking myself the same thing…" Rachel panted. "There was an eclipse. You didn't notice? Just before it began, I figured out that the king was about to proclaim that the sun would be blacked out unless we were all sacrificed. I tried to beat him to the punch, and claimed that it was because of my magical powers. I thought I could use the resulting panic to escape, but it didn't work. They know all about eclipses. The only thing it bought me was a few minutes of confusion.. I wouldn't have gotten away without a little help from T'ika." Rachel stopped, puzzled. "I'm glad we caught up with you, but what are you still doing here? Why aren't you already at the river?"

"You don't think we would leave without you, did you?" Max grinned.

"Yeah, right," Rachel said. *You would have left without your own child.*

"We had to figure out a different way to go," Dr. Gallagher explained. "Something's wrong with our directions. We thought we should intercept the Pinquina River by heading straight north. Instead, we ran into more buildings and Indians."

"But how could that be?" Tristan asked. "The map showed all three of the outposts as being to the south of Paititi."

"Except we weren't in Paititi," Rachel interjected. All three men stared at Rachel in surprise.

"Of course we were," Max said. "You saw the gold and the sculpted panthers in the plaza. What else could it have been?"

"Later…" Rachel insisted. "We're wasting valuable time. The king will still try to use the eclipse as a divine omen or something."

"If that was another outpost you saw ahead, there'll be warriors there, too," Tristan said. "We'll have to try to find a way between the two cities. We still should be able to head northeast and intersect with the Río Pinquina. Even if the map was wrong, the river would still have to flow west to east, as it comes down the eastern slopes of the Andes."

"Let's go then," Rachel urged.

Tristan still didn't want to use the machete, because of the extra noise it would make. This made the group's progress more difficult and indirect, as they zigzagged their way through what breaks in the foliage and animal trails they could find. Rachel was just beginning to feel a sense of relief when an arrow sliced through the air and pierced Tristan's right arm. He yelled out in pain as blood spurted from the wound.

"Nothing else to do," he grimaced "…except run for it!"

Max and Dr. Gallagher responded first, heading to the northeast as they dodged from tree to tree.

"They'll surround us too fast that way," Tristan shouted. "Just run!"

Rachel followed his orders and sprinted after the others with Tristan on her heels. *No use*, she realized. Just as she had told Max. This would never work. The foliage was still much too dense to put any distance between themselves and their pursuers. Rachel slowed, reached inside her jacket and unzipped the pocket. Wheeling around, she held the Tet out and shouted for the Indians to stop. More whooshing sounds filled the air near Rachel, as two more arrows whistled past her.

Max yelped as one of the arrows hit him in the back of his right thigh. He stumbled and fell forward into a grove of thorny bamboo shoots, which left deep scratches that began to well with blood. He howled in pain as he pulled the arrow from his leg, but quickly regained his feet and limped to the shelter of the nearest tree.

Rachel ran on, still holding the Tet in the direction of their pursuers, wincing in anticipation of the next flight of arrows, but trying not to cower.

"What the...? Forget that! Just run as fast as you can," Tristan shouted as he caught up with her.

"No, it's still working. They're still afraid of it."

True to her prediction, the rain of arrows had stopped. Rachel resumed flight, but repeatedly tripped and stumbled on the vines and underbrush.

Max had not seen the Tet. He shouted directions back to the others.

"It looks like there's a small creek to our left. Follow it downstream. That's our escape route to the Pinquina..."

Rachel continued to lag at the rear of the group with Tristan. She kept the Tet displayed where the Indians could clearly see it.

Ahead, Max led the way along the creek bed, followed by Dr. Gallagher. To avoid the worst of the brush, the four began skirting the very edge of the creek. Rachel heard a loud curse. She turned her head to see what was wrong.

Max was floundering over a muddy part of the creek bed. As he struggled to maintain his balance, he flailed his arms and accidentally released his grip on the bundle of belongings he had taken when he left the Inca city. It sailed out a few feet and splashed into the creek. Max fell to his knees and scrambled toward the water, a stricken look on his thorn-scratched and blood-streaked face.

"No!" he moaned, as he waded into the water.

"Forget it!" Tristan warned.

"You don't understand," Max sputtered. "It contains gems! Small gold figurines that I pocketed when T'ika wasn't looking. The Tet, too. It was inside. That bundle contains proof...several thousands dollars worth of treasure. I have to get it."

"Max, don't be crazy. Let it go!"

It was already too late. Max had begun to wade toward the spot where the bundle of trinkets had sunk. Suddenly he began to convulse and to splash wildly. His eyes opened wide in terror, and he began to scream in anguish.

At first, Rachel thought Max had been hit by a new barrage of arrows. Then, as the water around him erupted in a turbulent frenzy, almost like it was boiling, she realized what had happened. Piranha. Max had already been bleeding profusely when he had entered the water, and the piranha had instantly attacked.

Rachel stopped at the water's edge and realized in horror that Max was being eaten alive before her very eyes. She abruptly turned away and buried her face in her hands. Tristan savagely ripped a small branch from a nearby bush, then faltered in the mud as he tried to get to the water's edge.

"Grab hold!" he shouted, extending the branch in a futile effort to rescue Max.

Max continued screaming and thrashing in the water. Incredibly, even now he turned away from the proffered branch, alternately groping for the treasure and trying to brush away the ferocious flesh-eating fish.

He flailed madly, then fell sideways into the water. He resurfaced only once, screaming horribly in a half gurgle, half wail. Then, as he sank from sight, Max's cries were abruptly replaced by a sickening silence broken only by the splashing piranha. The water around Max's body continued to boil red with the blood-frenzy of the voracious meat-eaters. Tristan and Dr. Gallagher continued to stare in disbelief, pale-faced, silent and helpless.

Dr. Gallagher's knees buckled and he fell forward onto all fours, retching into the stream from the muddy shore. He screamed in shock and in fright, then scampered backward, crab-like in the mud, as the water in front of him erupted with a new onset of piranha going after the vomit.

Rachel remained turned away. She too felt violently nauseous, and doubled over as she threw up. Suddenly, another arrow whizzed past Dr. Gallagher, then another into a tree inches from Tristan.

Rachel recovered enough to shout another warning in the direction from which the arrows had flown. At least for a brief respite, her words again halted the attack.

"Rachel," Tristan called. "We've got to move on. I don't know how you happen to have recovered that thing, or how much longer it'll, but keep it visible and continue telling them whatever you want. Meanwhile, try to work your way along the banks of the stream. The current is flowing south, so we'll follow it and hope it leads into a bigger river. If we get to a faster moving source of water, we should get clear of the piranha. They stay in brackish, calmer creeks like this." Tristan called out to Dr. Gallagher. "Doc? You okay?"

"Yes...I think I can do that. I'll be...fine. It was just the shock, that's all..."

Rachel raised the Tet again. She took a deep breath and called out to the Indians, ordering them to stay away. No arrows whistled down upon her, so she began to make her way south along the stream. Tristan and Dr. Gallagher jogged forward to catch up with her. Only once, when

Tristan stopped to try to stem the loss of blood from his arm and lagged behind, did any of the Indians fire more arrows. Rachel retreated a bit and bullied the hidden snipers. She threatened to send a terrible plague that would fall upon the families of *all* the warriors, if any of the remaining three of them were harmed further.

Tristan caught back up and stayed close, until they saw a break in the trees ahead. Rachel saw that the water current in the stream had sped up. Near the break in the foliage there was even a mild stretch of rapids where the stream was shallower and dozens of rocks jutted from the water.

"The river must be just up ahead," Tristan shouted. Rushing forward through the vines and brush, at the same time as looking back over their shoulders, both Dr. Gallagher and Rachel nearly teetered over the edge of a precipice that suddenly yawned before them. The creek plunged over the edge and fell a thousand feet or more to the canyon floor.

"No! Not here!" Rachel exclaimed in frustration. "We're back at the Ucupacha—the canyon guarded by the Biba creature! We should have gone *up*stream, not down. This is where the tributary flows *out* from the Río Pinquina, not into it!"

Tristan came up to the edge of the cliff. He didn't look well. He had lost a lot of blood.

"Too late, now. Watch our backs Rachel," he huffed. "Keep the amulet in plain view. Doc, help me see if there's any kind of ledge we can take down the side of the cliff."

Tristan and Dr. Gallagher searched for several minutes without finding anyplace that looked safe enough to head down. Finally, they gave up. Tristan had removed the arrow from his arm, and had wrapped his belt around it to try to stem the loss of blood. Dr. Gallagher tore away one of his sleeves and fashioned as good a bandage as could be managed under the circumstances.

"We have to try to cross the stream," Tristan said. "Not here, the current's too strong, and not too far back upstream, otherwise there'll still be piranha."

"The Indians will be waiting for us on the other side, too," Rachel said. "They'll have just hacked down a couple a small trees for a bridge across."

Tristan nodded in agreement. "I know, but we don't have any choice. We have to see if there's any way down the wall of the cliff. There's nothing on this side of the stream…we have to try find a way down on the other side."

"Even if we do, you know what's down there," Rachel said. "…and we'd be no closer to the Pinquina than we already are now."

"We'll have to take the chance that the creature isn't near the falls. If we can get back inside the cavern behind the falls, we can try to sneak past the dual staircases. We'll have to try and find an exit from the cavern farther along. Somewhere it must rejoin the Río Pinquina."

Remembering how Chico and Raóul had died, Rachel reluctantly nodded her agreement.

They found a place where there were sufficient rocks to try to work their way across the current. Tristan went first. Rachel held her breath, but as Tristan had surmised, the piranha didn't frequent the stream this close to the rapids. She moved out into the water along with Dr. Gallagher. Tristan made his way across the rest of the stream and waited. The deepest part of the stream at the ford came only thigh-high on Rachel. She had to work hard to retain her footing in the swift moving water. She needed one hand on the rocks to steady herself, and the other to brandish the carnelian amulet.

Dr. Gallagher stayed close to lend a hand where he was able. "Whatever you do, don't let go of the Tet," he said.

Rachel ignored Gallagher's admonition and refocused her concentration on crossing the stream.

Finally, all three were on the other side. They quickly returned to the edge on the gorge. Tristan stopped to rest once they were at the precipice, but Dr. Gallagher immediately started to explore the side of the wall.

"Is there anything else we can do about your arm?" Rachel asked worriedly. Tristan looked exhausted and was still losing blood, despite the professor's previous attempts to bandage the wound.

"My arm's not what's worrying me," Tristan told her. He pulled up the leg of his trousers to reveal the wound from where the Am-mit creature's teeth had raked him three days ago.

Rachel grimaced at the sight. The leg was red and swollen. A couple of the cuts were obviously becoming infected. Only one of the small medical kits had survived the journey to this point. Most of their antibiotics had already been depleted treating earlier injuries. Tristan had taken what remained, but that had only been one day's supply. Tristan pointed at a short red streak that had just begun to creep out from one of the infected cuts.

"I'm starting to get blood poisoning," he told her. "It's already sapping my energy. I'm going to have to get some antibiotics in the next twenty-four hours or so. It's almost funny isn't it? I survived an attack by poison dart Indians, outran a mutant jaguar—or whatever it was, and narrowly escaped being pummeled to death by a lost tribe of Inca. After all that—the thing that could do me in? Blood poisoning."

"Why didn't you say anything about this before now?"

"There wasn't anything anybody could do about it. Besides, I didn't really start getting the blood poisoning until this morning. The best thing for it now is to quit wasting time and find a way down."

As if on cue, Dr. Gallagher called out that he had found a small ledge that descended along the wall of the cliff. He pointed it out to Tristan and Rachel.

"Ordinarily, I'd say you were out of your mind for even suggesting that," Rachel said. "If it doesn't get wider, we'll have to grow suction cups on our hands. I don't know about you, but I've already had a tough day."

"I'm afraid it's about to get tougher," Dr. Gallagher said, easing over the edge of the cliff and onto the ledge. "I'm not going back."

Tristan followed slowly, then Rachel. As she lowered her feet onto the ledge, she held up the Tet toward the trees and warned the Indians not to follow further.

The ledge was barely wide enough to stand on, but there was a bit of an inward incline. The three of them inched away from the waterfall and the top of the cliff. After two or three minutes, Rachel saw one of the Indians peer cautiously over the edge. She waved the Tet as a warning. As the sunlight caught the crystal, it briefly flashed a pinkish reflection onto the canyon wall. That was enough to cower the Indian, who immediately retreated from sight.

For a while the path got wider and they believed it might continue all the way to the valley. Minutes later, however, the ledge abruptly ended. Dr. Gallagher called out that it might be possible to slide to a small landing about fifteen feet below. "There's another ledge just below that," he told Tristan and Rachel. "I'm pretty sure we can make it."

"*Pretty* sure?" Rachel asked.

"Best I can do," Tristan said. "We don't have any rope for a safety line. You'll be on your own."

Dr. Gallagher was still determined to try. Using his good arm, Tristan helped Dr. Gallagher over the edge. "Good luck," he said, then let the professor slide down the canyon wall.

There was still enough of an incline that the professor slid slowly, rather than fell to the landing below. Rachel, whose view of the descent was blocked by Tristan, breathed another sigh of relief when the professor shouted a moment later that he was okay. Rachel thought it was a little too risky to try to change places with Tristan, despite the increased width of the ledge, a mere eighteen inches. She insisted that Tristan go next. She helped him maneuver over the edge, then watched as he slid down to join Dr. Gallagher. They were too far now from the top of the cliff for Rachel to tell if any of the Indians still watched from above. At least no one had followed them, so far. She stuck the Tet of Carnelian back inside the zippered pocket and worked her way over the side of the ledge. Without being able to see if she was lined up okay with the landing below, she would be sliding blindly, but Tristan and Dr. Gallagher called out encouragement that she was in perfect position. With her heart thumping wildly, she whispered a quick prayer and let go. She slid easily to the landing, amazed that the drop was much easier than it had looked. The new ledge trailing downward was only another meter below the landing and the three had no problem reaching it.

For about a third of the way down, they were able to zigzag back and forth from ledge to ledge or scramble from one bolder to another to reach a new route. Where possible, they angled back in the direction of the waterfall. In that way, they hoped to end up as close to the cavern entrance as possible. Eventually, however, they had to abandon sight of the falls as their only path onward led in the opposite direction. Matters deteriorated when the canyon wall became steeper and the ledge dwindled to less than a foot's width. Within sight, however, the wall of the canyon curved and the ledge broadened greatly. If they could just make it past the next fifty feet, the next ledge looked like it might take them well past the halfway point to the valley floor.

Dr. Gallagher felt that he would be more able to make it across the upcoming narrow section on all fours. "I'm way beyond caring how foolish that may look," he told the other two.

"If it works for you, who cares?" Tristan encouraged. "Just don't look down."

The professor started across on his hands and knees, and took it extremely slow. At the midway point, he called back that the ledge was only about nine inches wide. After an eternity, he called back a second time to tell them he was past the worst part. When it appeared obvious that he would successfully make it across to where the ledge widened, Tristan urged Rachel to go next. "I need to rest a bit longer."

There was just enough room for Rachel to brush past Tristan. As she moved her body across his on the ledge, he stopped her. "Just go as slow as you need to. We have all the time in the world."

Rachel looked into Tristan's eyes, and fought an impulse to kiss him. "I'll be fine. *You* be careful! You're the one with all the injuries." She decided she wanted to cross over standing up, facing the cliff. She knew she wouldn't be able to keep from looking down if she tried it on all fours like Dr. Gallagher, and was afraid she would lose her balance at the narrowest section. Concentrating on painfully slow and deliberate placement of her feet, Rachel willed herself out on the ledge. As she inched her way across, the image of the sloth's similar slow motion entered her mind. She hesitated, and cleared her head of the distracting thoughts. This was a moment for utter concentration. Having just watched Dr. Gallagher negotiate the ledge gave her confidence. If he could do it, she could too. When she came to the worst section, she pressed every inch of her body against the wall, and tried to imagine that the steep sides were at a comfortable slant. Reason told her that there was plenty of ledge below to stop her slide, and that nothing but panic would cause her to lose her balance. Rachel rationalized that the longer she spent on the section the greater the danger. She forced one step after another, until she heard Dr. Gallagher call to her that she was past the most dangerous part.

Tristan now had also already begun his way across. With one wounded arm and a swollen leg, there was no way for him to try crossing on his hands and knees. He moved across the ledge upright, as Rachel had, only more tentatively.

When Rachel could tell the ledge was safe again she stopped and turned her head back toward Tristan to watch his progress. From the expression on his face, Rachel could tell that Tristan had almost entirely tapped his remaining strength. He wouldn't be able to hold out much longer. She waited. She worried about Tristan's ability to cross the narrow section in his present condition. From where she now stood, it might be possible to help steady him at least on the final part of the narrowest section. As he reached the most perilous part, a premonition of disaster began to sweep over Rachel. She could now see; there was almost no way he was going to be able to stay on the ledge. He was wobbling too much and his foot placement was far too erratic to retain his balance. She began to work her way back toward him, suddenly oblivious to her own dangerous predicament. Before she could get close enough and reach out to steady him, the unthinkable happened. Tristan's knees buckled beneath him and he collapsed. As he fell, one foot slipped over the ledge, and Tristan rolled backward and over the side.

Rachel screamed. Tristan's body fell, slid, and bumped against the canyon wall a half dozen times, before finally skidding to a halt on a landing almost a hundred feet below. Rachel remained frozen on the ledge.

Dr. Gallagher stared into the chasm at the body for several minutes. When he finally looked up, Rachel had still not moved. Her head was turned away, and he could hear no sound from her, but from the slight shaking of her shoulders, Dr. Gallagher thought she might be crying.

"What do we do now?" he asked.

There was no response. Rachel was still fighting to maintain a fragile control. Though barely successful in holding back a flood of pent-up tears and emotion, she found herself unable to quell the spasmodic trembling that had besieged her muscles. She hugged her arms tight to her chest and rocked silently back and forth, breathing in tormented gasps.

Finally, after ten more minutes had passed without Rachel resuming the crossing, Dr. Gallagher called to her. Unheeded on the first try, he called again.

This time, Rachel murmured an incoherent reply, and seconds later managed her way across the remaining portion of the ledge.

"He could still be alive. We can't just leave him."

Tristan's body remained where it had landed, sprawled like a rag doll, arms and legs at unlikely angles. Dr. Gallagher peered down and shook his head gently.

"No way," he murmured. "I'm sorry. I liked him too, but we have to face facts. He couldn't have survived that. His neck or spine was probably broken. Look at how he's lying. Even if he was alive, there's no way we can reach him. There's just the two of us left, now."

Rachel continued to watch for any sign of life, but finally accepted the inevitable. Tristan was dead. She wiped away the tears forming at the corners of her eyes, and took a deep breath. Dr. Gallagher waited expectantly for Rachel to tell him what to do.

"Down," she said.

The rest of the ledge was easy. Without the need to pay as close attention, Rachel continued the descent in a trance. It occurred to her that of the entire expedition, the only two remaining members were the two most unlikely candidates to have survived. "So far…" she mumbled.

"I'm sorry—you said something?" Dr. Gallagher asked.

Rachel just shook her head; hardly aware that she had even said anything aloud. She had started to form a bond with Tristan, even begun to think of him romantically. The previous calamities during the expedition had repeatedly frightened her, shocked or astounded her, and drained her physically and mentally. His death was a devastating blow. He had symbolized renewed hope, and for the moment that had been the most important thing in the world to her. Hope that someone who knew what he was doing would get her out of this alive. Hope that there might be something more, once they had reached safety. Now she was alone, again. Dr. Gallagher didn't count. He was out of his element and knew it. If anything, he was depending on *her*. She continued along the ledge in silence, mechanically moving one foot, then the next.

Chapter Twenty-eight

am ḫeḫ: *"Everlasting Devourer"*

****

Ucupacha Valley, Thursday, February 26

"There!" Kenny said. "Did you see it? Somebody flashed a light at us. There's someone signaling from that narrow gorge down there."

"I didn't see," Amasu answered. "It could've been a natural reflection. Quartz, feldspar..."

"Not reddish-pink like that, could it? I'm going to see if I can fly inside on the next pass. It's worth checking out."

Today was the self-imposed deadline Kenny had set for ending the search. There had been no sign of the expedition since it had departed Boca Manu eight days earlier. Maybe the search had been hopeless from the beginning. Neither he nor Amasu had seen anything except the countless treetops and meandering waterways of the Madre de Dios. Minutes earlier, Amasu's learned and sharp eyes had detected what he believed *might* be abnormal patterns in the green canopy covering the plateau. There was the slight possibility that this could indicate man-made ruins beneath the forest. The tree cover was so thick he couldn't be sure. Yet, even as Kenny had started to head back toward Boca Manu, there was something that drove him to turn the plane around and try once more. There wasn't anything so special about the plateau and the narrow gorge that surrounded it; he just had a nagging feeling that wouldn't go away. He still had plenty of fuel, and it would make him feel a lot more comfortable knowing that he had exhausted all possibilities.

As he entered the canyon, Kenny was surprised to discover that the gorge was somewhat wider in places than it had looked at the higher altitude. He'd either have to land on the river or fly back out of the canyon to turn the plane around, but that shouldn't create any problems. The valley formed an almond-shaped ellipse around the plateau. He'd just make a couple of passes and get as close as he dared to the spot where he had seen the reddish reflection.

****

The ledge took Rachel and Dr. Gallagher, as they had hoped it would, halfway down to the canyon floor. Rachel continued to keep an eye out for a route that might take them to the landing where Tristan's body had hit. There was no such access that she could detect. Leaving Tristan's body behind troubled her, even though she knew there was nothing more she could do. Even if he had somehow survived the fall, and it had been possible to reach the landing, it would have been impossible for her and the professor to have transported him the rest of the way down the canyon wall. There was also her twin to worry about. Amidst all of the danger and excitement she had all but forgotten that Kenny was still lost—perhaps critically injured. She was still swimming in guilt and despair, and not paying much attention when Dr. Gallagher's exclamation shook her from her thoughts.

"Look! Is that a cave?"

She looked up and saw that their ledge had led them around a recessed part of the canyon wall. Facing them was a small cave. Or was it? The entrance was an almost perfect rectangular opening. She thought it looked manmade.

Upon reaching the opening, Gallagher glanced back at Rachel.

She shrugged and motioned him on. "Be on your guard. There are probably hidden traps like on the other side of the canyon," she muttered.

Dr. Gallagher didn't answer, but slowed perceptibly as he made his way into the cave. "Do you still have that little flashlight?" he asked. Rachel checked the pockets of her jacket. Incredibly, the small dive light was still in one of them. The small bulb produced only a meager amount of illumination inside the cave, but it was enough to guide them forward. They hadn't gone thirty feet when they entered a manmade chamber like those of the underground maze. Rachel shined the light around the room. Counting the one through which they had entered, doorways led from all four walls. This was part of the maze!

"Now what?" Dr. Gallagher asked. "We've been through this before, and it didn't have a good ending."

"I don't know," she sighed. Her composure was still a fragile shell around her.

Rachel tried as best she could to shut out her emotions for the moment. She took another deep breath and again returned her concentration to the problem at hand. She removed the Tet from her jacket and studied it closely, trying to decide where within the maze they might be relative to the intricate patterns etched into the carnelian cylinder.

"How did you get that back, anyway?" Gallagher asked.

Rachel quickly summarized how she had switched the Tet and the spearhead and her motives. She did not apologize for the deception, nor did Gallagher criticize her actions.

"I give up," she said, at last. "I can't find anything that begins to show whether it might be a kind of map or not."

"Maybe we're looking at it upside down," Dr. Gallagher suggested.

Rachel sighed and renewed her inspection of the Tet's carvings. She had seen many drawings or carvings of the Staff God. In every instance, when one of the staffs had a bird's head at one end, it showed the head positioned at the bottom.

"I suppose it's safe to say that the exit into the cavern from the maze is represented by the pea-shaped hole at the base of the staff," she ventured.

Dr. Gallagher nodded. "Which means that the exits ought to correspond to the other four holes at the middle of the staff and at the crocodile mouths. That's at least a start. But which opening is which city?"

The two consulted for several minutes, using Dr. Gallagher's recollections of the wording of the map hieroglyphics. By elimination, they narrowed the location of the city they had just fled to one of the holes on the Tet.

"Okay," Rachel said. "At least that's a start." She slowly traced a groove with her finger from the opening identified as the exit from that city. "There are only two rectangles along this groove all the way to the bottom of the Tet. The first one is near the top. I guess that could be the chamber where the Indians held us, before they took us to see the king in his audience chamber. That's where the maze begins, and that's where the lines start on the crystal as well. If it *is* possible to get to the alternate route, the other rectangle would have to represent this very room where we are now. Look how one of these lines only also goes a half-inch, then terminates at a smaller hole. That could be our cave out onto the ledge." Suddenly, the prospects of using the crystal amulet as a map looked much more promising.

"Which way would we need to go from here to get to the cavern?" Dr. Gallagher asked.

She traced the line back up from the base of the staff to the second rectangle. The groove ended at what would be the doorway to their left.

"Let's give it a try," she said. "What more do we have to lose?".

Rachel and Dr. Gallagher headed through the selected doorway and began to note their progress against the markings of the Tet. They encountered other doorways, branches, circular rooms, curves and sharp angles along the way. She found it encouraging that the corresponding markings on the cylinder matched what they found in the maze. Her pleasure abruptly vanished as they heard the unmistakable sounds of many feet clattering immediately ahead of them. Both turned and started to run back the way they had come. Suddenly, the sound of the footsteps passed straight by them, but on the other side of the stone wall.

"The duplicate staircase," she whispered to Dr. Gallagher. "They're on the twin staircase to ours. They're taking a different route."

"There's bound to be another group headed down the second staircase, as well."

"Probably, but if this is a *secret* route, the only places they should be able to intersect is at the second rectangular chamber, which we've already passed, and in the cavern itself."

"So, if we can beat them there…" Dr. Gallagher started.

"C'mon," she said, dashing back the way they had originally been heading.

The two of them rushed down the passages and stairs as fast as they could decide which was the correct way to go. The route was far more direct than the one they had taken as captives. She figured it would have to be, to allow the king a faster escape than anyone privy to the original route.

"This is the last turn—I think I can see some light up ahead," she told Dr. Gallagher. "It should lead us straight ahead to a fork in the passage.

We need to go to the right. That will take us down the last set of stairs to the underground river."

As they turned the corner, the source of the light became obvious. A large opening from high above allowed a generous amount of sunlight to penetrate the cavern. The sunlight also illuminated the floor and walls of the tunnel ahead of Rachel and Dr. Gallagher surprisingly well. A few steps forward, however, brought them to a stunned halt. A wide chasm yawned in front of them.

Rachel leaned forward cautiously and peered down. If there was ever such a thing as a bottomless abyss, this must be it. She pulled back from the edge in disbelief. The abyss was a huge volcanic chute that to all appearances reached endlessly upward toward the plateau above, and which gaped downward into infinity.

"I think I can see China…" said the professor, wryly. "Did we take a wrong turn?" His words echoed eerily into the high reaches above and the interminable depth of the chasm below, reverberating over and over. Rachel waited for the echoes to stop, before answering.

"I'm sure we didn't. I don't understand it. There's no way across this. It just doesn't make sense…the Tet got us this far. The patterns showed an exact match for all the passages we've encountered up to this point. We should be there in just a few more yards, right at the river, just beyond the next fork in the tunnel. How could the Tet be wrong, so close to the exit?"

Dr. Gallagher didn't have an answer. They stared into the chasm, at a loss for what to do next.

"If I didn't think it was such an extraordinary relic, I'd throw the damn thing into the abyss," Rachel muttered softly, in disgust. The echoes from the word 'abyss' made it sounding like a hissing of some giant snake.

Dr. Gallagher looked at her for a moment, puzzled. "Say that again?"

"I just said if it wasn't such a valuable relic, I'd throw it into the abyss."

Dr. Gallagher remained pensive for a few more moments, listening to the echoing hiss. Suddenly, he made a startling request.

"Do it."

"What?"

"Cast the Tet into the abyss."

Rachel blinked, and regarded the Egyptologist in amazement.

"Are you crazy? I was just venting my frustration. Are you forgetting what this artifact represents? If we wind up having to face the Indians again, it still might offer our only protection. Not to mention that it's a incredibly priceless artifact."

"I'm doubtful even the Tet would protect us from the king, now. Trust me. Throw it down. There's a passage in the Book of the Dead that tells what to do with the Tet of Carnelian after completing its primary use. It says that the crystal amulet is to be cast down where it will shatter into many pieces and a pool of water will arise where none was before. If that happens, we can swim across."

"*If* that happens? Are you losing it, Professor? Do you realize how much water it would take fill this hole? Where would it come from? I can't believe what you're saying. You think the Tet possesses some supernatural qualities? The only out-of-the-ordinary power we've experienced throughout this whole ordeal has been the strength of our imagination and perseverance. This artifact isn't some sort of magic wand and there are no ancient hocus pocus spells!"

"Just hear me out, will you? All I'm saying is that the Tet and the Book of Dead have provided all the clues we've needed to navigate these tunnels and secret doors...all the way until now. Why stop trusting them? Besides, are you so certain that the Tet has no special powers? Are you sure that it was just that Indian guard's fear that caused him to turn into a convulsing pile of jelly when you commanded him to suffer?"

Rachel hesitated, looking at the Tet in confusion. The crystal amulet was a beautiful work of art, and invaluable as a historic artifact linking two ancient worlds. Of course, it couldn't have been real magic...Yet, Dr.

Gallagher was right about the Tet and the Book of the Dead steering them correctly, so far. One thing was sure…there was no point in going back the way that they had come. The reddish color of the Tet was supposed to represent the blood tears of Isis. Isis, like Pachamama was an earth goddess. Once again, she was being asked to place trust in an ancient legend. A legend steeped in the mystery of an inner feminine strength.

"I can't believe I'm going to do this…," she said. Rachel raised the carnelian amulet slowly, and then, as if in a dream, cast the Tet into the chasm.

In astonishment, the two of them watched as the air around the falling Tet quivered and the carnelian staff shattered into several pieces. The echoing acoustics of the cavern oddly distorted the sound of the breaking fragments. Then, incredibly, the pieces began to come back together. As the shimmering air around the Tet returned to normal, both Rachel and Dr. Gallagher were astonished to see the Tet floating in mid-air, just at the brink of the chasm. Floating, like on water…slight ripples in the air surrounding it.

"Luray Caverns!" Rachel exclaimed with a sudden burst of enlightenment.

"What?"

Rachel laughed in delight. "I've seen this exact thing before—at a place called Luray Caverns, in Virginia. We're looking at an optical illusion! Look…" She bent and retrieved the Tet. "It's a natural mirror, formed by a shallow pool of water over the smooth rock floor!" She ruffled the water to demonstrate. As with the Tet, the ripples caused her hand to momentarily reflect from different fragmented points, like separate pieces. The echoing of the splashes caused a sound that did indeed resemble something breaking.

"There's enough light coming from that opening back there, but no draft and no movement on the water surface to cause a ripple, so it perfectly reflects the huge jagged opening above us. I think we can just walk across." She took a step out onto the apparent abyss. Her reflection was mirrored back to Dr. Gallagher.

"The water's only a few inches deep. It's eerie, but it's safe. C'mon."

Even with the knowledge that firm footing was right beneath the mirrored surface, it took a mustering of courage for Dr. Gallagher to join Rachel in stepping out onto the false chasm. He made his way gingerly across, following Rachel's path exactly, just to be sure. With much relief, he joined Rachel, moments later, in front of the final fork in the passageway shown on the Tet.

"The stairs and the exit to the river should be just a few yards farther," she warned.

Moments later, true to her words, they exited down the final few stairs and out to the subterranean river. They were alone on the pier. From the time it had taken them to descend the ledge and then to navigate the maze, Rachel guessed that they might have a twenty-minute lead on the Indians descending by way of the other route. Less, if the Children of the Sun had left behind any kind of copy of the Tet of Carnelian, before transporting the original back to Morocco.

"Now, we have to get out of here, before the Indians make their way down the other route. Should we take one of the small reed boats?" she asked.

"What if they notice it's missing? They'll know for sure we've been here. If we leave it and swim back to the opening, they may think we haven't found our way out of the maze. Plus we can hide easier in the water."

"You're probably right, but we can't go back out the way we came in. Remember how strong the undertow was from the waterfall? We'd never get past it. We have to head the other direction. The current goes that way, so it'll be easier to swim. It must also exit somewhere, otherwise there wouldn't be a current."

After quick consideration, Rachel helped Dr. Gallagher remove a couple of seat planks from one of the most inconspicuous of the moored boats. These would help the two of them stay afloat in the water, in case they had very far to go. They entered the water and quickly swam away from the pier. The current carried them along fairly easily, and whenever the warriors emerged onto the pier, it would be well after she and the professor had vanished from sight. They swam onward, aided by the current, until gradually a discernible light became visible ahead.

"We'll check it out cautiously," Dr. Gallagher suggested, as they got close enough to see that it was an opening to the outside. "We don't want to be too hasty, there could be more exits farther on."

The suggestion was more easily said than done. As the water swept Rachel toward the opening, the current became too strong for either to resist. She and the professor found themselves being drawn toward the edge of what proved to be another waterfall. There was no time to react. Rachel screamed as the current swept her over the edge. Dr. Gallagher plummeted immediately behind her. The drop was only about twenty feet high, and plunged into a relatively deep pool below. She struggled to the surface and swam free of a weak whirlpool effect created by the down draft of water. Dr. Gallagher popped to the surface a second later. Rachel reached out a hand, which the professor gratefully accepted. Rachel helped him out of the water, and the two climbed the sides of the pool to ground level.

"At least, that wasn't nearly as daunting as the way in which we entered that place," coughed the soaked, but uninjured professor.

"Yes, but look where we're back to."

She gestured at the canyon walls on either side with one hand as she smoothed back her wet hair with the other. "And how long will it take before that *thing* figures out that we're back?"

"Nothing about this could be easy, could it?" Dr. Gallagher acknowledged.

"We're alive, we're not captives anymore, and for the moment we're not being chased. The Am-mit creatures might even keep the Indians out of the valley. I'll take that for a start."

Chapter Twenty-nine

If thine eye be single,
thy whole body will be full of light.
—Matthew 6:22

✳✳✳✳

Ucupacha Valley, Thursday, February 26

As they made their way south, Rachel and Dr. Gallagher stayed close to the canyon wall. They kept an eye out for crevasses large enough to provide temporary protection, in case one of the "Biba" creatures showed up again. There was no telling what other beasts might also be lurking in the forested parts of the gorge. Despite their academic backgrounds, neither Rachel nor Dr. Gallagher wanted to find out. Both of them had already experienced enough field research the past two weeks to last them the rest of their lives.

"How can everything we've stumbled onto go undetected all this time?" Dr. Gallagher asked, as they stopped to catch their breath. "I feel like we've been running back and forth on some sort of time continuum!"

"There's a lot left to be discovered. People keep finding all sorts of things here in the Andes and in these jungles," Rachel nodded. "Some of the biggest Indian ruins were only discovered up north of here, a little over ten years ago. Still, we probably wouldn't have found anything, if it hadn't been for the map and the knowledge of where to look for the tunnels. Even with them, look at us. We're the only two left, and we're not out of this, yet. Think about it. Even in *your* field, thousands of years went by before Howard Carter discovered the Valley of the Kings. He didn't have to deal with anything comparable to the type of perils we've faced, or dense vegetation overgrowing everything like there is here. It's not so surprising no one has ever found it before." Rachel paused and listened. For a second she thought she had heard something.

Dr. Gallagher caught the look on Rachel's face and also stopped.

"I don't hear anything," he whispered.

"Maybe it was nothing. All the same, let's find a safe hiding place we can slip into, or a ledge we can scramble up for awhile. I could use the rest, anyway."

A little farther along, they came upon an overhang that went back far enough and was sufficiently low that it might provide some protection. They paused there and listened again for a while.

"I guess I could scout forward a safe distance to see if I can find the next place we could move to," Dr. Gallagher suggested. A tremor in his voice belied the confidence he was trying to show.

"Okay…but don't go more than about fifty yards. You remember how fast that Biba thing moved."

They continued onward in that fashion for another twenty minutes, moving from one spot to another, taking turns going ahead.

"No one will believe any of this," Dr. Gallagher said, as they stopped next to a cluster of huge boulders. "I don't have anything but a couple of clay tiles with scratched notes."

"I still have the Tet," Rachel said. "But that does bring up an interesting problem. You realize what will happen if we make it back and start talking about what we found. This will all disappear. I'm not saying all the Indians up there are sweet, gentle people. The king and the prince obviously want us dead. How they might go about that doesn't bring me much comfort, either. Still, that doesn't release us from our own moral obligations. Most of those Indians are just innocent pawns. T'ika even befriended us."

Dr. Gallagher looked unconvinced, so continued.

"The Peruvian government will either move in the army, or hundreds of other treasure-hunters just like Max will try to beat each other here. They'll bring in machine guns and all that kind of stuff Max was threatening. If they believe there's more to Paititi than just a myth, nothing will stop them. We can't tell anyone about this place. *Ever.*"

"But to keep it all hushed up…," the professor protested. "Think about what we now know. Absolute proof of an Egyptian discovery and settlement on the South American continent! A terrifying new species of carnivore. No other scientists have ever set foot here."

Rachel was quiet for a moment before responding. She too had wrestled with the conflicting appeal to share their astounding knowledge and discoveries with the world, balanced against the chaos that such a revelation would precipitate. It really came down to the same decision that had faced Max. Fame and power, or live and let live.

"Yes…on the one hand you're right, Doc. There *is* a fabulous lost civilization up there on that plateau. There are thousands of history books that ought to be re-written. But you know what? What difference does it really make? I remember watching you a day or two ago looking at the photo of your family, wondering if you'd ever see them again. You would have traded the knowledge of everything we've seen, any academic recognition or other profit that might come from it…for the chance to be safe and sound, at home next to those loved ones. I came here looking for my brother. I still haven't found him. For the last six or seven years I've just been reacting to life as it goes on around me. I've always felt like I've been victimized…not just during this expedition…long before…I never seem to have any options. I'm getting real tired of that. I'm ready to start creating some options."

Dr. Gallagher smiled weakly. "I think you started doing that a couple of days ago when you fished out the Tet and saved our lives. But what are you suggesting that we do? Turn our backs on all this? Act like we never saw it?"

"Why not? The world doesn't *need* to know what we've found. The information won't improve the quality of life for our world *or* the Indians. A lot more people will just needlessly be killed. This is your chance to be an anonymous hero. Those Indians up there have stayed hidden from the rest of the world for the past three thousand years. Haven't you ever wanted to save a rain forest? We can. *This* one! All we have to do is walk away from it and keep our mouths shut. We're both anthropologists. Our profession centers on the interpretation of human meaning, studying potentialities and intentionalities. If *we* can't leave those Indians up there alone, think how non-anthropologists will deal with them! I'm sorry. I don't need the fame and exposure. If I've learned anything these past couple of weeks, it's been what really matters and what doesn't. I don't want to try to change ancient history or make new history. I just want to find my brother and go *home*. My God, I *want* to turn thirty years old! I want to meet someone special, plant a garden, or take a cooking class. I want to start *enjoying* life again."

The sound of a sharp whack interrupted Rachel's explosive intro-spection. Rachel and Dr. Gallagher wheeled around just as an Indian warrior holding a wicked-looking battle club pitched forward, uncon-scious, onto the ground a few feet to their rear. Then, from behind one of the boulders staggered a battered figure holding a large rock. His face and body were covered in blood, scrapes and ugly bruises. For an instant Rachel stared in terror. The figure from the pit in her dream! Then recognition replaced imagination.

"Tristan!" Rachel shrieked. She threw herself on him, knocking them both to the ground.

Tristan cried out in pain. Rachel disengaged herself and studied him in alarm. "You're hurt?"

"Are you serious? I fell eighty feet off a damn cliff. I still have part of an arrow imbedded in my arm and I'm almost sure I cracked a half dozen ribs in the fall. My shoulder feels like it's separated, and I think I broke my left hand. Everything hurts so bad, it's hard to tell how serious any one injury is…and *you* just tackled me…"

"Yeah, but you're alive! We thought you were dead. There was no way for us to get to you, and you were all twisted up and not moving. If we'd known, I never would have gone on without you…"

"I probably would have thought the same thing. I was knocked unconscious. I'm not sure how long I was out. I must have slid and bumped most of the way down. If I'd hit something flat or jagged it probably would've snapped my neck or spine. As if that wasn't bad enough, I took a couple more shorter tumbles getting the rest of the way down." Tristan noticed that neither Rachel nor Dr. Gallagher bore any resemblance to his own battered condition.

"How nice for you two that you apparently found an easier route…" he added wryly.

"Alive…" Rachel beamed. She clasped Tristan's face between both hands and smothered his words in a kiss. Startled only momentarily, Tristan reciprocated awkwardly, then with added fervor.

"Ahem…" Dr. Gallagher coughed.

Rachel suddenly remembered they weren't alone and disengaged her mouth from Tristan's. Blushing, she sat up and made a futile attempt to neaten her jungle torn clothing and disheveled hair.

Dr. Gallagher began to tell Tristan about the maze and how they had used the Tet to get to the subterranean river.

"Very nice," Tristan sighed. "You two don't mind if I just lay here awhile, do you?"

"Just try not to bleed on my shoes," Rachel said, as she tore the remnant of one sleeve from her shirt and began to gently mop blood from a gash over Tristan's left eye.

"How in the world did you know where to find us?" Dr. Gallagher asked.

"Are you kidding? You were making so much noise, it was more like: how could I *keep* from finding you? After I made it down, I was still in sight of the waterfall. I found Raóul's pack and retrieved a couple of items. He was carrying one of the other medical kits, remember? I already took something for the blood poisoning. I didn't know which way you had gone, or even if you had made it this far. Walking was too painful, so I rolled a small log into the stream and hung onto it, drifting with the current. About ten minutes ago, I saw the Indian tracking you. When he started creeping up to ambush you, I floated as close as I dared, then came up from behind and got the drop on him. He was so intent on you, he didn't hear me until it was too late."

Dr. Gallagher stepped over and retrieved the war club, just in case the Indian recovered.

"And so you saved my life again," Rachel beamed.

"You mean the Indian? I doubt it. As best I can tell, you two were just about to talk him to death, anyway. What was that all about?"

Rachel grew serious again. "I was arguing that we should leave this all as big a secret as we found it."

"That's a little optimistic. You're assuming we're going to have a choice. We'd better get moving and see if we can find some better place to hole up. This fellow undoubtedly isn't the only one looking for us."

A familiar and chilling noise echoed toward them far from the direction they had come. The Biba beast was back.

"That wasn't what I meant, but it complicates matters even more. I'm in no shape to make a run for it."

"The roar sounded far away, but remember how fast it can cover distance," Dr. Gallagher said. "It'll be here soon enough, if it can smell us, or has some other way that it detects our presence. We need to stay closer to the places offering adequate shelter, if we're going to keep moving. I mean…wouldn't you agree?"

Tristan did not answer. He was watching Rachel, who had tilted her head and had a puzzled expression on her face. She again listened to some distant and barely audible sound.

"Another one?" Dr. Gallagher half-whispered.

"No…I thought, for a moment…it sounded like an engine noise, or a plane."

"Even if it was a plane, there's no way they'd spot us down here in the gorge," Tristan said.

She nodded in agreement.

Dr. Gallagher cautiously scouted the next safe haven, then waved for Rachel and Tristan to join him. As he had shown, Tristan could manage on his own, but he allowed Rachel to help support him as they moved forward. As they reached the crevasse the professor had found, the creature's roar sounded again. Still a little closer. This time, however, an answering roar came from the opposite side of the gorge, much closer than the first.

"It *is* another one!" the professor gasped. "We're going to have to hole up here."

"Maybe it's just an echo?" Rachel ventured.

"Wishful thinking," Tristan replied. "Remember what you told us before. There's no way these things could have survived if there was only one. This crevasse isn't narrow enough to provide adequate protection. We have to look for something else. But you're right, Doc, the next good spot we find, I think we better sit tight."

"Hmmm," Dr. Gallagher said. "Listen a minute…"

In the silence, Rachel again heard the sound she had thought might be an aircraft. This time she was sure of it.

"That *is* a plane! The sound is coming from up ahead and down low, not up above the canyon…"

"There's no telling what the acoustics of this gorge might be like," the professor said dubiously. "The canyon walls are probably channeling the sound from the sky farther south."

Again, the more obvious noise of the creature's roar interrupted their discussion. The closer animal might only be as far away as a few hundred yards, Rachel thought. *Much too near to outrun.*

"We're not going to make it," Dr. Gallagher choked, in disbelief.

Yet, the engine noise sounded to Rachel like it was getting even closer than the two beasts.

"I still think the other sound is coming from here in the canyon," she said, excitedly. "If we could just…"

Whatever wish Rachel was about to express was abruptly cut off by a blood-curdling scream that mingled with the terrifying thunder of the creature's roar.

"That Indian you conked on the head with the rock?" Gallagher croaked.

"Him, or one of his cohorts. Maybe that'll buy us a few minutes. Where's that damn plane?"

For the first time, both Tristan and Dr. Gallagher believed Rachel might be right.

"We should be able to see it," the professor said, craning his neck. He knew it was more a prayer than any reliable measure of accuracy.

Rachel left Tristan and moved farther away from the crevasse. She waded out knee deep into the stream to get a better look to their south.

"My God, Rachel! Be careful!" Dr. Gallagher warned. "That *thing* could get here in only a minute or two!"

Rachel, however, had already glimpsed a tiny speck of silver about a half-mile or less down the canyon.

"There it is! It *is* a plane." She began to wave her arms above her head. Dr. Gallagher rushed forward to join her, even though they were probably still too far away to be visible to the pilot.

When the plane got to within a few hundred yards, they could tell it was a seaplane of some sort, with the landing floats of such crafts. The pilot swooped low as he passed to show that he had seen them, then started easing down to land on the surface of the water.

"Oh, no! He's headed straight back toward the beasts!" Rachel shouted.

The plane touched down and skidded on the water. Rachel waded back onto the shore. She helped Tristan hurry, as much as he was able, back toward the north and the direction of the plane. The plane continued to move, but made a small circle on the water and slowly began motoring back toward Rachel and the two men. When it came to a stop, the pilot-side door swung open and a head peered over the top.

"Hey there, tourists! Somebody call for a cab?"

"Kenny!" Rachel screamed. She left Tristan with Dr. Gallagher and ran out toward the plane, gleefully shouting her twin's name over and over. The passenger side door opened as well, and as the man waded through waist deep water to the front of the plane, she recognized the old Indian, Amasu. Suddenly reminded of the rapidly nearing danger, she shouted at the Indian. "Señor Amasu! Get back in the plane, quick. Kenny, we have to get out of here *now*. Something terrible is close on our trail!"

Rachel waded urgently around to the passenger side, followed by Tristan and then Dr. Gallagher, who stopped to pump Amasu's hand in delight.

"Get in!" she yelled. "Kenny!" She hugged her brother around the neck ferociously, but started jabbering immediately. "We have to take off at once. There's no time to explain."

She turned and helped Tristan on board. Dr. Gallagher climbed in behind and Amasu climbed back into the co-pilot's seat.

"What's the hurry?" Kenny grinned. "We just got here. What happened to you, anyway? You know…it's great to see you all in one piece and all, Sis, but you're a mess!"

"Kenny, I'm not fooling around. Get this thing moving *now!*"

Kenny could tell that his twin was deathly afraid. He switched on the ignition to get the prop turning again. The engine sputtered and died.

"Shit! Start, you rusty old piece of tin!" Rachel screamed, slamming a fist against the side of the plane.

A startled Kenny looked over his shoulder at Rachel, who rarely used that kind of language. "Jeez, Rachel. It's okay…this is just an old plane, it takes a second try, sometimes, that's all."

A roar sounded in the gorge. The noise rattled the windowpanes of the plane.

"Shit! Start, damn it!" Kenny exclaimed. As he tried the ignition a second time, the engine coughed and kicked in. The propeller blade began to turn slowly. "What was that?" he asked.

As if in answer, another roar sounded, and the panes rattled again.

"Sounds big," said Amasu, a trace of anxiety in his voice.

"Big isn't the word for it. *That's* the reason we have to get out of here right this instant! "Kenny?"

"Almost," her brother answered. The prop was beginning to spin rapidly now, but not fast enough to take off. Nonetheless, the plane did begin to inch forward on the water.

"We better go faster than this," Dr. Gallagher stammered. "They're here. *Two* of them this time. I can see them."

The plane moved forward a little faster.

"They've seen us!" Dr. Gallagher shouted. "They're in the open and starting to run! They're only a couple of hundred yards away!"

"What is?" Kenny demanded. He had only gotten the speed up to about five miles per hour.

"Shut up and fly!" Amasu said. He, too, had stuck his head out and seen the monstrosities that were almost on top of them.

The plane accelerated but still far short of what was needed to take off.

"Oh God, oh God…," Dr. Gallagher kept mumbling. The pursuing beasts were rapidly closing the distance.

"Are we too heavy?" Tristan asked. "If you can get us far enough in front of them, Amasu and I can bail out and swim to shore. We can hole up nearby until you can come back for us…"

"*I'm* not bailing out," Amasu protested.

"Who is '*them*'?" Kenny asked. "What is this we're trying to outrun? This plane doesn't have a rear-view mirror…"

"They're very big, have lots of sharp teeth, and trust me…you don't want to have to find out in person," Tristan answered. "Can you take off, or not?"

"Is it me, or is everybody else in here kind of edgy?" Kenny asked. "We need just a little more speed. We'll make it…I think."

"You *think*?" Rachel asked.

"We *are* pretty loaded down," Kenny admitted.

"There's not much time left," Gallagher gulped. "These monsters are big enough to rip this plane apart, and they're still gaining ground…"

Rachel couldn't believe it. It still was like a dream. *Again,* she was running from a monster. She suddenly had an inspiration. *Turn the tables—like in her dream.*

"If we can't take off, turn around," she said. "Chase *them*."

The effect of this suggestion on the others was a stunned silence, which Tristan broke after a second or two.

"Rachel's right. Do it," he agreed. "We're giving these animals too much credit. They're chasing us, because we're fleeing. If we motor fast enough right back at them, it might momentarily confuse them; even frighten them away. Are you going too fast to turn around?"

"Maybe not," Kenny said. "Hold on." He turned the plane in as tight an arc as he dared. One sea float lifted, then bounced back down on the water. He aimed the plane straight at the charging beast.

"Whoa! Dinosaurs!"

The plane picked up more speed, and each one of them held his breath as the two creatures and the plane converged. With only a few yards before they would have collided, the huge predators suddenly veered away. As the craft zoomed past and continued to build speed, the animals stopped and turned, watching their erstwhile prey disappear in the other direction. Too late, the two beasts resumed the chase. This time, the seaplane's propellers had reached maximum velocity and the plane quickly reached sufficient speed to lift off.

"Please place your seat backs and tray tables all the way into the upright and locked position," intoned a much-relieved Kenny. "Stewardesses, prepare for takeoff…"

"Flight attendants," corrected Amasu.

Kenny glanced at Amasu quizzically and pulled the plane up off the stream and into the air.

A tear of joy streamed down Rachel's cheek. She lowered her face into her hands. The rest of the group celebrated with a great deal of hurrahs and backslapping.

After the commotion died down, Kenny had a few questions.

"All right, Sis. You're safe now. Mind telling me what the hell has been going on the last two weeks? And what kind of animals those were back there?"

"None of us know what they were," Rachel told him. "Something we never want to see again, though. As for what's been going on the last two weeks—I started out looking for *you*."

"Oh yes. I know all about that, now. That Max Arnold is one hell of a sorry bastard."

"Not anymore…" Dr. Gallagher said.

"Oh? Oh. You mean like…*dead*? What happened to all the rest of the group? Dr. Amasu said there were ten of you when he left you."

"Dead. Horribly. All of them," Rachel replied. "Snakes, poison dart Indians, piranhas, those creatures back there…The three of us were unbelievably lucky to have survived. Speaking of which, we need to get Tristan to a hospital…and soon. What's closest?"

"Boca Manu, but from the look of his injuries, I'd recommend Cuzco. It won't take that much longer, and he'll get the kind of attention his injuries need."

"Cuzco," Tristan agreed, then posed a question to Rachel. "What did you mean about that not being Paititi?"

"I should have figured it all out before, but I was looking for my brother, not Paititi. Then, one thing just kept happening after another. The Indians told the conquistadors where Paititi was, but no one ever paid attention. The jungle, they said. The realm of the Great Tiger. Perhaps they also meant the jaguar god Ccoa, or that creature in the gorge, but they were being even more simplistic than that. Paititi *is* the jungle. When the Indians talked about a place that contained far greater treasures than Cuzco or their other cities, they didn't mean a stone city with more gold and jewels—they meant the natural treasures provided by the rain forest. T'ika confirmed the truth. She said I alone knew the nature of Paititi's treasures. She didn't mean that as a puzzle. The Quechua word she used meant nature as in 'Mother Nature.' Her choice of words meant that the treasures were to be found in the gifts of nature."

"But surely that's just what she wanted you to believe," Tristan. objected.

"Pizarro must have had the same reaction," Rachel said, "...and all the treasure seekers since. People believe what they want to believe."

"Then the symbols spelling out the words ' *ɜbee-Ur*,' great panther, would be wrong," Dr. Gallagher said. "Paititi doesn't mean Great Tiger in Quechua?"

"No, anyone could have told you that," Rachel said. "I never realized you thought it was. Panther is translated as the Quechua word '*puma*.' Tiger would be '*uturungu*.' In fact, Paititi doesn't translate well into any Indian language, or at least not with a meaning that would make sense in the Great Tiger or El Dorado legend. It was just a place name."

"No," Gallagher said. "It does have one meaning that makes sense. Not an Indian translation, but an Egyptian one. Everyone told me it was the Indians' name for El Dorado, so I never even thought about an Egyptian translation." But there is one: Pa ɜtiti. Likeness of dawn. You both have said that the Indians claimed Paititi was east of Cuzco, in the realm of the great tiger, and the home of the Golden One. East is the home of the dawn...of the sun, Ra—the great Golden One. It looks like you were right, Rachel. Everyone wanted to believe so much in the legend that we over-interpreted the facts."

In the silence that followed, the three survivors shared the same thought. Even if the lost city wasn't Paititi, at least a part of the El Dorado legend was true. There was also the even more astounding proof of an ancient Egyptian presence in South America.

Regardless of whatever agreement she might be able to reach with Dr. Gallagher on the secrecy of the hidden gorge and plateau, there was still Tristan to think about. This had begun as his expedition. He was the one who had found the stone map and this talisman. He had risked all this on the *belief* that the legendary city existed. How could she expect him to abandon the project now that he knew about the Chinkana? Tristan must already know how she felt about the matter. He had over-heard at least some of her conversation with Dr. Gallagher.

Rachel felt something jabbing into her side, and realized it was the Tet. She pulled the amulet out and looked at Tristan.

"I guess this belongs to you," she said quietly. After a brief moment's hesitation, she reluctantly held out the Tet to Tristan.

"You had it all along?"

Rachel blushed, and nodded.

"And Max thought it was in his bundle because…?"

"I had switched it with one of the grooved spearheads T'ika brought me. In the darkness, he couldn't tell the difference."

Tristan studied her in silence for several moments, before speaking again.

"Why don't you hang onto it. You've been the right one to be in charge of the Tet, so far. I'm thinking the place it *really* belongs is in that new museum of yours, in Oklahoma. I'd just probably do something stupid with it."

"You're no longer concerned about lost treasures?"

"I wouldn't go *that* far…but I'm not a thief…and I'm not suicidal. There are small countries that have more money sitting in banks that would be easier to access than the treasures up there. This expedition was never really about the money, for me. Despite my many faults, I'm not Max. On the other hand, I'm not leaving completely empty-handed."

Tristan fished a golf ball-sized nugget from a pocket. Rachel recognized it as one of the gold nuggets like Max had fished out of the canyon stream.

"I picked up as much as my pockets would hold," he said in a low conspiratorial voice, "…as I was drifting downstream looking for you. I *could* always come back for more. I'd just have to work out a plan for getting in and out of the canyon without interference from the Indians or that dinosaur-wanna-be."

"How will I explain the Tet, without revealing the secrets of the Hidden Place?"

"The talisman was found in *Morocco*, remember? No one but us knows that it has a connection to Peru."

Dr. Gallagher leaned forward to join the conversation. "If we can work out some type of a loan, where I can have the Tet at UCLA for a time, I believe that between Mr. Sloan here and myself, we might be able to come up with a plausible story."

Tristan shrugged and nodded his acceptance.

Rachel looked at Dr. Gallagher, who held her glance for a couple of seconds. Rachel could read the unspoken capitulation on his face and in his eyes. To her very pleasant surprise, it looked like Tristan and the professor were both going along with keeping the secrets of the lost cities of the Chinkana.

"Hey, Sis," Kenny called, as he brought the plane up out of the gorge and banked toward Cuzco, "Not that I'm not satisfied just to find you…but, besides whatever was chasing the plane down there, didn't you stumble onto *anything* worthwhile?" He hadn't seen the gold Tristan had shown Rachel and Dr. Gallagher, or heard much of their hushed conversation over the sound of the plane's engine.

"You know, I think I just might have," Rachel shouted back, with a knowing glance at Amasu. "but probably not what you mean."

Rachel had come to Peru driven by the strong fraternal bond of twin to twin and an almost desperate belief that her brother was all that she had left. She had indeed found something else,—an inner sense of identity that had little or nothing to do with her twin. For the first time in a long, long while, all the "pieces" Amasu had cautioned her about were coming back "in sync" with one another. Like the eclipse, they were now transposed on one another—centered and quieted. Ordinary life had taken on a new and friendlier perspective.

"Don't tell me this was all just a wild goose chase?" Kenny asked.

"What a chase, though," Tristan answered. "This goose was the one that was supposed to have laid the golden egg."

"I heard about all that from Amasu. You didn't find Paititi?"

"Your sister just about has us convinced that it was mostly a myth," Dr. Gallagher said.

"No treasure," Kenny lamented. "It sure would have been something to have come back loaded with gold, jewels and stories of a lost city."

"This isn't the movies," Amasu said. "Not every journey has a 'Wow!' finish. It's what happens en route that makes the trip worthwhile, or not."

"What about all the tragedies and uncertainty along the way?" Dr. Gallagher asked.

"¡Waw! That's what keeps it interesting," Amasu snorted. "To be complete, life must contain both perfection and imperfection. Otherwise, by definition, something will be missing."

"Is all that some kind of Quechua Indian wisdom or something?" Kenny asked.

"Nah," Amasu answered. "I mostly stole it from Joseph Campbell. Quechua wisdom is more general. We'd say something like 'the longer you run, the farther you have to walk back.' You can adapt Indian wisdom like that to a hundred different situations."

Rachel smiled. She peered out the side window of the plane, in a final look at the plateau and the nearly invisible Ucupacha gorge. The expedition had covered only a narrow thirty-five mile stretch of jungle from

Puerto Definitivo to the plateau. Rachel's view from the plane showed the immensity of the jungle—an endless carpet of green, broken only by the snaking brown lines of infrequent rivers. She knew that the rain forest covered two and a half million square miles across Peru, continuing into Bolivia, Brazil and other surrounding countries. She thought about all the unbelievable things she had witnessed during the past two weeks. Ancient tunnels deep in the jungle...secret chambers and mazes with Egyptian hieroglyphics and cryptic puzzles...a legendary lost city...nightmarish carnivores. She shivered as she recollected the many narrow escapes and their companions who had not been as lucky.

Two and half million square miles... Rachel thought. *...and most of it impenetrable and unexplored. How many other secrets did this vast jungle hold? How fragile and threatened might this treasure of Paititi prove to be?*

She returned her gaze to Dr. Gallagher. What might be on his mind? His whole life was his work. Max Arnold had bought the Egyptologist's allegiance, lock, stock and barrel. What if word leaked out from one of the porters who had left with Amasu? If other treasure hunters who knew Max got wind of what he had been after, how long would it take for them to ferret out the professor? Sure, Dr. Gallagher was satisfied, now, just to be going home alive to his wife and kids. What about later?

What about Amasu? What did she really know about the peculiar old Indian? He might be full of insight, but both Max and Kenny had been able to hire his services as a guide. Who else might do the same?

And Kenny? Irrepressible, curious Kenny. He had seen the Am-mit beasts and already knew a part of the story. How much more could she tell without igniting some impetuous investigation by her twin?

She turned her attention last to Tristan. She smiled faintly for a moment, but almost as quickly, her emotions wavered.

Even though he had gallantly surrendered the Tet into her safekeeping, Tristan was still the biggest question mark of all. Now that he had been there once, he could find it again even without the Tet and the map. What was it Tristan had said to her the first time they had escaped the

Biba creature? *"This isn't the kind of adventure from which a man like me can just walk away. This is what keeps me going."*

As she continued to study him, she noticed that Tristan still held something in the palm of his hand. She recognized the gold nugget. Tristan was looking at it thoughtfully, and as he did, he began to pass the nugget back and forth, from hand to hand. Rachel looked at his face. Even in his weakened and battered condition, there was yet a spark in Tristan's eye.

A chill went down her spine as a mixture of sadness and apprehension crept through her soul. Sadness, not for herself; not even for Tristan or Kenny, but for the jungle. For T'ika. For the forests and the sloth…the beautiful jaguar…the birds…the Yaminhua.

Amasu was right. In the remote darkened regions of the jungle, she had rediscovered a part of herself that had been lost, discarded as irrelevant and without value. Within that darkness, despite, or perhaps even because of the misfortunes and trials she had endured, she had found a treasure more intangible, yet no less valuable than the gold in the shadows of the Chinkana. A part of her self was bound to the jungle—to the spirit of life that Amasu called Pachamama.

If thine eye be single, she thought. *How curious a concept for someone with irises like mine.*

"I could always come back for more," Tristan had said. Those words still echoed hauntingly. Tristan became aware of Rachel's scrutiny, smiled and dropped the nugget in a pocket. He moved closer, fondly studying her contrasting eyes and dirt-streaked face.

"So, what now?" The question popped out of her mouth even as the thought formed, and she immediately blushed. *We go back to our separate lives?*

Tristan shifted in his seat, causing Rachel's heart to sink as she anticipated the inevitable string of excuses certain to follow.

Tristan was painfully aware that his skills in the realm of romance were in almost as bad of shape as his battered body. Rachel's own apparent discomfort, however, put him at less a disadvantage.

"Well…you remember? I *do* have an assistant. I imagine she can handle things for a few more weeks. That is, if you've got any time on your hands…"

Rachel stared at him for a long moment, as all the worries and apprehension of only a second earlier flashed through her mind. Then, she returned Tristan's embarrassed half-smile.

If there is any certainty in life, it has to found in the present moment. Life is mostly an attitude, she realized. A circle had closed. She was going home. Home to a new life—one forever changed by her journey into the shadows. She was free to live. This was not the end of an adventure, she knew. It was a beginning.

"You looking for a nurse or something?" Rachel asked. "In your condition, I don't know if you're capable of much more than six weeks bed rest."

"That wasn't what I meant, but if it was an offer, I'm agreeable. Follow me?"

"Anywhere," Rachel answered.

About the Author

Michael Marcotte is a globetrotting amateur anthropologist with a background in computer systems management, interpreting and criminal investigation. He holds a second degree black belt in Taekwondo, and is an avid Scuba diver. He has authored several magazine articles and is at work on a second novel. He lives in Norman, Oklahoma with his wife and two children.

Printed in the United States
1197700003B/39